BAD ART

BAD ART

Quentin Bell

The University of Chicago Press

The University of Chicago Press, Chicago 60637

Chatto & Windus Ltd, London

© 1989 by Quentin Bell

All rights reserved. Published 1989

Printed in Great Britain

98 97 96 95 94 93 92 91 90 89   54321

Contents

List of Illustrations

Acknowledgements

The author and publishers are grateful to the following for permission to reproduce material:

West Riding County Council for 'Bad Art'; Cambridge University Press for 'The Art Critic and the Art Historian' (Leslie Stephen Lecture, 1973); The Registrar, University of Leeds, for 'Roger Fry'; The editor of the *Burlington Magazine* for 'Sickert', the first part of which appeared in the magazine, with some editorial changes, in April 1987; The University of Newcastle-upon-Tyne for 'Degas: *Le Viol*'; The University of Hull for 'Form and Content', an Inaugural lecture delivered on 3 November 1965 by the author, then Visiting Ferens Professor of Fine Art at the university; The University of Chicago Press for 'Art and the Elite', which appeared in *Critical Inquiry* 1 (1974): 33–46; The University of Southampton for 'Autolycus: A Demotic Art'; The University of Chicago Press and Sir Ernst Gombrich for 'Canons and Values in the Visual Arts', which appeared in *Critical Inquiry* 2 (1976): 395–410.

While permission has been sought to reproduce all the material appearing in this collection, in some cases it has proved unobtainable.

Preface

All save two of the essays in this book have a common ancestor: a book by me entitled *On Human Finery*, published in 1947. That book ended with an appendix concerning the dress of ghosts. An additional note, resulting from a later encounter with a different kind of spectre, may serve to begin this volume.

It was early in the morning. I happened to be in a cathedral, and had approached the cloisters. I seemed to have the place to myself, which at that hour of the day was natural. Then I saw the long shadow of a man. As I approached, I realised that something queer had happened. The visitor had walked out of the fifteenth century. He was of about the same age as the architecture around him and, like the architecture, he had survived. He could only be a ghost.

I did not believe in ghosts, but it was impossible not to believe in this gaily dressed youth. It did not look in the least like an hallucination; it was solid and undeniable. Two ladies had once walked into a former century when they were visiting Versailles – I had been suspicious of that story but now . . . My ghost walked out in the open air, and there I perceived a nun. It approached her. It offered her a cigarette. Then the camera crew and their impedimenta became visible, and I was, once more, free to disbelieve in ghosts. But why, for a moment, had my scepticism tottered?

If I had seen the nun alone I should have been untroubled. Nuns, until very recently, were practically unchangeable – like monks, beefeaters, flunkeys and fox hunters. But, in a general way, we dress to show our times. It is so usual to conform with the

1

fashions of our age that, unless we are forewarned by a proscenium arch, we can be astonished by a convincing disguise. Why we should suppose that an earthbound spirit should dress up to visit our century I do not know, unless it be that a ghost has in some manner to establish its ghostly character – for the wearing of archaic dress certainly is in most circumstances a startling event, and if a ghost cannot startle us, its occupation is gone. It startles us because the prevailing fashion seems inevitable and ubiquitous.

Here I would like to remind you of two pictures: *Work* by Ford Madox Brown, and *Music in the Tuileries Gardens* by Manet. (See illustrations 1 and 2.) I shall use these pictures to advance an argument concerning fashions in dress. But it is worth pointing out here that they relate also to our main arguments. They have both, at various times, been considered bad; today, they are both accounted good by a large public. Brown's picture had few admirers when it was painted, then it became very popular; its popularity declined sharply, and now its reputation is recovering. The Manet was also decidedly unpopular when it was painted but it has increased in critical (and monetary) value and continues to do so. Violent fluctuations of value such as these are usual in the history of art during the past two hundred years. *Work* shows us navvies digging up Heath Street, Hampstead, and with them are some ladies, gentlemen and intellectuals. The Manet shows us a fashionable crowd in the Tuileries Gardens, and here also are ladies and intellectuals. Morally and aesthetically Hampstead has as little to do with the Paris of Napoleon III as has Carlyle with Baudelaire (they figure on these canvases), nor could any pair of contemporary painters differ more completely in their methods and aims than these two.

Both pictures were painted in about 1860. In both, nearly all the gentlemen are clothed in black, sometimes relieved by white, and nearly all wear rather tall top hats. Manet uses them as a foil to the more highly coloured ladies. These all wear crinolines. Emma Ford Madox Brown, the blonde on the left of her husband's picture, carries a small sunshade; we can find its fellow in the Manet. Mme de le Josne, who sits in the foreground of the Tuileries, wears the bonnet of the period, set far back on the head so as to reveal the entire face and the hair and tied with a broad ribbon which dangles downwards beneath the wearer's chin. We shall find it in Heath Street. Another headdress, a hat which sits on the top of a lady's head and projects downwards both fore and aft, also occurs both in the Manet and in the Brown.

There are, of course, dissimilarities. The English workers are not men of fashion, nor is Carlyle (he stands on the right-hand side of the canvas with the Rev. F. D. Maurice). If we could look into the minds of the crowd, the differences would be far greater. Seldom have England and France been further apart than they were then, and it is precisely this vast difference in ethos which makes the similarity of dress so interesting.

Both countries were ruled by the fashion of the day. It is, in its way, a tyranny, even though there is no one tyrant to enforce its regulations. But, indeed, it is hardly a despicable power. There have been many attempts to enforce legislation intended to curb or to abolish the fashion of the day and even more attempts by leaders of public opinion to laugh or scold fashionable people out of the extravagant, immodest, unhealthy and ridiculous clothes that they wear. These attempts have failed. Fashionable people – the term in this context embraces the vast majority of the wealthier classes – have insisted upon their liberties and have preserved them.

But it is an odd kind of liberty that they have preserved. Return again to my two pictures. In both of them the artist has observed a fine and sunny day. For some of the elegant crowd in London and Paris it would presumably have been uncomfortably hot, but in neither have any of the gentry removed any of their clothes; even the dog in Brown's picture wears a little coat. The manual workers of Hampstead dress in a more rational way: they have their work to excuse a certain degree of déshabillé. But in Brown's foreground there is a young girl of the lowest class who wears some discarded finery that was once fashionable; in so doing, she displays her shoulders with a freedom which, in her betters, would be excusable in the evening when it is cool, but which would be quite inexcusable by day. But the penalties of being well dressed are much more considerable than those suffered by people who sweat in fine clothes. I have seen – and it was a grimly depressing sight – a young woman who in an age of long skirts would have been decidedly attractive, obliged by fashion to reveal legs of unspeakable horror.

This question of what to wear and what not to wear may seem a fairly trivial matter – one will hear the critics of fashion dismiss the whole thing as a frivolity and, not uncommonly, a feminine

3

frivolity. Historians of fashion know better. There is no extravagance, no immodesty, no unpracticality, of which men have not, at times, been guilty. But the main charge which has been laid against masculine dress is that it is atrociously ugly, and this brings me to the real nub and gist of this essay: the aesthetic element in dress.

If we take a fairly simple proposition: red is being worn this summer. It is clear that some kind of aesthetic decision has been made. It may be blue next summer, but for the moment red is beautiful and, I think, genuinely felt to be so, although to a painter the proposition may appear absurd. The more complex proposition 'this is a beautiful dress' may carry a much heavier load of emotions. It may describe all sorts of qualities which can hardly be thought of as aesthetic, and yet I think that in the total effect there will be an aesthetic element which, like all its other qualities, will be greatly affected by a change of fashion. When the dress grows dowdy it will become 'ugly', in a later metamorphosis it becomes 'picturesque' or 'historic'.

The most intriguing kind of value judgment arises when we say of a modern and fashionable suit that it is very ugly. This was something which never happened until the nineteenth century. The emotion was a product of, or a part of, the Romantic movement, a movement which disguised buildings as ancient monuments, a movement which was accompanied by a vast technological revolution. Now the architectural achievements of that astonishing industrial effort, although sometimes admired, were more usually shunned. The railway station, the gasometer, and the factory were indeed so much hated that they had frequently to be disguised as monuments of an earlier culture. In the same way, ladies and gentlemen might have disguised themselves in medieval dress – it is easier and less expensive to disguise a man than a suspension bridge. But this did not happen. Throughout the nineteenth century, a completely modern mode was worn by fashionable people and by that immense class which followed their example. The top hat, the crinoline, the frock coat and the bustle were accepted without question. Modern dress was certainly denounced; it was said to be hideous; nevertheless, it was purchased with enthusiasm and worn with pride.

G. F. Watts declared that he found it impossible to paint a pair of trousers; and, so far as I know, he never did. But did he ever wear a pair of trousers? I think so. I would go further and suggest that

Watts, or some of the other artists who felt as he did, might, when young, and when they first sold a picture for a good price, have purchased a pair of smart trousers and rejoiced in them. What had happened was that trousers, like crinolines and bustles, all of which were felt to be ugly by aesthetically minded people, were, in some other compartment of the aesthetic mind, admirable.

This confusion of feeling resulted from the fact that the fashion of the age was a novelty, which, of course, made it seductive. But at the same time fashion had taken so headlong a course that it was possible to compare one age with another and therefore effectively to criticise that which was modern.

I hope it may be granted, then, that fashion is a powerful and aesthetically disturbing social force. It is also a social convenience which usually serves to indicate the status of the wearer. Even in very primitive societies it marks the sex of individuals and usually tells us whether he or she has come of age, and whether the person concerned is a chieftain, a priest, or perhaps a warrior, and in more highly developed cultures a great number of different occupations may have some appropriate form of dress. But in European or modern societies there is a difference so great as to be of fundamental importance: we are mobile; as mobile as our technology, our social structure and our art.

A trained and attentive eye may perceive that dress in older societies also changes, but the rate of change is so much slower than ours as to be almost negligible. We are capable of changing our dress so rapidly that the whole appearance of men and women may be radically altered. Forms of dress which would have seemed unimaginably shocking to people of a former generation may now be introduced, abandoned, and reintroduced within a single lifespan. Not only is the rate of change prodigious, but the frontiers of fashion are immensely enlarged, involving in our restless and violent commotions classes which previously were almost excluded from fashionable mutation and, at the same time, whole cultures which formerly had adhered to more or less immobile patterns.

I have already hinted at another characteristic of fashion: where other arts may express national feelings, fashion remains international. It is engendered in comparatively few centres and it divides us, not in accordance with international frontiers, but into classes.

The motor force of fashion as it affects the individual is

5

something with which we have for long been familiar in writings concerning fashion. It arises surely from the desire for respectability, the desire to take one's place, decently and yet unobtrusively, in good society – and perhaps in a rather better society than that to which we are accustomed. More adventurous spirits, particularly those of the young and the beautiful, may take a much more aggressive stance and seek by a reckless pursuit of the extremes of fashion to rise superior to the common herd. But obviously social adventures of this kind, and indeed the whole process of emulation only becomes possible when the upwardly mobile individual is favoured by political and/or by economic power. In a rigidly stratified society such conduct would be not merely impossible but unthinkable.

An explanation of fashionable change which used to be common was that it is an expression of restless human nature, a fickle desire for something new. This would be a more convincing explanation if fashion occurred wherever human beings are to be found, but it does not. Fashion, in the sense of change, can exist only in a mobile society. It seems that human nature can itself be changed through the operation of social forces. Our notions of propriety, decency and beauty can be related to our economic environment.

My concern here is with beauty. Any study of fashion, or indeed of art history in general, suggests that there must be some degree of aesthetic unanimity, either mobile or immobile, within a given culture. But, as we have already seen, this situation, although it is normal, is not inevitable. It is possible for two opposing ideas concerning beauty to flourish simultaneously. This occurred in the nineteenth century and persisted until quite recently. In the eighteenth century and the more distant past there was, no doubt, a difference between educated and uneducated taste, but there was nothing at all like that sharp rejection of modernity which developed after the Industrial Revolution.

I suspect that that adoption of a dual standard in the judgment of works of art may have engendered a further and more important schism. About the middle of the last century a new phenomenon was created: the taste of the establishment (the academies, salons, art-loving and art-buying public being virtually one and the same). But it, in turn, was challenged by what we now call the *avant garde*, expressing a view of art which, although it varied, was invariably hostile to the establishment. The establishment, on the other hand, considered that the artists of the *avant garde* were either negligible or despicable. In the eyes of the vast majority, theirs was bad art.

Within half a century this judgment has been reversed. In popular esteem and in the market place, it is now the art of the establishment which seems bad, while the art of the opposition has become good. It is this drastic and astonishing revaluation which provides my point of departure.

Bad Art

═══════════════════════════════════════

I

This may seem an eccentric and wrong-headed theme. Why, it may be asked, should we devote attention to that which, manifestly, does not deserve it? There are two answers to this question: one, which might lead me far from my main argument, is concerned with art history, for history, so it seems to me, cannot afford to neglect any major historical phenomenon. The other answer, which, in fact, defines the purpose of this essay, is that our perception of the goodness of good art is determined by some opposite quality with which we compare it. If this be accepted, the utility of such an enquiry will at once be apparent; it is always useful to take an object and look at it from a new point of view, to consider it, so to speak, backside on or upside down.

In order to avoid confusion, it must at once be conceded that arguments concerning bad art are no more conclusive than arguments concerning good art. In the last analysis, they must rest upon assertions that cannot be proved. Nevertheless, I think that we can advance further upon common ground if we approach the matter from this direction than would be the case if we started by considering that which we admire. Lovers of art are likely to be fiercely divided when they discuss the work of their more distinguished contemporaries; but when it comes to the illustrations in a woman's magazine or the design on a box of chocolates they will be more or less unanimous. Unanimous judgments are not always reliable, but they do at least provide a point of departure.

I would like to begin by considering what happens when a picture is copied. There are many kinds of copy; the copy which is better than the original, the copy that is worse, the copy that is different – but the kind of copy of which I would like to remind you is that which you may see if you go into any of the great Continental galleries where you will find a certain number of assiduous imitators who, with masterpieces before them, attempt to produce facsimiles. Some of these copyists are highly skilled, they match their tones with infinite care, they copy line for line even to the last *minutiae* of the brush. And yet, as they themselves would be the first to admit, some vital element of the original escapes them. No special knowledge is needed in order to distinguish between the masterpiece and the counterfeit; the second resembles the first only as a corpse resembles a living body.

Obviously the difference between the copy and the original must lie in the paint: a painting, whatever its content, is always a material thing, yet the difference, howsoever striking, is so minute that it may be hard to point to any one part of the picture that has not been perfectly reproduced. It is as though a glaze has been floated over the entire canvas, distorting and corrupting everything through the interposition of an alien personality. We can measure the extent of this drastic though impalpable metamorphosis by comparing a photograph with a copy such as I have described; the impersonal machine preserves far more of the original – even though it works through a different medium – than does the personal care of the imitator.

Now certain facts about bad art immediately become clear when we look at an example of this kind. There are certain qualities which the bad copyist can take from the good original without apparently making his own picture any better. The copy may be as carefully painted, as well composed, as faithful a mirror of the external world as that which it feigns, and I think we may conclude from this that excellence in dexterity, verisimilitude and composition will not make a bad picture good. This, indeed, is sufficiently apparent from the original works of many lesser masters. None of the excellencies which we can enumerate will survive even the most careful transposition, although every quality that can be described in words may also be described by the copyist in paint. An essayist having in front of him a good coloured reproduction of a Rembrandt may write as complete an account of the picture as he could do in front of the original. But he will know very well that there is an immense, an indescribable, difference between the thing itself and the printed image.

If we want a word with which to describe this incommunicable element, then I think that the word must be sentiment. Even here we must be careful; when, for instance, Van Gogh copied Gustave Doré's miserable engraving of a prison yard he undoubtedly attempted to conserve Doré's sentiment. And yet the sentiment is not the same. And it is here, I think, that we may come nearest to discovering the essential quality in bad art. The expression of sentiment as opposed to the pictorial narration of a given story is something which derives from a state of mind and just as, obviously, the same story illustrated by, say, Rembrandt and Rubens or even by artists who are comparatively close together, as for instance David and Prudhon, will undergo a profound metamorphosis as it passes into different hands, so a landscape by Constable or a still life by Cézanne is virtually uncopyable, except by mechanical means, because the sentient copyist must inevitably, and however much he attempts to subordinate himself to his original, retain sentiments of his own and these must inevitably affect his work.

So far I have probably commanded your assent rather than your attention. But the next stage of my argument is more questionable and less commonplace: I believe that the quality of badness in a work of art derives from an awareness of beauty, or rather, of that which society at large considers beautiful and which I will here call social beauty. I must return and consider the implications of that word 'beautiful', but first let me offer two examples which may help to clarify my meaning. The sentiment in a Van Gogh is in the highest degree personal, he is moved by a pure and uncalculating desire to make pictorial statements. Even today, that which he says has a brutal and unexpected quality; in his own time, his work was almost universally condemned for its ugliness and its ineptitude. Gustave Doré, on the other hand, refers continually to a whole common market of ideas; at no point are we disturbed by an original or a surprising sentiment. In fact, his work was socially acceptable and was for many years widely and enthusiastically accepted; unlike Van Gogh, he was considered 'artistic'.

Or again, take the work of almost any three-year-old child and compare it with the productions of an adolescent. The picture by the adolescent will almost certainly be more workmanlike, more intelligent, and, in certain respects, more profound than that of the child, but it will also have a quality of badness, of insincerity, which is completely absent from the first drawings that we make. The badness of the adolescent's drawing arises from what we call self-consciousness, but which is in fact consciousness of others, not necessarily an awareness of the teacher so much as an awareness of society, of the qualities society deems beautiful.

The situation of Gustave Doré or of the adolescent is that he is forced by his perception of social values to modify that frankly unconscious approach which belongs to those who are untroubled by social exigencies – the genius and the child. He is the victim of a dual standard of excellence which leads him, almost inevitably, to a compromise or to a capitulation which necessarily vitiates his sentiments.

Here I am led naturally back to the question of beauty. It is not necessary to define the term but merely to remind you of the existence – in certain historical conditions – of two standards of excellence. Return, once more, to the example of Van Gogh and Gustave Doré. In a sense it may be said that both artists sought beauty and that both achieved it, even though their aims seem to be diametrically opposed.

The beauty of Van Gogh is of a kind which, at first sight, seems to the general public to be the very negation of beauty, to be, in fact, unmitigated ugliness. Only by degrees, as we learn to understand the meaning behind the violence of the artist's language, do we learn to accept it. When once it has been accepted we think, not, I hope, unreasonably, that it has become a permanent acquisition (but even in this we may be wrong).

The typical life history of every artistic movement of the past hundred years has consisted of a struggle against hostility and indifference, the good artist has fought against the popular conception of beauty, the bad artist has accepted it at once or after a brief struggle. There have been two measures of excellence and, as a necessary result, a struggle in which the artist must be continually driven to a compromise, to an insincere bargain which results in falsity of sentiment, in bad art. The typical aesthetic history of the child, that is to say, the suppression of pure emotion untroubled by any conscious pursuit of beauty and its replacement by an attitude of social deference allows us to suppose that, in modern society this conflict, and the almost inevitable victory of social taste, makes bad art a normal, if not a universal, phenomenon.

I think that we shall have come about as far as we can come towards an incontrovertible statement if we say that bad art arises from a failure of sentiment, that this is caused by some form of insincerity, and that this, in its turn, results from a form of social pressure in favour of that which society at large calls beauty.

II

Art history is a record of change. Pictures, like fashions in dress, are first liked and then disliked. If we examine the history of taste during the past two hundred years, this pattern is repeated in a most violent fashion: that which was loved and admired becomes hateful and ridiculous. Consider some obvious and overwhelming examples of the last century: *The Monarch of the Glen*, *The Boyhood of Raleigh* and *When Did You Last See Your Father?* Why is it that they appear so appallingly bad? We should most of us agree that Landseer, Millais and perhaps Francis Yeames showed great talent as young men. Why should they look so dreadful in middle age? In each case, the demands of society were met, and met with enthusiasm. These artists had completely accepted the opinion of their age as to what constituted a beautiful picture, and, having done so, addressed themselves to the beautiful with horrifying success.

If we look further into the nineteenth century and consider that work which, without being of the heroic stature of the Impressionists, is still valued for its charm – the dresses, the fashion plates, and the cheap ornaments of the period – we find them far preferable to the great historical machines of the academies precisely because they attempt far less. We can perceive the same law in operation even within the *oeuvre* of the most portentous masters. If we compare the book illustrations or the rough sketches of a Millais, a Poynter or a Leighton with their finished easel pictures, we shall realise that they could only do their worst when they really exerted themselves.

Take another example, this time from our own epoch. Go into a big department store and look at the more expensive and highly decorated objects, the garlanded lampshades and the moquette television suites (trad. or contemp.), the apparatus of gracious living and the reproductions of works by artists who paint a socially acceptable pastiche of the Impressionists. There, if you have a grain of sensibility, your heart will sink. But it will rise again as you leave this abominable abode of beauty and enter the hardware department. Here you may enjoy yourself for here there is no art. Take a spade and admire its clean, athletic, trenchant appearance. It has only one blemish – the manufacturer's label, for here there will be some little pretence at ornament, some paltry shield or feeble scroll, some artful distortion of the maker's name adorned in the cause of art.

Put the case in another way. *The Monarch of the Glen* has become bad because it is attempting to be so good; the conflict between social and personal valuations is therefore exceptionally acute; the fashion plate or the spade succeeds at its own level because the maker is relatively unambitious and is therefore not compelled to seek beauty with any large measure of enthusiasm. We may, in fact, postulate a simple law of aesthetic gravity: the higher you fly the harder you fall.

If bad art results from an awareness of social demands, then we should expect to find that the incidence of bad art varies according to the social situation of the artist and in response to historical changes. I believe that a clear correspondence can be seen between historical developments and the growth or decline of bad art, and indubitably, bad art is a variable not a constant phenomenon. Therefore, in using the word 'bad', I refer to a real but not an unchangeable sentiment.

At first sight, indeed, it appears that one of the advantages of discussing bad art lies in the abundance of material that lies ready to hand, and, of course, it is true that we do not have to look far in order to find great quantities of miserable work produced in every part of the civilised world during the past hundred and fifty years. But, if we go back to the eighteenth and then to the seventeenth and sixteenth centuries, we shall, if we continue to apply the same standards, discover a substantial diminution of output, especially in architecture and the applied arts. In fact, the abundant production of bad art, which we now regard as a normal feature of European culture, hardly begins before the Renaissance. Implicitly we recognise this fact in our day-to-day judgments concerning art. If I were to say: there is some thirteenth-century glass in such and such a church, you would know without being told that it was good or very good. If I were to say that the glass was nineteenth century you would know that in all probability it was bad; it is only if I were to put the glass in some intermediate period between the fourteenth and the nineteenth centuries that you would require information concerning its aesthetic value. In other words, there are long periods in which the statistical probability of a thing being good or bad is so great as to make further information superfluous.

Nor is this simply a matter of periods nor, indeed, of cultures; in a stricter sense, the social context of the artist determines his standards of achievement. While vast inequalities exist between one painter and another in a period such as the sixteenth century, only very slight differences will be found between masons, potters or cabinet makers of that epoch.

Here let me add a rider which, in truth, follows naturally from what I have already said. Social forces are nearly always inescapable. The whole method of art history is based on the assumption that one can usually date a work by its style. A nineteenth-century copy of a sixteenth-century painting will almost invariably be recognisable for what it is. One may see this principle of aesthetic determinism at work in historical reconstructions for stage or films where, despite the careful efforts of the designer to render a true image of the past, the present – the designer's present – constantly emerges. The date is 'given away' by the fact that the artist cannot but want to make his work beautiful and that in so doing he must make concessions to the standards of his period. It is not until these standards have lost their validity that we perceive the shortcomings of the imitations. The case of art forgeries is particularly instructive here. The Van Meegeren Vermeers, forgeries of a most ingenious kind, did at first deceive a great number of experts. Today we are amazed at their gullibility. This is not simply hindsight: the forger's deficiencies as an artist have become visible, as a patch on a piece of cloth becomes visible when it fades faster than the surrounding material. His style has begun to 'date' and we see that, despite all his efforts to conjure himself into the seventeenth century, he remains always in the 1930s. Benedict Nicolson has even shown that his facial types are drawn from film stars of the period. Once again, the artist is prevented from achieving his object by an inescapable deference to beauty.

Clearly, at this point, I am in some danger of contradicting myself. If the taste of any period is inescapable, then it is not only the bad artist who is affected by it. This is true enough, and it is true that the work even of a nonconformist like Van Gogh dates in the sense that we can place it historically; but it dates far less than does a work by Gustave Doré. The emotional insincerity which makes Doré's work so deplorable arises from an enslavement to the standards of his age. Van Gogh was liberated from this because the intensity of his vision was such that he could rise above it. The twelfth-century artist required no liberation because he could accept his age without inward questioning, for him there was no conflict, hence no insincerity.

Bad art, if this analysis be correct, arises from a rather sophisticated state of mind. In order to be insincere the artist must have some kind of choice and his choice must lie between two kinds of excellence, such as will occur only in certain conditions. We need not and should not imagine the bad artist deliberately setting out to please his public, we need not even think of him saying to himself: that looks attractive, that will please the critics. The damnable thing about bad art is that the insincerity which lies at its roots is not perceived by the artist himself.

It is not within my purpose, and perhaps it is beyond my capacity, to write a history of bad art. I will go no farther than to suggest that such a history would be confined to periods of high culture – I think we might discover examples of bad art in the Egyptian and later Chinese dynasties, the Hellenic world, some forms of Islamic art and European art after Giotto. It follows or co-exists with very good art, and this for the simple reason that very good art creates a destructive admiration for beauty. A typical instance would, I think, be the Italianising art of the Low Countries in the sixteenth century. If one were to take Messrs Thieme-Becker's solid tomes and count the number of good artists who have flourished since the death of Michelangelo one would, I am afraid, be forced to the unwelcome conclusion that the great majority have been bad. This melancholy but most important fact about art is obscured by our tendency to forget those artists whose work no longer interests us.

In the case of the late nineteenth century, where we are interested only in a few rebellious figures who stood outside the mainstream of contemporary work, we have today a completely distorted view. Look at the Encyclopaedia Britannica for 1912. A special section is devoted to recent developments in France. It was written by M. Léonce Bénédite, curator of the Luxembourg. He makes no mention of Seurat, Signac, Gauguin, Van Gogh, Vuillard, Berthe Morisot, or any of the Fauves, and for him the great French artists of the period after 1870 are Robert Fleury, Bastien Lepage, Meissonier, Rosa Bonheur, Gérôme, Bouguereau, Fromentin, Bonvin, Cormon and Henner. The article on British painting is even more striking. You may perhaps have heard of Herkomer, Luke Fildes and Frank Dicksee, but you will surely be surprised to learn that 'in marine painting no one has appeared to rival Henry Moore, perhaps the greatest student of wave forms the world has ever seen', although apparently even he had a competitor in the late Edward Hayes. Pass from the vast catalogue of English and French nonentities to the equally numerous and even more undistinguished multitude of Belgian, Dutch, German, Swedish and Norwegian and Russian painters and you will, I think, be appalled by the spectacle of misused paint and wasted effort. The French *indépendants* then appear in perspective, as a little candle in a vast and naughty world. They were bright indeed, but to most wanderers invisible. How could it be otherwise if we remember that the aim of painting is the production of beauty and that which these painters produced appeared ugly and inept.

This disquieting pattern of production and achievement is less obvious when we turn to more remote ages and, certainly, the nineteenth century is peculiar in having neglected nearly all its great painters and in having produced a school of art which finds no echo in the architecture and applied art of the epoch. Nevertheless, something of the same inequality of performance and rarity of merit will be found in all the periods subsequent to the High Renaissance.

But the nineteenth century even now, when we are learning to consider it with more sympathy than was possible a generation ago, is still in a class of its own. I cannot account for this beyond saying that it seems to me clear that the reasons are to be found in the history of society itself; but I do want to point to the intensity of the nineteenth-century concern with beauty. No other age sought it with such assiduity, it clamoured for beauty as a child clamours for sweets; it produced beauty by the ton and by the square mile, it applied beauty with reckless profusion to every available surface in the form of frills and flounces, stucco and gutta-percha mouldings, buttons, beading and Berlin wool, lincrusta, papier maché and Britannia metal, crockets, buttresses, cherubs, scroll work, arabesques and foliage. Look at any board school or bustle of eighty years ago and you will find more beauty than you know what to do with. It is true that the century produced some gaunt metallic structures which we can now admire, but from these, lovers of beauty – from Ruskin downwards – turned shudderingly away.

Here, perhaps, we may obtain a glimpse of the social mechanism that creates bad art. The mischievous sense of beauty arises from a corresponding perception of ugliness and a rejection of that ugliness. The art of the High Renaissance and, still more, that of the seventeenth-century academicians results from an aristocratic dislike of mean, base or villainous subjects; beauty here may almost be equated with 'nobility'. The idea was replaced by that which, first suggested by Diderot and then developed by Ruskin, asserts that beauty is indissolubly connected with morality. In both cases the critics were reacting against something that their society had made for itself – the vulgarities of plebeian life or the apparatus of industrialism – and they set against it an aesthetic ideal of a more tolerable kind. Thus we have a preoccupation with beauty which is eminently social in that it arises not from any delight in the visible world but from a species of social anxiety and social ostentation. I am not arguing that such motives are not productive of good art but that, while producing works of lasting value, they also engender much that is bad – the pretentious and histrionic confections of a Lebrun or a Van Loo, the sickly pomposities of Ary Scheffer or Joseph Albert Moore. These were an escape into social beauty and represented not personal feelings but polite evasions.

III

So, although there may be unchanging values in art, there is also much that is volatile. Indeed, it is possible to discover a pattern.

The clearest example of regular and predictable variations in aesthetic feeling is provided by the history of fashion. The word derives from, and is most clearly associated with, the history of costume and it is in the case of dress that we can most clearly see and measure our variations of sentiment. Any man and still more any woman who has reached a certain age will experience a feeling of amusement, of dismay, of disgust almost, when she is confronted by photographs which show her in the fashionable dress of a generation ago. What frights, what frumps we were in the twenties and thirties! Nevertheless, in the twenties we considered ourselves most becomingly got up; *then* it was the clothes of our parents at the beginning of the century which seemed ludicrous. In the same way M. Octave Uzanne writing in the 1890s considered that the crinoline was the most hideous thing that women had ever worn. In the 1850s it was the Directoire style which appeared abominable. Although our feelings concerning current fashions are not usually perfectly straightforward and vary a good deal in accordance with personal factors, nevertheless they are obviously and in a very palpable way approved, while their predecessors are equally clearly rejected even though they may be, and after a suitable interval usually are, restored to favour. This continuous process of change, with its accompanying process of admiration and disgust, is matched, although not exactly reproduced, in all the arts of the Western world. The continual search for new forms and the continual rejection of old ones, the period of neglect and the subsequent revival of interest in old styles, all suggest that there may be laws of change which will hold good for frescoes as well as for flounces. The laws of change forbid us ever to stay still, they forbid us to move too quickly and they forbid us to step back.

Perhaps I may elaborate on this, partly to show what these laws imply and partly to make it clear that we do in fact take their existence for granted – that they are in fact evident.

The law of movement is not entirely inexorable, the history of art can stand still, so still at least that its movement is imperceptible. Nevertheless, within very wide limits it applies to all Western art and European art history is the history of its operation. It would seem to be an ever accelerating process and just as there has never been a period in European history since the Crusades when there has *not* been a latest thing in dress, so there has *never* been a time when there has not been a latest style of architecture or, since the fifteenth century at all events, in painting. In the same way, there has never been a completely radical break in art. At times the rate of change has been comparatively rapid; but we are all of us the creatures of our own aesthetic, we imbibe the feelings that have been given us by our predecessors, even the greatest innovations start from somewhere – that is to say from the art of their own times, which is itself related to the past. I believe that it would be possible to put this more strongly and to say that there has never been a revolutionary who did not start as a traditionalist. At all events, it is just as unbelievable that the crinoline should become a bustle in six months as that art should develop from Renaissance to Baroque in a year, that the thirteenth century should produce a Rembrandt or the seventeenth a Seurat.

More remarkable is the fact that we can never step backwards, for artists have at times made strenuous efforts to do just this.

The so-called reactionaries of art are usually those who attempt to remain in the same place and to attempt a short step back is almost as rare in painting as in dress-making. Who today wants to wear the dresses or paint the pictures of yesterday? But it is by no means uncommon to attempt to follow a style which through the lapse of time has become, as we say, historic or romantic. This, as we have already seen, is surprisingly difficult. Pugin's Gothic, Wedgwood's classicism, Poiret's Directoire, remain subtly but unmistakably of their own time. Almost everything that Western man has made bears its inevitable date-stamp; this is the assumption of all *expertise* and it seems on the whole to be a justifiable assumption. Broadly speaking, art history never repeats itself.

Why then is the historical process so potent? Why can we neither stop still nor go backwards? Human beings are ingenious. On the face of it there appears no reason why this should be beyond human ingenuity and a great many of us – forgers, reactionaries, film producers, artists in search of originality, and so on – want for one reason or another to evade the workings of art history. And yet they find the task if not impossible, exceedingly difficult. Why should this be the case?

We may prove the rule by its exceptions. We shall not find societies which succeed in leaping forward or creeping backwards, but we do find some which succeed, very nearly, in staying still.

In Western art, and I suppose in the art of most of the more highly developed cultures, we deal naturally in time, we identify a thing by its period or dynasty; but when we consider simpler societies we think not of time but of place – Manesis, Tanagra, New Guinea. Only in a few comparatively rare cases do we find temporal change in primitive art. Relatively speaking, the art of primitive peoples is static and for the same reason it is of a uniform quality. Just as the personal adornments of savages seem to remain unaltered from generation to generation, so too the totem maker makes very much the same totem that his father and his grandfather made before him and that his son will make after him. And all the totems of the tribe will have very much the same aesthetic quality. No doubt some primitive artists are better, more skilful, more inventive than others; but in most primitive societies the magical quality of the work of art depends upon the exact repetition of formulae which exclude anything that we should class as self-expression or originality, while in many societies the artist is not even a specialist in his craft but all members of the tribe may be expected to join the business of image-making and the very idea of the artist as a person distinguishable from the rest of the community is something alien, almost inconceivable. In no primitive society, so far as I can make out, do we find that modern phenomenon, the man of genius, with his accompanying phenomena, the imitator, the *avant garde*, the very good and the very bad artists coexisting within the same society.

We may say then that, aesthetically speaking, there are two kinds of society – the static homogeneous society and the dynamic heterogeneous society, and between them, no doubt, a great many intermediate types. And yet, having said this, it is immediately necessary to make qualifications for it is not so much the society as the economic unit within the society which determines the range of aesthetic variation. The range of achievement which in Western societies is typical of the art of painting since the High Renaissance is not typical of the applied arts, at all events until the Industrial Revolution. Again in societies which have for long been predominantly heterogeneous, we shall find certain economically backward groups: peasants, craftsmen or workers in small industries, who have more or less maintained traditional methods and standards.

The determinant of aesthetic variation would seem then to be economic, and the determinant is the homogeneous or the heterogeneous situation rather than the homogeneous or the heterogeneous society. The importance of the 'situation' can hardly be exaggerated. So much of our aesthetic thinking is based upon the idea of discrimination that it is not easy to envisage a state of affairs in which the quality of an artist and his artefact would be taken for granted; again the idea of genius and with it the idea of exceptional intellectual or spiritual excellence as a natural concern of the artist – even though it may be attained only by a few particularly fortunate practitioners – is so familiar that we cannot readily accept the idea of a condition in which all artists are equal. It is at all events arguable that the idea of beauty in works of art is itself a product of the more complex type of social organisation. The savage cannot see his own works as being beautiful partly because he is without the power of discrimination but also because, so far as we can tell, he is solely interested in their practical efficiency as a means of influencing the course of nature or of bringing good fortune.

Before attempting the next leg of my argument I would like to offer two other facts which seem to me to support my contentions. Firstly, then, the homogeneous situation can at once be destroyed by an attack upon its economic substructure. Introduce modern methods of production and distribution to no matter what homogeneous group and you can kill its art overnight. This has been done so frequently and in so many parts of the world that it is hardly necessary to adduce examples. Secondly, an individual living within our own society but not fully aware of its standards may produce work which approximates to the homogeneity of the simpler economies. Thus, again, young children, whose work is of surprisingly uniform quality; but as they grow older and learn to conform to adult standards they become unequal in performance. It may be said that the savage in this respect retains throughout adult life the uniformity of achievement of the child. That there is some kind of causal connection between social development and patterns of aesthetic feelings seems to me sufficiently clear. I believe that our aesthetic sentiments are profoundly modified by the structure of the society in which we live and this belief is based upon what seem to me some extremely trite observations. If I now go on to consider the mechanism of this relationship I do so in a much less confident spirit and I am very well aware that I am omitting a great deal.

The history of art may be regarded as the history of a consumer-producer relationship. This remains true even when the producer is the sole consumer, when he is, so to speak, attempting to satisfy his own demand without regard for anyone else. There are, in fact, situations in which the artist is doing this even though he is working for quite a large market. The savage is in this position in that he is bound by regulations which oblige him to be intensely conservative but which, we may surmise, are not felt as a restriction in that he himself is fully identified with the tribe, clan or society to which he belongs. This very simple homogeneous relationship can change when a society accumulates enough wealth to make it possible for the consumer to demand an especially big, elaborate or costly work of art. It is at this point that the individual or the community is likely to start competitive consumption. In the history of costume we find a continual effort on the part of individuals and classes to keep up with the Joneses or whoever else may set the standard of sumptuosity, grandeur and refinement, and a continual effort by the predominant individuals and classes to maintain proper distinctions by changes of fashion. I have already attempted to describe this process as it relates to clothing. Here I must ask the reader to accept this extremely brief allusion to what is an extremely complex process, adding only this: that whereas I have no doubt at all that the process which we call fashion arises from the workings of a competitive society, the workings of fashion, involving as they do our feelings concerning decorum, decency and beauty, come to have a kind of moral force so that, for instance, it is not unreasonable to imagine a sartorially conscious Robinson Crusoe dressing each night for dinner without even having a Man Friday to lay out his black tie for him. Fashion, in fact, is born of competition but may take highly sublimated forms. Having made this reservation, I would suggest that a similar force makes itself felt in the history of the other visual arts, that city states, cathedral towns, princes and guilds have used art for competitive purposes and that this process of emulation gradually brings about that dynamic process to which I have already referred. At the same time it modifies the relationship between the consumer and the producer. A desire for pre-eminence undermines conservatism. The difference between the skilled and the semi-skilled worker becomes more noticeable, the master and the journeyman become differentiated and the way is opened for the supremely skilful artist, the man of genius. For a long time, however, aesthetic discrimination would remain comparatively undeveloped. The master and the journeyman are both trying to do very much what the public wants them to do, only some of them are better at doing it than others.

A radical break occurs when the artist gains such technical mastery that he can enjoy a much higher degree of freedom than had hitherto been possible, so much so that he need no longer respond to the consumer's requirements but rather begins himself to dictate the nature of the demand. This sets up two quite different consumer-producer relationships. On the one hand, you have Michelangelo producing works of art that are intended to please Michelangelo; on the other hand, you have consumers who want works by Michelangelo or by artists who are attempting to be as Michelangelesque as possible. The idea of beauty is no longer a purely communal idea, it is an idea very largely formed by a handful of exceptional individuals. From being an integrated part of a society the artist is now a potential genius or a potential imitator; his own individuality, his own powers, decide his fate. Moreover he is obliged to discriminate. The leaders of his profession have differing personalities; he may choose to be a Titian rather than a Michelangelo, or he may seek for some eclectic style which presupposes an abstract idea of beauty.

At this point we may glance at two phenomena characteristic of Western society since the Renaissance: regionalism, a situation in which a whole area or a whole industry is so far removed from the influence of fashion – is so economically backward – that the old consumer-producer relationship persists; and provincialism, in which the market for whatever may be the latest form of art has been established but in which the demand is met either by importation or by the imitation of foreign wares. Given sufficient economic growth a provincial centre may finally establish itself as a metropolis, as has happened in the Low Countries, France, England and the United States.

Thus the Renaissance produced an extraordinary diversity of achievement and response in the arts. Nevertheless, there still is a certain persisting homogeneity in architecture and painting. Despite some notable examples of nonconformity, the great European styles – Mannerist, Baroque, even Rococo – do give a certain measure of common purpose to the visual artists of the sixteenth, seventeenth and eighteenth centuries. But by the nineteenth century that homogeneity had been almost entirely destroyed. We can just perceive the temporal quality that unites Victorian gothic to Victorian renaissance – perhaps we may even discern some kind of community of feeling between Renoir and Sir John Millais, Van Gogh and Gustave Doré – but the aesthetic diversity of the last century is far greater than that of any preceding age.

The reasons for this profound revolution lie, I think, in the evolution of both the producer and the consumer. The patron was, in the Middle Ages, an institution; by the nineteenth century he had become a market, a market composed of innumerable individuals most of them united by a prevailing taste in art but with many varieties of individual feeling. The painter might make direct contact with individuals but he might also dispose of his wares through a dealer or an academy acting as a marketplace. Already, in seventeenth-century Holland, we can see how this resulted in the development of a multitude of different *genres* and of an earnest attention on the part of the artist to the business of finding that kind of form and content which would please a large section of the public. In the nineteenth century this vast heterogeneous clientele was even more important and created an even greater diversity of manners, all the more so in that it contained a certain number, statistically minute but aesthetically important, who were ready to subsidise eccentricity.

The situation of the artist underwent an equally radical change. In the nineteenth century, he enjoyed an unheard of freedom. He was free not only because the diversity of the market enabled him to choose his style in a way that had never before been possible but also because, sometimes, he had a high degree of economic independence. And yet, generally, he used that freedom to seek a profitable market, to conform as nearly as he might, given the heterogeneity of the age, with its prevailing tastes. The artists who are today remembered and valued were the few who took a different course. It would seem that the aesthetic fashions of the nineteenth century were different from those of previous centuries. The dichotomy of taste was so absolute, the artists in their opposing camps were so completely opposed in aim and in method – and, most important of all, we have rejected the majority tendency so violently. It is this last peculiarity of the nineteenth-century situation which I find most interesting. I do not want to suggest that it is entirely new; no doubt in the High Renaissance the Quattrocento looked pretty old hat, certainly the words mannerist and baroque, both of which have a pejorative origin, imply that there was a time when these styles became dowdy. But the rejection of the acknowledged giants of their time, Delaroche, Meissonier, Böcklin, Leighton, has been more complete than any previous reversal of taste in art history while the apotheosis of the

25

rebels – of Cézanne, Seurat, Gauguin, etc. – is an astonishingly novel phenomenon.

The reason for this peripety of taste may be that what we may call the salon painters were particularly well able to meet the requirements of the consumer in that they had no object save the satisfaction of the customer, and the customer was particularly interested in sentiment, so that today, being unable to share the sentimental attitudes of, say, Lord Leighton's public, we can find very little else to admire in his work. The rebels on the other hand seem to have shown a wilful disregard for public feeling and in fact to have escaped, as nearly as an artist can escape, from the influence of fashion. This ability to resist the dynamic forces of taste, or (to put the thing positively) this power to say something personal, comes pretty near to a definition of what in the present century we find admirable in art. So that today we enjoy the work of the child, the savage, or the artists in a homogeneous situation, all of whom escape the operation of fashion because for them it does not exist, and we can also enjoy the work of those masters who could rise above fashion either by controlling it or by rejecting it.

In our present situation, a situation in which painters seem to have come to terms with the demands of society and art seems more and more to be a part of the apparatus of fashionable life, it is permissible to wonder whether we too will see some drastic revaluation of present values. At this point, however, speculation becomes altogether too foolhardy and it is wiser not to proceed.

The Art Critic and the Art Historian

I will begin with a quotation from Leslie Stephen. He is describing the effect upon him when he was a young man at Cambridge of the first volume of *Modern Painters*.

People who shared the indifference to art of those dark ages (I can answer for one) were suddenly fascinated, and found to their amazement that they knew a book about pictures almost by heart. They did not foresee the day when a comfortable indifference to artistic matters, instead of being normal and respectable, would be pitiable and almost criminal.

Stephen, writing at the turn of the century, utters what sounds like a half serious *cri de coeur*, for by that time the literature of art was becoming formidable and, as one may well believe, in his view, oppressive. And yet it was but a beginning; our age has made the image, in an astounding way, accessible and ubiquitous and the literature, or perhaps one should say the dissemination, of the visual arts has attained almost frightening dimensions. While the coffee tables of the rich groan beneath the weight of glossy facsimiles – or at least of what purport to be facsimiles – the rest of us are surfeited with an almost equally glossy and even more misleading array of paperbacks and Sunday supplements, not to speak of the cultural offerings of the cinema and the goggle box. If 'a comfortable indifference to artistic matters' was 'pitiable and almost criminal' at the beginning of the century, today it is almost impossible, even in Cambridge.

But while the literature of art is, in publishers' terms, booming, it has in one respect suffered a loss. During the past two hundred

years there has usually been some important figure who acted as a
censor and an apologist of the contemporary scene, a Diderot, a
Baudelaire, a Ruskin or a Roger Fry. Who amongst our living
authors plays this important role? What name springs to mind? I
would suggest that no name actually springs; the last of our
grandly influential critics was Sir Herbert Read and since his death,
whatever else modern art may or may not possess, it has no
prophet. This is not to say that aesthetic prophets are necessarily
desirable nor that there are not some very conscientious and
extremely perceptive critics at work today. But it is, I believe, true
that for better or for worse we have no grand pundit of living art
and I believe that this lack may be connected with what I see as a
certain diminution in the role of the art critic. It is a tendency which
I regret and the causes of which I want to try to discuss. It arises, I
believe, from a misunderstanding concerning the proper functions
of the critic, and this confusion of purpose will be my theme. First,
however, I think that I should glance at two important circumstances which make the work of an art critic particularly difficult
today.

In the first place it has to be acknowledged that the character of
modern art itself makes critical discussion difficult. During the past
sixty years, ever since the introduction of completely abstract
painting, the visual arts have become increasingly estranged from
literature (indeed we can trace the beginnings of this process to a
much earlier date); as a result, art has become increasingly
indescribable. The familiar theme and the comprehensible anecdote have ceased to interest painters or sculptors. The critic finds
himself called upon to assess objects and operations which, to a
previous generation, would have seemed to have nothing to do
with the fine arts and which an art critic would not have discussed.
The task is not easy and it is accomplished only too often by the
production of important sounding but almost entirely meaningless
verbiage. This, however, does not seem to me to be a capital
difficulty; there have always been critics who were ready to talk
nonsense about art. It is only, perhaps, that in the present situation
the temptation to do so is rather greater.

A much more important difficulty arises from the fact that the
dissemination of images to which I have already referred has, to a
large extent, altered the critic's function. The critic has, in some
measure, been replaced by the photographer. There was a time

when an important part of his business consisted in showing the public – through the medium of literature – things which it could not actually see. Art criticism, unassisted by accurate illustrations, was a peculiar and very exacting literary exercise in which the author had to conjure up the image of that which he wanted to discuss. Under such conditions the art critic was at an enormous disadvantage compared to the literary critic, in that he could never support his arguments with anything like positive verifiable evidence. And yet this weakness was also a source of strength; if a critic had the descriptive powers of a Ruskin he might produce the prose equivalent of a painting, and it is this necessity which makes *Modern Painters* so memorable as literature. At the same time, of course, it was a disability which led critics, consciously or unconsciously, to distort facts for their own ends. It gave them a command over their readers which is not enjoyed by their successors.

With the advent of efficient methods of reproduction the task of the critic gradually began to change. He became aware of the image as an alternative to his own descriptive powers and this was the case whether he was, or was not, actually able to make use of photography. Indeed the situation of the journalist working for a daily or weekly paper carrying few illustrations or none at all is particularly lamentable (this at all events was my sentiment when I worked for a newspaper), for he cannot but feel that he is at a disadvantage: he envies the lecturer who is armed with two projectors, the speaker who commands film or video tape, or the author who is furnished with all the resources of modern book production.

And yet all these are not only served but hampered by the abundance of their illustrations. They need no longer describe in words that which, even in a poor reproduction, is evident; they tend to become commentators and theorists. As such, they may have much to offer, but sometimes their text is less interesting than the aspect of the work of art itself, particularly when it is of a kind which must be allowed to speak for itself; that is to say, one which seems to depend upon purely formal relations. When once we have been supplied with an image, we may undertake the critical task for ourselves and it must often be the case that the author will be powerless to add much where we feel admiration and even more incompetent to persuade us when we feel disgust. It is not, perhaps, surprising that the public shows more interest in those authors who can give us information of a kind which the work itself cannot supply. When once our interest is engaged by a picture we are anxious not so much to be told *why* we are interested but rather who painted it, when it was painted, how it relates to the history of art and indeed to history as a whole.

I have said, I hope not unfairly, that there seems to be no outstanding figure amongst the critics of contemporary art, but amongst the art historians there are many. Here, indeed, there are names that *do* spring to mind and which, therefore, I need not mention. The availability of the image makes it possible for us all to be critics of art; it does not provide but rather stimulates our appetite for the kind of information that the art historian can give us.

Am I making an unreal distinction between the critic and the historian? Is it not true that the critic may sometimes venture into the past and that the historian must, inevitably, undertake some of the functions of the critic? It is true; and yet there is a distinction which, if we forget it, leads us, I believe, to bad history and to muddled criticism. I think that I can best explain what I mean by taking a fairly well known example.

Titian's *Sacred and Profane Love* in the Borghese Gallery is an oblong picture almost three times as wide as it is high. Titian has insisted upon its character by means of a series of very emphatic horizontals. In the foreground are two women seated at either end of a marble tank. One of them is very sumptuously dressed, and behind her there is a dark, rather stormy landscape crowned by a fortress. The other is almost naked and behind her we see the calm waters of an estuary, pastures, a church spire and a shepherd with his flock; she holds in her left hand a Roman lamp which burns against a cloudy but serene sky; she leans towards the clothed figure who, while facing away out of the picture, is also slightly inclined towards her companion; between them a putto dips one hand in the waters of the tank which is carved with the figures of men and horses.

Now it has been suggested that these figures represent two kinds of love, that the clothed figure symbolises the Venus of this world while the nude *beltà disornata* represents a more spiritual passion, the landscape echoes their characters (on the one side is mundane power, on the other spiritual repose), they are different and yet they are in harmony; the putto between them alludes perhaps to the waters of truth while the tank itself, a sarcophagus, reminds us of death.

This kind of information, even if it fails to convince, does seem to me helpful; for it engages our curiosity concerning Titian's purpose, it may give the work an historical resonance which would be lacking if we were to go no further than the admirable geometry of the picture, or, for that matter, the splendid way in which Titian can, with so little internal drawing, suggest density and move- ment. But although the information that the scholars can provide may and probably will help us to a deeper enjoyment of a work of art, it cannot be considered essential. The essential qualities without which the critic is impotent are sensibility and the ability to communicate his sentiments. And it is precisely his ability to proceed without external evidence which enables the art critic to venture into a field vaster and more various, more accessible and more comprehensible, than that enjoyed by any other kind of critic. For the art critic is not hampered, as the literary critic must be, by the narrow frontiers and the mortality of language. He needs no translator to explain the beauties of Scythian or Islamic work. The anthropologist as he carries his researches further and further into the remote past must soon lose all trace of the musician and the poet; but the materials of art criticism remain vividly and excitingly abundant in the caves of primitive man.

Nor is this all; I would claim, although perhaps with a shade less confidence, that our knowledge of the visual arts can have an intimacy which is seldom possible in the field of literature. We may sometimes be fortunate enough to have several versions or drafts of a literary work, but it is surely very rarely that we can witness the actual operation of an author's mind. I can indicate my meaning by pointing to an exceptional case where we do have this privilege: there *are* records which show us Henry James talking to or rather elaborately and impressively thinking aloud to his secretary, building phrase upon phrase until finally with what one might almost call a verbal ejaculation he unburdens himself of an entire idea. But this is a literary curiosity; whereas a sheet of drawings by Raphael or Leonardo, a brief notation of landscape by Claude or by Rembrandt, any kind of pictorial or sculptural thinking in wax or clay or upon paper is sufficiently common. So that there is a sense in which we know Rembrandt better than we can ever know

31

Shakespeare, for we have the record of his idle, his half-conscious thoughts. Nor is it simply that such records can give a vivid idea of what was passing through an artist's mind: there is a further degree of intimacy, not easily described in words, but familiar enough I think to anyone who has handled a pencil or a riffler; it is founded upon a community of experience, that fellow feeling which enables us to know, or, at least, to imagine that we know, just what a Chinese painter who died two thousand years ago felt – in his fingers so to speak – as he described the silhouette of a bamboo, how the loaded brush responded to his pressure upon the shaft, the way in which the hairs stroked the paper as they expanded to form the belly of the leaf and contracted to achieve the final calculated flourish of the stem. The historian points, very properly, to the enormous differences which divide age from age, culture from culture. It is true that these differences exist; it is true that we have no right to imagine that the artists of other periods shared our problems, our ideas about imagery; the very concept of art as we understand the term may have been unknown to many of them. But it is also true that many of the processes of making works of art remain as constant, as communicable from generation to generation, as are the physical processes of eating, drinking or suffering pain.

The legitimate theatre of operations is, for the critic, much wider than it can ever be for even the most encyclopaedic of art historians, also the operations themselves are of an essentially different character. Return for a moment to Titian's *Sacred and Profane Love*. I must ask you to imagine that I have talked about it with the tongues of angels, with the poetic fire of Ruskin, with the sweet convincing reasonableness of Roger Fry and said all that can be said in praise both of its form and of its content. And then imagine, as my splendid periods reach at last their magnificent peroration, that some one of you remarks: 'The trouble about that picture is that it makes me feel sick.'

Such a statement does not leave much room for conversational manoeuvre because it is, in its way, a valid criticism. It is almost as though my hypothetical interrupter were to say: 'I cannot see the beauties of that picture because I happen to have been born blind.' In fact, I think that most of us would admit that there are certain works of art, works it may be that are highly esteemed by reputable critics, to which we *are* blind; with the best will in the world and the most persuasive advocate to help us, we cannot overcome our disability. Tastes do change and critics may help to change them, but there are some points on which we remain 'invincibly ignorant'.

But now consider the historian: how does he deal with an objection of this kind? Surely he ought simply to disregard it? It is no concern of his, for what matters to him are not our feelings, but the facts. Titian's painting is one of the facts with which he has to deal and our feelings about the facts only become important if they happen to alter the course of history. That Titian was very much admired by subsequent artists is a matter of importance to him; whether they were right to admire him is not.

Now this seems a truth almost too obvious to be stated, and yet observe how easily this strong commonsensical position can be outflanked. Suppose a rather different kind of adversary were to say: 'I admire Titian but I have doubts about this picture, in fact, I am convinced that it is not by Titian.' At once it becomes necessary to meet the objection, for if we accept it our whole conception of Titian as an historical phenomenon would have to be altered. It is still true that a sentiment of this kind matters less to the historian than documentary evidence which establishes the authenticity of the work; it is true also that the identification of a picture by an examination of the artist's stylistic habits need be no more aesthetic than are the attributions of the handwriting expert; but there are cases where the quality of the work has to be taken into consideration and the aesthetic valuations of the critic, although they must always be treated with particular caution by the scholar, have at some points to be taken into consideration. To that extent art history is necessarily and inevitably dependent upon value judgments.

It must also be allowed that historians are likely to feel some emotion when confronted by works of art; it is likely that they will work in those fields of study where the flowers are fairest and, when they come to write a monograph on a favourite artist, that they will insist, not only upon the historical significance but upon the exceptional gifts of their 'discoveries'; no one will think the worse of an essay upon Raphael because it includes a rhapsody upon the School of Athens.

All this is no doubt very right and proper. But it is not right and proper when we allow our value judgments to lead us into a falsification of history, that is to say, when the historian allows his own personal predilections to determine which facts should and which facts should not be recorded, and this is what has happened.

Here is an example of what I mean. I take it, well aware of my own audacity, from the citadel of art historical studies, from the very Palladium itself. I refer, of course, to the leader columns of the *Burlington Magazine*.

The number of the magazine from which I am going to quote was mainly devoted to articles upon the Pre-Raphaelites; the editor seems to have felt that this was a circumstance which called for some kind of apology and he apologises thus:

this obsession with Pre-Raphaelitism . . . becomes really mysterious when it is judged by the highest and most unswervingly orthodox standards; when there is ample room for a *catalogue raisonné* of Botticelli, why bother with men who often provided, at best, but a pale and decorative reflection of his sublime qualities. The question is intellectually valid but emotionally unsound. Unlike the Victorians, we do not feel obliged, even theoretically, to devote ourselves to the highest and holiest whenever we come across it.

I do not think that one needs to reflect deeply in order to perceive that the leader writer, when he says that the question which he has proposed is intellectually valid but emotionally unsound, is stating the exact reverse of the truth. For him at least it is clearly emotionally valid, but it is so unsound intellectually that one wonders whether he has ever thought seriously about art history. Obviously he has; this is a slip, a *lapsus*, a nod from Homer and after all that number of the *Burlington was* devoted to the Pre-Raphaelites. In itself this minor aberration would not matter. But it does not stand by itself; effectively it endorses, lends authority and confers an air of intellectual respectability upon a kind of art history which deserves no such protection. There is, as I hope to show, a kind of semi-mythology masquerading as history which is confidently imparted to students both at secondary and higher levels of education and then, as any examiner knows to his cost, is regurgitated in the form of almost pure misinformation. It is this which is here characterised as intellectually valid and this which we are told follows unswervingly orthodox standards. I feel as a pious Catholic might feel who heard the Pope uttering heresy and although, as a pious believer in the *Burlington*, I am well aware that to attack that journal on art historical grounds is madness, I am sufficiently maddened to do so.

Let us then begin with the unswervingly orthodox standards in so far as they concern Botticelli. Were his 'sublime qualities' recognised during his lifetime? I imagine that they were; but I rather doubt whether they were still very highly valued at the time of his death, in 1510. Writing about half a century later Vasari praised his paintings and, to a lesser extent, his drawings in terms which are well enough but which fall rather short of sublimity. Thereafter nobody seems to have much to say about him. Karel van Mander gives him a brief mention and about a hundred years later De Piles in his *Abregé de la Vie des Peintres* allows him a short and non-committal paragraph. In the eighteenth century the general indifference continues. He was left to be rediscovered by the nineteenth century, but the nineteenth century was in no hurry to do so. The first signs of enthusiasm are in the works of Mrs Jameson and of François Rio although they neither of them reach Burlingtonian standards; these are not attained, in England at all events, until about 1870 when Ruskin, Pater and Swinburne began that enthusiastic appreciation which was continued by Ulmann and Horne. These last produced, I think, the first serious art historical studies to be devoted to this artist. Thus, for about three hundred of the four hundred and fifty years that separate us from Botticelli, his sublime qualities were ignored. What then became of the unswerving orthodox standards of art history? They look about as unswerving as a well oiled weathercock.

Now what about the 'pale and decorative imitators' of Botticelli, the Pre-Raphaelites? The comparison seems to me a little odd. I could wish that Holman Hunt were rather more decorative and certainly it would, to my mind, be an advantage if he were rather paler, nor do I see much trace of Botticelli in Millais, in Ford Madox Brown or even in Rossetti; Burne-Jones fits the description best, although even here I should have thought that Mantegna was a more important influence. Never mind, I do agree that they do not appear as great as Botticelli and twenty years ago I would have agreed heartily. But does this justify the wilful neglect of them that has been displayed by art historians? I use this term in order to describe a silence which arises, not from ignorance, such as we might find in a nineteenth-century historian who failed to mention Georges de la Tour, but from a sort of contempt well described by the *Burlington* leader writer in the phrase 'why bother?'. That the Pre-Raphaelites should not have been the subject of many serious studies until quite recently is no doubt an inevitable result of the prevailing taste in art; but there are some histories in which we have the right to expect that the author will rise above personal taste. An author who gives us a conspectus of the world's art should not pass over in silence a movement which, howsoever deplorable it may be, was, in its day, important and influential. The student has the right to know what happened even if in so doing he knows, as it were, the worst. It seems only right to say that two authors of world histories of art, Sir Ernst Gombrich and Helen Gardner, do precisely this; that is to say, they give us the essential facts. There may be others who do likewise; I do not know. But the student who relies on Professor Janson's large and handsome history of art, published in 1962, or on Upjohn Wingert and Mahler's *History of World Art* (1957) – both popular and in many ways deservedly popular works – will not discover that the Pre-Raphaelites ever existed. He will not be much better off with Robb and Garrison or Bernard S. Myers, both of whom briefly acknowledge the existence of the Pre-Raphaelites in passages remarkable for their inaccuracy. This is what I call misinformation, and it is the kind of misinformation that I have described as being regurgitated in examination papers. I do not see how it is to be justified.

Imagine a history of the reign of Charles II in which no mention was made of the Plague of 1665 and suppose that, taxed with this omission, the historian were to reply: 'I have followed the highest and most unswervingly orthodox standards. When there is ample room for a complete account of the Black Death, why bother with plagues which often provided, at best, but a pale and imperfect reflection of that sublime disaster?'

I have a notion that such a reply would not altogether satisfy other historians; why should it satisfy art historians? Historians, surely, should not exclude events because they don't like them and there are some happenings of such magnitude that they must be included in any history that pretends to be complete. What then do I mean by magnitude? I mean statistical size. It is the numerically important fact with which the historian is concerned. If the Plague of 1665 had killed only ten people any but a highly specialised historian would be justified in disregarding it, unless, of course, those ten people had been in positions of such importance that their death affected the lives of a great many other people. Exactly the same rule, so it seems to me, applies to art history. Michelangelo and Rubens are important to the art historian not only because they directly affected a great many other people but because they influenced the entire course of art history. As it happens, a great many art lovers today – but by no means all of them – admire these masters. Salvator Rosa is not, I think, regarded by most modern critics as a very great or even a very blood-curdling fellow, but because he did curdle the blood of several generations, he is an historical fact with which we have to reckon. I think that we do reckon with Salvator; he has at least a place in the history books. But there is another respect in which I think that historians are less historical, that is to say, less statistical than they should be. They look at the highest peaks of achievement and barely glance at the foothills on which, after all, the highest peaks usually rest. The minor artists, the lesser arts, because they are not, from an aesthetic point of view, very exciting do not receive very much attention, but do they not tell us as much and sometimes, perhaps, more about an age than do the masters and the masterpieces? In fact, in saying that the normal and typical art of a period tends to be overlooked in favour of that which is abnormal and eccentric I am not perfectly exact, for, in truth, our value judgments lead us in this matter into a strange inconsistency of approach. Where the common standard of achievement is high we *do* look at the work of an entire culture or dynasty; it is only when standards are uneven that we decide to disregard the greater part of the evidence.

Now, if we apply a statistical method of judgment to Botticelli and to the Pre-Raphaelites, we shall, I think, discover that, although Botticelli is an intensely interesting individual from a critical point of view in relation to the general history of Florence and Italy in the late fifteenth century, still, being at a kind of dead end in painting and out of sympathy with the ideas of the High Renaissance, he is not important in the way that a painter like Michelangelo or Rubens is important. He has no great immediate impact; in fact, he only becomes really influential thanks to the Pre-Raphaelites, or at least to the forces that made them what they were. The case of the Pre-Raphaelites themselves is rather different: in their earlier phase of development they exerted a very strong but not very permanent influence upon English painting; in their second stage, that of William Morris and Burne-Jones, they were closely connected with developments in painting and, even more, in the ornamental arts which are still affecting us today. Thus, like Botticelli, they passed through a period of oblivion; like Botticelli they have revived. It would certainly appear that they have created a more persistent commotion in the mainstream of art history than he did; historically speaking, neither of them ought to be considered negligible.

What I am trying to say is so very obvious that it would hardly be worth so much repetition were it not for the fact that it is hard to take; it is hard to take because it is emotionally unacceptable. We are drawn to the study of art by reason of an aesthetic emotion, an emotion which makes it very difficult to admit that what we call bad art may be just as important, historically, as that which we call good art. I use the phrase 'what we call good art' because as we have already seen, things which have been accounted bad become good and vice versa. But although we are aware of this and although we know that changes in style result necessarily from a change in our ideas of what is valuable in art, still it is hard to view art history – or at least recent art history – except through the distorting glass of aesthetic enthusiasm.

Aesthetic enthusiasm is a lovable and a forgivable characteristic but surely the struggle between rival conceptions of art, like the conflicts of nations or of political parties, is one which the historian should endeavour to understand even if he cannot sympathise with both sides. Where the ancient wars of art are concerned, the historian does not find this a difficult exercise. The quarrels between Rubenists and Poussinists, between Ingres and Delacroix, are not likely to engage the passions of a modern writer, nor could any contemporary scholar show himself a violent partisan in such disputes and hope to escape ridicule. But the history of the art of the past hundred years is *still* seen as an heroic encounter between the forces of light and those of darkness, a battle in which we still take sides, an issue which is still alive.

Read almost any art student's essay on a late nineteenth- or a twentieth-century topic and you will become aware that art history is seen as an unending struggle between the baddies and the goodies. The goodies are easily identified: they are the young, the *avant garde*, the bold, sincere, gifted revolutionaries, the men who shake the confidence of the dense, materialistic bourgeoisie; they are the Courbets, the Manets, the Cézannes, Picassos, Mondrians, Pollocks and whoever the latest hero of the *avant garde* may be; probably the essayist himself is on the way to becoming a goodie. The goodies have only one fault: they grow old and in so doing tend also to lose something of their goodieness.

But who are the baddies? They appear to have been born old; they are rotten time-serving salon painters, photographic fuddy duddies who paint what they see or worse still, being portrait painters, insincerely paint what they don't see; until quite recently the Pre-Raphaelites were baddies. It is, above all, the academy which is cast in the role of Lucifer; but who the academicians may be, what they teach or stand for we never discover. It is, as we have already seen, a characteristic of this kind of history that you do not look at your opponent; he is to be condemned upon no evidence. And so we get the very strange picture of nineteenth-century and twentieth-century art consisting of a series of assaults by a heroic minority upon a powerful enemy who seems hardly to exist.

This grotesque travesty of history is sustained not simply by what I have called aesthetic enthusiasm, but by something even stronger. The myth of nineteenth-century art history is played out by the young artist and the critic, both of whom are eager to take up the role of 'goodies'. To this end, it is impressed upon young artists that they must at all costs be 'contemporary'; I must confess that I find it rather difficult to imagine how they can contrive to be anything else. To be shocking, rebellious, revolting – in every sense of the word – becomes a duty. The possibility that a reactionary might have virtues or that a revolutionary might have faults is barely entertained. In the same way the degree to which an artist has advanced in the *avant garde* is held to be the grand criterion of merit. The critical question: 'Is X a better artist than Y?' is confused with the historical question: 'Which of them was the first to invent such and such a device or technique?' If X was making sculpture out of contraceptive appliances in the last weeks of December 1972 then he was more *avant garde*, more of a goodie, than Y who did no such thing until the beginning of February 1973. In fact, of course, the sequence of events may be of art historical interest but it is of no critical importance whatsoever.

These considerations have brought us back from the art historian to the critic and I think that we are now in a position to understand some of his present maladies. In the bad melodrama which passes for the art history of the past hundred years the critic is the baddest of all the baddies. There are, to be sure, a few shining lights, a few heroes, but they are far outnumbered by the villains – once again a largely anonymous band – who sneered at Cézanne, who denounced Manet, who couldn't see the point of Picasso, who declared that the *avant garde* rebel was flinging a pot of paint in the face of the public. These were the blackest wretches of all – the lackeys of the academy.

The unhappy academicians of our own day have no lackeys, no critic would dare to praise them, for to do so would be reactionary. When the latest young man hurls a pot of paint in the critic's face, the critic murmurs, as he squeezes the polyvinylacetate out of his whiskers, that he is in no way alienated by what has, he considers, been a total experience in commitment to an environmental situation. To protest would be to class oneself with the enemies of progress. We fear the judgments of history; our timidity is such that we dare not say boo to a goose for fear that it should turn out to be a swan.

This is no doubt too sweeping and I am sure that it would be possible to produce examples of modern criticism which would make it necessary to allow that there are critics of contemporary art to whom my words do not apply. It is on them, the critics who are not afraid to appear reactionary, that our best hopes for the development of healthy art criticism depend. For the prevailing tendency not only amongst critics but amongst artists and the public at large is one of nonconformist conformity. Surveying the field of modern art there must be many of us who inwardly condemn much that we observe as pretentious, affected and downright silly; but there are few who have the courage roundly to declare their feelings. Others have made this 'mistake' before and they have been proved wrong. But does it really matter if a critic is, as they say, wrong?

This brings me to what is perhaps the most important difference between the historian and the critic. It is the business of the critic to tell the truth about the kind of facts which cannot be verified, that is to say, about his own feelings. It is the business of the art historian to tell the truth about the kind of facts that can be verified and, if necessary, to disregard his own feelings.

There are then two different kinds of truth about works of art, the one dependent upon evidence acceptable to everyone, the other based upon sentiments which derive from the relationship between the work of art and the spectator, a personal relationship varying from person to person and a variable relationship varying from time to time. This surely is something that we all know. Equally surely it is something that we forget or disregard, for it is because this distinction is not made that the historians produce history which is not true and the critics produce criticism which is not sincere.

Allow me, therefore, at the risk of being tedious, to point out that Burne-Jones was born in 1833 and that this is a fact; it is also a fact that when I was 17 I thought Burne-Jones a very bad painter. But whereas everyone is and was in agreement as to the date of his birth, *not* everyone agreed with my estimate of his work nor, today, do I agree with it myself. I am not sure that this implies that I either am or was *wrong* about Burne-Jones; but it certainly does mean that the relationship between me and his painting has changed. It is true that circumstances could arise which would oblige me to believe that Burne-Jones was not born in 1833, but if I were to change my opinion on this point it would be necessary for me to convince not only myself, but other people, that my arguments were sound.

To state the case in other terms: it is possible to imagine a man born incurably blind who, nevertheless, could make a valuable contribution to the history of art; but a blind art critic is not imaginable. Please don't misunderstand me: I am not saying that art historians ought to be blind; I am not even suggesting that they should be devoid of aesthetic feeling; indeed, I am all for having them passionately in love with that which they think good and strongly hating that which they think bad, provided always that they are aware, as a good historian should be aware, that their feelings are themselves a part of history, interesting precisely because they fluctuate and are fallible and not to be considered as immutable laws. Aesthetic emotion only becomes a danger to the historian when it leads him to rearrange facts in order to suit his emotional needs, when he is led by passion and by prejudice into falsehood.

The situation of the critic who is unable to distinguish between the facts of feeling and the facts of history is more perilous than that of the historian who makes the same error. For, after all, the historian need not be involved in a situation in which his judgment is likely to be distorted. But for the art critic the danger is nearly inescapable.

There have, no doubt, been critics who were so confident in their own aesthetic rectitude that it never occurred to them that they might defer to the opinions of others or even to their own former views. It may even be that there *are* such critics. On the whole, I suspect that these happy few are characteristic of an aesthetically confident society, one which was able to accept aesthetic regulations without difficulty. In our own society, shaken by the aesthetic shocks of the last hundred years, doubts must surely arise. One would like to imagine that the critic feels that there are but two questions for him to answer, firstly: 'What do I feel about this work of art?'; secondly: 'How best can I express my feeling?' But I think one must imagine a rather more complicated and agitated inward debate developing more or less in this manner:

Ego: What is that meant to be? I don't care for it at all.
Super Ego: Look again. Everyone is talking about the chap who did that.
Ego: I can't honestly say that I like the thing.
Super Ego: Oh, but you ought to like it; it's so *Modern*; and if you don't say that you like it everyone will laugh at you and set you down as a reactionary.
Ego: I think it's a leg-pull.
Super Ego: But that is what they said about Cézanne and Matisse and Picasso and Marcel Duchamp.
Ego: Come to that, I think Marcel Duchamp is a leg-pull.
Super Ego: For shame! Don't you know that he's a classic, his work fetches thousands on the art market. Why, at this rate, you'll be saying that you don't like Mondrian . . .
Ego: Well, if you want to know the truth . . .
Super Ego: Stop. I can't bear it. You mustn't say such things, even to yourself.
Ego: Well, all right, I'll accept Mondrian; but in the case of this particular work, I cannot honestly say . . .
Super Ego: We might hedge a bit. Say: it's profoundly interesting in its way, although the idiom presents certain difficulties. That doesn't commit us too deeply.

Now in this dialogue it is clear that what I have called the *Super Ego* is appealing to authority. The question 'Am I wrong?' implies in this context that there is somewhere an authority with powers of judgment superior to one's own. This authority may take the form of an academy, or a doctrine, a tradition or a consensus of critical and educated opinion. In one form or another it is a necessary court of appeal, for without some such tribunal, which in its turn supposes the existence of a law-giving body, it is hard to see how the critic can believe that his judgments have any objective value or can be more than expressions of personal opinion.

The critic, in fact, wants to have his opinions and eat them. That sensibility which in the first place drew him to the task of criticism makes him also the natural and proper mouthpiece of his own views. But the strength of his aesthetic beliefs makes him try to vest his feelings with objective authority, an authority which derives its power precisely from the fact that it does not simply represent the critic's own feelings but those of something that you might call an 'external examiner'. Hence the painful and not very productive colloquy which I have attempted to describe. In that discussion, the keenest thrust of the *Super Ego* was its appeal to history, for it is a remarkable fact that, whereas we usually treat the judgments of the past with some contempt, the judgments of the future, even though we know that these too must eventually become the judgments of the past, are awaited with anxious respect.

'History will say that you were wrong' – that is the threat; and in that threat is implicit the idea that the critic is a kind of tipster, someone who is expected to give us all the winners and who, if he backs a non-starter, must be a bad critic.

A very slight acquaintance with art history should be sufficient to undermine this view. Consider the Tattenham Corner of criticism at the turn of the eighteenth century: Raphael taking the lead from Correggio, Lebrun coming up close behind the first four, then Annibale, Ludovico and Agostino followed by Carlo Dolci leading Domenichino by a short head . . . And then, a century later, nearly all those past favourites left far behind by dark horses from another stable: Fra Angelico, Filippo Lippi, Masaccio, not to speak of Botticelli. But were the Bolognese out of the race? Not a bit of it; fifty years later we see the Carracci coming up strongly beside the rails past Benozzo Gozzoli.

In the history of art there are no winners because there is no winning post. How then is it possible for punters to find a 'good thing'? In the short run, it is perhaps possible; there are critics (and dealers) who can tell us with reasonable accuracy what to buy and what to unload. In terms of the immediate future it is reasonable for a critic to discern tomorrow's opinion of today's assessments; but neither the critic nor anyone else can tell whether such reversals may not themselves be reversed, so that that which will seem foolish tomorrow may appear wisdom the day after tomorrow.

Granting, however, that critics do make judgments which seem to us clearly to be mistakes, do we really believe that such errors invalidate their criticism? Let us agree that Diderot was wrong about Greuze, that Baudelaire was wrong about Ary Scheffer, that Sickert was wrong about Cézanne and that Roger Fry was wrong about Turner.

To what extent is their reputation as critics damaged by what seem to us to be errors of judgment? The mischief, so it seems to me, is small; it amounts to no more than this, that we find criticism more enjoyable when we can agree with the critic; the writer who can match our sentiments in words and perhaps explain to us why we like what we do like, must write more enjoyably than he who condemns that which we love and extols that which we detest. Nevertheless, even at their most wrong-headed, Diderot, Baudelaire, Sickert and Fry can delight and teach us or, if they do not, I fancy that the blame lies with us and not with them.

Let me, in conclusion, compare the work of a critic who was almost continuously right, with that of a critic who, as often as not, was violently and impressively wrong: I refer to Émile Zola and John Ruskin.

Even Zola made mistakes, the blunders of romantic youth and of bourgeois maturity; but still, if one considers the *Salon* of 1866, the article on Manet, the review of the *Exposition Universelle* of 1867 and the *Salon* of 1868, how wonderfully right he appears. His heroes – Manet, Monet, Boudin, Sisley, Degas, Pissarro – are our heroes, and his villains – Gérome, Cabanel, Meissonier – are our villains. Very few writers on art have been so completely justified by the opinions of posterity, certainly not Ruskin.

Ruskin could indeed write eloquently about artists whom we most of us admire today: Turner, Tintoretto and the Gothic builders; but he was unable to do so without making detestable remarks about others whom we also admire. To praise Turner he had to blackguard Constable; he could love Tintoretto only by hating Michelangelo; his admiration for Gothic forms had to be combined with a loathing for Palladian architecture. Nor was this the end of his silliness: while venting his spleen upon Rembrandt and Caravaggio he had to strip every laurel in his grove in order that he might lay tributes enough at the feet of Miss Greenaway and Miss Alexander.

And yet, when we measure Zola against Ruskin it must surely be allowed that there is a point of view from which Zola looks the smaller of the two critics. Certainly he is very readable, he says things which are acute and amusing, he knows how to plead and how to be insolent. But compared with Ruskin he seems hardly more than a first-rate journalist, involved rather in the party political warfare of art than in any very deep emotion.

It may seem that I am in some danger here of applying to criticism exactly the kind of judgment values which seem to me so unreliable when applied to art itself. Let me therefore admit at once that there will be many highly respectable critics who do not share my admiration for Ruskin's prose and to them it may well appear that my view concerning his greatness as a critic is mistaken. How can I persuade them that Ruskin uses the English language with such force and such sincerity that he becomes admirable even when he is talking nonsense? But the fact that Ruskin's critical achievements were of the greatest art historical importance is something that can be demonstrated, for it is a matter of historical truth that, in the middle of the last century, an undergraduate at Trinity Hall, who had no great interest in any art save that of literature, was suddenly fascinated by Ruskin and found to his amazement that he knew 'a book about pictures almost by heart'.

Conformity and Nonconformity in the Fine Arts

The artist is, in popular mythology, a nonconformist. He is thought to diverge from the group and to be, in every way, eccentric. His art will, very likely, be incomprehensible save perhaps to the members of a small coterie. He is less fixed in his habits and in his habitat than is the business-man or the manual worker. In short, he is a Bohemian.

This popular conception of the artist is, of course, inexact; there are a great many painters and sculptors who, in their social habits, are almost indistinguishable from their fellow men, and a great mass of painting and sculpture is always in perfect conformity with current tastes and current conventions. Most art is, perforce, socially acceptable and socially comprehensible.

Nevertheless, the popular conception does correspond to a reality. The social status of the painter has, since the Renaissance, been much more fluid than that of the members of most other professions. His work calls for the public expression of his most intimate feelings – a sale, so to speak, of his dirty linen – and this certainly imposes emotional strains that are severe in proportion to the intimacy of the artist's confessions. Moreover, for the past hundred and fifty years the fine arts have been in a state of permanent revolution, and that revolution, which has been an insurrection of individualists, has had the effect of making painting more and more a means of intimate public exposure and hence of public incomprehension. Those works that we now think most valuable in the output of the nineteenth century were produced by a small minority of rebels acting in defiance of public opinion, including the opinion of the vast majority of their colleagues. To some extent this aesthetic nonconformity has been associated with social nonconformity, so that the use of the word bourgeois as a term of abuse belongs as much to the terminology of romantic art as it does to that of Marxism.

There are therefore sufficient grounds for the habitual judgment of the man in the street who believes that the behaviour of artists is strange and unpredictable. At the same time, this view of the artist is a comparatively new one in the history of art, and there is no reason to suppose that it existed, or had any foundation in reality, before the Renaissance, or, at all events, before the time of Giotto.

Within the guild system the status of the painter was as clearly defined as that of the goldsmith, the fuller, or the harness maker, with whom, indeed, his guild contracted corporate alliances. The idea of genius, or rather of the man of genius, which is so firmly embodied in our modern conception of the artist, was not provided for by guild regulations, and the 'masterpiece', which we now think of as the exceptional work of an exceptional performer, was no more than the craftsmanlike production that every individual presented to his guild when he was received as master. The art of painting was a trade clearly placed amongst the lower, or mechanical, arts, and this position was perfectly well understood by all parties.

In this tradition-directed social context the innovator or revolutionary did not enter into the scheme of things. The idea of individual pre-eminence was itself extremely limited – formulae were repeated from generation to generation and the artist continued to do what was expected of him to the best of his ability. Although his name was legion and he survived for centuries, the peasant craftsman of a given culture may be considered as one person, and is thus treated in works of scholarship. One has only to think of the fantastic diversity of talent and of style in the painting of the past hundred years, as compared with the uniform achievements of many generations of Han potters, to see how radical the change has been. It is no exaggeration to say that there is less variation in style and aesthetic quality in a hundred years of medieval sculpture than Picasso alone has shown in his lifetime.

Until we come to a fairly recent period, the evidence concerning the social behaviour of artists is not extensive; but it would appear that the changing pattern of behaviour is closely linked with the aesthetic fragmentation to which I have referred. This process arises when a certain number of artists, breaking with tradition, present the public with new techniques and new ideas. Good workmanship then becomes of less importance than talent. The painter ceases to be a pure craftsman; he becomes a pictorial poet and demands a status such as that enjoyed by the liberal artist. Already we find this claim made for painters by Petrarch in the fourteenth century; but I think that it was not until the middle of the fifteenth century that society was ready to listen to it. The treatise of the fifteenth-century architect and humanist Alberti, with its insistence upon the mathematical nature of the art, upon humanism, and upon the historical and poetical functions of the painter, marks the change. But it was the painters themselves who made it inevitable. The artists of the High Renaissance were, in fact, so eminent, there were amongst them so many great men, that it became necessary to find a new social apparatus that might contain them, rather in the same way that it became necessary to find a new social apparatus for the engineer and the industrialist of the nineteenth century. In the one case, as in the other, the process of social readjustment created difficulties. 'I have never been a painter or a sculptor,' said Michelangelo, 'in the sense of having kept a shop.' The wife of a freshly knighted grocer could not have been more haughty.

The social aspirations of the post-Renaissance artist eventually found expression, first in Rome, and then in Paris, with the establishment of academies of art. The academy was a professional association imitated from those that had been created by the philosophers and the literati. It was established in opposition to the guild; it gave the artist a professional hierarchy and provided an education in taste that could supplement, and eventually replace, the purely manual training of the workshop.

Libertas restituat artes may seem, to modern painters, to have been a strange motto for the Academy of Louis XIV, but in fact the Academy did liberate the painter from the restrictive practices and the plebeian associations of the Guild of St Luke; it enabled him freely to seek his fortune as a graphic poet or a pictorial philosopher and, with the example of Raphael and Sir Peter Paul Rubens before him, to live and to paint like a gentleman.

The style of the academies was, or was intended to be, free from the frantic distortions of Mannerism, from the striking verisimilitude of the followers of Caravaggio, from the gaudy colours of

Venice or, in fact, from any of those artifices whereby a painter might gain the favour of the crowd. It was an art for the highly educated, its programme being aptly expressed in five words: Nobility, Decorum, Regularity, Chastity, and Restraint. It forms a coherent part of the age of Racine, which was also the age of Poussin, and of that 'regime of status' which flourished in the seventeenth century, decayed in the eighteenth century and perished in 1789.

But already, contemporaneously with the French Royal Academy, we find in the free society of Holland painters who escaped, not only from the bondage of the guilds, but from the conventions of the academies; and it is here, in the work of Rembrandt, that we may perceive the first tremendous insurrection of the human spirit that was to burst out again so violently in the nineteenth century. In his later work, Rembrandt owes allegiance to no one; he is a 'self-directed painter', bound only by his own conscience as an artist.

The guilds were destroyed both by the emergence of a professional association that was socially more attractive than a trade corporation and, in Holland, by the development of free enterprise. The training of apprentices in the workshop outlived the guild and continued until, for economic reasons, it became unnecessary. But, at an early stage, the teacher-pupil relationship was modified.

Before the Renaissance, the main task of the pupil was to learn to imitate his employer until the work of the apprentice became indistinguishable from that of the master. Therefore, for so long as the articles of apprenticeship lasted, the master could sell the pupil's work as his own. As the art of painting developed, the work of the pupil might, as he achieved mastery, diverge a little, be a little more 'modern' than that of his employer. But the distinction between the two would in general be slight, and their common character would be strongly imprinted by the community to which they both belonged.

In the sixteenth century, the local and paternal relationship was increasingly replaced by international and ideological 'schools'. We find Italianising northerners; schools, such as the 'Roman School', which were not strictly local; and those of the Mannerists and Naturalists, which were schools of thought. This was not a wholly new development in the history of art; ideas have always travelled. But the tendency of the smaller centres to accept foreign influences and to become provincial instead of being regional was greatly strengthened and accelerated.

As this process developed, the role of the teacher diminished. Painters found their masters, not in real life, but in museums; and the school, despite some persistent local affiliations, became an ideological phenomenon.

By the time this stage had been reached, that is, by the nineteenth century, the academies had long ceased to be of use to the progressive artist. Like the guilds, which by then were to some extent idealised in the minds of painters, they had outlived their purpose. Now it was the academies that were seen as the enemies of individual expression. Originality was now the grand desideratum. The academies claimed the right to teach, to assess and to regulate the affairs of the fine arts, and this was felt to be an intolerable infringement of the rights of the individual.

The painting of the nineteenth century has been classified under a number of headings: Romanticism, Realism, Impressionism, Neo-Impressionism, and so on; but these schools, or movements, as we might more truly call them, correspond only in a very rough and ready way to the actual work of the painters, and there were a great many eccentric figures, some of them by no means undistinguished, who, in reality, defy classification. The main currents of artistic feeling are definable; but the only common quality of the great artists of that period was an intense belief in the right of the painter to express himself as he saw fit. They were attacked by and opposed to 'official art', and they were all *indépendants*.

The idea of genius, of native abilities finding expression without the assistance of teaching or the help of 'rules of art', was one that had already perturbed Sir Joshua Reynolds when he founded the Royal Academy. In the late nineteenth century the emergence of the 'autodidact' in the person of the 'Douanier' Rousseau, a Sunday painter who by academic standards was quite untaught and quite inept, together with a new child-centred doctrine of art education and a new belief in the supreme value of 'self expression', completed the process.

Deprived of all rules, the artist had now to regulate his conduct entirely by his personal conception of what was right or wrong in art. Nor could he do this by looking to the example of those masters who had followed the 'grand style'; certainly he looked at the museums, perhaps more than ever before; but he could no longer find in them a coherent development, a true apostolic succession from the Greeks to the High Renaissance and from the High Renaissance to the great academicians.

In truth, that academic path which avoided the Venetians, the Flemish, and the Dutch had always been too narrow for comfort; but with the growing taste for Gothic and primitive work, for the peasant and the child, the artist was left with no path of any kind; the world was all before him. In aesthetic theory it became necessary to search for some common denominator, for 'significant form' and 'plastic values', which, in fact, left the painter to the dictates of his own artistic conscience, to what Cézanne called '*sa petite sensation*'.

Thus, the twentieth-century painter or sculptor finds that he may express himself freely with no outward censor to thwart him, while the inward censor has but one question to put to him: 'Are you being honest with yourself?' It is a terrible question to answer.

This freedom from aesthetic restraints was purchased at a heavy price. The typical life history of the independent painter of the nineteenth century is one of conflict maintained against the indifference or the hostility of the public; insults and ridicule had to be faced, and, unless he could depend upon extraneous financial support, the painter was likely to starve. As his mode of expression became more comprehensible to the general public and became, as one may say, part of the pictorial language of the century, the rebel might establish himself with a small clientele; but for many there was never any public recognition.

The reasons for this solid opposition are comparatively clear. A number of the revolutionaries affronted public opinion by adopting an attitude explicitly or implicitly critical of the social system of their day; but their greatest fault was that they were too frank concerning their own feelings in an age that valued social dissimulation. An outburst of violent emotion expressed in an unfamiliar idiom cannot but appear brutal, offensive, and obscene. It is hard for us today to understand the outcry against painters such as Manet or Renoir, because we have grown too accustomed to their manner of address to be affronted. But if we compare the work of these painters with that of their prosperous rivals, the men who gave the public what it wanted, we shall, I think, understand why the *indépendants* seemed insufferably sincere.

51

They were telling the truth about what they saw; they were guilty of making personal remarks.

One effect of this revulsion of feeling on the part of the great public was to divorce the most interesting painters of the period from those patrons who, in the past, had made abundant use of works of art for instruction, propaganda, and conspicuous consumption; in particular, divorce them from the Churches.

The great religious bodies had probably made comfortable patrons because they had not, until very recently, felt it necessary to demand sincerity from the artist; in a medieval or in a savage society they could take his work for granted. The tradition-directed artist did not have to worry about 'feeling'; he was given his assignment – his Buddha or his Virgin – and knew perfectly well, down to the last gesture and the last fold of drapery, what he had to do. The religious form was accepted by both parties.

This ecclesiastical framework continued to function and to provide an adequate container for the artist long after he had ceased to take it for granted that the chief part of his work would be religious, and long after he had developed sufficient spiritual autonomy to acquire a quite personal notion of sacred art. In the fifteenth century, the Church seems to have found no difficulty in accepting sacred art that was completely frivolous and worldly in treatment, and, in the High Renaissance, paganism established a comfortable *modus vivendi* with Christianity. It was not until after the Counter Reformation that the Inquisition raised some objections to Veronese's translation of the New Testament into the proud and flaunting opulence of Venice, and this was but a first unemphatic protest.

How completely the social situation has changed may be judged from the fact that from about 1860 to 1930, a period in which many great artists flourished and in which many of them were intensely religious, there is hardly one instance of a great master being asked to decorate a church. For the first time in history a great aesthetic movement has developed without at any point making contact with organised religion. There have indeed been numerous religious painters, but their works have not been used to advertise faith; they have painted easel pictures to be sold by dealers to private individuals.

The reason for this estrangement between the Church and the artists is, I think, clear; the Churches are social institutions and the artists, living in an age of permanent revolution, have employed an idiom that is not socially acceptable.

Within recent years a fairly widespread and determined effort has been made to bring experimental art into the service of the Churches; but these efforts have encountered very strong resistance from both the laity and the hierarchy. Opposition of this kind is very understandable. To the ordinary churchgoer the decencies and proprieties of worship are a matter of the first importance: a man smoking or a woman dressed for church in a bikini are as repugnant as heresy, and the works of modern artists, howsoever religious, are shocking in proportion to their sincerity.

The traditional patrons of the arts, the aristocracy, the monarchy, and the great municipal bodies, were also alienated from that which was most interesting in the art of their time. The baroque glorification of contemporary history or, for that matter, the rococo decoration of the life of the leisure class required a certain measure of social adjustment by the artist, which could not be achieved by the individualist painters of the nineteenth century. The court painter was working for a public, and the independent was painting for himself; whereas the former was socially integrated to a point at which he could achieve his ends without loss of sincerity, the latter was not. The work of the courtier painters of the nineteenth century betrays, it seems to me, an uneasy consciousness of the artist's predicament; the painter was forced to assume an attitude he did not altogether feel.

The nineteenth-century rebels, when they sold at all, sold to the middle classes; but even here their clientele was very restricted. To some extent this may be attributed to the fact that members of this class were culturally dependent on their 'social superiors'. It is interesting, in this connection, to note that the American industrialists were more ready to purchase works by the Impressionists than were the more tradition-directed magnates of Europe.

But there are certain qualities in the visual arts that are valued by the customers of almost every age and class: expense, workmanship, technical efficiency (which may sometimes take the form of verisimilitude). These essentially economic demands have produced a number of seemingly contradictory impulses, which must be examined.

We have seen that, in the social context in which the artist simply did that which was expected of him, ideological considerations hardly occurred either to the producer or to the consumer; that which the patron (and the guild) demanded was hard work. The labour expended upon a work of art is, in an aesthetic sense, wasted because it is socially required that the artefact (which is, after all, a thing for show or an instrument of conspicuous consumption) should manifestly have been expensive to make. Amongst very primitive peoples this 'honorific waste' of labour can take very naive forms: the piling of stone upon stone to build a pyramid or a megalithic structure in honour of a monarch or a deity. Something of the same mode of displaying power may still be seen in advanced cultures that exhibit their power by the construction of colossi such as the Empire State Building or the Palace of the Soviets.

But the subtler notion of embodying labour power in skill, as in the fabulous intricacies of late Gothic architecture, must be almost equally ancient, and the unsophisticated observer may still express his admiration for a piece of lace or finely carved wood by exclaiming at the amount of work that has been 'put into it'.

In representational painting as we know it in the West, the usual assessment of skill has been based upon the artist's ability to achieve verisimilitude, and the works that earn the praise of the majority are those which, being highly finished in every detail, are immediately convincing as representation.

Legends, such as the story of Zeuxis and the grapes, show how important the public has felt this to be. There can be little doubt that, in the consumer-producer relationship, the demand and the supply of skill have – until very recently, at all events – been the chief consideration. It was the main business of the artist to supply the patron with a polite artefact.

The word polite is, in this connection, of great convenience because it suggests a highly finished surface and also a socially acceptable manner. Works of this kind have been valued in every culture of which we have any record, and it would not be hard to discover examples of this tendency in the products of schools that are, in every other respect, perfectly opposed. Amongst these examples are some of the greatest masterpieces of painting and sculpture. In the twentieth century we value politeness less than we used to. We see in it a form of dissimulation particularly reprehensible in an artist. But considering the work of past ages it must be allowed that when the artist was sufficiently at ease in his social environment, he could be both polite and sincere.

It is once more in the Renaissance that we find the first manifestations of the now common notion that a rude, imperfect, and unfinished work might be as valuable as a correct and impeccable performance. It was then that the drawing, which for the medieval artist was no more than a means to an end – a mapping out of the main forms in the picture – became valuable for its own sake, and was presented to friends and collected by amateurs.

The drawing or sketch is frequently a more intimate thing than the finished work of art; it is, as it were, the *extempore* conversation of art, less elegant but more personal than the balanced periods of a carefully prepared address. In the later works of Titian and in the paintings of Tintoretto the sketch makes its appearance in the finished painting, and from that time forward the charm of a loose, personal handling of pigment becomes a major feature of European painting.

This cavalier disregard of finish – as that term would have been understood by the Van Eycks or by Ingres – characterises nearly all the important painting of the past hundred years, and with it goes a disregard for verisimilitude, or at least for the kind of verisimilitude that is associated with the mirror-image. The Impressionists, observing light and attempting to record its effects with scientific accuracy, were not untrue to nature; but they were completely at variance with contemporary standards of craftsmanship and, until the public had become accustomed to their mode of vision, their mingling of red and blue in grass, their splashes of green and violet upon the human face, seemed a grotesque travesty. But it was not, I think, the apparent untruth of their statements that shocked the public so much as the brutality, the impolite, uncraftsmanlike directness of their manner.

The middle-class culture that had produced the startlingly personal contribution of Rembrandt also produced one of the most impersonal art forms that have ever been created: the Dutch still life. Here we have the kind of art that, despite some attempts at emblematic significance, and despite its astonishing potentialities in the hands of genius, is capable of being a mere exhibition of manual dexterity: the painting of lifelike flies upon lifelike grapes, the placing of a highlight within a wine glass, the restatement of every tiny detail upon a patterned curtain.

The Victorian middle classes seem to have had the same taste for exact workmanship, for painting that has the quality of highly polished furniture combined, in their case, with sentimental piety. It is interesting, in this connection, to note how quickly the great British public came to terms with the Pre-Raphaelites. The Pre-Raphaelites began by giving offence; they were original, sincere, and, in a sense, revolutionary. But their belief in scrupulous exactitude, in the virtues of labour and unremitting attention to detail, were too perfectly in accord with the middle-class ethos to be rejected. Ruskin himself, for all his sincere admiration of Turner and Tintoretto, could not resist the temptation to apply the gospel of hard work to art criticism. In the Whistler-Ruskin trial this conception of art as honest toil – as opposed to art as a careless outpouring of the spirit – emerges with the greatest clarity. The solid, almost unanimous opposition of the middle classes to Impressionism was based upon the view that it was the business of the painter to produce a recognisable and edifying image of nature in an honest and workmanlike fashion, and this conception of the painter's duty seems hardly to have been modified until the second quarter of the present century. I am speaking here of the opinions of the man in the street.

The history of art in the nineteenth century is one of a growing disassociation between the general public and a small but formidable minority of artists. The self-directed painter found himself invariably and increasingly in conflict with society. But it is necessary to qualify this view – in the first place, by pointing out that the general public can learn to tolerate a new idiom; and, in the second place, by admitting that the majority of artists, those who design our advertisements, our furnishings, and the pictures that hang in salons and academies, *do* live by pleasing the public, although in my opinion, their susceptibility to the existing situation is made manifest by the patent insincerity of their works. They may claim to be tradition-directed artists, but in fact they are self-directed artists who are untrue to themselves, the only tradition-directed artists now living being members of very poor, backward, or savage communities.

But, when all allowances have been made, the pattern is still recognisable, revealing an ever increasing emphasis upon individual, as opposed to communal, expression. History shows us first an almost complete identification of the artist and his public, then the emergence of talented individuals within the accepted artistic formulae of the age, then the man of genius, who might be more or less misunderstood by the general public, and finally the completely intransigent declaration of personal independence, the rejection of all rules and all controls and the nonconforming artist opposed to all but a very few enlightened members of the public.

Such was, and such to a large extent still is, the social situation of the artist in the stage of inner-direction. Is it possible that a new phase is now beginning and that we are witnessing a reintegration of the artist into society?

There are reasons for thinking that something of the kind is happening. But what follows is in the highest degree speculative and is certainly not offered in a spirit of dogmatic assertion.

1. From the sociological point of view, the most striking change that has occurred in the history of the fine arts during the first half of the twentieth century is the transformation of the typical life history of the nonconforming artist. Before 1910 there was no independent artist, save Monet, who had ever come near to achieving the financial success of the 'academic' salon painters. And even in that year painters such as Derain, Matisse, Picasso, Braque, and Vlaminck were far from affluent. By 1930 all these painters and many others of the same rebel band were selling at big prices, and the boom is still on. The independent artist no longer dies in a garret, he dies in a suite of rooms surrounded by doctors, secretaries, and journalists. He achieves not only wealth, but also fame in his own lifetime.

An unsophisticated public still supports a large number of conforming painters (in the old sense of the word) who can produce acceptable works, especially portraits, and make a good living; advertising agents likewise. But the position of these artists is rather similar to that of the writers and illustrators of the comics; they have a vast clientele, but they remain, to a large extent, anonymous. The great names in contemporary art are Matisse and Picasso, Braque and Henry Moore, and although not everyone may like them, everyone has heard of them. Among a thousand Americans to whom these names are familiar, is there one who could supply the name of the actual President of the Royal or any other Academy? There may be, in fact there obviously are, thousands of unknown 'nonconforming' painters, but it is not their nonconformity that stands between them and fame.

Obviously, this change implies a change of public temper. In fact, there is today a kind of rival establishment that plays a part not unlike that of the old academies, and which is, to a large extent, international. Prizes and awards are given, exhibitions are held with a generous use of funds by bodies that, clearly, are more afraid of being old-fashioned than of anything else.

The museums of modern art, the glossier magazines, the designers of sets for stage or films, the interior decorators of new business premises, even some of the Churches, all those who make it their business to be in the swim, now offer patronage to the 'rebels', and not merely to those rebels who with age have become established, but also to the young and relatively unknown.

Broadly speaking, we may say that there are today two main roads to fortune for a young artist. He may learn to please that still large and naive public that demands a flattering handmade photograph disguised as an old master, or he may squirt his canvas with creosote, scour, scratch, blast and excoriate it, until it hangs in fashionable tatters upon the walls of one of our principal art galleries. The former method may still command a steadier sale than the latter, and it calls for less salesmanship; but the latter is the true highway to glory and to wealth. The painters who run to neither excess may think themselves lucky if they can keep body and soul together, because, whatever their talents, they are very unlikely to achieve worldly success.

2. I have suggested that one of the reasons why independent art in the nineteenth century was felt to be offensive was that it was too personal to be endured. Perhaps we may ascribe the acceptability of much contemporary work to a reverse tendency. The Fauves – the wild beasts – who came to maturity before 1914 adopted an extremely offensive style; but their successors have, in different ways, reduced the personal element in their art to a bare minimum. This is not an easy thing to achieve in graphic art. The faithful reproduction of an old master by a modern copyist can rarely be mistaken for an original, and experts can, with a surprisingly high degree of unanimity, attribute a slight sketch to a period, a school, or in many cases an individual. The quality of the artist's vision is made evident in some incomprehensible but clearly recognisable manner, in every stroke that he makes. But this applies only to a line drawn free hand. A line drawn with a ruler, whether it be drawn by Sir John Millais or by Giotto is, or at least can be made, completely impersonal.

There are abstract works consisting simply of geometrical forms and flat areas of colour, or of evenly tinted wood or plastic, which could be copied with a high degree of accuracy by a student who had never seen the original but had been furnished with a series of measurements. This, of course, does not mean that the artist has eliminated the personal quality from his work, but only that he has placed himself in the same position as the architect, surrendering that power of intimate communication that is peculiar to the pictorial arts.

Within recent years, however, painters have adopted techniques that have the effect, if not the intention, of abolishing that quality of design (I use the word both in the sense of pattern and of intention) that is still preserved in abstract art. The painting can now be reduced to an accident. Throw a bucket of liquid paint at your canvas and you rid yourself, at one blow, of the personal quality that results from the manipulation of brush or pencil, and also of the sense of directed effort that appears when any attempt is made at arrangement. It would seem to be possible, with a little ingenuity, to remove the personal quality altogether from action painting by the use of machinery. These endeavours reach the ultimate Nirvana of impersonality in the work of those Parisians who content themselves with the exhibition of a rectangle of plain, tinted wallpaper within a frame.

The idea of the artist as an individualist is still too strongly held by the artists themselves for them to be able to contemplate complete immolation. Each man entertains the modest hope that his accidents may be better than those of his neighbour. Nevertheless, it does appear to me that there is a clear tendency towards impersonality of style; the means adopted, whether they involve the use of the ruler or of the watering can, must, of necessity, tend toward uniformity of style and achievement.

3. The great flowering of independent art in France during the nineteenth century was unique in that, unlike any other great artistic movement, it was accompanied by no corresponding development in architecture and the applied arts. It was, as one may say, socially isolated. To some extent, this was made inevitable by the revolutionary character of the various movements; but it is also true that Impressionism, both the Impressionism of Monet and that of Degas, consisted in the observation of life and had practically nothing in common with decorative art.

59

The painter surveyed the world impartially, not looking for those things that were deemed beautiful, but for those that could be restated in terms of reflected light. A girl dressed for a ball, a railway station, a row of suburban houses or a dish of onions would all serve his purpose equally well. It was left to Morris and his disciples, to the apostles of Art Nouveau and later to Roger Fry in England and Gropius in Germany, to attempt a reconciliation of modern art and modern life.

In a sense, these efforts have been successful, and the twentieth century has its own style. 'Contemporary' wallpaper, furniture fabrics, and interior decoration derive clearly from contemporary painting, although frequently as the result of vulgarisation in the worst sense of the word. At the same time, architecture and engineering have exerted a notable influence upon the arts of painting and sculpture. Both abstract painting and action painting have a congruous relationship with what may be called functional architecture, the former as an extension, almost a parody, of the structures of the machine age, the latter as a decorative foil to the regular unbroken surfaces of the modern building, giving relief to the eye, but at the same time harmonising by reason of its similarly impersonal character.

Thus the nonconforming painter (if the term can still legitimately be used), unlike his predecessors of the last century, fits well enough into the style of the age.

It would appear that the artists of today may be returning to a position in which they can be fully integrated in society. They are swimming with the current; they give the public what it wants and are rewarded accordingly. To an ever increasing extent they are ready to submerge their personalities in the common artistic personality of the age. Their art is no longer a protest; it has become part of a general assent.

In all this the artists may seem to be returning to the position of the medieval painter or the craftsman of primitive society. But their conformity is of a new kind: they remain, in a sense, revolutionary, because they explicitly reject tradition and have little or nothing to do with the past. Their revolutions are quasi-unanimous movements, however, and they change direction in the manner of a shoal of fish, a flight of starlings, or the designers of women's clothes. Their nonconformity is essentially conformist and provides less and less scope for the lonely eccentric or the pre-eminent leader.

If this tendency continues we may perhaps see a progressive disappearance of the man of genius and an ever growing conformity in manners, morals, and ideas until the artist is indistinguishable from the rest of the community.

Roger Fry

In an autobiographical work entitled *The Dream*, Lucian describes how, as a boy, he was confronted (like Hercules) by two ladies each of whom invited him to make his future career under her guidance. Of these, one was a dusty, horny-handed, hoydenish sort of woman who represented the art of sculpture; the other was in every way her opposite: elegant, charming and altogether ladylike, she introduced herself as Education. This lady implored the youth to have nothing to do with the practice of the fine arts. It was, she said, socially disreputable; even if he should prove to be another Phidias, Lucian would still be one of the *hoi polloi*, a craftsman, a mechanic . . . The boy took her advice, he rejected art and sought education; he ends the poem with a rather smug appraisal of his growing reputation as a successful literary man received even in the most exclusive circles.

I do not know whether Lucian's assessment of the social standing and educational attainments of the artist was generally accepted amongst the ancients; but I suspect that it was. Painting and sculpture had no muse, and when after many centuries Olympus was disbanded, they found, despite the patronage of St Luke, no place amongst the seven liberal arts, no chair within our ancient universities. It is true that the Renaissance provided them with a corporation, but that situation has not proved altogether congenial; the academy of fine art became a working reality just when the idea that made it what it was had ceased to be of service to artists; as a school the academy could not be compared to any institute of higher learning; as a professional association it too easily became the refuge of mediocrity.

A feeling that academies of art had somehow failed in their mission is evident even in the *Discourses* of Reynolds, and the hope that somehow the 'gowned academic' might succeed where the academician had come to grief is not new. In the late eighteenth century the Reverend Peters, chaplain to the Royal Academy, a painter more celebrated for his enthusiastic treatment of the female form than for his piety, learning, or talent, approached the University of Oxford, but without lasting results. Half a century later Benjamin Robert Haydon entreated Lord Melbourne to establish chairs of fine art at our universities so that future legislators and patrons should be able to withstand the blandishments of a venal and depraved academic body. But the government of the day (1836) was so far in agreement with Lucian that, when it created schools of art, it placed them under the tutelage of the Board of Trade. Colleges of art had to wait more than a century before they could offer degrees.

The slow incursion of the artist into British universities has taken place partly through accident, partly through design and partly through the action of enlightened benefactors. It is as a result of deliberate policy that London and many other universities have included fine art in their courses. Such courses, however, are frequently of a sort of which even Lucian might have approved. They involve no actual handling of paint or clay, no dirty process of aesthetic parturition. The student does not look at a painting while the pigment is still moist, he waits until it has been dried, varnished, restored and perhaps adorned with interesting *pentimenti*. He approaches it as a connoisseur and an historian, a biographer and a student of the history of ideas; he takes his stand upon the same respectable territory as the archaeologist and the palaeographer.

In this *Kunstforschung* which has for long flourished in Germany and is now excellently established at the Courtauld Institute, the pure art historian need have no connection with the practice of the art that he studies; his own discipline is self-sufficing and requires no extrinsic justification. He is a pure scholar and, as such, in every way respectable. Nor is he useful simply as a man of erudition; he may be of enormous service to the artist and to all who are in any way sensible to visual art; he may help us to feel more deeply, to see more clearly and, passing over all barriers of language and historical distance, to participate with a peculiar intimacy in one of the most important and moving of human occupations. When the historian pursues this course the artist cannot be indifferent to his activities; he has too much to offer, too much to explain that is of immediate relevance to our own problems in the studio and the workshop. No artist, however single-minded his devotion to nature, can disregard art itself, and the lessons of the past may be as critically important to the creative worker as are the experiments of the present. But there are historians and critics who can come still nearer to the creative experience of the artist, who are, in fact, both scholars and artists and can mediate between the practitioner and the historian; it is a curious fact that two great critics of this genus both found chairs in our universities. That they did so is due to the munificence of a proctor in Doctors' Commons, Felix Slade, who endowed the school which bears his name in the University of London and the chairs of Fine Art at Oxford and at Cambridge. The first Slade Professor at Oxford was Ruskin; the most distinguished professor of Fine Art at Cambridge was Roger Fry.

It is my purpose here to discuss Roger Fry, my own first teacher, and to do so as he would have wished, objectively and critically. But it may be helpful at the outset, both in explaining the character of my subject and in reinforcing my argument, to look at both these remarkable men.

Roger Fry was born in 1866 when Ruskin was forty-seven. Like Ruskin he wanted to be an artist, became a critic *malgré lui* and continued to practise his art until the end of his life. Like Ruskin he came of puritan stock and like Ruskin he abandoned the beliefs of his parents, although he did so more easily, more happily and more completely. Like Ruskin, he carried something of his early moral training with him through life, for, although he ceased to believe in God, he kept something of the intense belief in humility and honesty of his Quaker ancestors. Like Ruskin, but to a far lesser extent, he kept a social conscience and was interested in the social purposes of art; like Ruskin, he loved France and Italy better than he loved Flanders and Holland; like Ruskin, he dominated the aesthetic thinking of a generation and, like Ruskin, he has suffered from a sharp reversal of public esteem.

Both Fry and Ruskin began life not only as artists but as scientists. Ruskin was, I think, the more considerable artist of the two; certainly, he had far less of the scientific virtues. He displays all the intense, narrow, intolerant yet volatile partisanship of which the artist-critic is capable; writing with a force that sweeps one off one's feet, he proclaims with passionate certainty the transcendent virtues of those whom he admires and the utter baseness of those whom he does not admire; he can touch no subject without enthusiasm and few without indignation; his voice rises to a scream as he discusses the wrongs of Governor Eyre or the iniquities of Charles Darwin; very seldom in his voluminous writings does he consider that he may sometimes be in the wrong and there is no trick of special pleading or verbal legerdemain of which he is not guilty.

Fry is in almost every way the exact opposite. Certainly, he had his enthusiasms and his prejudices. He believed too much in Marchand and van Dongen, too little in Turner and Delacroix; he could find very little to say for the English portrait painters, for the Pre-Raphaelites or the Mannerists. But the catholicity of his taste was, by Ruskinian standards, fantastic. The doors of his pantheon were open to all the great European schools, to the Africans, the Scythians, the Chinese and the cultures of Pre-Columbian America, to children and to peasants as well as to the Impressionists and Post-Impressionists. His reluctance to dismiss anything without giving it a fair trial made him both credulous and sceptical; he would never reject an artist or an idea, or for that matter a patent medicine, on *a priori* grounds. He would never leave a judgment unquestioned. 'In art we know nothing for certain,' he once said to me. 'Consider the enormous reputation of Landseer amongst highly educated people in the nineteenth century. Were they mad, or have we misjudged him?' And then, after a pause, 'I might be equally wrong about Cézanne,' and then, after a further pause, 'But I really don't think I am.'

And yet, despite his caution, he had a far bolder spirit than Ruskin. Ruskin discovered very little; he summarises the aesthetic discoveries of his time and gives them noble expression. Fry was to a far greater extent an innovator, a pioneer. His temperate and sceptical attitude makes Fry a less overwhelming writer than Ruskin. He cannot indulge in the fierce Ruskinian philippic nor can he achieve the fantastic poetical dressmaking with which in *Modern Painters* Ruskin adorns and yet disguises the beauties of Turner. Fry will analyse and, as far as he can, explain his intense emotion before a Poussin or a Cézanne, but his prose is under constant scrutiny; nothing must be falsified, nothing obscured and, in the end, he realises the limitations of language, the inability of words to express that which can only be said in paint.

In this essay I have tried to press as far as I could the analysis of some typical works of Cézanne. But it must always be kept in mind that such analysis halts before the ultimate concrete reality of the work of art, and perhaps in proportion to the greatness of the work it must leave untouched a greater part of its objective. For Cézanne this inadequacy is particularly sensible and in the last resort we cannot in the least explain why the smallest product of his hand arouses the impression of being a revelation of the highest importance, or what exactly it is that gives it its grave authority.

This, it seems to me (he is concluding his study of Cézanne), is good but not great prose; it has neither the tempestuous force of the *Seven Lamps of Architecture* nor the enchanting lucidity of *Praeterita*; yet it approaches more nearly to the central mysteries of painting than do the writings of any other critic whom I have read, for it has the rarest of all critical virtues, humility, a humility that is born of the very power and insight of the critic. 'Grave authority' does exactly describe the quality of a Cézanne drawing and another author would have been happy enough with such a *trouvaille*; but Fry knows too much to pretend that he has said all that he knows.

Less well armed by nature for the manufacture of verbal felicities, restrained always by a scientific conscience, Fry was also through a great part of his career hampered by a theoretical reluctance to make use of those devices to which the literary man naturally turns when confronted by the difficulty of writing about pictures. The discovery of sentimental connections, of hidden anecdotes or messages, the discussion of the overt and manifest 'story' of a picture, seemed to him to show a preoccupation with inessentials. For him the plastic harmonies of a work of art, the qualities that come nearest to musical form, were of pre-eminent importance; it was therefore to the arrangement of formal quantities – that in art which it is hardest to describe – that he addressed himself.

It is said that when Roger Fry was giving a lecture on handwriting he came, after showing examples of Renaissance and medieval scripts, to a slide on which he had reproduced a page from a letter written to him by Virginia Woolf. While discussing the problems raised by that lively, elegant, idiosyncratic hand Fry, for once in a way, lost touch with his audience, for the example of handwriting that he had chosen provided a spirited, highly scandalous and perhaps mendacious story involving several people who were present in the lecture room. With characteristic innocence he had completely forgotten that handwriting might be considered rather for the message that it conveys than for the forms it assumes; he had chosen the letter at random and prepared the slide without ever actually reading the words formed by those interesting characters.

Se non è vero è ben trovato; the story certainly gives a notion of Fry's careless indifference to anything save the matter in hand, his inability to conceive that other people could treat an aesthetic question with anything less than his own fine seriousness. It is less true if it be taken as an example of his attitude to art as a whole. Certainly in the period between 1910 and, say, 1925, Fry was deeply and almost exclusively concerned with plastic values; I have heard him describe the agonised body of Christ upon the cross as 'this important mass'. It seemed to him then that the contemplation of form could be isolated from our other emotions when we examine a work of art, that it was a 'constant' more profound and more significant than any of the emotions that have to do with life. It is a view of art which was forced upon him and his generation by the catholicity of taste to which I have referred, a view which it is hard entirely to accept or entirely to reject.

To divorce the pattern – or, to speak more accurately, the frantic tumultuous convulsion – of the Antwerp *Deposition* from the operatic drama of Christ's martyrdom as Rubens so enthusiastic-ally presents it, to separate the play of light and shade in Goya's *Execution* of 1808 from the horrifying spectacle of human cruelty and human terror, would hardly seem possible. But while re-cognising that most artists have told some kind of story – using the word in its fullest possible extension of meaning – and recognising also that this 'literary' sentiment may, perhaps must, affect everything that the artist does, it still remains true that the results of art, however they may be achieved and howsoever great the story embodied therein, *can* be apprehended and measured without reference to legend or content.

Most of us do not know, none of us can fully understand, the 'story' that an artist living in an ancient and alien culture wished to tell, but that ignorance does not prevent us from receiving very intense emotions from the work of his hands. It is questionable how much is gained or lost when we are offered a new explanation of Giorgione's *Tempestà* or Watteau's *Cytherea*. We create almost always with the invisible in mind, but it is, of course, the visible that remains. And, while the tendency of modern scholarship takes us away from Fry's method and inclines us to a deeper investigation of the symbolism and philosophy of the old masters, painters have turned ever more completely to an entirely obfusc expression of their feelings, to the harmonious but reticent geometry of Mondrian, the enigmatic calligraphy of Rothko.

Fry, in fact, pointed to one of the great dilemmas of art criticism, our ability to feel so much of what an artist is saying when we can understand so little of what he intends to say. No one who looks much at works of art and shares something of the taste of our century can escape this problem; we must live with it, and Fry's enunciation thereof was a necessary stage in the development of aesthetic ideas.

His views were never static; like most critics he changed them, and unlike many critics he made no attempt to conceal the fact. In 1891, when he was twenty-five, he went for the first time to Italy. As might have been expected, he went with Ruskin as his guide; he returned with opinions of his own almost exactly opposed to those of his first teacher, for whereas Ruskin was entranced by the savagery, vigour, irregularity and 'redundancy' of Gothic art, Fry, even when he admired the same masters, was attracted above all by their ability to impose order upon nature. The word design, with its related ideas of purpose, plan or drawing (*disegno*), expresses well enough that which he most admired in the visual arts, that which he could always find in the compact harmonies of Poussin or the architectural felicities of Piero della Francesca. But at this stage he was ready to allow that design might also be of a psychological kind. In his very sympathetic introduction to the *Discourses* of Reynolds he suggests that the Ghent altarpiece, in that it shows us the convergence of many sacred personages towards a central mystery of their faith, has a sentimental confluence and hence a unity, a unity no less secure than that of the great masters of the High Renaissance.

Now this insistence upon design, upon the regulatory and co-ordinating functions of the artist, made him unsympathetic to Impressionism. 'I don't like to have undigested facts thrown at my head in that way'; he said this of Bastien Lepage, and we may therefore agree with him, but the same criticism might have been applied to Monet or to Sisley – both of whom he did admire, but I think in a rather unwilling fashion – and he was very much out of sympathy with the doctrines of Impressionism as propounded in this country by the followers of Whistler, to the doctrine of Art for Art's Sake and to the conception of painting as a direct, factual transcription of nature. It is a measure of current doctrine in this country at the turn of the century, and of Fry's attitude, that he felt it necessary almost to apologise for his nonconformity in discovering the spiritual content of Giotto's art. And it was with a sense of conscious provocation that he found a literary element in the work of that paragon of objectivity, Velàzquez. In his own early painting he is seeking, clumsily, for ordered poetry, while his rapidly growing reputation as a journalist and a lecturer was largely built upon a study of the old masters. It is not surprising that the younger members of the New English Art Club thought him reactionary. It was in April 1902 that he first became aware that his views on the primary importance of content might be mistaken. He then saw a still life by Chardin which gave him the feeling that here was something 'immensely grave and impressive'; this, he reflected, 'is just how I felt when I first saw Michelangelo's frescoes in the Sistine Chapel'. That which Chardin began, Cézanne completed; the change, however, was not rapid. In 1906 he could still write, 'We confess to having been hitherto sceptical about Cézanne's genius but these two pieces reveal a power which is entirely distinct and personal, and though the artistic appeal is limited, and touches none of the finer issues of life, it is none the less complete.' These reservations were presently to vanish; he learnt to look with greater love and understanding at Cézanne; he perceived that it was possible to achieve a sublimity equal to that of the great masters and yet to leave these 'finer issues' on one side. Cézanne's own programme – *refaire Poussin d'après la nature* – had been achieved, and, because such an achievement was possible, because those painters whom Fry himself christened the Post-Impressionists were able to restore the artist to his old position as a designer and not a mere observer, and had done so without any of the theological or literary machinery of the past, Fry found it necessary to reconsider his position in the light of the facts.

Such a re-examination, such a jettisoning of firmly held theories was what one would have expected of him. What does seem to me remarkable is that Fry, with his training and temperament, should have seen that Cézanne and his followers were not simply innovators but represented also a return to the great traditions of the past, for such a conviction, which does not seem wonderful today, required an extraordinary effort of the mind in the year 1910.

If Fry had been a professional revolutionary of the arts, if he had been a younger man, if he had been one of those who seek modernity for its own sake, then it would have been understandable; but he was none of these things; he was middle-aged, conservative-minded, a pillar almost of the artistic establishment. He had nothing to make him see the point of Cézanne save his own sensibility, and how rare such acuteness of feeling was may be judged by the reactions of Fry's contemporaries when he brought the first Post-Impressionist exhibition to London. There were those who, when confronted by these unfamiliar works, were able to dismiss Cézanne as a bungler and Fry as a deluded puzzlehead – such was the attitude of the greatest English painter of that age, Walter Sickert. There were a few critics who were ready to find some virtue – in Gauguin at all events – but the vast majority of the public, more particularly of that cultivated public which had provided an enthusiastic audience for Fry's lectures on the old masters, was affronted, dismayed and disgusted. Charlatan, mountebank, maniac were some of the milder terms with which they described 'the reckless prophet . . . of this rotten league'. The savage violence of feeling engendered amongst artists and patrons was something more bitter and more extravagant than had hitherto been seen or has since been known amongst English artists and critics. It is a measure of the strength of these ancient quarrels that Roger Fry's character as a man still has to be defended. I would like to add, more or less in parenthesis, that where attempts have been made to support such personal attacks by concrete evidence it has not been hard to confute the voice of calumny.

It is characteristic of Fry that he was considerably puzzled by the outcry that he had provoked. He heard Cézanne described as an anarchist and Van Gogh as a pornographer, and to him – as to us – such accusations seemed utterly ludicrous; their achievements lay precisely in the fact that they had restored order and chastity to the art of painting. He concluded that, essentially, his critics were not interested in art as he understood it; a genteel familiarity with the fine arts, an ability to discuss the 'correggiescity of Correggio' lent polish and brilliance to the conversation of a lady or gentleman. 'The accusation of revolutionary anarchism was due to a social rather than an aesthetic prejudice.'

The observation was true as far as it went; but I do not think that Fry, going straight to the simple heart of the matter – the essential worth of the pictures – ever realised how deeply such brutally sincere expressions of aesthetic emotion shocked the smug, prurient optimism of 1910. If Brangwyn, Dicksee and Sargent were great masters, then indeed Gauguin and Van Gogh were the most dangerous and the most reprehensible of revolutionaries; they destroyed the whole tissue of comfortable falsehoods on which that age based its views of beauty, propriety and decorum. Fry's own assumptions concerning 'the finer issues' had been sacrificed unreservedly on the altar of intellectual honesty; with the devastating ruthlessness of a saint, he expected the rest of the world to behave with his own uncompromising integrity. That the public should be unable to understand the terms of a new pictorial language was something that he *could* see; in a notable correspondence in the columns of *The Nation*, in December 1910, he showed very clearly what these difficulties were and showed with exactitude how they would in future be surmounted. But the fierce *emotional* reaction of the cultivated world was something that he could not comprehend and for which he could make no allowance.

Despite all calumnies and misunderstandings I think that the years between 1910 and 1914 were the happiest in Fry's life. If he lost old friends, he made new ones, particularly amongst the young painters who welcomed the innovations of Post-Impressionism. To Fry this seemed a momentous development, for not only were the artists liberating themselves from the mere imitation of nature, but also – and this was implicit in the whole process – they were rediscovering style. Where the Impressionists had been confined within the frontiers of the picture frame, the Fauves – like the great masters of Italy – could adventure upon the wall and upon the furniture. Art could again be harmonised with architecture; the painter need no longer explain the world; he could change it. Considering the artistic character of the world as it existed in 1910, Fry decided that it certainly needed changing and that the process of changing it would be exhilarating. He got artists to work upon the Borough Polytechnic, he organised the Omega Workshops and he began to consider the whole function of art in society.

Writing a lecture – typically enough – in a railway station refreshment room, he describes the scene thus:

The space my eye travels over is a small one, but I am appalled at the amount of 'art' that it harbours. The window towards which I look is filled in its lower part by stained glass; within a highly elaborate border, designed by someone who knew the conventions of thirteenth-century glass, is a pattern of yellow and purple vine leaves with bunches of grapes, and flitting about among these many small birds. In front is a lace curtain with patterns taken from at least four centuries and as many countries. On the walls, up to a height of four feet, is a covering of lincrusta walton stamped with a complicated pattern in two colours, with sham silver medallions. Above that a moulding but an inch wide, and yet creeping throughout its whole width a degenerate descendant of a Graeco-Roman carved guilloche pattern; this has evidently been cut out of the wood by machine or stamped out of some composition – its nature is so perfectly concealed that it is hard to say which. Above this is a wallpaper in which an effect of eighteenth-century satin brocade is imitated by shaded staining of the paper. Each of the little refreshment tables has two cloths, one arranged symmetrically with the table, the other a highly ornate printed cotton arranged 'artistically' in a diagonal position. In the centre of each table is a large pot in which every beautiful quality in the material and making of pots has been carefully obliterated by methods each of which implies profound scientific knowledge and great inventive talent. Within each pot is a plant with large dark green leaves, apparently made of india rubber. This painful catalogue makes up only a small part of the inventory of 'art' of the restaurant. If I were to go on to tell of the legs of the tables, of the electric light fittings, of the chairs into the wooden seats of which some tremendous mechanical force has deeply impressed a large distorted anthemion – if I were to tell of all these things, my reader and I might both begin to realise with painful acuteness something of the horrible toil involved in all this display. Display is indeed the end and explanation of it all. Not one of these things has been made because the maker enjoyed the making; not one has been bought because its contemplation would give any one pleasure, but solely because each of these things is accepted as a symbol of a particular social status. I say their contemplation can give no one pleasure; they are there because their absence would be resented by the average man who regards a large amount of futile display as in some way inseparable from the conditions of that well-to-do life to which he belongs or aspires to belong.

If everything were merely clean and serviceable he would proclaim the place bare and uncomfortable.

I imagine that Fry must have read Veblen's *Theory of the Leisure Class* and that his thought here is influenced by Veblen. He saw that the horrors of modern art and architecture are produced not by a hatred of beauty but by an injudicious love of it; that the trimmings and refinements added for social reasons, the polite suppression of sensibility, the falsifications of fashion, are more fatal to art than any crudity or ineptitude.

This acute understanding of the effect of social forces upon the history of art is evident in nearly all his later writings; it provides an element of great and lasting importance that we neglect at our peril. I am sorry that he never managed to develop his ideas in a complete and systematic form. One essay, written in 1917, and many passing allusions give us a notion of what he might have done. Far more sensitive and a good deal more level-headed than Veblen, he would have produced a more coherent and useful book than the *Theory of the Leisure Class*, and my own generation, which in the thirties attempted to reconcile a taste for what was then modern art with an affection for the *analecta* of Marx, Engels and Plekhanov, would at least have had something solid and formidable against which to try its strength. But he was too busy, always too busy; he had his own painting, a great deal of journalism and his memorable lectures on Flemish, French and Italian art to complete. And then from about 1925 he was busy pulling his own central theory to pieces. Could one really consider the paintings of Rembrandt as pure form and without reference to their content? With his usual honesty he decided that one could not; once again it was necessary to reconsider his theories in the light of the facts. He began to look for a new formulation of his ideas; that formulation was not complete when he died as a result of an accident in 1934. Thus, appropriately enough for a critic who questioned everything, the story of his development ends on a note of interrogation.

I am well aware that this slight adumbration of Fry's character as a critic and theorist gives but a very imperfect notion of his thought and no notion at all of his greatness as a teacher. Fry was not a great painter or a supremely great writer. His true genius – and it was genius of the highest order – was revealed when he began to talk.

Unfortunately, he was never filmed and, if his broadcasts were recorded, the records have been lost. Of his performance in the lecture theatre we have a moving description by Virginia Woolf which it would be foolish to paraphrase. I would, however, like to conclude by giving some kind of notion of what it was like to be taught by him in the churches and galleries of Europe.

In this connection the word taught may perhaps convey the wrong shade of meaning. Fry would answer any question that you might put to him, but his manner certainly was *not* didactic. In fact, the magic of his teaching lay precisely in this, that he assumed that you were on an equality with him, that he was in no sense instructing or performing. It was *your* opinions, *your* ideas that were called for. He even assumed that his companions had his own fantastic appetite and capacity for absorbing works of art and was mildly astonished when, after five hours' strenuous sight-seeing, they suggested that it might be time for lunch. The 'teaching' came when after a moment of silent, open-mouthed inspiration the work itself, or his interlocutor's comments, would provoke him into an expression of feeling. It might be very laconic, but sometimes that gift, derived perhaps from generations of Quaker ancestors, for being 'moved by the spirit', would lead him to talk at length. Then indeed the whole structure of a picture could come alive. One would realise with amazed delight the existence of unsuspected harmonies and unheard-of subtleties. At such times Fry could make the whole working of his wonderfully acute sensibility beautifully and completely public; he was experiencing things in one's presence, telling one extraordinary things that were happening to him as he looked and understood more and more completely the intentions of the artist. The great masters spoke to him and he repeated the message as it came. But I should entirely misrepresent this experience if I were to suggest that his hearer felt that he was at the receiving end of a chain of communication. Fry's experience was not presented as his own property; it belonged as much to his listeners as to himself. His observations carried such instant conviction that they could at once be annexed and, in speaking, it seemed that he did no more than give audible expression to joint discoveries.

In learning to ride a bicycle one may at first be dependent upon a teacher who holds the machine upright and maintains it, as the pupil learns to travel, by only the slightest pressure of his hand. A time may come when this restraint will be so gentle that the learner fancies that he maintains his balance unaided, and presently he will in fact do so and in doing so become able to sustain and direct himself. It was thus that Fry taught, and it should be added that it was always his wish to see the pupil take his own course, even when that course appeared to him to be in the wrong direction.

Fry could impart something more reliable than information and far more useful than any system of 'correct' taste; he gave the power to see, to feel, to discriminate. He could not have done this if he had not been a charming, wise and persuasive person. I think that it may also be said of him that he derived his astonishing insight into the nature of painting from a species of sympathy which is given only to those who are themselves painters. He could never say all that he would have liked to have said on canvas, but the practice of what he always liked to think was his true profession did, I believe, give him the power of genius elsewhere. For him, Lucian's choice between the practice of art and the pursuit of education did not exist; and I have very little doubt that he would have blamed the writer, not only for his snobbery but for not understanding that there *are* circumstances when it is best to court two ladies at the same time.

Sickert

There are taciturn painters, painters who are perpetually at a loss for words and, when they find them, have very little idea what to do with them, painters of whom it may truly be said that they should be seen and not heard. Sickert was not one of them. For the greater part of his working life he was expressing himself in words both publicly and privately. He always had a great deal to say. He was very anxious that the world should have his opinions on a wide variety of subjects. The world got them. But what really were his opinions? Had he, in fact, anything that could be called opinions? It has been doubted.

'The opinions of Walter Richard Sickert, what were they? They boxed the compass between a first and a third glass of wine. Sickert was a chameleon . . .'

Thus Clive Bell; and he goes on to say that Sickert was a poseur, an actor: 'one day he would be John Bull and the next Voltaire; occasionally he was the Archbishop of Canterbury and quite often the Pope. He was an actor in all companies and sometimes a buffoon. He would dress up as a cook, a raffish dandy, a Seven Dials swell, a bookmaker, a solicitor, or an artist even.' In no sense was Sickert a scholar; for, if his acquaintance with books was scrappy, his acquaintance with pictures was not much better: 'Nevertheless, reading Dr Emmon's book,' Bell continues, 'I discovered that his serious criticism and advice are far more interesting and better expressed than I had supposed.'

That Sickert was in this sense a chameleon can hardly be denied. Sickert was, and in literal truth had been, an actor; it should be added that, of the many roles that he chose to play off the stage, most were comic, some were wildly funny and, although at times he played the tease and the angry dogmatist, the characters that he adopted were never, so far as I am aware, mean, sly or malevolent. On the whole, his 'parts' were genial and jovial even if sometimes a little absurd. In his writings, many of these disguises make their appearance and, frequently when he indulges his passion for parenthesis, he resembles that celebrated gentleman who mounted his horse and rode off furiously in all directions.

And yet, behind the jokes and the disguises there was, as most people would admit, a serious purpose. To quote again from my father's memoir: 'Only the pictures were there to prove that a temperament, with an eye and a hand, called Sickert or Walter Sickert or Richard Sickert or Walter Richard Sickert existed and throughout a long development from Whistlerian days to the last could be recognised.'

I would go much further. There was not only a painter, but a teacher behind all the fooling and posing and fun of his writings and of his conversation; there were indeed opinions, carefully considered opinions from which Sickert could not easily be moved. He might appear to be a chameleon or, if you like, he was a chameleon, but chameleons change colour for a reason, and so did Sickert. There was an unchanging body of opinion behind the many disguises. I would say that Sickert is remarkable amongst painters for the coherence of his doctrinal position and for the fact that he so rarely moved from it.

Many painters, I fancy, paint as seems good to them, following, perhaps, an idea or general notion, but only discovering that they have some coherent doctrine when the character of their own work forces them to this conclusion. Most, I imagine, look for a good selling line and stick to it. But Sickert, so it appears to me, had a fairly precise notion of what he wanted to do quite early in life. He must have got a great deal, but he also discarded a great deal, from Whistler. I think he listened attentively to Charles Keene, but his true master was De Gas.* Degas taught him partly by example and partly by certain notions concerning movement, memory, spontaneity and truth which are for the most part

---

*I spell the name thus for one of the things that Sickert told me was that nothing irritated him more than the English habit of pronouncing him 'Daygah'.

connected with the theories and teaching of Lecoq de Boisbaudran. To these theoretical influences I will return. But first I must try to dispose of, or at least properly to situate, this image of Sickert the joker, Sickert the poseur.

In this connection it is fair to say that the writings of Sickert and the conversation of Sickert are all of a piece.

In an article in the *Art News*, February 1910, Sickert discusses Manet and the Impressionists. He is reviewing M. Duret's book. He agrees that the Impressionists were the lineal descendants of the great European masters and discusses the opposition that they encountered in Paris. He continues:

I remember thinking of these things one morning at four o'clock, as I lifted a corner of the Venetian blind in the hotel of Paddington station to watch the stream of young men in identical green caps swarming up the arrival slope into Praed Street, on the morning of the Cup Tie. I'll warrant none of them were thinking either of Sir William Richmond or of me! I doubt even if the name of Frank Rutter would have spelt anything very definite to their eager, happy morning eyes. None of them recked, I'll bet, that Mr Berenson, after making us feel small, and breaking our heads for years with his '*inis* and '*iccios*, had come down heavily and imprudently into the field of modern art, and plumped for Matisse, carrying with him deeply moved spinsters who had never heard of Monet, and dowagers to whom Degas was nought! None of them knew, I'll bet, how relieved were those of us, including the present writer, who had hitherto modest and chilly doubts as to the sufficient length and weight of our kilt of culture, when we saw Berenson prone and bare in the field of modern art, revealing deficiencies we had long suspected, but dared not hint at. *Ouf*! There is one at least whose works I shall not have to read!

And here he is discussing the violent letters to the *Morning Post* protesting against the First Post-Impressionist Exhibition. This article appeared in the *Fortnightly Review* for January 1911.

Monsieur Blanche, in a letter to the *Morning Post*, thinks it of critical relevance to emphasise the theory that Van Gogh was a Jew, and, what appears to make the matter worse in the eyes of my brilliant and talented friend, an apparently intolerable aggravation, a Jew from Holland at that! Truly it is difficult for the fashionable portrait-painter to be a just critic. A life time spent in *tête-à-tête* with the *femme du monde*, his customer, cannot but tinge his views of life and art. Mr Ross struck in the *Morning Post* with no uncertain trumpet, the protectionist note on this exhibition. Mr Ricketts, I suspect is merely naughty and knows better, a delightful and witty *advocatus angelorum*. I said to myself, 'We shall have Sir William

Richmond and Sir Philip Burne Jones.' *'Pan!'* as they say in France, *'ça y était.'* 'There remains now,' I said to myself, 'only the regularly recurring Mr Wake Cook.' *Tac* which I must explain is the Venetian for *'Pan!'* (I have lived so much abroad.)

In both these extracts we have, very obviously, Sickert the cosmopolitan, even his English is translated from the French – 'there is one at least . . .' In each case he is embarking upon a digression; this is particularly so in the article on Manet and the Impressionists where he goes entirely out of his way in order to be rude to Berenson and Matisse. In each case, both in his manner and his matter, he has a serious purpose.

Sickert, for reasons which I will discuss later, had grave doubts about the value of Matisse, of Picasso and of Cézanne; he wanted to attack them from a position of knowledge and authority and he did not want *his* objections to be confused with the more simple-minded utterances of the pure reactionaries. At that time, an English art critic who could claim to have spent much of his life in Italian but principally in French studios had a distinct advantage. To assert, as Sickert could, that he had been a close friend and in some sort the pupil of Degas was a very great advantage in the critical battle. Sickert talks to the public as one who knows. He is going to say some very reactionary things but he says them, not as one who is astonished and outraged by modernity, but as someone who has known all about it for years; who is already bored by the business; who regards it as *très vieux jeu* (the manner is catching).

Whether these passages are, in a strict sense, 'well written' may be doubted; Sickert is not a stylist. But they are effectively written, and their effect is one of conversation. A garrulous, unbuttoned post-prandial style full of wandering reflections and scandalously imported anecdotes, sometimes – like this sentence – without a principal verb. This was Sickert's way of writing, and also his way of talking.

The evidence of the written word is sufficiently abundant. Sickert's conversation has also been recorded, and the reader may gain a notion of it from Osbert Sitwell, from Denys Sutton and from Marjorie Lilly, amongst others. Since our subject was a great enough man to justify even a slight memorial I here take the liberty of adding my own testimony.

It was, I think, in the year 1925. My brother and I were home for the holidays and the exigencies of life had left us upon my father's hands. He took us to dine at what was then a humble but entirely sympathetic little establishment called *L'Etoile* in Charlotte Street. We dined well and there was a bottle of which, we boys being still fairly juvenile, I imagine Clive took the lion's share; no doubt there was brandy with his coffee so that, by the end of the meal, he would have been slightly flown and, as always in such circumstances, a benign, benevolent and very entertaining host; a very different person from the sober, slightly acid author of *Old Friends*. He was a man who loved to entertain – even a pair of schoolboys – and who knew how to be vastly entertaining.

But that evening the entertainment was to include more than a solo performance; indeed, it might almost have been called variety, for presently Clive began to make signals to a distinguished old party who was dining with a quietly attractive lady at the other end of the room. Presently they joined us, another bottle appeared. We boys were introduced to Sickert and Thérèse Lessore. The conversation soon turned to the stage, the stage, that is, of Dan Leno, Little Titch and Lottie Collins.

> Lottie Collins has no sense,
> She shows her arse for eighteenpence.
> Sixpence more the people pay,
> She turns it round the other way.

I am not sure, but I think that this was one of the flowers of ancient verse which either Clive or Sickert culled from the *hortus siccus* of the past. But most of their numbers were joint efforts sung with great enthusiasm. I wish it were not the case, but the only melody and the only words that remain with me after half a century are 'Daisy, Daisy', an air which I can hardly claim to have rescued from oblivion. Clive assisted with less musical precision than Sickert, but with that astonishing verbal memory which allowed him to recall lines which Sickert was delighted to recognise as old but long-forgotten friends.

I have a notion that the recital grew more and more libidinous; I am certain that the vocal renderings became ever more joyfully emphatic, with Clive worrying less and less about the melody while Sickert bothered less and less about the words. They were both perfectly happy and neither was conscious of, or at least neither was at all abashed by, what had now become an extremely attentive audience.* This audience consisted of my brother and me, of Thérèse, who, I dare say, was well accustomed to Walter's dramatic exploits, the waiters, the proprietor, and some fellow diners – of these, I remember distinctly a nice young man, a bank clerk, perhaps, who had with him a very pretty girl to whom, I fancy, he was showing the sights of Soho. That night they certainly got their money's worth; they were half delighted and half embarrassed. So was I.

I had been brought up amongst painters; my earliest criminal activities consisted in stealing the fruit off still lives. But in addition to the painters whom I knew, there were, it appeared, others of a different make. My own home-grown artists and their friends were, to be sure, eccentric. They wore odd clothes, they did odd things; but this, I supposed, was simply because they were themselves rather odd, rather eccentric people. They were not, how shall I put it, professionally eccentric. These others, whom one met in books, in the pages of *Punch*, in advertisements, invariably wore smocks, they were bearded, they sported flowing ties; they were ostentatiously and overwhelmingly Bohemian. By those standards, the standards of *La Vie de Bohème*, the painters I knew hardly qualified at all. But Sickert did. Not that he wore a smock, or, at that moment, a beard; his tie didn't flow, his trousers were not patched; but he was emphatically a Bohemian; he was acting like an artist and I found this disconcerting. It may be argued that his behaviour was almost exactly like that of my father; but it wasn't; Clive was bottled; Sickert was only slightly bottled and I somehow divined that, whatever his condition, his conduct would have been much the same. Naturally shy, I felt a certain awkwardness at making one of a party which was so noisily defying the conventions of the quiet English diner, with his hushed conversa-

*As I write these words another ditty returns to my mind. Again it is connected with a well-known tune, but the words may be unfamiliar; they recall the tragic death of H.R.H. The Duke of Clarence in 1894 at the time when he was affianced to Princess Mary of Teck, later consort of George V:

> The Duke of Clarence has passed away,
> No more kisses for Princess May;
> Gone to hear the angels play,
> Ta-rar-rar-rar-ra *boom* de-ay.

tion and reticent manners. And yet, although Sickert, because his conduct was so clearly calculated to defy all social timidity, did in a way shock me, I found it impossible not to like him. There was something expansive, generous and benevolent about his tomfooleries which could conquer even a rather priggish, easily embarrassed boy of fifteen. In each subsequent meeting with Sickert I felt the same thing, but as my own inhibitions thawed I felt with ever greater force that here was someone who was an actor, an entertainer, almost, despite his real genius, a mountebank, but also someone who was on affectionate terms with the world; who joked because he wanted one to be amused, to be happy in his company. As I have said, the poses that he assumed were never disagreeable and to the sheer pleasure of his company was added something else: a dazzled admiration for one who could so brilliantly carry off whatever impersonation he had for the time chosen to adopt.

Well, it grew late; the greater part of the audience drifted away, the rest began to put away the silver, whip up napkins and pile chairs upon tables. Eventually, with much genial banter the painter and the critic wished each other good night vastly pleased with each other's company. The point is perhaps worth making. Theoretically they were opposed, indeed they were enemies. Sickert thought that Clive, together with Roger Fry, had corrupted the youth of his day; in conversation and in print he loved to mock him. Clive did not always take his sallies in very good part and replied, sometimes with acerbity. Sickert was, in his view, an absurd old stick in the mud and the memoir from which I have already quoted was but a summing up of attitudes which I think must have been pretty well known to Sickert during his lifetime. Historically, and on paper so to speak, they were diametrically opposed. Their manifest pleasure in each other's company was not the less real for that and it was in a spirit of perfect charity that they moved away unsteadily even though in different directions. The pavements were hard and frosty, Clive had no support save that of his giggling offspring. Sickert, safer on the experienced arm of Thérèse, continued to sing cheerfully down Charlotte Street until he was out of earshot.

I saw him again in December 1929. The Maynard Keyneses gave a party at 46, Gordon Square; there were a great many people. Bernard Shaw sat on a sofa with Virginia Woolf, flattering and being flattered; I longed for the courage to go up to them and be introduced, but lacked it. I was, however, introduced, for the second time, to Sickert. I was able to tell him how much I admired his painting at the London Group Exhibition; he replied that it was not his invention but that of Leech (I think), the work being, in effect, one of those 'echoes' which he was then producing, a theatrical scene taken from perhaps the *Illustrated London News* and by him converted into a painting entitled *Entente Anglo Russe*, that being the name of the ballet which had formed the subject of the drawing. He said at once that he wanted to paint me as I was; that is to say, in evening dress. I was wearing a black tie and a boiled shirt for the first time (whose black tie and whose boiled shirt I cannot recall). Thus, after some further negotiation, I found myself early one cold foggy Sunday morning in January on the underground railway, dressed as though for a dance. I felt exceedingly uncomfortable and concealed my awkwardly assembled finery beneath a very shabby overcoat. I had been told that the master would meet me at Highbury Station but felt that it was very unlikely that he would, and the prospect of waiting for him and probably missing him in that rather desolate spot and in that unsuitable disguise did not attract me.

But there he was dressed, as I recollect, in a brilliant green tail coat, sponge-bag tartan trousers of a reddish hue and startlingly patterned carpet slippers. The sight of him cheered me immensely. We must have made a pretty remarkable looking pair as we left the entrance to the station and I dare say it was our aspect no less than his violent exclamation which visibly shook a melancholy, cornet-playing band of salvationists on the station – 'God damn Christianity' was what he shouted at them. He must have been in a naughty mood that morning, for when the door was opened for us by a sluttish looking maid he turned to me and said, 'Beautiful as a Pinturicchio but an awful bitch really.' The girl was much less put out than the salvationists had been, but she gave us a dirty look.

Sickert's studio was large, dusty and chaotic – very much, in fact, the kind of thing with which I was familiar; but it differed from the establishments which I knew mainly because of its many books. In recollection, it seems to me that volumes of all shapes and sizes had accumulated to such an extent that the visitor had to make his way between precipitous cliffs of literature which threatened at any moment to fall and leave the painter imprisoned within an impenetrable wilderness of printed matter. Probably I exaggerate; I do remember Sickert, looking for some volume, thinking against all probability to find it and saying as he lifted it, 'No, German, I can tell by the weight' – with which words he let it fall back into the general detritus of books, its pages open to show that it contained erotica. In the midst of this chaos there still remained a clearing at the centre of which rose a model's throne. To this I ascended and with no attempt at setting me in a pose, Sickert took pen and ink and began at once to draw.

That it was an honour to be Sickert's model I had no doubt. Nevertheless, I had sufficient experience of this form of service to look forward to the next few hours without enthusiasm. I was standing; I had no book, my legs would ache abominably after a time; it would be a long business and thoroughly uncomfortable.

I soon discovered my mistake. He kept me about ten minutes, certainly not more than a quarter of an hour, in which time he executed a small full length drawing, a study of my face and a detail of a hand and arm. After many years this drawing has returned to me; it was for some years at my mother's studio at 8, Fitzroy Street. It was one of the very few things to survive an incendiary bomb. I don't think that it is very like, except in the pose and generally rather shabby aspect of the model. Sickert has been kind enough to provide me with eyebrows, things which, to all intents and purposes, I do not have. But he was quite prepared to use it as a basis for a full length, life-sized portrait, nor did he seem to think that it would be necessary for me to return for further sittings.

To an art student of that epoch this seemed a very strange method of working. I had been brought up to think of a painting as something that resulted from a process, often a prolonged process, of correction and recorrection. One discovered what one really wanted to do while one was actually engaged in the act of painting – and the canvas was, as it were, a laboratory in which, after a multitude of experiments, one might at last discover a picture. The idea of making a preliminary sketch, a drawing which might be squared up for use in the final work, was not encouraged. 'You never stop drawing': from the moment when you start your picture to the time when you put the final touches to it, you are discovering and describing form – such had been the thesis of Jean Marchand. Sickert's method of picture making was so entirely opposed to these teachings that I was a little scandalised but also, for who could say that *his* teachings were entirely at fault, exceedingly interested. I was later to discover that they constituted an essential part of his doctrine.

The sitting being finished, I prepared to take my leave, congratulating myself on having escaped the kind of prolonged torment and tedium that I had anticipated. To my delight, I found that I was expected to stay for lunch; I was enormously flattered. The rest of the morning was filled, splendidly filled with talk. In my time I have had the good fortune to listen to many people who could talk well, people who were intelligent, lucid, amusing and, in some cases, brilliant; but I have never heard anyone who could produce the kind of dazzling performance with which Sickert entertained me that day. It was the conversation of one who had been on the stage and never quite got off it, talk that was conceived as performance rather than argument, and it appeared to me to echo, in some degree, the sallies and the felicities of another age. It was the rhetoric of one who had been on intimate terms with Wilde and Whistler, Beardsley and Max Beerbohm and all their no doubt numerous imitators and epigoni, people for whom, I think, conversation, for better or worse, was an art, for whom malice was amply excused by wit, and for whom each observation was a pyrotechnic device, at the very least a squib. For them dullness was an unforgivable crime; they had no patience with the long thoughtful silences, the clumsy but sincere adumbrations, the inarticulate groping for truth which was to be so much cultivated by a later generation reared, not in Oxford or the Café Guerbois, but beside the deep, slow Cam. The thought that I was listening to a vanished age of brilliance and decadence added to my pleasure in the encounter. It was for me a day of unforgettable delight, the talk – the monologue rather – which filled the morning and flowed majestically over chicken and champagne, continued in splendid abundance through the afternoon until presently the lamps were lit and I could make my way home, no longer a sartorial oddity, but rather a normal if battered ingredient of the urban scene. Throughout that long session Sickert proceeded on the theory that he was developing a single observation, but one which was diverted by rather a large number of very considerable digressions. 'Thérèse will gather up my parentheses all in good time,' he observed.

I wish I could remember more of that magical day. Those who knew Sickert better than I will probably be able to divine the nature of the subjects on which he touched.

He talked about the greatness of J. F. Millet and of Degas; he spoke at length about his belief in the honesty and integrity of the Tichborne claimant, the innocent boy from the outback who claimed to be the long lost heir to a baronetcy – he ended by doing penal servitude or, as Sickert put it, was sent to prison for signing his own name. And how did Sickert know that Orton was really Tichborne all the time? Why, he could tell you what each witness said, or what he might easily have said if he had been Sickert feeling much the better for half a bottle of champagne, but, above all, there was the testimony of Whistler. Jimmy had been in court when a sealed document was handed to the claimant and he had seen him unconsciously, un*consciously* mark you, grope for a paper knife. Now only a man reared in a gentle home and bred as a gentleman would have done that; it settled the matter. There were a good many matters which Walter had, in rather the same manner, settled to his own satisfaction – the greatness of Poynter, the necessity of washing (or was it of never washing?) one's hair and of daily public baths; heaven, he declared, would be a public bath with mixed bathing and music; also, he was quite positive that one should always smoke a cheroot with the thick end between one's lips, the best tobacco was at the thin end. At one point he diverged into literary criticism: 'Tell your aunt that I admire her novels but there was one in which she opened a parenthesis and never closed it. Now a lady should always know when to open and when to close her legs.' I found him most rewarding when he was talking about painting. Nothing, he said, is harder to paint than a young face, and why? Because there are no violent accents. Any fool can paint age and deformity, even beauty is not too hard, but a rather undistinguished youthful face, that is the test. And here again he was enunciating a cardinal principle. But he wandered at such a rate that he was hard to digest, from the uses and abuses of the palette knife to David Low (a cartoon by Low adorned his walls). He had met Lansbury and, being a reactionary by conviction, had complained that democracy was an error: you can't do without blood and breeding. 'But isn't a cart horse nobler than a thoroughbred?' And, said the painter, 'He had something there, you know.'

And here I would observe by the way that all I know of Sickert suggests that, although his family connections were Liberal, he himself was the most convinced and the most logical of Tories. He loved the impoverished classes, they were the subject of his art and he had no desire to see them made tidy, comfortable and prosperous: why educate the masses when they are so beautifully, so interestingly ignorant; why disturb the splendidly discordant relationship of classes, for ever different from one another, for ever divided by every kind of interesting snobbery and factional hatred. He would not have spelled the matter out in these words, but he did, most emphatically, rejoice in a world which was infinitely divided and subdivided by differences of wealth, education and ethos – a world of shoddy and satin, seedy and posh.

He embarked on a long story of his relationship with George V and Queen Mary. Sickert had sent loyal and encouraging messages to the sovereign and his consort at the time when the King, slipping off his horse at the front, was for a time confined to his bed. Sickert found the royal couple less responsive than he could have wished. In view of the fact that most of his loyal telegrams to Windsor Castle were in German (this was in 1917) and that Sickert made a great deal out of the fancied similarity between the King and a frog, the frog being the hero of a ballad by Wilhelm Busch, this reticence is not altogether surprising.

Then I must look at some of his paintings. There was a picture by Leech of two young ladies on the front at Brighton (an illustration, I think, to *Plain or Ringlets*) and this I was called on to admire; weren't they darlings? I had private doubts; I even had some doubts concerning the variations that Sickert had played upon that old tune. At all events, I much preferred the *Raising of Lazarus* which I saw at about that time, perhaps on that same visit. But for Sickert the echo was a new passion, a new toy, an infidelity (so I see it) to his muse, but perhaps not the less exciting for that, so that when, presently, he told me how to paint a picture, the picture for which he provided a recipe was another echo.

'*Mon petit*,' he said (or at least he said something of the kind, for this, it must be remembered, took place more than half a century ago), 'mon petit, it's dead easy. There's nothing to it. You look through old copies of the *Illustrated London News*, or *Punch*, or, better still, some paper like *Judy*, something the bloody critics will never have heard of, find a cut that you like, square it up, paint it in monochrome using white and ultramarine and then let it dry for two or three weeks. When it is quite hard take an old silk handkerchief [I hadn't got an old silk handkerchief, and it seemed to me that it was only people like Sickert who had such things, but I determined on the spot to buy a silk handkerchief and age it as fast as I could] then take some linseed oil and rub down the picture until the surface is quite smooth. Then, using a very restricted palette, you paint the thing, but swiftly with rare and discreet touches, like a girl using lipstick.'

This was all received with attentive awe. I hope that I was never failing in respect, but belief did fail when, having told me that his father had known Ludwig of Bavaria well, he went on to give a graphic account of the funeral of the Duke of Wellington – an event which must surely have taken place some years before his birth. But at this point it is hard not to suppose that Sickert was curious to see how much would be swallowed by a rather owlish and over-eager art student and one who was, surely, a legitimate subject for a little teasing mystification. Sickert was, in fact, an arch tease. He hung *The Monarch of the Glen* in his studio. Did he admire it? Oh yes, but also 'c'est pour emmerder Roger Fry.' In the same way, he was always eager to extol the bêtes noires of the young: Poynter, Orchardson, Ruskin.

But with the teasing went genuine feeling. Instruction, education, indoctrination, in the strict sense of these words, might be used to describe much of Sickert's conversation and much of his writing. This, at least, was his purpose. He was a didactic artist. One who thoroughly enjoyed the politics of art, he very much wanted to teach the young, to set them on the right path and perhaps even, in my case, to snatch a brand already half consumed by the infernal combustion engine of Cézanne. Indeed, my last sight of him, some years after that memorable sitting-cum-lunch party was of Sickert as a lecturer.

There were some intervening interviews and some telegraphic communications, but after ten years I did again see him, and in that time he had attained in my eyes and in the eyes of some of my contemporaries a new stature. Quite unconsciously he had become involved in a revolution or at least a movement informed by a revolutionary purpose, and he had been in some measure canonised by the revolutionaries. Perhaps it would be more exact to say that in this, the last stage of his career, there was a party among the young which regarded him as one of the heroes of modern painting.

I suppose that Sickert's happiest and most productive epoch

belongs to those years when an earlier generation of young English painters, those who were to form the Camden Town Group, regarded him as the mentor of the moderns. At that time, all that was new and lively and progressive in British art tended to fetch up at 19, Fitzroy Street. He himself was doing his best work and they were following lines of which he could approve. Then came Cézanne and the Post-Impressionists. The erstwhile leader of the young found himself the commander of the Old Brigade. Thus, when I met him in 1929 about twenty years after the First Post-Impressionist Exhibition, he must have been somewhat shaken by the success of his opponents, by the growing influence of the followers of Cézanne and the school of Paris, by the war and certain private griefs. Still respected and applauded even by his adversaries, he was in some measure a cult figure, but also a back number.

By the late thirties, there had been a reaction. It seemed that the 'movement' in Paris had run out of steam and had lost touch with reality. Some of the lesser figures had turned to facile decorative effects and fashionable airs. Sickert had remained true to himself and to reality. Someone at the Euston Road School invited him to lecture.

There was a good deal in both the principles and the practices of the Euston Road which Sickert would have rejected. *Male gut und schnell* was emphatically *not* the motto of William Coldstream or Claude Rogers. But whoever it was who decided that Sickert should be invited to address the London School of Drawing and Painting was fundamentally right; it was entirely suitable that Sickert should preside over the destinies of the nascent school; like him, they sought truth, and in that search were ready to abandon easy dexterity and decorative grace. Like them, he still marched under the old banner *disegno*; it is the drawing which, above all else, demonstrates the honesty, the integrity of the artist.

Thus it came about that an anxious party awaited the arrival of Sickert at 8, Fitzroy Street at about one o'clock in the afternoon of 6 July 1938. It was here that he was to lunch and whence he would proceed to the studios and lecture. It grew later and later and still there was no sign of him. Presently from the metallic covered passage which connected the studio with the main entrance of the house we heard a strange confusion of sounds, a confusion composed of laughter, fluent Tuscan, and the clanging murmurs of which that passage was always alarmingly productive. It was Sickert with Thérèse and our neighbour Signor Ferro; Sickert was explaining the manner in which an active man could use the passage as a latrine.

The lunch was hurried but gay; Sickert seemed in excellent form, and I don't think that he drank too much. It was some genuine senile confusion which led him as he took his place beside the chairman to ask in a stage whisper, 'Is that Roger?' Fry had been dead for five years and more, but from this rather disquieting remark I judge that Sickert could not rid his mind of his old opponent.

After Clive Bell had introduced the speaker as the greatest living British painter and promised that if Sickert took the occasion to attack him, he, Bell, would reply in kind, Sickert gave his lecture. Once more I was told how to paint a picture; but now the master had returned to his true principles: he reverted to the doctrine of speed, although it had to be admitted that he also dilated a little on the advantages of using photographs. If you wanted to paint something – say a house – it might be well to take a photograph of the house and square it up. But there was a more heroic way of tackling the job: you might take a taxi and drive past the house and as you flashed by make your drawing. 'Of course,' he conceded, 'if you are a beginner you can tap on the glass and ask the man to drive past slowly.' I think that some of his audience, not being familiar with the Sickertian doctrine of speed, may have been a little puzzled.

At a later period, after the beginning of the war I think, a deputation of the Euston Road School went out to Ramsgate in what was a deliberate act of homage. The excursion has been described by one of the visitors. I am glad of that visit; it must surely have been gratifying, after so many years, for Sickert to receive such an assurance of youthful admiration.

But I never saw him again after that lecture. If these few and imperfect records of what was, after all, a comparatively slight and fleeting relationship with Sickert are at all to the purpose it is because certain things become more obvious in the light of my story. It does seem to me that Sickert's *obiter dicta*, his prejudices, his very jokes were indicative of a serious programme which is evident in his painting and very evident in his writing.

Again and again, so it now seems to me, he was making a case, defending a thesis; behind the *facetiae* and the banter there was a coherent and consistent doctrine.

From this follows an assumption that would, I think, have been made by most of Sickert's contemporaries but to which we, today, accede only with great caution. The assumption was that there was a right way and a wrong way of painting, a right objective and a proper means. Hence a duty to be didactic. It was typical that Sickert, in entertaining me with his foibles and fancies, should have thrown in a lesson in painting. He wanted me to follow the right path and to avoid error. He had a passion for teaching. He believed in his doctrines with a seriousness which was in its way admirable, but which can hardly be shared by our own doctrine-distracted age. This view, that there was a right way of painting, was shared, perhaps, but with less conviction, by his adversaries and between them there was a doctrinal battle. But it was an absurd encounter. A follower of Sickert, even such a zealot as Osbert Sitwell, might make excellent fun of Clive Bell or Roger Fry, but when it came to making fun of Cézanne he fell silent. Conversely, the followers of Cézanne might hold Sickert up to ridicule – Sickert the critic, that is, but not Sickert the painter. To find a doctrine that will admit the claims of both is not easy, but to believe in a doctrine which excludes either is impossible. In truth, the opponents of Sickert in that they admired him did, tacitly, concede the case; but I can assure the reader that in the year 1929 this was by no means so obvious and indeed there must be many people even now who remember when a like claim of absolute and exclusive artistic rectitude was still advanced by the more dull-witted practitioners of abstract art.

We will consider presently the consequences of this polarity of artistic opinion but first it will be convenient to look at another side of Sickert's conversation and literary work. Sickert, it must be obvious from these slight memoirs and from all the more extensive records of his life, was a joker. His conversations, his opinions, his dress, his behaviour were funny. It was only in his painting that he was not funny at all. And even in his paintings jokes were tied on to the pictures, like tin cans to a dog's tail, and with a complete lack of seriousness.

Frank Rutter may or may not have said that a painting originally entitled *The Camden Town Murder* was later exhibited over the title *What Shall We Do for the Rent?* and eventually found a purchaser as *The Germans in Belgium*. There was even a flippant inconsistency in his manner of signing pictures and, it is said, of dating them. But should we assume, as some people have assumed, that those dark Mornington Crescent interiors, those enigmatic groups of figures on beds or in shabby rooms, were simply exercises in luminosity and tonality? Surely not. When Sickert told Virginia Woolf that he was a literary painter like all decent painters, he was telling the truth about himself at all events. The flippant title may be of little service in discovering the true character of the obfusc dramas which he delighted to paint, but there was a drama there, of some kind, perhaps of a kind which Sickert himself would have found it difficult to put into words. In this, he follows his master Degas whose 'genre' paintings have received many titles, who is too reticent to do more than to express a mood, the immanent presence of some human catastrophe, but who, when he chooses, is the most 'literary' painter of his age.

If this be true then it would seem that the function of the joke is defensive. Sickert rides away on a witticism from a situation because he either cannot or will not commit himself to the kind of explicit and overt title which served the Pre-Raphaelites. He laughs that he may not weep.

These considerations bring us also to our starting point in considering the Sickertian doctrine. Sickert is concerned, despite a few still lives and a few landscapes, with man and man-made things. But man must be truly depicted; he must be shown not as he ought to be, but as he is. Think for a moment of the greatest of the academicians, the genius of things as they ought to be. Look at the *Incendio in Borgo*, a scene in which the Pope is miraculously extinguishing a house on fire, and you will discover that there is not a single actor upon that wall who really feels the effect of haste or of agitation, every single movement of every single limb is beautiful, graceful, exactly and exquisitely placed in its architectonic position, every group is made to cohere with the architecture and the most absurd inventions, as, for instance, the man who is apparently engaged upon pointless gymnastic exercises, are acceptable because not for one moment does Raphael suggest that we are in the real world, rather we are called upon to observe a miraculously subtle balletic performance.

The *Incendio in Borgo* is a masterpiece, but after the death of Ingres there was no one anywhere who could even begin to paint in that manner again. The master of modern life, to adapt Baudelaire's phrase, had to look elsewhere and to find another place from which to take his point of departure. It was not difficult. He could find what he needed in the face of a laughing Dutch gipsy, on the walls of the Louvre, or, since we are dealing in masterpieces, consider the *Night Watch*. Here we have the rich, the human, the Shakespearean masterpiece with nothing of the ballet about it, no hint of planned disposition but everywhere accident, disorder, confusion, irrelevance, life. This is where Sickert starts. It is here in Amsterdam, not in Rome, that we shall find his spiritual ancestors, the gods of his particular cult.

Accident, disorder, confusion, irrelevance – this is what life is really like, this is what, if you have the right kind of apparatus, you may catch in an exposure of a thousandth of a second. If only he can learn to look hard enough, to remember well enough, to draw well enough, the painter may become that instantaneous camera, but one that is driven by a sudden passionate excitement so to seize life that he may take from it, not all that is there, but all that matters, all that is useful to the artist.

The idea of training the mind and the hand to record appearances with the utmost speed was one which interested a great many of the French pioneers of modernism. Lecoq de Boisbaudran, who had a considerable influence upon Rodin, Degas and Whistler, attempted a systematic and progressive training of the memory in order that that which had once been seen might for ever be retained. Sickert was less ambitious and less systematic, but he was certainly in general agreement with the idea of the very short pose above all because it outflanked the methods of the academies. For him, there was something abnormal and unnatural about the nude unless she were on a bed or in a bath. The life class fails to stimulate or at least it most emphatically ceases to stimulate as we go on peering, plumbing, measuring, correcting and recorrecting. The painter of modern life rejects the enthroned model altogether, or if that for some reason be impossible, he sees to it that she shall be draped so that the folds of material that cover her will never again be reassembled. Thus, the student is again filled with a sense of urgency, impelled by a desperate need to state that which can only be stated once.

Tilly Pullen of 16, Inkerman Villas, London NW3, is real enough, but take away all her clothes, set her in one of those ham poses into which experienced models fall by second nature – the Niobe, the Odalisque, La Source – and she becomes a monument;

we can no longer see her because the entire history of art has become an opaque barrier between her and us. Inevitably, we find ourselves looking at her through the spectacles of the masters, quoting from and alluding to all those who in former times have ridden this particular war horse.

Perhaps, during the past sixty years, we have wandered so far from nature that she has again become a mysterious and an enchanting stranger. In 1900 it would have been different. The nudes of the salon and the academy were indeed overpowering, abundant and profoundly disheartening, and ever so distant from Tilly Pullen. She, whether undraped as Artemis or richly and abundantly adorned as *La Princesse du Pays de Porcelaine*, was emphatically not herself; she was, as far as disguise could make her, a pictorial falsehood, and so away with her. Let her catch the first bus back to Kilburn, and let us follow her, then, for a moment in the dingy glimmering illumination of the shared bedsitter, standing against the ludicrous roses of the grimy wall paper and preparing herself for rest on the equally grimy cast iron bedstead, with its unwashed sheets, its dubious chamber pot, the cheap cosmetics and cigarette stubbs – in fact, all her natural habitat. She stretches, yawns and pulls out a hat pin. And you cry: Stop, hold it!

At that instant, that is to say the moment when your eye is caught by some magnificent conjunction of pictorial facts, you must get the model to pause; she can't hold the pose for long, and, even if she could, the light would change, and even if the light didn't change, your mood would. There is nothing for it then but to draw. You begin at the 'eye catch', the point that commanded your interest, and then, without bothering to correct or to take the pencil from the paper, you work outwards towards the margins of your picture looking to the spaces that lie between the objects that you see. Using the neutral information that they supply, you rapidly complete a sight sized drawing; that is to say, a drawing in which objects appear more or less at the size that you would record, if they were traced upon a sheet of glass about an arm's length from your nose.

Given skill, given honesty of purpose and given just a few minutes of Tilly Pullen's time, you can make a record which in its very imperfections is so much alive that when you bring it home and square it up you have that fertile grain, that fragment of reality which is somehow all the better for being so fragmentary, what

Henry James called the germ, the *donné*, from which perhaps you may make a masterpiece.

But supposing that we are not dealing with Tilly Pullen, but with a duchess. Is she not also to be presented in her natural habitat? No doubt she is, but it is far better for painters to have no truck with duchesses, particularly if they happen to be young and beautiful. The painter's business is with reality and a young and beautiful duchess hardly counts as real; she belongs to those two Sickertian categories 'the august site' and 'the smartened up young person', and is therefore abnormal. Equally abnormal and equally unusable by the painter are the magnificently ugly and the utterly horrific. The great aim of Sickertian realism was to find beauty in the dull, the tawdry, the commonplace.

I think that it is necessary to assess this attitude within its historical context. In those years – the years between 1890 and 1914 – the Royal Academy was to an extraordinary extent devoted to beauty, beauty as depicted by Lord Leighton and by Burne-Jones and by a host of lesser men. There were bevies of duchesses, yards of satin, acres of lace and gentle English landscape scenes populated by cows which, one can't help feeling, would have felt it indelicate to produce milk. The New English was no doubt a little more restrained but in the life decorative, as presented by Sargent and in his later works by Orpen, the wistful urchins, the brave fisherfolk and deeply sentimental collie dogs were very much in evidence.

The unreal drama of the rich, of the 'gooseocracy', that is to say, a government of beings in matinée hats that detests art as it detests all realities, or of the poor, as touchingly presented to the rich, all rags and tatters and pathos, was not for Sickert. His art was a protest against it, a protest against the crushing weight of beautiful beings, beautiful furniture and beautiful sentiments.

His art was also a protest against easy solutions and this was evident not only in his choice of banal subject matter and unposed nature, but also in his manner of painting. Sickert, being well acquainted with Degas, must also have known the Impressionists fairly well, but although he did enrich his palette around the year 1908 it was under the influence, not of the Impressionists, but of his junior Spencer Gore. What he seems chiefly to have gained from the French, apart from Degas, was a readiness to convey forms through accent rather than through outline; and in this he followed a procedure which, like the choice of his subject matter, was sufficiently heroic. I use this word with intention for it seems to me that there is something more than a little courageous in the disdain he shows for all that is immediately charming and graceful in nature and for the secure comfort that derives from the ability to work at length and at leisure upon a subject. But again, look at his contemporaries – the by no means ungifted or at all negligible painters of the New English Art Club – and observe their handling of paint. How deftly, how descriptively they manipulate their sables, how impressively they build rectangles of wholly convincing firmness with one bold stroke of the chisel-headed, hog's-hair brush, how well they pass from one smoothly painted phrase to another, how fluently and with what pleasing skill they indicate the soft luminous shadow beneath a jaw, the highlight on a porcelain vase, or the broken glitter of a satin dress. When it pleased him Sickert could do likewise: he knew all the tricks that ever were thought of and some that were not. But, again and again in his portraits and interiors, in just those passages where we should expect the planes to be drawn together by suave handling and a flow of paint that follows the direction of the drawing, he seems, almost wantonly, to work *against* the contour so that his paint surface becomes a ruthlessly abrasive system of blobs and dashes and abrupt asperities of paint. It almost looks as though he had set out somehow brutally and swiftly to obliterate his own beautiful drawing and he appears to achieve his description, for his paint is indeed in the strongest way descriptive, simply by being utterly and entirely right as a statement of tone.

There are paintings in which Sickert allows himself to be almost gentle in his transitions, and there are others in which he will follow a contour with all the strong descriptive verve of Hals; but even in these there is a degree of self denial which exhibits the highest form of technical self discipline. The thing is done in the very hardest way, it is done triumphantly and rightly and without the slightest concession to sentimentality of thought or feeling. Even Degas in his fiercest descriptions of the old hacks of the ballet is less ruthlessly austere.

If the reader can agree that the words triumphantly and rightly are appropriate, if, in fact, he can agree that Sickert has his place amongst the great painters of the past century, then it will surely be allowed that the pictorial doctrine which I have attempted to adumbrate, the doctrine of realism *à l'outrance*, of rapid statement and emotion recollected in tranquillity, was at least useful to him. It is a doctrine from which he sometimes departs. Nevertheless, it does provide a fixed point to which he returns; something about which, for all his chameleonlike capers and tomfooleries, he is serious.

Nor was it only for Sickert that it was valuable. If we look at the work of his friends and contemporaries – Walter Bayes, Spencer Gore, Harold Gilman, R. A. Bevan, Malcolm Drummond – we shall discover that, although they were many of them to part company with him and, as he saw it, to go whoring after strange gods, he did teach them something valuable. There is in the work of all these painters a kind of drawing which is based upon an idea of integrity. Put a Sickert drawing beside one of the most brilliant of Augustus John's confections and you can at once see the quality of thought that was expressed by Sickert's hands and, to a surprising extent, transmitted to those who felt his influence. Compared with John, Sickert looks almost inept, he fumbles, he hesitates, he gropes; but in the end he says, or rather he brutally blurts out the truth that he has discovered – while his younger contemporary has managed beautifully and dexterously to say the kind of thing that a reputable old master would have said if faced by the same motif. In Sickert's work there is a passionate pursuit of truth, and this same quality does find its echo in the drawings of an artist like Drummond. What is less communicable is that astonishing visual curiosity which enables Sickert to find truth in such surprising places. Again in Augustus John's work, there is rather a pursuit of beauty, which in his followers or indeed in his own weaker productions, degenerates into the search for a pleasing manner.

The Sickertian doctrine, therefore, is something more than a personal explanation of art serviceable only to the artist himself. It was a sufficiently influential doctrine and one which, it may be claimed, had a tonic effect upon the young; it did help young artists to avoid a certain kind of fluent and facile generalisation which at the beginning of the twentieth century was sufficiently common and contagious amongst those who had been taught at the Slade. It was, then, a doctrine, which, like all artistic doctrines, could be mischievous, but it was also a doctrine worth studying and, when it was attacked, worth fighting for. One of Sickert's chief motives in writing was precisely this: to defend his doctrine.

Sickert had begun to write early in life; in this Whistler set him an example. Indeed, Whistler was probably the person who first led him to commit sentiments to print, for although Sickert never imitated the precious ornamentation of *Ten O'Clock*, his style being always simple, direct and unaffected, save by the habit of quotation in foreign tongues, he must have caught from Whistler the notion of communicating with the press and it was as Whistler's supporter and henchman that he first began to fire off squibs. More seriously, and at some length, he contributed a long essay on Bastien Lepage to a memorial volume dedicated to that painter; it was one of the strangest offerings ever left on a newly covered grave for, although it did contain a reference to that painter's own personal integrity, it also contained a root and branch denunciation of the particular brand of 'studio' realism, the carefully painted, sentimentally loaded realism which at that time seemed to be the chief French contribution to British painting. Bastien Lepage, he concluded, was painting the wrong things in the wrong way. I still do not understand how this essay ever got published. It is important, for it contains the first of Sickert's statements concerning doctrine, and from it we may judge how consistent he was throughout the years.

From the first he was discursive. Journalists in those days received an amount of space that would astonish, delight and perhaps embarrass their modern descendants. With so much room, Sickert could wander unashamed from topic to topic and in this respect, as in some others, his writings resemble his conversation. As in conversation, he built himself a character. This was important if, as so frequently happened, he was going to preach, to denounce, to defend his own point of view. For all these purposes it was necessary that Sickert should give the public a notion of his qualifications. As an advocate and a witness Sickert needed to exhibit himself in a flamboyant manner, nor, I think, did it worry him at all that in the process he was obliged to make some large, indeed, some overweening assumptions concerning his omniscience and the crass ignorance of the rest of the world. It must be allowed that the perils of such an attitude are great. Nothing is more irritating than to have to listen to a catalogue of writer's attainments except perhaps that species of humour which relies for its effect upon the fact that lesser mortals are not so well informed as we. All the vast literary skill of Evelyn Waugh, even the genius of Rudyard Kipling can hardly make it tolerable that an author should dwell upon his superior knowledge; as a literary device it is both pompous and mean.

That Sickert escapes a similar charge, despite the fact that he insists so much on his credentials is, I think, something very much in his favour, even though a part of the reason why he is so readily forgiven is that we do not take his vainglory very seriously; but for the rest, our indulgence is based upon the fact that, without great skill as a writer, he has the art, or perhaps the artlessness, of keeping our sympathy and that he maintains, almost always, a playful and engaging tone.

To the modern reader the most unpalatable aspect of his writings is his inability either to accept or wholly to dismiss Cézanne. Cézanne, as he rightly saw, was the arch enemy of the perceived, as opposed to the conceived object, the great practitioner of infinitely prolonged research, of drawing through colour as opposed to drawing through tonality and, in the popular view of the time, of the neutrally architectonic, as opposed to the human and narrative painting. From Cézanne stemmed all the other heresies of the age, all the forces that seduced Sickert's followers into error. In consequence, Cézanne is described as a tragic failure, a pathetic bungler, the 'master of how not to do it'. But he could not be entirely dismissed; he was an artist with personality enough to make him disturbing. Again and again Sickert returns to the attack, again and again he beheads the hydra only to discover that new heads have sprouted.

As the years went by, Sickert found himself increasingly forced by circumstances into the position of the old reactionary. It is not a happy position for one who, like Sickert, wanted to persuade the young, and this attitude has indeed done him a disservice. And surely if we undervalue him for this reason, it is we who are wrong.

Sickert himself said, apropos the Whistler-Ruskin affair: 'The pretension of a great critic is not like the pretension of the ridiculous modern being called an expert. A great critic does not stand or fall by immunity from error.'

Like so many of Sickert's remarks, this is profoundly true and, indeed, it may be doubted whether, in this department of thought, the word error means very much. Sickert's writing is full of errors, full also of inaccuracies, dangerous generalisations and absurdities. But he had the cardinal virtue of an art critic: he loved and was passionately interested in painting. And he writes about it with genuine feeling and with splendid impetuosity. If, because the current of contemporary feeling was against him, he may be called wrong then, as the eddies of fashion reverse old judgments he may equally well be called right. His admiration of the work of Sir Edward Poynter might look silly enough in 1920; now it is becoming increasingly acceptable. In the early twentieth century Sickert's insistence upon the value of 'literature' in art was hard to accept; the beginnings of the century had seen so much 'literature' that it passed easily from the statement that bad literature in art makes bad art, which is indeed very nearly a tautology, to the much more dubious statement that literature in art is either meaningless or reprehensible. There would be few today who would not agree with Sickert that the critics of the year 1910 were wrong to throw out the baby of sentiment with the bath water of sentimentality. Sickert was surely right to protest and, in his last years, Roger Fry had begun to come round to his way of thinking.

Sickert's fault as a critic in the eyes of the young was that he was on the wrong side – as we now see it – in a great controversy. He was against Cézanne because Cézanne could not be accommodated within his theory of painting. But the theory of painting, if this analysis be correct, was for his own purposes admirable and tremendously productive. By being wrong he became, as an artist, superbly right.

Degas: Le Viol

Ever since I first saw it, in 1933, *Le Viol* has puzzled me (see illustration 3). It puzzles me, both in respect of its form and of its content. Of its form I really will say very little. Degas can be left to present his own structural mysteries. One's first and most obvious impression is of space, of an enclosed and illuminated space. We are looking into a room, the orthogonals meet near the head of a seated or crouching woman, we are therefore about at her level. The reflection in the mirror suggests that the room is not large and that the lamp on the pedestal table is its only illumination. The light that falls from this lamp does not behave in a perfectly logical manner; in consequence, the position of the table is not easily determined. When Degas repainted parts of this canvas in about 1900 he added the flowers on the lampshade which serve to unite it with the wall, thus adding to the enigmatic quality of the space. There is, so to speak, plenty of room in which to move about, and yet the sense of confinement is very evident. Turn the picture upside down and the claustral sensation will be intensified. The tonal design will also become more evident, the frontier between light and shade then appears as a straight line drawn almost midway across the picture with one great, deep, rectangular re-entrant; this pattern of illumination reinforces the sensation of a deep central projection. But over, and as one may say, playing against this composition in space, there is a linear pattern; a line may be drawn from the crown of the woman's head to that of the man and it will fall tangentially upon the dark oval frame of the little picture on the wall; yet the inward thrust of the composition is so strong that this is hardly apparent; in rather the same way, a series of parallels – the woman's dress, her corsets, the man's feet – all very clearly suggest a corresponding diagonal making two sides of a triangle, the base of which is the man's body, the apex a point well outside the picture.

The central axis from which all the drawing grows is, surely, the pedestal table, the open box and the lamp. I cannot express my sense of the importance of this passage better than by saying that I can well imagine Degas feeling that if only he could get *that* part solidly stated the rest would fall into place. Everything, it seems to me, is governed by this central axis, the mirror balancing the shape of the bedstead, the strong horizontal that is broken by the top hat and the girl's head, which itself terminates a majestic series of curves made by her arm and her petticoat – note in passing that the arm itself is a miracle of integrity – who but Degas would have dared to describe such inexplicable contours? From the same nexus the fringe of the counterpane, produced by the angle of the box, is itself integrated with the carpet and the floorboards. This, the vital element in the composition, is surely one of the great feats of painting of the nineteenth century.

But, when I speak of the lamp and the table as the vital element of the composition am I not guilty of an absurdity? For here we have, not the innocent decorative peacetime manoeuvres of abstract art, but the bloody and terrible encounters of a painter who has engaged in the warfare of human relationships. The 'vital' elements in the psychomorphic – as distinct from the purely abstract – design are a man and a woman, the woman averted from the man and between them a void in which the lamp and the table play a not unimportant but psychologically subordinate role. Now this couple in this not very distinguished bedroom have not come hither for the purpose of playing a quiet game of chess or discussing the arguments for and against proportional representation. For reasons which will presently appear, I am being as cautious as possible in my conjectures, but I think I am not going too far when I say that this is clearly an erotic transaction: the characters are involved in some business of affection or of lust. An intelligent but uninformed observer, seeing *Le Viol* for the first time said to me: 'I have never before seen a picture in which the feeling of emotional tension was so strong.'

In Manson's list and again in the catalogue of the French

exhibition at Burlington House in 1933, the picture is discreetly styled *Intérieure*. Nevertheless it had already acquired an alternative name, for it was then, at the London exhibition, that Roger Fry told me it was also known as *Le Viol*. According to him – and unfortunately I do not know how close he was to first hand sources – the story about this painting, to use his expression, was pretty generally known at the beginning of this century, so much so that when the picture was offered to the Metropolitan the Governors took fright and refused it (remember that Degas' *Absinthe* had already caused a terrible outcry in London). Degas, hearing what had happened, remarked with characteristic wit: 'Mais j'aurais donné un certificat de marriage avec.' The anecdote may be true; we know from Sickert that Degas enjoyed making fun of the Anglo Saxons, and conceivably – as we shall see – the joke may have had a deeper meaning; but it does not prove very much, save that the alternative title has for long been current. It is used by all the more recent authorities, including Lemoisne, who also agrees with other writers in ascribing it to the year 1874 or 1875.

Here for a moment I would like to digress. The dating of works of art is a fascinating but perilous occupation. I know far too little about Degas' stylistic development to attempt, on that ground, an emendation of Lemoisne's chronology. There is, however, what appears to be a first study for *Le Viol*, a study which is fairly close to the final work and which M. Jean Adhémar believes to have been made in 1867 or 1868. The ascription is made plausible by the fact that the sketch was drawn on the back of a document dated December 1867. This, of course, does not necessarily date the drawing apart from the fact that it could not have been made before the document was issued. Nor is there any compelling reason why this sketch should not have been executed six years before the picture was finished. On the other hand it does make it seem possible that *Le Viol* is rather earlier than we had supposed. Another study will be found in Degas' notebooks for 1871 and 1872. All that I am concerned to show here is that whatever the date of the completion of the finished picture, the thing was conceived between 1868 and 1872. Miss Jean Sutherland Boggs dates the picture *circa* 1871.

To return now to my main theme, the subject of the picture has for long been supposed to be a rape, and several authorities have gone further and found in it an illustration to a novel *Les Combats de*

Françoise Duquesnoy by Degas' friend Duranty. Duranty is an author who might fairly be expected to have an influence on Degas: they knew each other well, and Duranty as a critic found none of the independent artists of the time more to his taste. It seems natural that Degas should have, so to speak, returned the compliment. Nevertheless an element of doubt remains, an element which has not been dispelled by the critics. M. Camille Mauclair in his study of Degas puts it thus: 'Was Degas touched by an intimate drama unknown to us? Was his object to depict, as has been suggested, an episode in a novel by his friend Duranty . . . that remains an enigma.'

But why should it remain an enigma? Why not, as a first step, get hold of a copy of Duranty's novel and read it? In England, where I can find no copy, that is not so easy, but M. Mauclair had the Bibliothèque Nationale at his disposal. Why did he not use it? The reason was, I think, that he had a particularly juicy passage of fine writing in prospect:

Amidst the poetic lights and shades of the little bedchamber of a neat and virginal working girl – a room softly lit by a lamp near an embroiderer's work basket, and here again how can one help naming Vermeer? – we find ourselves in the terribly heavy silence which followed on the brutal struggle: a silence broken by the sobbing of the semi-nude victim, bowed down by grief, whilst, with his back to the door, the man, who, now that he has satisfied his lust, is once more correct, but mournfully so, contemplates her despair, though, despite his ennui and remorse, with a glint of madness in his eyes.

Here is the pathetic sobriety, restrained pity, and sadness in the presence of a young girl soiled by the egoistic, epileptic bestiality of the male, which in a singular manner contradicts the legend, if not of the misanthropy, at least of the caustic insensibility that is connected with the painter's name. But all this is suggested by the painter's means. The young girl's head, the lamp shade adorned with flowerets, the pink-lined work basket, and the naive pictures on the wall are so many elements to bring home to us the position and the soul of the little victim, and to these are added her sorry linen corset, torn from her and lying there on the ground – her slim shoulder caressed by the light. The still-life parts of this picture speak to us the language of her home and form a whole with the tragedy . . . one can easily imagine how other painters, by a calculated and lascivious disorder, would have emphasised this scene. Degas' infinite tact counselled him to leave everything in its place, one might think that nothing had happened. After a few abominable moments we see nothing more amidst these now peaceful surroundings, save a guilty man and a wretched girl.

'One might think that nothing had happened.' But in that case what leads one to suppose that anything in particular *had* happened?

M. Tabary in his study of Duranty writes thus: 'M. Wilenski in his book *Modern French Painters* has advanced the view that a masterpiece by Degas, *Le Viol* sometimes more discreetly called *Intérieure* was suggested by a passage in the last of Duranty's novels *Les Combats de Françoise Duquesnoy*; we cannot subscribe to this hypothesis. Degas' picture shows the aftermath to a scene of violence which will not be found in the work of our author.'

If we turn to the book itself we shall find nothing in any way similar to M. Mauclair's spirited account of the matter. There is, to be sure, one scene of conjugal violence which might just conceivably be likened to *Le Viol* although it has nothing to do with a rape. The book contains a rather colourless portrait of an impossibly virtuous young woman who lives with a brute of a husband and conducts a platonic affair with an impossibly high-minded young man. Duranty is not a descriptive writer but it is clear that he situates his action in the wealthiest Parisian society during the reign of Louis Philippe. I feel that we need very strong proof that Degas had Duranty in mind before we can believe that the picture has anything to do with the novel. A further difficulty arises, if the picture was conceived in 1868. This is that *Françoise Duquesnoy* was not published until 1872. A first version did, however, appear in *L'Evenement Illustré* in 1867.

Degas himself referred to the picture either as *Intérieur* or: 'mon tableau de genre'.

I hate to disappoint my readers, but it seems to me doubtful whether the picture, which I shall continue, for convenience sake, to refer to as *Le Viol*, has in fact anything to do with rape. My doubts are augmented by the observations of M. Jean Adhémar. M. Adhémar sees the picture as an illustration not to Duranty but to Zola, and M. Lemoisne is inclined to accept his view. Here again we have a very probable literary source. We are told that Degas was at times overwhelmed by the genius of Zola, and again Zola's connection with the Impressionists and with the realist movement is well known. M. Adhémar finds the subject of *Le Viol* in the crucial chapter of *Madeleine Férat* where a married couple – Degas *could* produce a marriage certificate – meet, not in the virginal bedroom of a working girl, but in a hotel. The story is not one of rape but of frustration. The woman is deeply alienated by the unexorcised spectre of a former love. The bedroom turns out to be that in which she had slept with her husband's predecessor. And although she loves her husband and no longer feels any affection for her former lover, the revival of buried memories, the recollection of carnal intimacies forced upon her consciousness by the associative power of the furniture, the pictures on the walls, the bric-a-brac on the mantelpiece and a dozen other evocative trifles creates an inhibition strong enough to undo the bonds of mutual love. Madeleine rejects Guillaume and the evening, which marks the catastrophe of their drama, ends in misery and a course of events which leads finally to her suicide.

The mood of the picture seems very close to Zola's novel, the quiet despair of the woman, the tense exasperation of the man are true to Zola's meaning, while the round table and the narrow virginal bed are actually mentioned in the text.

It is tempting to look no further, all the more tempting in that Guillaume, in the earlier chapters of the novel, is drawn from Zola's recollections of the young Cézanne. Might we not discover in this picture a commentary upon the private life of the master of Aix? M. Adhémar suggests no such thing, and we had better be equally discreet. Some authors have already tried to find Cézanne's features in a Degas portrait. The resemblance is not great but it is greater than that which subsists between Cézanne's self portraits and the head of the man who posed for *Le Viol*.

Undoubtedly, M. Adhémar's suggestion is very much more convincing than anything that has been advanced by Professor Wilenski or M. Camille Mauclair. Nevertheless, I cannot accept it without reservations; if Degas did have *Madeleine Férat* in mind, then, certainly, he has taken extensive liberties with his text. Zola describes his heroine with some particularity and, as Edouard Herriot has said, she looks like a Manet (the novel was in fact dedicated to Manet). Zola describes the bedroom in the *Auberge du Grand Cerf* with even greater care and at every stage in the action he indicates the situation of his characters. Degas disregards this detailed scenario at almost every point. Perhaps we should not expect too close a correspondence between the novelist and the painter. But do we, in fact, need to find a specific text for this picture? The legend has grown up that the painting was suggested by a novel; the particular novel suggested fails to support this theory, and so we hunt for another and more probable source. But there is no hard evidence that Degas looked for or needed to look for literary inspiration. Of those of his works which verge on history or anecdote – *Sémiramis, Les Malheurs de la Ville d'Orléans, Bouderie, l'Absinthe, La Fille de Jephthe, Les Spartiates* – only the two last have a recognisable programme and these belong to the stock in trade of academic art.

It is true that the genre pictures show, in a general way, a sympathy with current literature. And it is true that *Le Viol* captures, more completely even than Manet's *Nana* – how vulgar the Manet looks beside him – the atmosphere of the French realist novel of the nineteenth century. But for my part, if I had to find a literary equivalent for it, I think that I should look to the sensuous but restrained naturalism of Maupassant – remember that Maupassant said to Degas, 'You paint as I would like to write.' But if Degas wanted to tell a story he was quite capable of finding his own and I believe that this is what he has done here. Look, for a moment, at illustration 4 in which, clearly, we have the man of *Le Viol* and a woman, perhaps the same woman, dressed for the street and, as it would seem, entering or attempting to enter a room. There is nothing to suggest that she is Madeleine Férat or Françoise Duquesnoy. The picture is mysterious in its space, its illumination and its meaning, but, taken in conjunction with the final version, it does suggest an imprecise purpose, it is as though the artist was looking for a solution, a solution which was, therefore, of his own making. If this be the case, the meaning of *Le Viol* is to be found not so much in the literary history of his age as in Degas' own personality.

Degas was in, not *of*, the Impressionist movement; he was divided from those who became his allies in the struggle against 'Le Salon de M. Bouguereau' by profound differences of temperament and training; he came from a more nervous and more privileged environment; his approach to life and to art was more intellectual and more complicated; he had neither the wise simplicity of Renoir, the assertive ebullience of Courbet, or the simple, unselfconscious worldliness of Manet; he was a wit and his conversational acerbities are keen, dry, cold and splendid as the aphorisms of M. de la Rochefoucauld. It was natural that he should have been trained by a pupil of Ingres, the very symbol of the artistic establishment, and that he should have remained faithful in his admiration of that master. After his death, at a time when the greatness of Cézanne and the Post-Impressionists still had something of the strength of novelty, Degas' reactionary beliefs damaged his reputation. Meier Graefe, who rates him as a draughtsman lower than Menzel, can find very little to praise save the late pastels. Degas was altogether too *pompier*; Degas' genre is in his view 'a variation of a well known theme practised by the lower grade of academicians and Degas' employment of modern means does not make the attempt less distasteful.' And yet to his admirers he seemed a painter who detested literary effects; 'No modern artist,' declared Liebermann, 'has so completely subdued the anecdote'. Both statements are in a measure true. Degas did not easily abandon the history picture of his early years; he is always nearer to literature than is a painter like Monet or like Pissarro. He was relatively unmoved by inanimate things. 'I do not,' he said, 'find it necessary to go into ecstasies over a pond.' His subjects are human: they live in the streets, the racecourse, the coulisses of the Opéra, dressmakers' shops or brothels, places where people amuse themselves and make money. There Degas observes them, not without irony. But his literature is inferential; although his pictures were most carefully composed and resulted from numerous studies assembled and rearranged in the studio, he never explains, he never provides the sort of easily comprehensible drama of which Hogarth, Daumier and Frith were masters. His is the art that conceals art: in his dramas we seem to be witnessing something that has been taken exactly as it was found. Nothing is posed, nothing has been contrived, and yet this effect is produced by the most careful disposition and the most subtle contrivance.

There is, in truth, no such thing as a neutral attitude in painting, the refusal to dramatise, to elucidate or to beautify – and Degas refused all these three capital demands of romantic art – in itself betrays a positive attitude towards art and towards nature; it results from a critical position which Degas' contemporaries found sufficiently disconcerting. 'M. Degas, why do you make your women so ugly?' 'But, Madame, women generally are ugly.' As though to aggravate the fault he devotes himself to a ruthless examination of that art which affords the most enchanting medium for feminine display and dissimulation and this, to many people, seemed utterly perverse. Listen for a moment to the cultured protest of the nineteenth century. Max Beerbohm, on Brandard's *Carlotta Grisi* (see illustration 5) writes:

Below the stark ruff of muslin about her waist, her legs are as a tilted pair of compasses; one point in the air, the other impinging the ground. One tiptoe poised ever so lightly upon the earth, as though the muslin wings at her shoulders were not quite strong enough to bear her up into the sky! So she remains, hovering betwixt two elements; a creature exquisitely ambiguous, being neither aerial or of the earth. She knows that she is mortal, yet is conscious of apotheosis. She knows that she, though herself must perish, is imperishable; for she sees us, her posterity, gazing fondly back at her. She is touched. And we, a little envious of those who did once see Grisi plain always shall find solace in this pretty picture of her; holding it to be, for all the artificiality of its convention, as much more real as it is prettier than the stringent ballet girls of Degas.

And yet, might we not almost reverse Max Beerbohm's statement and, laying profane hands upon his divine prose, say of Degas' painting that we hold it to be, for all the realism of its treatment, as much more seductive as it is convincing than the flaccid coryphée of the print maker?

Degas' fault in the eyes of his contemporaries lay in his unwillingness to satisfy a need which was, in truth, ephemeral; with the passage of time, his figures gain rather than lose interest by reason of the fact that they are not marked by acquiescence in a passing fashion of beauty. Thus it is that the pungent acid with which Degas painted his female sitters appears to have been a volatile fluid of which hardly a trace remains.

Writing, it would seem, with a portrait of herself in mind, Miss Mary Cassatt declared, 'I wish above all *not* to leave it to my family as something of myself. It has aesthetic qualities, but it is so painful and shows me as so repugnant a person that I would not wish it to be known that I posed for it.' And yet as Miss Jean Sutherland Boggs says: 'It has the expressive face of an intelligent, humorous woman, painted with great tenderness by Degas; to us it seems to have a stronger and happier character than the portrait she painted of herself.'

Degas charms where once he repelled. We see that which was latent in his work though hidden. And this union of opposing qualities agrees with what we know of his character. An amiable, tender-hearted misanthrope, he was also a celibate, a misogynist who mocked at, despised and was obsessed by women. With the example of M. Mauclair in mind I will forbear from attempting to deduce too much from his pictures. But the written word is more explicit than the painted image and Degas, fortunately for my purposes, has committed his emotions to verse.

> Elle danse, en mourant, comme autour d'un roseau,
> D'une flute où le vent triste de Weber joue;
> Le ruban de ses pas s'entortille et se noue,
> Son corps s'affaise et tombe en un geste d'oiseau.
> Siffle les violons. Fraiche, du bleu de l'eau.
> Silvana vient, et là, curieuse s'ébroue
> Le bonheur de revivre et l'amour pur se joue
> Sur ses yeux, sur ses seins, sur tout l'etre nouveau,
> Et ses pieds de satin brodent, comme l'aiguille,
> Des dessins de plaisir. La capricante fille
> Use mes pauvres yeux, à la suivre peinant.
> Mais d'un signe toujours cesse le beau mystère:
> Elle retire trop les jambes en sautant;
> C'est un saut de grenouille aux mares de Cythère.

'Poetry,' as Mallarmé said to Degas in a celebrated exchange, 'is made not with ideas but with words;' and so I have given you Degas' words. Nevertheless, in the context of my argument, it would appear that there is something to be said for Degas' view that it is the ideas that count, therefore, even though I must change the words and murder the prosody, I think that a translation may be useful:

> Dying, she dances where stage rushes grow
> And Weber's woodwind wails.
> She twines and binds the ribbon of her steps.
> Birdlike she droops and fails.
> By violins revived, she breathes again
> Quits the blue water, fresh with eager life
> By love adorned, love on her eyes and breasts
> Silvana lives in love with her new self.
> Now, satin-shod she threads with needle toes
> Designs of joy, whose leaping 'broidery

Amazes, dazzles and torments the eye.
But a mere touch will always break the bond,
She jumps and jumping lifts her legs too high
To plump, froglike, in Cytheraea's pond.

This, surely, is plain enough. The octave is a pure, romantic, unqualified tribute. The sestet begins with a veiled reproach: 'la capricante fille/Use mes pauvres yeux, à la suivre peinant' – this, from a man who lived in mortal terror of blindness, is not mere gallantry; and then at the end he turns his subject to ridicule; he takes back the bouquet that he has almost presented and retires into the safety of a joke. This complex emotion compounded of affection and repulsion is, so it seems to me, discernible in his painting. If you look at those of his works in which members of the same sex are grouped together, you will find that his characters may often face each other and converse; but this is very rarely the case when he painted men with women.

Here either one party is averted from the other, or both look out of the picture either in the same or in opposite directions. This is so marked a feature of what I have ventured to call their psychomorphic design that one critic maintains that the Ducros portrait is an angry scene comparable to *Le Viol*. It is indeed a strange portrait, if it is a portrait, and it has its affinities with *Le Viol* and with three other *tableaux d'attention*, *Bouderie*, *Les Spartiates* and *Les Malheurs de la Ville d'Orléans*. In all these pictures the left is, so to speak, the female side to the canvas – it is separated from the right by a central element across which Degas sets a unifying diagonal. In most ways *Les Spartiates* (see illustration 6) may serve as a pattern for the rest. The picture has sometimes been called 'Spartan Girls provoking Boys'. It derives probably from the 'Anacharsis' of the Abbé Barthélemy. 'The girls,' says this author, paraphrasing Plutarch, 'excite the boys to glory, either by their example, or by flattering eulogies, or by caustic remarks.' Whatever form the war of the sexes may here be taking, it would seem that the girls must almost inevitably confront the boys; but, in a first study, Degas contrived that the boys should not, in fact, look at them but fall into the usual averted pattern of the other pictures.

In *Bouderie* the order is the same but the central space is much diminished and is, I think, less interesting than in *Le Viol* or *Les Spartiates*; but stylistically and, I think, sentimentally, it is very close to our subject. This is almost the reverse of *Le Viol*; now it is the woman who is the aggressor, the man who turns away. Finally, in *Les Malheurs de la Ville d'Orléans* (see illustration 7), the last of Degas' academic pictures, we have a much more complicated spatial organisation but one in which I think it is again possible to discover a feminine element to the left and a male element to the right, although the division is by no means so tidy as elsewhere. Nevertheless, in the relationship of the man shooting at a woman we find something of the same pattern of diagonals from right to left as in *Le Viol*. In these three paintings the element of hostility between the sexes is apparent and it is perhaps because we sense their psychomorphic affinity to *Le Viol* that that picture has earned its title. But *Les Malheurs de la Ville d'Orléans* is much more explicit. Protected by the conventions of academic art Degas shows his hand, for this is unashamedly a scene of murder, torture and rape. It is pertinent to ask where Degas found this ferocious subject. M. Pierre Cabane has searched the records of medieval history and cannot find that the picture relates to any real event. Like *Le Viol* it seems to be a private fantasy of the artist's own invention. *La Ville d'Orléans*, M. Cabane continues, was historically, sentimentally and politically connected with the Degas family. May we, then, regard it as a symbol of this family? According to Mlle. Fèvre, the painter's niece, Degas' mother often told him of that other Orleans across the Atlantic from whence she came. Degas, says Mlle. Fèvre, adored his mother and gradually formed a longing to visit her home, a longing which he realised when, acting perhaps on a sudden impulse, he accompanied his brother to America. This journey was undertaken in 1872; at the same time there was a notable crisis in the artist's private life, for it was then that he was stricken by the fear of blindness. The symptoms of his malady suggest the development of senile macular degeneration. Nevertheless, there is reason to think that the progress of the disease was not entirely regulated by physical causes. Degas' friends used to declare that he could see what he wanted to see – the accusation is, on the face of it, absurd, for manifestly Degas wanted to see the model and could not. There is evidence, however, that suggests that they may have been in a sense right. The complexities of human motivation are such that it is not entirely fanciful to suppose that the painter's vision may sometimes have been occluded by the shadows of unconscious thoughts and prohibitions. Most biographers ascribe this malady to hardships suffered during the siege of Paris in 1870, but Degas also said that it was caused by privations suffered when he left home to become an art student after quarrelling with his father. However this may be, there can be no doubt that the symptoms became really alarming about 1871, that is to say at the time when he was working on *Le Viol*.

Le Viol also marks a turning point in Degas' art. Thereafter, the literary content of his work becomes more and more difficult to detect, save in his savage treatment of women. He remains celibate as far as we know, his pictures of brothels certainly do not suggest that he visited those establishments with a lascivious intention; he had a number of sentimental relationships with women friends, but they were inconclusive. As he grew older he became more and more lonely. Affectionate and considerate, he nevertheless separated himself from the world by a kind of proud, half involuntary misanthropy, increasing blindness effected a more terrible isolation and he ended an old man wandering about Paris alone, obsessed by the idea of death.

What conclusions can we draw? None, I think. The framework of verifiable fact is too fragile; at best, it may serve as a basis for guess work. The mind of a painter is too secret a thing to be explored with confidence. If Degas had private and personal reasons for hiding his meanings, there were also strong aesthetic and social forces making in the same direction. He was, so to speak, coming into line with the Impressionists. The future lay with them and Degas was, in a sense, the last of the great literary artists. But he is also the first of the enigmatic painters, those who, while shunning anecdote, give us mood without narrative. *Ennui, What Shall We Do for the Rent?*, *Father Comes Home*, stem directly from Degas and, above all, from *Le Viol*, and through them come the paintings of Sickert's followers. A certain directness of approach, a certain dramatic simplicity which was still possible in Degas' youth has been lost. Picasso, Stanley Spencer, Francis Bacon, Rauschenberg may allude or suggest or hint; but there is that in the climate of our age which forbids them to tell a plain tale without equivocation. *Le Viol* marks a turning point in European art after which painting falls silent.

When I was hastily seeking material for this essay I met Anthony

Blunt, who observed that *Le Viol* is a very mysterious picture and expressed the hope that I would not rob it of its mystery. I assured him that I would not, and I can, at least, conclude by boasting that I have kept my word.

The Life Room as a Battlefield

Educational Controversies in England from
the Eighteenth Century to the Present Day

REYNOLDS *v*. HOGARTH AND BLAKE

Let us begin with the model. To those of us who have worked in
the life room that image – the naked figure in the north light –
comes to mind as vividly as the smell of turpentine or the gentle
scrape of charcoal upon paper. An art school without a life room is
for most of us an unfamiliar idea. There is something blasphemous
in the notion that we should now dismiss the model for ever.
Nevertheless, it is to that consummation that we are now moving.
Two years ago I was in an art school in New York; in front of me
was one of the most paintable subjects I have ever seen. A dusky
girl lying on a sofa in something of the attitude of the Rokeby
Venus, the sofa a dirty green, behind her an old mirror in which
was reflected an astonishing pattern of easels and students. It was
one of those scenes where every accident of nature seems to lead
the eye into fresh and more beautiful juxtapositions of form, where
almost too much is given and yet where every gift presents a fresh
problem. But of the twenty students one only was paying the
slightest attention to what lay before him. In that school, at all
events, the model had become an anomaly and I could not help
feeling that she was doomed. Doomed because she appears simply
as an art historical monument. She is only there because the

Renaissance put her there; she belongs to the whole apparatus of academic art and there is nothing, apparently, in the forms of painting now [1962] fashionable on both sides of the Atlantic to justify her existence.

I do not know when people began to use the naked model. Leonardo speaks of the advisability of working from the nude in summer in order to save fuel. Benvenuto Cellini describes the manner in which he and other young men would obtain the services of a youth, who would sit in poses which gave effects of great foreshortening and how Cellini and his friends would draw from the shadowed outline of his form upon a wall. Certainly, by the time that public academies of painting began to emerge, that is to say, towards the end of the sixteenth century, the model had become an obvious and essential property of art education.

The life room had, by this time, become the centre and, as one may say, the throne room of the academic school. The student would learn the craft of his trade, the preparation of canvas or board, the grinding of colours, the actual business of painting and, very likely, the translation of the master's conceptions from a mere pochade to a vast canvas. But all this he would acquire in his master's studio; the cultivation of taste – of the grand style – would be the business of the academy school.

Taste meant the taste of the great Italians, of Raphael and Michelangelo, of Correggio, of Titian and Leonardo, or perhaps, better still, that moderated and corrected combination of their best qualities – Michelangelo without his extravagance, Titian made sober – which might be found in the work of Guido, or of the Carracci, or above all in the chaste and scholarly inventions of Poussin.

All academic theory agrees that a simple imitation of nature is the lowest and meanest form of art. The painter who would work nobly and for a noble public must seek abstraction. His work must be sublime both in theme and treatment. He shows things not as they are, but as they ought to be.

It is sufficient to state this theory in order to show its limitations. To say that it is inadmissible as a complete explanation either of art or of beauty is hardly necessary. Here I want rather to point to the degree of truth that it contains.

The proposition to which I would like you to accede is simple: it is that a woman with a hump, a hare lip, a double chin and whiskers is, in a quite clear and unmistakable fashion, less beautiful than

Raphael's Galatea. Undoubtedly a drawing of such a woman may be very fine; nevertheless, in choosing a model for his Madonnas and his nymphs, Raphael will look elsewhere, and we see why he should do so. Moreover, even when he represents an aged philosopher, a simple fisherman or an uncouth triton, Raphael may be trusted never to show us a shocking or a distressing human being. Beauty – in the sense in which we use the word when speaking of a beautiful woman – is an integral part of his art, as it is of the main stream of Italian art.

It is with that limited but important sense of the word beauty in mind that I want to consider the practice of the academies.

The student in the academic school did not come straight to the life room. First he had to learn how the model was to be seen. He would begin by making careful copies of eyes, noses, ears, faces, arms, legs and finally entire figures. These he would take from engravings. When he had learnt to imitate these works 'from the flat' he would be set to work from the cast, again starting with fragments – noses, ears, etc., and then attempting whole figures: the Antinous, the Venus de' Medici and so on. Sometimes also he would use casts from dead or living bodies. Thus, in the Academy schools in London, there was for many years a cast known as Old Smugglerius taken from the body of a smuggler of heroic proportions set in the pose of the dying gladiator.

I hope that you will not think me too desperately reactionary if I say that I think that the cast still has its uses in art education, that is, if you grant that work from the human figure has its uses. Admittedly, the usual art school cast confronts the student with a problem of some difficulty, for whereas we expect an object to reflect the maximum amount of light at its point of maximum convexity, the art school cast has so much dirt on its temples, its cheeks, its eyeballs and its lips that it has very much the air of a photographic negative. Nevertheless it can, if well kept, be of one uniform colour and texture, it keeps still, it can be placed in almost any position, and it does not complicate the student's problems (nor for that matter, it must be added, enrich his work) with the psychological tensions that must arise, when the clothed and the naked meet – for however businesslike a purpose – in one room.

But it was not with considerations such as these that the masters of the seventeenth- and eighteenth-century academies enforced the study of the cast – or of antique sculpture – upon their students.

Seeing that the antique invariably contains all that is most beautiful in proportion and is also the source of all the graces, all elegance and all expressive sentiment, it is a study all the more necessary in that it leads to the understanding of beauty in nature (*la belle verité*). It must be studied without consideration of the time that it takes to acquire mastery, for since the antique is the rule of beauty one must draw it until one has a strong and perfect idea thereof. Thus one may see nature properly and bring her back to her original intentions, from which she often departs.

I must do De Piles the justice of saying that he adds to his text those famous words of Rubens to the effect that the antique should be used with discretion lest the work of the student come to 'stink of the stone'.

The idea that Nature departs from her own intentions gives us the key to the whole of academic theory. If Nature intended us to look like the Apollo Belvedere or the Capitoline Venus it is clear that in the vast majority of cases, at all events, she has bungled the job horribly. Without descending to those 'wrinkles, pouches and other small imperfections', to borrow the words of Sir Kenneth Clark in his admirable study of *The Nude* (I have also borrowed extensively from his ideas), without dwelling upon those hairs, blotches, knobs and lumps which we find almost invariably in the naked body of a mature model, we have only to glance at the faces around us to find deviations from the norm. Think of any meeting – a board, a committee, a class, it makes no odds – and of the faces you will confront. Would there be one that could for a moment be confused with the plaster faces upon the art school wall? And if we were indeed all formed in an antique mould, what then? We should no doubt be a very handsome company but shouldn't we also be rather dull? If the fault of naturalistic art lies in its tendency to become mere hand-made photography in which the painter or sculptor loses himself in multitudinous trivialities, the fault of abstract art – whether it be the abstract art of a Canova or the abstract art of a Sam Francis – is that it ends by becoming insipid.

Nevertheless, the idea that the human body is beautiful in the measure that it is free from abnormalities has its validity. When we draw from 'chic' – placing the pupils of the eyes above the corners of the mouth, the lobe of the ear on a level with the nostril and so on – we are taking bearings which will enable us to construct a face which approximates roughly to the Graeco-Roman ideal and which we may, in a very special but very true sense, call beautiful.

1. Ford Madox Brown *Work*

2. Edouard Manet *Music in the Tuileries Gardens*

ABOVE 3. Edgar Degas   *Le Viol*

LEFT 4. Edgar Degas   Study for *Le Viol*

RIGHT 5. John Brandard   *Carlotta Grisi in 'Giselle'*

6. Edgar Degas *Les Spartiates*

7. Edgar Degas *Les Malheurs de la Ville d'Orléans*

8. Jean Baptiste Greuze   *Le Fils Ingrat*

9. William Powell Frith   *Many Happy Returns of the Day*

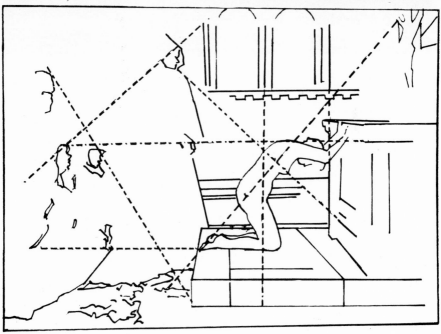

10. Philip Calderon   *Renunciation*

11. Diagram of the above

12. William Dyce   *Francesca di Rimini*

13. Francisco de Goya   *Saturn Eating his Children*

P. 19.

l'Amour Simple.

P. 43.

Extreme Desespoir

ABOVE **14, 15. Charles Le Brun**
Têtes d'expression

LEFT **16. Anon** *La Grue*

At the same time, these same formulae, even if we work them out with a ruler and compasses, will give us a 'normal' face; in fact, in making a portrait, we may begin by indicating very lightly an ideal form of this kind and make it true to the model by marking its deviations from the norm. It is surprising how slight they are; a likeness may be caught or lost by a barely perceptible pressure upon the shaft of a no. 2 sable, a minute deviation in the drawing of an outline may transform the whole structure of a face. In short, we all seem to approximate to that norm which can be found, without looking, by means of a simple calculation of the effect of known rules, rules that were new when Piero della Francesca worked out his perspective heads in the 1460s, but which are today the stock-in-trade of the art student.

But De Piles does not speak of nature approximating to our simple schema, he speaks of nature's intentions – 'bring her back to her first intention from which she often strays'. Why is this?

Let me give you the answer obliquely: suppose yourself to be a painter at work in Italy or Flanders about the end of the fifteenth century. Rather a pleasant situation you think? Not a bit of it. You have social aspirations and social feelings, but what are you? A tradesman in a small way of business, a man without a muse, a base mechanic excluded from the liberal arts, in short, you are non-U. What then will you do to improve your social standing? You will set out to prove that the art of painting is every bit as genteel, as grand, as poetical, as the respectable arts of literature – indeed you will proclaim that painting is silent poetry: *ut pictura poesis*. This business of mapping-out the main dispositions of nature, this making of beauty by rule, will be no mere convenience for the draughtsman seeking to construct a probable appearance of the body, it will be an effort to find that divine prototype of the human frame that existed in the mind of the Deity when man was first created out of chaos, and God made man in his own image. The repetition of that primal creative event is no mere journeyman's task.

The perfect human proportion is given us by heaven. Nature, corrupted by her inevitable association with matter, produces human forms in which we can at best divine an occasional hint of her *intentions*. The painter takes these hints and from them he deduces the divine plan. Nor is this all. Remember that you are living in an age obsessed by the idea of harmonious measurement and by neo-platonism, when the proportions of man are worked out upon the drawing board it will be found – with the aid of Vitruvius, a little ingenuity and some contrivance – that they correspond to the two perfect geometrical figures, the square and the circle, from which, if you will but read the 'Timaeus' in the right spirit, you may discover that the structure of the universe itself is compounded.

In the age of Michelangelo and Raphael, of Correggio and Leonardo, it would not have been very difficult to suppose that the painter and the sculptor might have been a poet, a philosopher, even, perhaps, a gentleman and a scholar.

Long before any academy of art could actually be established, academic theory in its simplest form (and I have oversimplified it), had been challenged, though rather by the practice of the painters themselves than by the precepts of theorists.

Go back to that schematic drawing of the human figure by which we can discover the normal configurations of man. It derives, obviously, from our experience. We see the normal relationship of eyes and nose, breasts and navel, hips and ankles and we may, like Dürer, actually derive our drawing from average measurements. But when the first light statement of forms is made we may add beauty, *not* by working strictly to our mathematical average but by a judicious departure from the norm. Watch the fashion artist, or the fashionable portrait painter at work. He enlarges the eyes, reduces the size of the head, elongates the neck and the legs, diminishes the waists of girls and broadens the shoulders of men. This, roughly speaking, was the practice of the Mannerists. And just as the first process – the omission of imperfections – has a certain validity, so has the second, the addition of particularly admirable features. And just as the search for normal man could be given a philosophical basis, so could Bacon's statement – which is practically a summary of mannerist doctrine – that 'there is no excellent beauty that has not some strangeness in the proportion', in that, by referring to the imagination, we may launch into heaven knows what mystical speculations, leaving material things behind us.

At first sight, the experience of the Mannerists seems to destroy the whole basis of that theory which looks for perfection in the average. And yet it does not. Stretch Mannerism far enough and it breaks. Go back to your improved drawing and improve it again.

Pull out the neck until it is twice as long as the body, a pin-head at its extremity, elongate the legs until they are like telegraph poles and you will have something which in this century may do well enough in the hands of a Giacometti but which, within the framework of mannerist art, was unsatisfying and which we might reasonably call ugly or monstrous if we found it in a living human being. The operative words in Bacon's sentence are *some strangeness*; implicitly he recognises that nature has claims which, at a certain point, must be respected.

It was perhaps this feeling, together with an apprehension of that opposite face of naturalism, the violent, subversive naturalism of Caravaggio, which led in the seventeenth century to the elaboration of aesthetic theories, theories which sought a happy mean between base realism and vulgar mannerism. And it was on the basis of these theories that the French Academy of Fine Art was established.

I would like to try to describe the aspect of the life room in that academy as Reynolds saw it when he visited the Académie Royale de Peinture et de Sculpture on his way home from Italy in 1752.

Imagine a fairly big room, big enough to hold about a hundred people, high too, but it is hard to estimate its proportions, for all the light comes from one vast lantern suspended above the model. The students sit in a semi-circle around the throne and on two raised tiers. The model has been set in a pose taken from the antique. He is a man, always a man. In fact, always the same man – M. *le modèle du roi* he calls himself, and he is entitled to wear a sword when he wears anything at all. He has held his job for forty years and in that time has passed through countless avatars – Hercules, Ganymede, Apollo and Dionysus, the students being instructed to plump him up a bit if he is to be Herculean, to fine him down when he is a mere stripling. Nor is that the extent of his metamorphoses – he has been Ceres, Diana and Venus. For if you look amongst the boys and young men who crowd the benches you will see some elderly, unsuccessful academicians who come here to get a free model. If for their historical pictures they require a nymph then, like the students, they must make additions and subtractions, for to the academic artist, nature is only a starting point after all. Only once in all the year does a lady sit on the model's throne. She is a virtuous young person elegantly dressed and, in drawing her, the young men compete for the *prix d'expression* established by M. de Caylus.

If we look further into the establishment we shall find ruin and disorder. Anatomy and perspective are neglected, the students are riotous, the casts are defaced and broken, the very skeleton in the academic cupboard lacks half its bones. And, if we listen, we may hear from beyond its walls the voice of criticism. 'Since we have had an Academy of Painting,' says Voltaire, 'we have had no great artists.' And 'These seven cruel years at the Academy,' exclaims Diderot, 'what does the student learn from them? – a manner.'

By 1768, when the Royal Academy came into existence, the great battle against academies had begun and Reynolds, its first president, was also the first academic theorist to take a defensive attitude. I will not enter into all the complicated and rather squalid disputes which preceded the foundation of the existing academy. But this much should be said: whereas in other countries the academy was an instrument of royal government – Charles I would have given us an academy of this kind if he could have managed it – and whereas foreign academies were not unusually connected with trade schools, our own Royal Academy was founded, typically enough, as a private commercial venture, it having been noticed that exhibiting societies made money. It was the most successful and, it should be added, the most talented of several competing societies, and that which finally gained the ear of royalty. One result of that competition may be noticed; the short-lived academy of Cheron and Vanderbank employed a female model 'to make it', as Hogarth puts it, 'more inviting to subscribers'. Others (including the Society of Artists which later became the Royal Academy) followed suit. It was not until the nineteenth century that the rest of Europe followed our private enterprise.

Portrait painting ever has, and ever will, succeed better in this country than in any other. The demand will be as constant as new faces arise, and with this we must be contented, for it will be vain to force what can never be accomplished at least by such institutions as Royal Academies on the system now in agitation.

Thus Hogarth, and certainly he knew what he was talking about. The time had passed in which an academy could usefully be started and the Academy itself belonged to the apparatus of absolute monarchy. The Royal Academy has never been a truly academic institution. It has been a market place rather than a college. This certainly was not Reynolds' intention, and, in the *Discourses*, he argues continually and persuasively for the grand style, for the establishment in this country of a school of historical painting worthy to be compared with that of Florence.

The whole tendency of the age was against him, but he had also to encounter other adversaries. Of these the first was Hogarth. Hogarth, it is true, attempted works in the grand style himself. How grand and, alas, how empty his history paintings could be may be judged from the enormous altar piece now in Bristol Art Gallery, where the Holy personages, angels and all the rest of his *dramatis personae* have the air of unskilled actors playing parts in a charade the meaning of which they do not understand. But the best of Hogarth, that which we all know, is Dutch in its inspiration and Dutch in its care for the particular. It deals not with sublimities but with character and the human comedy. It is, unlike academic art, concerned with practical morality. It belongs to the same tradition as Richardson – the novelist, I mean – and the Victorians. It rejoices in the fashions of the day, even though it may mock at them. It abounds in those singular and particular details which, as Reynolds pointed out, should be avoided by the student of the sublime. And I think the presence of Hogarth, certainly the liveliest figure in British painting until the middle of the century, was the first obstacle to the creation of an academy of painting. In addition to all this, Hogarth had a theory of beauty, a line which he believed capable of giving beauty to any form, which looks forward in its principle, if not in its application, to the unitary theories of our own day. Apply this theory and the whole necessity for seeking sublimity through abstraction falls to the ground. Finally, Hogarth was himself a sturdy John-Bullish sort of character with a certain gift for blasphemy, as, for instance, in his statement that 'nature is finer than Raphael', a statement which to the generation of cultured dilettanti, of wealthy young men who had made the Grand Tour and returned with Roman busts such as you may see on the mantelpiece of the third scene in *Marriage à la Mode* with blackened copies of Guercino and the Carracci, found quite inadmissible. In fact, Reynolds crossed swords with Hogarth in *The Idler* when he first enunciated his theory of ideal form and in argument got the better of it. Hogarth, then, was an initial obstacle that had to be cleared away before the Academy could be born. Thereafter, a more serious difficulty lay in the general mistrust of academies which now existed. In his first *Discourse* the President raises and meets the objections that might be made. 'Raffaele, it is true, had not the advantage of studying in an Academy; but all Rome and the works of Michel Angelo in particular, were to him an Academy.'

The academies of the continent had indeed failed, not because they pursued wrong ends but because they adopted the wrong means. 'One advantage, I will venture to affirm, we shall have in our Academy, which no other nation can boast. We shall have nothing to unlearn.'

In the Royal Academy the student would learn to look at nature, he would make no attempt to idealise but would work directly from that which he saw. Generalisation – essential though it was – would come later. The Royal Academy was therefore to become a reforming body, a new model which would re-establish the authority of art teaching, an authority which had of late been seriously shaken.

The eighteenth century, turning from the fierce theological pre-occupations of the seventeenth, looked towards those two rather amorphous conceptions – nature and natural man. 'Everywhere man is born free and everywhere he is in chains.' Give men liberty, take from them the hampering restrictions that are imposed by society and they will become wise and virtuous. Translated into aesthetic terms this meant that a man of natural talent might paint as a bird sings – freely and beautifully, all the rules and precedents of the academies being no more than obstacles in his path. Rousseau's Emile was to have no 'drawing master who would set him to copy from copies'. He would be brought face to face with nature and would work directly. Here was a profoundly subversive doctrine and one that was to have enormous effects in the nineteenth century. Reynolds attacks it in his first *Discourse*:

– it may be laid down as a maxim, that he who begins by presuming on his own sense, has ended his studies as soon as he has commenced them. Every opportunity, therefore, should be taken to discountenance that false and vulgar opinion, that rules are the fetters of genius; they are fetters only to men of no genius; as that armour, which upon the strong is an ornament and a defence, upon the weak and misshapen becomes a load, and cripples the body which it was made to protect.

Finally, in considering the obstacles which Reynolds had to surmount, one must include Reynolds himself. Reynolds, in his own art, belies his opinions. His efforts at the sublime were, as he himself knew, far from being his best work, while his most successful portraiture was not always that in which he attempted to apply the grand style to what he himself considered an inferior department of painting. In his fifteenth, last and most moving *Discourse*, speaking of Michelangelo, he says:

. . . it will not, I hope, be thought presumptuous in me to appear in the train, I cannot say of his imitators, but of his admirers. I have taken another course, one more suited to my abilities, and to the taste of the times in which I live. Yet, however unequal I feel myself to that attempt, were I now to begin the world again I would tread in the steps of that great master . . .

But indeed it was the taste of the times in which he lived which would have prevented Sir Joshua from ever successfully following Michelangelo. His was a sceptical temper and his taste was too catholic for him to be able to enunciate academic doctrines with the bland fervour of his seventeenth-century predecessors. He could admire Rubens and the Venetians, Rembrandt and even the Van Eycks. There was in his manner a diffidence, a modesty, a tolerance ill-suited to his authoritarian task. But, above all, his version of academic theory was altogether too practical, too materialist to suit the ardent temper of his juniors.

Let me return once more to the central academic theory, the idea that there is a perfect image of man to which all actual human forms aspire with greater or less success. Apply this theory for a moment to cats: we have a notion of the human beau-ideal but what about the platonic puss? Is he black or white, tabby or tortoiseshell, or must he be of some indeterminate grey? The Renaissance was too much concerned with human affairs to become involved with generalised cats, and too mediterranean to reflect upon the difficulties presented by a great variety of racial types. But the eighteenth century was much more conscious of this problem.

. . . to speak my most secret sentiments, most reverend Fum, the ladies here are horribly ugly; I can hardly endure the sight of them; they no way resemble the beauties of China . . . how is it possible I could have eyes for a woman whose feet are ten inches long.

Thus Goldsmith in *The Citizen of the World*. Reynolds felt the force of this argument and in looking for an explanation of the nature of beauty he deprives it of all theological, all superlunary authority, ascribing it simply to the effect of custom. For him deformity is ugliness and if deformity becomes habitual – as in the case of the Chinese lady's foot – it becomes beautiful. This concession is of the utmost theoretical importance in that it opens the door to a whole galaxy of aesthetic concepts far removed from the Hellenic tradition. I would also venture to suggest that it is a matter of direct political importance to us today. For all that Reynolds might say, Europe continued to equate fairness with beauty and to consider a dark skin and a flattened nose as being something essentially inferior to golden hair and blue eyes. A hundred years later it was still necessary for Plekhanov to confront the Venus de Milo with the Hottentot Venus and point out that the former no less than the latter owed her fame to particular social conditions and not to any abstract superiority.

It may seem far fetched to suggest that this stubborn aesthetic predilection has played its part in that fatal racialism, that *damnosa hereditas* of the West, for which we are paying hourly as I write these words. But I would like to point out one significant fact: Ruskin, who rejects Reynolds' teachings on this matter, declares that it amounts simply to saying that black is white, that yes and no should change their meanings, was in fact unable to see any virtue in 'exotic' art. For all his essential nobility of character and despite some fine protests, Ruskin could seldom accord to coloured races that enthusiastic sympathy which he showed for the Poles or the Danes. Indeed, he has left some pages that seem to condone the worst excesses of colonialism.

What shocked Ruskin in Reynolds' *Discourses* – and shocked him all the more in view of his admiration for Reynolds as a painter – was the underlying materialism of his attitude. A contemporary critic, William Blake, was even more disturbed thereby and reacted even more violently.

In Blake we have an example of the kind of painter who was to become familiar in the nineteenth century; the painter who is agin the government, who despises academies and academicians as such and who measures the whole world against his own talent and finds it wanting. Pevsner has shown us such a one in the German painter Carstens, who cheated and reviled the Berlin

Academy in a most disdainful fashion – the type of the artist of the Sturm und Drang movement. Blake was just such another and it is worth pausing for a moment to consider his sallies against the P.R.A., for they too give a taste of the individual's reactions against authority:

Reynolds: As I have formerly observed admiration seldom promotes knowledge.
Blake: Enthusiastic admiration is the first principle of knowledge and its last. Now he begins to degrade, to deny and to mock.

Here, surely we have the nineteenth century talking to the eighteenth. Seeing the world in black and white, living in a perpetual fever, Blake could attack Reynolds with religious fury. He is far less tolerant, far narrower in his views than his adversary.

Why should Titian and the Venetians be named in a discourse on Art? Such idiots are not artists.

> Venetian, all the colouring is no more
> Than boulstered plasters on a crooked whore.

The fact that Reynolds had been to Italy while he, Blake, had not, made no difference. Blake knew, was sure, that he was on the side of the angels while Sir Joshua was on the side of Satan.

The most astonishing thing, and the most interesting from our point of view, is that, although Reynolds and Blake both admired Michelangelo, Reynolds advocated a rational middle form while Blake returned to the Mannerists and pushed their views to the greatest possible extremity.

Reynolds: It is not easy to define in what this great style consists, or to describe, by words, the proper means of acquiring it . . . there neither are, nor can be, any precise rules . . . yet we may truly say that they always operate in proportion to our attention in observing the works of nature . . . perfection and beauty are not to be sought in the heavens, but upon earth.
Blake: A lie!
Reynolds: They are about us and on every side of us.
Blake: A lie!
Reynolds: But the power of discerning what is deformed in nature, or in other words, what is particular and uncommon, can be acquired only by experience; and the whole beauty and grandeur of art consists, in my opinion, in being able to get

above all singular forms, local customs, particularities and details of every kind.

Blake: A folly. Singular and Particular details is the foundation of the sublime.

Reynolds: It is from reiterated experience, and a close comparison of the objects in nature, that an artist becomes possessed of the idea of that central form, if I may so express it, from which every deviation is deformity.

Blake: One central form compounded of all other forms being granted, it does not follow that all other forms are deformity. All forms are perfect in the poet's mind, but these are not abstracted, nor compounded from nature; but are from the imagination.

Reynolds: In the midst of the highest flights of the imagination, reason ought to preside from first to last.

Blake: If this is true, it is a Devlish Foolish thing to be an Artist.

Here we have the now familiar quarrel between the rebel and the academician, a quarrel which, because all the great movements of the nineteenth century were essentially rebellious, has made the word academic a term of abuse amongst artists.

Blake's diatribes bring us back to the old controversy to which I have already alluded, the controversy between the painter who seeks everything from the imagination and him who insists that nature shall be our constant guide. The debate continues but so far as it relates to the academic idea it was virtually concluded in the nineteenth century by Benjamin Robert Haydon.

HAYDON *v.* DYCE

> The world's great age begins anew,
> The golden years return
> The earth doth like a snake renew
> Her winter weeds outworn:
> Heaven smiles, and faiths and empires gleam,
> Like wrecks of a dissolving dream.

That, as you know, is Shelley; now let us have some Keats:

> Great spirits now on earth are sojourning;
> He of the cloud, the cataract, the lake,
> Who on Helvellyn's summit, wide awake,
> Catches his freshness from Archangel's wing:

> He of the rose, the violet, the spring,
> The social smile, the chain for Freedom's sake:
> And lo! – whose steadfastness would never take
> A meaner sound than Raphael's whispering.
> And other spirits there are standing apart,
> Upon the forehead of the age to come;
> These, these will give the world another heart,
> And other pulses. Hear ye not the hum
> Of mighty workings –
> Listen awhile ye nations, and be dumb.

And if you want to know whose steadfastness would never take a meaner sound than Raphael's whispering, the answer is Benjamin Robert Haydon's.

I will return to the happy relationship between Haydon and the Romantic poets later on. What I want to insist on at this point is the note of expectancy and optimism – qualified, it is true, in the later stanzas of 'Hellas' – which informs these poems. The poets feel that they stand at the threshold of a great age, that time will soon bring a change, a prosperous revolution. But for Shelley there was something else – for him the revolution was indeed to be a return. In this, Shelley was close to the whole tendency of art in his day. Return once more to Jean Jacques Rousseau, to the notion of a happy primitive state of man, of man innocent, perfect and uncorrupted. That virtuous and natural man was the first and greatest of artists; he is the psalmist or the homeric poet. The demand for him seemed to beget the supply, and this was provided by the Hellenic world. From beneath the Italian vineyards men had brought to light the arabesques of Pompeii. The greatness of Paestum and Agrigento was rediscovered; when Bonaparte invaded Egypt, Europe found a new and still earlier style; while that enterprising Scotsman Macpherson supplied a new, an intoxicating and a phoney elixir in the form of bottled Ossian.

Some of these sources might be tainted, like Ossian, but all were welcomed, all represented the glorious primitive infancy of mankind, all could be used in the task of regeneration. (Matthew Arnold was still trying to believe in the authenticity of Ossian in the mid-nineteenth century.)

When, for a brief, terrible moment, it seemed that society was going to be purified with blood and fire, when the Bastille had fallen and Louis XVI had been sent to join Charles I, there occurred the most remarkable event in the whole history of art. (Although it is not usually mentioned by art historians.) In those days, half the population of France disguised itself as Graeco-Roman sculpture. Casting aside their wigs, their stays, their hoops, their high-heeled shoes and their stiff brocades, clad only in a plain, unpatterned, high-girdled chiton, sandalled, wearing their own natural hair *à l'antique*, women walked the streets looking as though they had escaped from museums.

In so far as any one man was responsible for this astonishing aesthetic peripety, it was Jacques Louis David. It was his *Oath of the Horatii* and, still more, his *Lucius Junius Brutus* which set the style, not only in dress, but in architecture and furniture, for a generation. David, himself a student of the academy and an academician, was responsible for the destruction in 1790 of the academic body (which was recreated by Napoleon). As a pupil of Vien he was one of the first products of a new type of art teaching, art teaching based not on workshop practice, but on whole-time study of the modern kind. David's own school, established in the Louvre, was in the same way a modern art school, modern in most of its details of organisation, save that there were no women and the students took it in turns to be the model.

With so much emphasis upon antiquity it may appear at first sight that David and, in its wider sense, the school of David was simply returning to academic practices. But there is a certain difference between neo-classicism and the classicism of the Renaissance. The artists of the Renaissance and, even more, the academic teachers of the seventeenth century found what they wanted in Graeco-Roman sculpture, but the generalisation that they sought could, in theory, have been obtained from other sources and in fact was best provided by the school of Raphael. Theoretically their practice would have remained the same even if nothing had remained of Greece or Rome. David and his friends were not predominantly interested in generalisation. They approached the antique in an archaeological spirit and David himself saw in his pictures not ideal scenes, but evocations of the past as accurate as his learning could make them or else monuments of the present conceived in terms of the past. In some cases, for instance in the *Marat* and the *Mme. Récamier*, the present seemed to play into his hands, to be so perfectly attuned to the heroic style of republican Rome, that he could achieve his ends simply by an accurate depiction of that which lay before him – and it is here, I think, that he is at his greatest. Once again we have in his own paintings a symptom of that concern with the past, the pure and excellent childhood of man, which we notice everywhere at this period.

There was, however, more than one way of arriving at that sacred fount. While the great majority of the pupils of David were content to follow their master in the pursuit of classical antiquity, there was one pupil – and the most gifted – who for a time strayed into another path and sought excellence in the earlier manifestations of Italian art. Ingres could look back beyond Raphael and in his *Paolo and Francesca* produce something that seems much nearer to the Quattrocento than to the classical prototypes of his master.

I am, perhaps, reading too much into the earlier works of Ingres. But his contemporaries in Rome, the German Nazarenes Schnorr von Carolsfeld, Peter Cornelius, Pforr and Overbeck, were certainly engaged in the same quest for ancient purity, in their case Christian, hence medieval, purity.

Long after the Nazarene brotherhood had become an established part of the artistic life of Rome the brethren were joined by a young man from Aberdeen. His name was William Dyce. Already at the age of 19 he had been to Italy and had painted his first important picture, *Bacchus Nursed by the Nymphs of Nyssa*. He had an extraordinary fluency of line, a brilliance that reminded one of Etty, a talent quite amazing in so young a man. Then he went back to Scotland and under his parents' influence abandoned painting, took an M.A. at the Marischal College, and wrote an important thesis on electromagnetism. He returned to Rome and as I have said, on this, his second, visit fell in with the Nazarenes, underwent an artistic conversion and painted a Madonna in the manner of Giovanni Bellini.

William Dyce returned to Scotland in 1830 with a new sense of mission, a new purity of drawing, a new enthusiasm for the religious incentive in art (none of which prevented him from painting very delightful portraits in the manner of Raeburn when he settled in Edinburgh). He returned also with a doctrine of art education, or perhaps one should more truly say, an attitude towards art teaching which resulted naturally from the Nazarene attitude to art.

If you take the view that art should above all things be Christian and that the Renaissance was a beastly corruption of Gothic virtue, a filthy spreading of pagan impurity, then it follows not only that you should turn to the tidy simplicity of an Angelico or a Van Eyck but that you should get rid of the academic school, a vile and mischievous child of the Renaissance, and return to the guild.

Here, so it was at all events imagined, a happy paternal relationship between teacher and pupil, bound alike by wise and benevolent regulations, seemed to bring forth great artists, not by any wretched copying of pagan antiquity but by the practice of honest craftsmanship. It was in this manner that the teaching of art was to be reformed, and the day was to come when young Mr Dyce would have a chance to put his ideas, or something like his ideas, into practice. But now for the moment I must leave him.

Let me turn to another young man, a handsome, Byronic figure with a good deal of nose, a very large head, a very short upper lip, a sensual mouth, a firm chin, flowing locks, eyes already a little myopic, a glance that is already a little wild. The year is 1808. He is drawing a statue by candlelight beneath a tarpaulin at the back of a house in Park Lane, and he trembles so much with excitement that he can hardly manipulate his portecrayon, for the statue is the Theseus from the Parthenon, the house belongs to Lord Elgin, the young man is Benjamin Robert Haydon and he has discovered the whole secret of art.

In searching for ancient purity it was well enough to look at vases and wall paintings, the marbles of the Vatican or the Aldobrandini Marriage, but what was all this compared with the Athenian root from which all art, all science and philosophy had sprung, the sculptures of the Parthenon itself. Here indeed was the very source from which all the mighty river of art – all that Haydon deemed valuable – derived.

But that was not all. For Haydon, the Elgin marbles were not simply the great and splendid achievement of Hellas, not simply the perfect type compared with which all later achievements, even those of Raphael, even those of Michelangelo, were but faint echoes; for him they were a sign from Heaven, a divine confirmation of his own theories and, implicitly, of his own mission as the regenerator, the creator indeed, of British art.

Haydon had begun by accepting the theories of Reynolds only to feel their insufficiency. The average was too base, too mediocre a thing to act as a foundation of the grand style. But neither could he accept the distortions and eccentricities of his master, Fuseli, he who would 'paint a figure with six toes and call it nature as she

132

ought to be'. Where was the solution to this secular problem? Haydon found it in the function, the anatomy of man. The perfect man was the most human man. In the imperfect man there would be something always of the brute. To find that which was essentially human and therefore essentially beautiful, you must dissect both men and beasts, and from this you might learn to discern those formations which were notably human. Most human beings are not perfectly adjusted to material existence and are therefore neither beautiful nor serviceable in providing the material for an average type, hence the poverty of Reynolds' solution. But the exaggerations of Mannerism or of Fuseli failed also in that they were not based upon an understanding of the healthy functioning of the body. The true way lay in the middle, neither binding the imagination to a mean habit, nor permitting it to indulge in illegitimate licence.

Here was Haydon's doctrine and looking for the ultimate authority of Greek practice he found it in the anatomical treatment of bone and muscle in the metopes of the Parthenon.

With such an instrument in his hands – the final solution of the academic dilemma sanctioned by the first, best art of man – Haydon felt ready to conquer the world; nor did he ever doubt that he had the strength to wield that two-handed engine. Years of failure, of debt, of neglect could not destroy – though it may secretly have undermined – his faith in his own genius. He was still, he believed, the superior of all the Academicians and the equal of Michelangelo. Nor should his fantastic vainglory be accounted mere paranoiac folly; no artist ever had a better press. Hazlitt and Leigh Hunt, Wordsworth and Keats believed in him as did many of his fellow painters. Nor was he without talent, however far his apocalyptic desires might outrun performance.

I must not lose myself in the absorbing irrelevancies of Haydon's life and misfortunes. He himself found the source of every calamity in his first grand quarrel with the Academy when his *Dentatus* – the picture that was to exhibit his newly rediscovered principles of art – was badly hung in the exhibition of 1809. Thereafter, although he had his hours of triumph, his progress was blocked partly by the Academicians, partly by his own fiercely unreasonable temper. In 1823 we find him in the Fleet prison and thereafter the bailiffs are never far from his door. It was in that year that he first began to consider whether government should not intervene to do something for the artist, and drafted the first of his numerous petitions to Parliament.

His proposals fell under two heads. First and foremost he wanted government to spend money on history paintings for public buildings. Secondly, he wanted some kind of national art education. Both these schemes were in the end to be realised and both were to bring bitter grief to their originator. The scheme for art education was made a practical possibility by Haydon's association with the Whig leaders, particularly Lord Melbourne, and with the Radicals, of whom William Ewart, the M.P. for Liverpool, was the most important for his purposes. At this time there were no municipal art schools in England, whereas most European countries had large and elaborate schemes of art education. English manufacturers purchased foreign designs or pirated them; despite the technical excellence of their wares they were forced from the market, in all those fields involving ornament, by the works of foreigners, and in particular by the French. The moral seemed clear. In 1835 a Select Committee was appointed to enquire into the Arts and their connection with manufactures. The Select Committee was used by Haydon and his radical friends as a stick with which to beat the Royal Academy against which they were waging a lively campaign (which came very near to landing the President, Sir Martin Archer Shee, in Newgate). But the main part of its business was concerned with art and industry and it led to the establishment of what was called a School of Design in 1837.

Haydon had a perfectly clear idea of what this School of Design was to be. It would be an art school, indeed an academy, teaching all art on the basis of the study of the human figure and the antique, and from this basic course some would go on to develop as artisans while a few would continue to become fine artists and even historical painters. A great central school of this kind would be established in London, branch schools on the same pattern would be set up in the provinces and the whole apparatus would be under the wise management of a painter, not an Academician but one who was perfectly imbued with the correct principles of teaching the human figure – who would of course be Haydon himself. Nor was this all: in Haydon's scheme of things, schools of fine art would be established at the universities by means of which the wealthy youth of the nation would be set on its guard against academic humbug, and the Royal Academy itself would be dissolved, its schools taken over, its exhibitions managed by a 'constituency' of artists.

In a bloody and terrible revolution, a time when all things seem possible, changes of this kind might have been made and Haydon might have been established as dictator of the fine arts. But in 1837, under the government of Lord Melbourne and with Mr Poulett Thomson at the Board of Trade, a very different solution was envisaged. A school as inexpensive as might be would be established in the capital and, in deference to the known wishes of the radical gentlemen, provincial schools might be subsidised if they could also be maintained by local subscriptions. Certain manufacturers, certain patrons of the arts and certain Royal Academicians would be invited to form a governing body for the metropolitan establishment; needless to say, Mr Haydon – who was not disposed to co-operate readily with members of the Academy – would *not* be invited . . .

And thus, much to Haydon's chagrin, it was managed. He, the originator of the scheme, was to be excluded from its management. There was worse to follow. The council decided that the human figure should not be taught in the schools. By this they did not simply mean that there was to be no living model, but that there was to be no working from statues, casts, pictures or engravings that represented the human figure.

There were two reasons for this 'regulation' – in the first place the Academicians were very anxious that there should be no rival to their own school, in the second place this was, after all, to be a school for manufacturers, the apparatus of 'High Art' was unnecessary. Indeed, in the minutes of the schools of design we find the fear frequently expressed that the school would produce 'artists'. An idle fear.

But if the council of the new school knew what it did not want to do, it knew very little else. It found an architect, John Buonarotti Papworth, and put him in charge; it found plasterers and paper hangers to act as teachers; it even found a few students; but it had no coherent doctrine.

In this situation it looked abroad for guidance and it also looked to Edinburgh where, for many years, there had been a small school of art, and in Edinburgh it found a young teacher who had just proposed a revolution in art education, a revolution that would make the art school a preparation, not for the practice of high art, but for industry. This young teacher was William Dyce and in 1838 he was brought to London and placed in charge of the School of Design at Somerset House.

Dyce was resolved to make the art school not a studio, but a workshop, indeed a factory. The student would learn the processes of industry and would make designs which would in fact be sold to industrialists. His earliest training would be concerned not with eyes and noses but with abstract and geometrical shapes and he would be guided by a paternal hand, not into the dangerous realms of Fine Art, but into various trades. Thus Dyce found it his first duty as principal to make an enquiry into manufacturing processes and almost his first act was to install a Jacquard loom in the premises of the central school. Dyce was principal for five years and thereafter he was inspector of the provincial schools which were making from 1841 onwards. During this time he had to fight a battle on two fronts: he was much plagued by the governors of his school. I will not go into the details of that struggle beyond saying that in the 1840s the governors of art schools had not realised that an artist, if he is to be the efficient principal of an art school, needs some time in which to do his own work. (Let us not enquire as to whether governors are any wiser today.) But of the outward struggle something must be said: he was tormented by Haydon.

Haydon, when he saw how matters would be decided by the Minister, began to stump the country. He visited the manufacturing centres, he assisted in the creation of independent schools of design. The government, he told the mechanics who would be the principal clientèle of the new schools, the government is determined to prevent you from acquiring knowledge. You might become artists but you will be denied the power to advance yourselves. Moreover the method employed by Mr Dyce, a follower of the dry, hard, Gothic German school – is faulty, it is based on the German Gewerbeschule, whereas my proposals are based on the practice of the school at Lyons – and which do you think is best, German design or French? In London he, with the help of Ewart, went further. He established a rival school of design with a model, drawing students so fast from the government school that Dyce, almost immediately, had to allow the figure to be taught at Somerset House.

In the provinces the greatest battle was fought at Manchester. Here Haydon had been largely instrumental in establishing a school in which the teaching would be on principles laid down by him. As usually happened, the town soon found that it needed funds from the government and government, in the person of Dyce, demanded conformity with its own practice. Let Haydon describe what followed:

Only think what has happened. I had established here, as you know, a School of Design, with the figure as the basis. Some time since, again influenced by those obstinate ignoramuses in London, the council here allowed itself to be persuaded to abolish the figure. The young men behaved admirably well. They met together, subscribed, and continued the figure privately, and waited for my coming down. Now that I have arrived they brought me their drawings, which are admirable for their accuracy, breadth and finish. This is going on like the early Christians. Persecution like this will make the thing. These councils and pupils are doing here what is being done by councils and pupils in many great towns at which I have lectured. Such is the baneful and mischievous influence of that blot of centralised ignorance in London, the moment my back is turned they seek to undo all the good I have done. But if the young gentlemen only remain sound, and continue to draw the figure, those gentlemen in London will one day be brought to acknowledge their error. It is pitiable to find such obstinacy and ignorance, wilful intentional ignorance, of what is for their great country's good, in high places.

It should be added that the setback to the Haydonian party was partly due to the tactlessness of a female model who threw a fit in a public corridor of the school.

The new regime brought a new leader who replaced the model with exercises in form, relationship and rhythm, culminating in actual problems of design for manufacture. But this victory of the central authority was only partial and temporary for, in fact, Haydon had powerful allies in the provinces. Those manufacturers on whose goodwill the schools depended were by no means pleased by the idea of a school that would, virtually, be a factory for making patterns. They considered that technical education could be far better given in their own workshops and that the schools should in fact be academies, the more academic the better.

Thwarted in the provinces and compelled to compromise in the central school, Dyce withdrew from the principalship. He was replaced by an Edinburgh colleague, C. H. Wilson, but he remained inspector until 1845.

It was in that year that Haydon had his last fling at the Council of the School of Design.

Those who know the painting school of the Royal College will remember an ornate plaque on the stairs just above the first floor. In the centre of it is a bearded Victorian gentleman. His name was Richard Burchett and he was at one time a principal master at South Kensington. In the year 1845 he was a student and the ringleader in an insurrection. It was an insurrection that very nearly led to blows, if not bloodshed, and one of the most spirited chapters in the history of British art schools.

You will remember that I said that Dyce was obliged by the example of Haydon's rival school to allow the creation of a class in the human figure at Somerset House. This department flourished, in fact it flourished too much. Students, it was found, came thither and used it as a preparatory establishment for the Academy school. Its Master, J. R. Herbert, was popular. Wilson, the head of the school, was not. A petty warfare of small vexations, gas lamps turned out, casts removed, regulations enforced to the letter, was waged against the master and students of the figure school, until at last there was what the president of the Board of Trade called 'an unseemly altercation'. Haydon described the matter thus:

The Figure Master, more enthusiastic than discreet, felt indignant at an order put up in his schools which appeared to him to reflect on the conduct of his scholars; angry words took place before the scholars; the Decorative master called the Figure master into his room, angry words again went on, the figure master elegantly called the decorative master 'a snob', and the decorative master still more elegantly called the figure master 'a liar and a scoundrel'.

Tantaene animis etc.

Luckily, neither master having the organ of combativeness very largely developed, separated, bowing, and swearing vengeance before the council – a very pretty way of occupying precious time, spending public money, and advancing the refinement of the mechanic.

There was, as may be imagined, a great deal of public outcry. The *Art Journal*, the *Builder*, the *Spectator*, the *Athenaeum*, were full of indignant letters. There were questions in the House and the matter was raised on the adjournment. The government stood by the school, refused an enquiry and expelled the mutineers; but in fact, although they may not have known it, the students had won their victory. Never again would the director dare to outlaw the human figure; the pressure from students, and, even more, from the manufacturers in the provinces, was decisive, and from 1845 onwards it became clear that the School of Design would have also to become a school of art.

How much Haydon realised of all this it would be hard to say, but certainly he had the satisfaction of being proved right, of hitting his opponent a blow that sent him staggering back against the ropes and of enjoying a signal triumph in the pages of *The Times*.

Alas, his moments of triumph were few enough now. When the great schemes of public decoration for which he had so long agitated at last took form and the new House of Commons was to be decorated, it was Dyce who triumphed, Dyce the representative of the 'hard, dry German style' that was gaining ground every day. Haydon was rejected in the competition without a prize or an honourable mention.

Then at last Haydon despaired. One last effort to attract the British public by the exhibition of his *Banishment of Aristides* was defeated by a rival attraction: General Tom Thumb; alas, for the academic doctrine, alas, for ideal beauty and divine proportion. The public turned from the correct and perfect image of man as deduced from the study of anatomy and sanctioned by the example of Hellas in her greatest age, instead it gaped at a mis-shapen dwarf.

This was the end, Haydon could bear it no more. On 22 June, 1846, he tried to blow his brains out, failed, and cut his throat with a razor.

COLE AND RUSKIN

There is a direct conflict, an open war, between Hogarth and Reynolds, Reynolds and Blake, Dyce and Haydon. Between Cole and Ruskin the antagonism is inferential. Cole's own position was never entirely clear; Ruskin never examined it, although he frequently adverts to the shortcomings of his system. Cole was not a man of principle but a man of method, an empiricist with an extraordinary genius for practical affairs, he knew perfectly how to come to terms with his age. And in this he was the precise opposite of Ruskin. It is hardly wonderful therefore that Cole ended his days comfortably with a knighthood in a pleasant villa in the Home Counties, having accumulated a fortune, while Ruskin, having dissipated a still greater inheritance, died under a load of grief, defeated, despairing, and mad.

Henry Cole started life as a civil servant in the Record Office. He found that office in confusion; with fearful energy he purged it, replaced his own superior and made it a model of efficiency. This, however, was but one of his youthful employments. Penny postage, the single gauge railway, Grimsby Docks, the Corn Laws – all engaged his attention and where his attention was engaged his energies were also engaged to the full. During the 1840s he became interested in the applied arts, he organised a sort of Design Centre – Felix Summerly's Art Manufactory; there were also Felix Summerly's books for children, guides to places of historic interest, maps and plans – and this prosperous activity brought him into touch with the Schools of Design.

After the rebellion of '45 the Schools of Design had entered into a state of semi-permanent crisis. While provincial schools fell into debt and lost students, the metropolitan school was afflicted, first by a revolt of the staff, then by a long period of internal dissension ending with the removal of the director (with him went the only distinguished teacher, Alfred Stevens); then followed an uneasy period of government by a triumvirate in which Dyce returned but in which he was so quarrelsome and so unhappy that he soon resigned. It was during this period that the Board of Trade asked Henry Cole to assist them. He made three reports in the last of which he said, in effect, that the schools were so ill governed, and managed – in so far as they were managed – on such false principles, that they ought to be entirely destroyed and entirely remade.

From this time (1848) Henry Cole's interest was engaged, and he set to work to reform and incidentally to make himself director of the schools.

I might amuse you by a description of the methods employed by Cole; the manner in which he obtained a Select Committee to investigate the schools in 1849; the way in which he briefed the chairman and influenced the witnesses; the way in which he arranged what questions should be put and what answers given; his thoughtfulness in writing the chairman's first, second and third reports; his ingenuity, when members of the Select Committee proved recalcitrant, in arranging with another member to double-cross the majority; his foresight in founding a Journal of Design, the main object of which was to attack the management of the Schools of Design, and his tact in using the inside information that he obtained to give that Journal special reports on the work of the Select Committee. All this, as I say, might prove entertaining but I must cut the matter short by saying that through the Select Committee, through the *Journal of Design*, through his manipulation of the Society of Arts, and through his ability to make himself wellnigh intolerable to authority and, above all, through the really valuable work that he did in connection with the Great Exhibition of 1851, Cole did at last succeed in gaining his end. He obtained for himself a Department of Practical Art – later the Department of Science and Art – organised as he wished it to be organised and, in truth, very much more efficient than the old Schools of Design with their divided control and maze of bureaucratic entrenchments. By 1852 Henry Cole was in power and he held that power for twenty-six years, becoming eventually Sir Henry Cole, K.C.B. or, as he was irreverently called, Old King Cole.

On the material side, his reign was prosperous. Art education became a part of primary school teaching and art schools proliferated throughout the country. The Metropolitan school, after various displacements, was established at South Kensington, where it still is.

What, then, was its policy?

In his long fight against the Board of Trade, Cole adopts the point of view of Dyce, but in a more brutal fashion.

I apprehend that the assumption in starting these schools was, that the benefit should be strictly commercial. I do not think that the schools were created for aesthetic purposes, or for general educational purposes. I apprehend that the age is so essentially commercial, that it hardly looks to promoting anything of this kind except for commercial purposes. In this case, I think it was specially commercial.

Study of the human figure was to be excluded, the schools should approximate as nearly as possible to factories, the teaching should be severely practical. This, Cole was convinced, was what the manufacturers wanted. It was not until he was in control of the schools that he discovered his mistake. His first reaction, typically, was to try to bully the industrialists and he actually established a museum of false design at South Kensington in which manufacturers were pilloried. But he soon had the good sense to realise that he must withdraw from that position.

Thwarted in his first objective, Cole found two main tasks for the Schools. They could train teachers and they could provide a recreational course for amateurs.

The training of teachers was made possible by the inclusion of drawing in the curriculum of national schools. Cole made the useful discovery that for this purpose artistic talent was not necessary. All that the children had to learn was the steadiness of hand and accuracy of eye that would make them useful in factories; a master with no qualifications save nerves of steel (and a heart of stone) could set them first to the freehand description of straight lines and the placing of regular intervals on those lines, then to the reproduction of angles, then curves and finally cubes, cones, spheres, cylinders and conventionalised flower forms. An ingenious arrangement of payment by results ensured the efficient working of the system. The teacher who attended an art school and passed examinations received certificates which bumped up his pay; these certificates were graduated. He was also paid on the results of his students' work. Thus he had a direct incentive to work in the art school, to prepare pupils who would do likewise and to follow, obediently, the lines laid down by the examiners.

Dyce had had in his mind's eye something like a modern guild with workshop training, Haydon had envisaged a reformed Academy. How noble and how great their conceptions appear in comparison with this mindless copying of unlovely forms. It is hard to estimate how much this system cost in terms of human drudgery and children's tears. I have myself seen something of that old system of South Kensington teaching. The long hours spent with a hard pencil, the sweaty hands patterning the paper with greasy stains while the pupil anxiously and laboriously imitates the shape of a parallelepiped or an ivy leaf, a leaf itself depicted without joy or curiosity, serving merely to provide another exercise in judiciously calculated severity. No shade of deference here even to Raphael or the antique, no art worthy of the name, nothing in view save the production of abundant cheap labour:

The main thing was to make the children accurate. That was the moral of the whole thing. Some sentimental objections had been made to a hard and fast and repulsive method of teaching drawing; that was all very well, but they were hardly dealing with sentiment. It was necessary to be very matter of fact in training artisans to be accurate in understanding any drawings that might come before them.

Such was the mainstay of the South Kensington system. Its other secondary function was hardly more fruitful, this was the provision of a cheap, but fee-paying establishment for the amateur. Here was an alternative for all those daughters of the middle classes who had artistic longings but whose parents could not quite run to the expense of a drawing master. Here too the profit motive was not absent, for the great voiceless unemployed class of Victorian England was female and in those days, before the invention of the typewriter, there was a chance of pin money, of genteel remittances, from lampshades and embroidered tea cosies. Like the impoverished teachers, the impoverished gentlefolk went in for art largely for what they could get out of it.

The tap root of all this mischief is in the endeavour to produce some ability in the student to make money by designing for manufacture. No student who makes this his primary object will ever be able to design at all; and the very words 'School of Design' involve the profoundest of art fallacies. Drawing may be taught by tutors; but design only by Heaven; and to every scholar who thinks to sell his inspiration, Heaven refuses its help.

That, as you may have guessed, was Ruskin, and, as you may also have guessed, I have here been somewhat haunted by the ghost of that prodigious Victorian – you will have seen the fringe of his whiskers around my dependent clauses, the faint marks of his geological hammer in my oblique approaches, my wilful divagations, my far too frequent efforts at fine writing. He is, in truth, an infectious author which does not, alas, mean that he communicates his strength.

Consider now where that strength lies. It is not simply a gift for stringing words together, a hauling in of phrase after phrase, metaphor after metaphor, a rounding up of the whole with a great sweeping biblical analogy. Not simply then a control of words – not simply that, but a moral force, a power that sweeps everything before it. Ruskin spoke with an advantage denied to all subsequent critics; he spoke in the pulpit, with all the authority of a priest. You think perhaps that I exaggerate – listen to this from the *Laws of Fesole*:

And the purpose of this book is to teach our English students of art the elements of these Christian laws, as distinguished from the Infidel laws of the spuriously classic school, under which, of late, our students have been exclusively trained.

Nevertheless, in this book the art of Giotto and Angelico is not taught because it is Christian, but because it is absolutely true and good: neither is the Infidel art of Palladio and Giulio Romano forbidden because it is Pagan; but because it is false and bad; and has entirely destroyed not only our English schools of art, but all others in which it has ever been taught or trusted in.

Just compare this for a moment with Sir Joshua Reynolds, Reynolds speaking as President of the Academy and as the greatest – or very nearly the greatest – painter of his age, talking to second-year students:

I flatter myself, that from the long experience I have had, and the unceasing assiduity with which I have pursued those studies in which, like you, I have been engaged, I shall be acquitted of vanity in offering some hints to your consideration. They are, indeed, in a great degree founded upon my own mistakes in the same pursuit. But the history of errors, properly managed, often shortens the road to truth. And although no method of study, that I can offer, will of itself conduct to excellence, yet it may preserve industry from being misapplied.

It is, I think, important to make this point because here in Ruskin we have an attempt to assert authority, to direct the student as surely – though in a quite different direction from – that in which De Piles wished to direct him. Ruskin, as I hope to show, was the grand executioner of the academic idea; he destroyed it more thoroughly than any other theorist, but it was his intention to put something in its place, something that the Nazarenes and Dyce had already glanced at and which he, Ruskin, in fifty years of thought and writing, sought to define. On the Continent the blunt destructive mind of Courbet was engaged in a similar task; similar, that is, in its anti-academic tendencies, but dissimilar in that it put nothing in its place – nothing theoretical, that is, but something eminently practical. So that, whereas Ruskin left a literary structure in which the academic system was exhibited and displaced but in which the shrine of a new faith was at last left empty, Courbet was building realism, a great solid muck heap upon which the flowers of Impressionism were begotten. Take, if you like, a Ruskinian comparison: in 1871 when Ruskin was exhorting the young men at Oxford to behave like truly Christian gentlemen and was shrinking in horrified disgust from the spectacle of the Paris Commune, Courbet was pulling down the Vendôme column. All good sense, good morality and good art seemed then to be on Ruskin's side; but the future lay with Courbet.

And yet this is not all the truth. Ruskin is enormously influential, and something of what he said has developed and is of the utmost importance to us today. His execution of the academic idea was a thing that had to be done.

Let us look first at his equipment for the task. We have already seen that he had an astonishing gift for language and a prodigious moral force with which to drive his words home. He had something else: a natural disposition to admire that which lay outside the academic canon; a love first of landscape and of art in the age before Raphael; a love of colour rather than of line; a natural aversion to the nude; a deep hatred of the High Renaissance – or at all events of the High Renaissance outside Venice – and a still deeper hatred of the seventeenth century. Thus he was predisposed from the outset to reject a school of thought which made the nude its palladium and the antique its guide, which placed history painting upon a special eminence and which began the history of painting with Raphael.

At this point I think it may be helpful to describe in a very few words the nature of Ruskin's various opinions for, like everyone else, he changed them. As a boy he responded naturally to landscape, and to the poetry of landscape, and in his first visits to Italy it was landscape, the landscape of Turner, which was for him also the landscape of Byron and Rogers, that he saw. The first volume of *Modern Painters* is an enthusiastic vindication of Turner and a rejection of the classical, the academic, landscape of Claude and Poussin. Then in 1845, escaping from the family influence, he enters into that long second period in which, while losing the fiercely and narrowly Protestant faith of his mother, he discovers Tintoretto, Titian and Veronese and, at the same time, the Quattrocento. It is at this point that he has to perform the most difficult gymnastics in order to accept the Venetians and yet to reject anything that might savour of Palladianism or the Roman school. The final phase marks a kind of return to his original position. He discovers that Michelangelo is bad; and worse than bad – pernicious; that he is responsible for all that is amiss with the great Venetians and that truth, pure, good, Christian truth, lies after all with Bellini, Carpaccio, Cimabue, Fra Angelico and Giotto.

It will be appreciated that these successive discoveries could not fail to have a certain effect upon Ruskin's theories and upon his practice as a teacher of art. The surprising thing is how consistent he managed to be. To many of his contemporaries it seemed that he was as destructive as Courbet, that he, like his friends of the Pre-Raphaelite Brotherhood, advocated nothing more or less than an abandonment of the ideal – of all Raphaelesque beauty and the substitution of ugliness.

This, however, as I have already hinted, was far from being the case.

For Ruskin the making of a picture was, essentially, a moral transaction, the artist's first business was to attain such discipline of hand and such humility of spirit that he could and would transcribe the appearance of anything whatsoever with the utmost patience and dexterity and without any dishonest facility of execution, but always with sober delicacy.

But this, when achieved, was but the beginning and the first great object of the student. Dutch exactitude, when applied to unworthy ends, was the meanest and most contemptible form of art.

True excellence lay in the exact delineation – a free delineation based upon an exact apprehension – of that which was most beautiful and most edifying in nature.

By Nature, Ruskin meant something quite different from that which most modern painters and critics usually mean. For us, Nature is the world outside the canvas – the world of natural appearances. For Ruskin, Nature was that which had been made not by men but by God. The works of man were all too frequently ugly and the painter was not to accept them without reservations. Turner himself was sometimes at fault in this respect. His view of Margate –I think one of the loveliest of the 'Harbours of England' – seems to Ruskin 'capricious'. Of all the English ports:

there will hardly be found another so utterly devoid of all romantic interest as Margate. [It is] simply a mass of modern parades and streets with a little bit of chalk cliff, an orderly pier, and some bathing machines. Turner never conceives it as anything else, and yet for the sake of this simple vision, again and again he quits all higher thoughts . . . It is certainly provoking to find the great painter, who often only deigns to bestow on some Rhenish fortress or French city, crested with gothic towers, a few misty and indistinguishable touches of his brush, setting himself to indicate, with unerring toil, every separate square window in the parades, hotels and circulating libraries of an English bathing place.

But more than this – not only was the modern house, still more the modern factory, railway train or pithead, a subject unfit for painting, there were flowers, rocks and animals of vile and misshapen form stained with vicious and vulgar colour, things corrupting, things base or sinful, things not to be rendered by the artist. It is true that in his middle period, at the moment when he was most indulgent to the Renaissance, he believed that an awareness of sin, the awareness of a Titian – that worldly yet sublimely religious artist – gave to his work a moral tension which placed it above the childish innocent delight of Angelico, but in later life he concluded that he had been mistaken, the true artist must neither hear, speak nor know of evil.

It will be seen that an attitude of this kind leads us far from the impartial observation of facts, takes us back instead to a new form of academic theory. But where the old theory dealt essentially with dignity, the new was concerned with morality.

Ruskin, who had a considerable admiration for Reynolds as a painter and a man, felt nevertheless that he must reject the *Discourses* altogether – or, if not altogether, at least in so far as the central doctrine of idealisation was concerned. In the first place, he distrusted the idea of generalisation in that it was a convenient subterfuge for the slovenly artist. But, more importantly, he, with his eyes upon the mountains, could see that it would not apply – as it was intended to apply – to rocks or trees; that is to say, to large classes of objects. You cannot have a tree which is both olive and cypress, it must be one or the other. What then is it to be, if it is not to be – as, on the whole, Ruskin did not think it need be – a particular olive or a particular cypress? It must be typical of its species, showing all the tender aspiring nature of the cypress, all the strength and mysterious colour of the olive. These qualities may be rendered rather larger than life – but still truthfully.

This was his position, roughly speaking (and I am inevitably doing injustice to a subtle and penetrating mind by such generalisations as these), this was his position at the time of the first volume of *Modern Painters* (1843).

In his second volume he gives a more precise meaning to this when he considers ideal form. What, he asks, is an ideal oak? Is it the finest oak that we can find, say, in a gentleman's park, where it is looked after and all competing plants are cut down? But this is an abnormal oak, in no way typical of its species and certainly not the average oak. Is it then the oak as you find it in the forest half crushed by other plants? But here each plant is in a different situation and averages become meaningless. Ruskin therefore comes to the conclusion: 'So then there is in trees no perfect form which can be fixed upon or reasoned out as ideal; but that there is always an ideal oak which, however poverty-stricken, or hunger-pinched, or tempest-tortured, is yet seen to have done, under its appointed circumstances, all that could be expected of oak.'

The ideal is, therefore, not to be found by any form of calculation but by an examination of the moral situation of the object under discussion. The oak is satisfactory if it is doing its duty in that state of life to which it has pleased God to call it. So, too, with the artist attempting the 'Grand Style'. In the third volume of *Modern Painters* he makes a thorough-going attack on Reynolds and points out that:

He has involved himself in a crowd of theories, whose issue he had not foreseen, and committed himself to conclusions which he never intended. There is an instinctive consciousness in his own mind of the difference between high and low art; but he is utterly incapable of explaining it, and every effort which he makes to do so involves him in unexpected fallacy and absurdity. It is *not* true that Poetry does not concern herself with minute details. It is *not* true that high art seeks only the Invariable. It is *not* true that imitative art is an easy thing. It is *not* true that the faithful rendering of nature is an employment in which 'the slowest intellect is likely to succeed best'. All these successive assertions are utterly false and untenable, while the plain truth, a truth lying at the very door, has all the while escaped him . . . namely, that the difference between great and mean art lies, not in definable methods of handling, or styles of representation, or choices of subject, but wholly in the nobleness of the end to which the effort of the painter is addressed.

Before looking to see how this critique of academic theory worked out in terms of practical teaching, I think it is worth pausing to consider whether, after an interval of a hundred years, they hold good. I think that there is no doubt that Ruskin demolishes Reynolds; we stand with him, both in his sympathy with the first president and in his refusal to accept the arguments of the *Discourses*. Nevertheless, in the matter of generalisation, Ruskin proves a little too much. We may, if we choose, attribute moral purpose to trees, but it can hardly be denied that every oak is in truth, whatever its situation, doing all that could be expected of an oak. A lazy, despondent, procrastinating oak does not exist. It follows, therefore, that all oaks are morally excellent and all equally beautiful. In fine we can paint any oak and each will be as ideal as its fellow; but what then does the word ideal mean? In fact, it seems to me that Ruskin has argued it out of existence without realising that he has done so.

In his dissection of the Grand Style he seems to me equally radical, the difference between great and mean art is certainly to be found nowhere but in the sentiment of the artist. It is not a matter of canonical rules, but neither is it a matter of morality, or at least of morality in the simple terms that Ruskin uses. Once again his argument is more destructive than he had intended it to be.

Ruskin wrote two elementary drawing books and a great many lectures intended to assist students who were doing practical work. In addition, much of his general criticism is essentially pedagogic. *The Elements of Drawing* was intended for the use of his many admirers, particularly female admirers who wanted to learn to draw. He had also in view his pupils of the Working Men's College in London, a body the nature of which is sufficiently explained by its name and which was organised by the Christian Socialist F. D. Maurice. Here Ruskin taught an enthusiastic class; like all his other pupils they were not being trained as artists and also they were adults. It is very necessary to make this point, for Ruskin's methods, which were severe, were not intended for children of twelve or under, these – and it is enormously to Ruskin's credit that he said this – these were to be left to 'the voluntary practice of art'. 'It' (the child) 'should be allowed to amuse itself with cheap colours almost as soon as it has sense enough to wish for them.'

In other words, Ruskin's training begins almost at the point where Cole's National School training would leave off. When it does begin it is indeed severe. The student goes from exercises in shading and washings, through pebbles to twigs; his temper is tried not only by infinite minutiae but by a great mass of improving talk. Nevertheless, this is much better than South Kensington and, from what we can discover of the average drawing master's practice in the nineteenth century, it would seem that such teaching had an astringent and bracing effect. The working men, who also had Turners to copy, lichen, twigs, fluorspar set in a glass of water, seem to have fallen in love with the subject – or at least with the teacher.

At Oxford where, as Professor of Fine Art, he founded a Drawing School, Ruskin had less success. His lectures were indeed packed by a delighted, though sometimes bewildered and exasperated audience, but his drawing class was seldom visited. Here he made abundant use of examples, engravings after Turner, engravings by Holbein, Botticelli and Dürer.

It was at Oxford that he finally rejected the High Renaissance and Michelangelo in particular. 'That dark carnality of Michelangelo's has fostered insolent science and fleshly imagination.' With Michelangelo he rejects all the apparatus of academic teaching, in particular the study of anatomy which he considered one of the most fatal influences in the history of art. Already in the *Elements of Drawing* it was clear that the cast or the engraving from established academic sources was in his eyes useless. Now he went much further. Students should draw only from what they saw in life around them. To open up a body with a scalpel was both horrible and misleading, it showed the student things that he couldn't actually see but which he would draw because he knew that they were there; and here he made a point of considerable importance. But if it was wrong to strip the flesh from the bones was it not also wrong to strip the clothes from the flesh? This was a matter on which Ruskin could not quite make up his mind; he was bothered and embarrassed by the nude, even though he did himself at one time make life studies. With the example of the Italians and his beloved Botticelli and Tintoretto before him, he could not quite condemn the use of the naked model. But then, the Italians lived in a warm climate where nakedness and semi-nakedness were more natural and therefore less indecent. In the end he compromised. There should be no nude model in the Ruskin school, but for artists it was on the whole proper and perhaps necessary.

The *Laws of Fesole* was written in 1878 and is one of the strangest works ever written on art education. It has its part in Ruskin's curious Guild of St George, an organisation that was to reconstitute social justice, honest toil and hand-made things throughout the Kingdom, and behind it an unhappy love affair, a gradual drift into the world of make-believe. It is written really for use in the schools of a private utopia.

It is in all respects less useful and less practical than the *Elements of Drawing* and its severity is more purposeless, more wilfully eccentric. *Laws of Fesole* marks the beginning of Ruskin's defeat at the hands of Cole and at the hands of the nineteenth century. For fifty years he had been telling England what was wrong with it, talking about beauty, talking about social justice, talking about religion, and talking with the tongues of angels, with the thunder and volume of a Hebrew prophet. Audiences had rushed to hear him, he was famous and influential, he had spawned a multitude of Venetian gothic municipal buildings and yet – what had been the result? Comfortably, prosperously, irresistibly, the mines and the mills, the villas and the railway stations had arisen. The lower classes were brutalised, the upper classes were frivolous and unfeeling. Everything, it seemed, had been in vain, his life and his work had been wasted. Overwhelmed, his indignant soul covered its eyes in madness.

And yet, much had been done, and there was an inheritance. While Ruskin lay plunged in the darkness of insanity at Brantwood, his social work was taken up by Morris; not, it is true, as he would have wished it, but with a new uncompromising intellectual materialism. His ideas in education were applied and adapted by Walter Crane.

A guild, very much on the lines of the Guild of St George, was started by one of his disciples, Ashbee. It failed, but it was restarted in the new century and now, for the first time, an attempt was made to come to terms with the realities of the age, and the machine found its place in the studio. At the same time, the Arts and Crafts movement, of which Ruskin was certainly the founder, spread from this country to Germany and Belgium, to Van der Velde, Muthesius and Gropius.

Some years ago when I was in Boston I had the pleasure of meeting Gropius. I asked him to what extent he had Ruskin in mind when he founded the Bauhaus. 'Well of course,' he replied, 'I was very much against Ruskin.' 'But still,' I persisted, 'for that very reason one could say you had him in mind.' And to this he agreed.

Of course the Bauhaus was 'against Ruskin'; it rejected the notion from which he could never depart, that the machine is immoral and its products ugly and it was this – the determination not to face the realities of the age – that was Ruskin's undoing. Nevertheless, in its social aspirations the Bauhaus was Ruskinian and perhaps its teaching may be fairly said to belong to the School of Dyce and Ruskin as against the 'infidel school of Palladio, Giulio Romano' – and the nude.

WALTER SICKERT, ROGER FRY AND THE TWENTIETH CENTURY

It is, on the face of it, surprising that the model survived the nineteenth century. Ruskin looked at her askance, Cole brought her in only for fee-paying amateurs or advanced students, and, as I shall try to show, neither Courbet, the Impressionists, Degas, or his English followers had much use for her – in the life room – and yet she flourished.

The nineteenth century was, in fact, the great century of the artist's model and particularly of the female model; already enthroned in England she was given the entrée to Continental schools by M. Ingres and everywhere in the official, popular, successful art of the period you will find her – in Etty and Leighton and Alma-Tadema, in Delaroche, Bouguereau, Cabanel, in the mythological paintings of all the worthy, prosperous, decorated academicians she, the *genius loci*, presides, and one is intensely conscious, as one never is with Titian or Rubens, let alone Poussin or the Carracci, of the personable young woman taking her pose under a north light in a well appointed studio and, in so doing, giving that incredibly overdressed – I should rather say upholstered – society an opportunity to indulge in a form of prurience that might be called 'high art'.

I was sitting one night, sadly, in one of the two-houses-a-night Empires in a distant suburb [writes Sickert] when a 'living picture' act was put on the stage. *Diana, The Three Graces*, we have all seen and smiled at the naiveté of these doubly edited and anodyne incitements to the worship of beauty, and to the culture of the masses. *The Wave* is an unvarying item. Clad in pink tricot from the neck downwards, not only as to her five-toed feet, but to the tips of her pointed stays and the tips of her ten fingers (tricot does not wash as easily as flesh and costs more to wash), a somewhat stiff little packet, like a second-hand lay figure of the cheapest make, floats, not without a strand of gauze, on the crest of the property billow. The only human thing is the pretty little face, fixed in a discreet and deprecating smile. A friend who was with me said, 'There you have it. There is the academic nude. There is the simplified nude'. The audience, nourished for generations on the Academy and Chantrey bequest nudes, responded with enthusiasm, convinced that here was Art without what the papers call 'vulgarity'. The Puritan and the artist may well join hands and cry, both equally shocked, 'If this is the nude, for heaven's sake give us the draped and let's say no more about it'.

Yes, there she was, the descendant of Raphael's Galatea and Poussin's Muse, fallen on evil days, representing neither a platonic idea nor a scholarly invention but the precariously balanced libido of the Victorian middle classes. The reaction against the Academy, which was already troubling Sir Joshua Reynolds, had now reached a new stage of intensity, and the independent artist was now ready to dispense not only with the institution but with the apparatus.

Away with the model and away with the art school itself, such had been Courbet's doctrine; when finally he acceded to the desire of a certain number of dissident *beaux-arts* students and established a school of a kind he did so on the understanding that, although he might give advice, there would be no formal teaching. As for the model, he was an ox tethered in the middle of the floor and his activities were such that the unfortunate landlord of the building rented by Courbet declared that the damage caused in three weeks' occupation far exceeded six weeks' rent.

Courbet's school, with its co-operative methods and its live-stock, did not last very long. Moreover, it did not altogether satisfy the needs of his successors, the Impressionists. What their needs were may best be described by the art critic Philippe Burty, who in his novel *Grave Imprudence* gives a very clear picture of what a young Impressionist might have felt about the apparatus of his art in 1880. I will endeavour to translate:

What he wanted was to see a woman moving easily naturally and spontaneously in the open air and the sunlight, to find his nude in nature.

That kind of truthful vision is denied to the modern artist and one of Brissot's best founded complaints against the bloodless Academy was that it maintained the use of mythological painting – although neither the painter nor the public are in any way familiar with the principal subject matter of that art. Gavarni found what he needed in the medical examinations for conscripts. Delacroix studied the foreshortening of acrobats, Daumier went in summer to the public baths. The students of Lecoq de Boisbaudran hired an enclosure where artillerymen wrestled naked at the price of one litre each per dozen of them. All the pioneers of the modern movement have tried to see the model otherwise than in a set pose, in a grey light and amidst dull surroundings. But it might be hard to persuade the guardians of public morality that, by playing the mandoline out of doors with a naked girl, one was merely attempting to recreate a Giorgione.

This was, in fact, what Manet and Renoir did, and what Cézanne dreamed of doing, but it represents only one aspect of independent art in France, and that which is least concerned with the human figure; for many of the Impressionists, a stream, a haystack, a row of vines, a railway station was sufficient. But for Degas and his followers, Toulouse-Lautrec, Whistler and Sickert, human life was everything; they were of the school of Ingres, they were draughtsmen before they were painters.

I have said that they were of the school of Ingres. This is of course particularly true of Degas, whose early historical paintings are, I suppose, the last great academic works in the history of painting. And when he turned from classicism to realism, Degas might have become the one great nineteenth-century painter of anecdote. He was drawn instead to the more reticent art of Japan, he remains close to life, but too faithful to what he can actually see to rearrange, to moralise or to dramatise his scenes.

Ukiyo-ye, the pictures of the fleeting world – these could be found in the Paris Opera or at the races as well as in the pleasure gardens or Kabuki theatres of Yedo. The art of seeing life as it flies, of capturing some momentary concatenation of figures with snap-shot rapidity, led to a search for a new technique of drawing, a technique involving the cultivation of memory. Lecoq de Boisbaudran attempted a method of training students of drawing so that they could, eventually, take one steady look at an object and then return to the studio and reproduce it. Undoubtedly this had its influence upon Rodin, Degas, Whistler and Sickert.

It is to Sickert that I must now turn. Sickert at the beginning of this century represented 'modern art' and French art in England. From him a whole generation of students – Gilman, Spencer Gore, Drummond – received a coherent doctrine based entirely on Degas and completely disregarding everything that had happened to French painting since 1880; and this doctrine was accepted as being the last word of the *avant garde* until about 1910.

It amounted to this – I exaggerate as Sickert himself did. All good painting is literary; that is to say, it deals with human situations. But it is not anecdotal, that is to say, it is not *arranged*. You must take it as you find it – and no cheating. Walk, on a winter's evening, through the streets of Camden Town, the gas lights illuminate each room and, before the curtains are drawn, you may see a scene ready set. Ghastly wallpaper, cheap prints on the walls, the high tea with kippers and scrambled eggs half ready on the table, the potted plants the desperate symbols of mediocre gentility, a man saying something to a woman, leaning against a mantelpiece. What is happening? You don't know, life won't give you the clues that Hogarth provides. It won't tell your stories in dumb show for you, but this is life, and therefore your proper subject. The homes of the rich and the refined, the beautiful face and the old English garden, these are ready made art and of no service to you, these are the props of the life beautiful with which you, as an artist, have nothing to do. 'The artist is he who can take a piece of flint and wring out of it drops of attar of roses.' (Here we have the exact negation of Ruskinian doctrines.)

This, then, is the kind of literature in which you must deal, a literature of mood rather than of narrative, of real rather than of ideal life. You will render it first by drawing swiftly that which you see, drawing at sight size and drawing with a purpose – never for the sake of making a drawing. And you will use your drawing, and nothing else, in order to make your painting – painting in which tone will predominate, for bodies in movement are most accurately described by tone, and the drawing and the tonality of your picture will make its structure.

Now, to prepare a student for this kind of art hours of laborious study from the model will be worse than useless; so too still life and, in a lesser degree, landscape – for before the still object the mind stagnates, the first vivid impression is lost, the student ceases to feel that urgent need to set down the essential facts, now, at once, before 'the sun sets behind the house in Stanhope Street . . . before the fizziness of his momentary mood becomes still and flat.' What then shall we do with the model? Fire her, throw her out of the art school, find her again if you like in a bar parlour, a grubby bed sitter or up with the girls in the gallery; there you may draw her if you like, and if you can mix with your colours some incalculable element of genius you may paint a Sickert.

As a general art teaching this is clearly absurd, much more absurd than anything that Ruskin ever said, for Ruskin, whatever else he may have wanted his pupils to do, was not trying to get them to paint Ruskins.

Sickert, in fact, suffered from the intense narrowness of sympathy that afflicts the good artist. That which was not grist to his mill must grind for no one else. It is this unreasonable simple-mindedness which makes the painter the best and worst of critics.

Ruskin, so much broader in outlook, was still, by twentieth-century standards, incredibly limited in his range of appreciation. He condemned all art that was not European, and even in Europe he could tolerate only a few schools and a few periods.

Roger Fry dismissed all the salon painting of the last century, all the Pre-Raphaelites save Burne-Jones; he also had a few notorious 'blind spots' – Dürer, Delacroix, Turner and a few others, but, having said this, we may almost say that he could find merit in everything that anyone had ever done anywhere.

This difference in scope resulted from a natural predisposition to enthusiastic admiration, it resulted also from a growing awareness (which had been in progress since the end of the nineteenth century and the beginning of the twentieth) of the virtues of long neglected schools. This new catholicity of taste killed the academic idea once and for all, Greece and the Renaissance became parts, valuable and important parts, but only parts, of the development of art as a whole. With it went all arguments based upon the moral purpose of art. The Aztec mask, the Easter Island statue, stands sublime, awful and expressive. Expressive of what? We don't know; all we know is that they are admirable just as the Kings of Judah upon the walls of Chartres are admirable and perhaps for the same reason.

Thus with the destruction of the academic idea one is forced back upon some unitary theory of art, something analogous to

Hogarth's line of beauty or, more probably, to a wider conception: Clive Bell's significant form, Roger Fry's plastic values, or Berenson's ideated space.

This cut across Sickert's whole system of ideas. But the antagonism between him and Roger Fry centred around a more immediate question. Fry was mainly responsible for bringing to London two exhibitions in which the British public found itself confronted for the first time by Gauguin, Van Gogh, Matisse, Picasso, Rouault, Derain and Cézanne. It was, above all, on the subject of Cézanne that Sickert and he quarrelled.

Sickert spent a great deal of time attacking both Clive Bell and Roger Fry, but was hardly attacked in his turn. Both critics admired his work, both tended to laugh at his criticism. May I enter here a personal reminiscence which may seem to be in very bad taste. In 1945, on the occasion of Ginner's seventieth birthday, a large dinner was given at which I found myself sitting next to Nina Hamnett who had been the mistress both of Roger Fry and of Walter Sickert. 'The difference between Roger and Walter,' she said, 'was this: Walter knew I was a bitch; Roger, bless his heart, never did.' The story is instructive, and in more ways than one. For in the opposition of those two remarkable characters, the one so brilliant, so knowing and so much an artist, and the other so wise, so gullible and so much a philosopher, lies much of the story of those years. Sickert was gifted with acute powers of observation and, though genial, was entirely self-centred. For him there was only one kind of painting, his own, and only one purpose in society, to allow him to paint and live as he pleased. Fry, on the other hand, was essentially a philanthropist; in a sense, one may call him 'academic', in that he always held to the view that painting should be something nobler and more profound than a mere imitation of life. He was distressed by the aesthetic squalor of the world, that squalor in which Sickert took a horrid delight.

The aesthetic theories of the two men corresponded very exactly with their temperaments and talents. Sickert was indifferent to questions of decoration. He could take anything and use it for his own pictorial purposes. Fry was indifferent to pictorial anecdote and rejoiced in the fact that in the work of the Post-Impressionists he could find a style which, like the great styles of Italy and Byzantium, was as applicable to a chair or a carpet as to a great painting. For him, the easel picture was only one medium and he always wanted to get painters to cover the walls of some great public building. He turned also, as Pugin and Morris had turned before him, to the applied arts, and seeing in them both the means whereby the young artist could live and the public be given something decent wherewith to furnish its homes, he founded the Omega Workshops.

Roger Fry never propounded a pedagogic doctrine and although he befriended and helped Marion Richardson he was, I think, sceptical about all forms of art teaching, even his own, but his own should I think be mentioned. Kenneth Clark says of Fry in the dedication to his *Looking at Pictures* (1960), he 'taught my generation how to look'. In considering pictures, we do not usually reflect with gratitude upon the fact that we are able to see them, and this unconsciousness of sight is even more apparent in a generation which has never needed to be taught to see the merits of Cézanne.

There cannot now be many people who heard him lecture, but when we die the memory of that extraordinary experience will not die with us. To take extracts from or to summarise Virginia Woolf's recollections of those evenings when Roger Fry filled and dominated the Queen's Hall would be an ungrateful, almost a criminal undertaking, but perhaps her conclusion may be quoted without impropriety.

For two hours they [the audience] had been looking at pictures. But they had seen one of which the lecturer himself was unconscious – the outline of the man against the screen, an ascetic figure in evening dress who paused and pondered, and then raised his stick and pointed. That was a picture that would remain in memory together with the rest, a rough sketch that would serve many of the audience in years to come as the portrait of a great critic, a man of profound sensibility but of exacting honesty, who, when reason could penetrate no further broke off; but was convinced, and convinced others, that what he saw was there.

As a theorist, he was less convincing, for he himself was less convinced. His method, it seems to me, was to ride his theories until they dropped. Here he is in a letter to Robert Bridges:

I very early became convinced that our emotions before works of art were of many kinds and that we failed as a rule to distinguish the nature of the mixture and I set to work by introspection to discover what the different elements of these compound emotions might be and to try to get at the most constant, unchanging and therefore I suppose fundamental emotion. I found that this 'constant' had to do always with the contemplation of form (of course colour is in this sense part of artistic form). It also seemed to me that the emotions resulting from the contemplation of form were more universal (less particularised and coloured by individual history), more profound and more significant spiritually than any of the emotions which had to do with life (the immense effect of music is noteworthy in this respect though of course music may be merely a physiological stimulus). I therefore assume that the contemplation of form is a peculiarly important spiritual exercise (your 'spiritual mirth'). My analyses of form-lines, sequences, rhythms, &c. are merely aids for the uninitiated to attain to the contemplation of form – they do not explain.

But agreeing that aesthetic appreciation is a pre-eminently spiritual function does not imply for me any connection with morals. In the first place the contemplation of Truth is likewise a spiritual function but is I judge entirely amoral. Indeed I should be inclined to deny to morals (proper) any spiritual quality – they are rather the mechanism of civil life – the rules by which life in groups can be rendered tolerable and are therefore only concerned *directly* with behaviours . . .

I find that in proportion as a work of art is great it is forced to discard all appeal to sex. Only bad art can be successfully pornographic. It may have been the *point de départ*, it is no longer visible when the work of art has arrived. Of course those people who are insensitive to the artist's real intentions may go off on even the slightest hint of a more accessible appeal. As for instance a man reading a great poem which he did not understand might occupy his mind with the *double entendre* of words it contained. I can imagine that to some people Velasquez' Venus might excite sexual feeling; to any one who understands the picture such an idea is utterly impossible, it is too remote from the artist's meaning to be even suggested. As regards painting I think you are quite wrong in thinking that the preoccupation with the female nude is the result of sexual feeling. It is simply that the plasticity of the female figure is peculiarly adapted to pictorial design; much more so, on account of its greater simplicity, than the male – though of course the plasticity of the human figure in general is peculiarly stimulating to the pictorial sense – perhaps not more than that of a tiger but it is the most stimulating of easily accessible natural phenomena.

In its purest form I must confess that I have found this doctrine untenable. So did Roger, he soon found it impossible, in considering the drawings of Rembrandt, to divorce form from content and said as much in a lecture delivered in 1929. For him it seemed in the end that there were forms of art that could not be properly explained without reference to their 'meaning' – just as the melody of an aria may be irrevocably married to words. But although, as a medium of criticism, the theory of pure form has been found too rarefied to allow the critic to breathe, as a form of art it has flourished. The American students whom I mentioned had effectively and decisively turned their backs upon the seductions that lay before them. Of *their* pictures it might truly be said that sexual feeling was 'too remote even to be suggested' and, if I appear to be unsympathetic in my estimate of their endeavours, it is not that I do not appreciate the heroic chastity with which they can avert their eyes from all carnal delights, but because in so doing they sometimes appear to me to arrive at a degree of purity which is academic, not only in the sense that it is magnificently remote from the facts of life, but because it is a little dull or when not dull a little inclined to degenerate into something purely decorative.

OURSELVES *v.* OURSELVES

Coming to the actual controversies of the present age it is best to be circumspect and to be brief. In considering the question shall we now (1962) fire the model, one can hardly do more than adduce the arguments on both sides of the question and leave it to the reader to decide where he, or she, now stands, always remembering that fashions in art can change.

First then, the basic course as it exists is not simply a gimmick for teaching abstract art, it does not necessarily involve the abandonment of the model; but it does put the model in her proper place, which is *not* the centre of the art school. Art teaching in schools of general education tends at present to fade out in weak, undisciplined, cosily imaginative prettiness and has no relation to the world in which we live. Neither has teaching in colleges of art any such relevance; it follows, hesitatingly, in the footsteps of the Renaissance, without conviction or purpose. All teaching relates to the model, or to that dreadful amalgamation of models called 'pictorial comp', and every curve, every shape in the model is hackneyed and cliché-ridden.

Just as the painters of the Renaissance needed a new form of teaching, so do we, and our teaching, like theirs, must relate to the philosophy and science of the age, must be as applicable to the product designer as to the painter or the sculptor, must be integrated with the entire aesthetic of the twentieth century.

To this end we must teach our children and our students to consider shapes and colours, rhythms and spaces, abstract and natural forms such as will provide them with a grammar of design, and upon that basis, with the grammatical knowledge, they may learn to speak for themselves.

Now let me put the case for the opposition. The first objection arises precisely from this idea of teaching a grammar of design. It involves the oldest of educational fallacies, the elementary fallacy, that which supposes that you should learn the parts of a thing before learning the whole: the eyes, the ears, the noses of the antique head before the head itself. The basic elements of design were exactly what Henry Cole taught in his elementary schools – with what results we know, for the mind of the young person is synthetic, not analytic and, although some teaching of grammatical work may be necessary in the college of art, it should certainly not be allowed in the school of general education.

Bound up with this is a second aspect of the elementary fallacy: the belief that a simple shape is easier to describe than a complex one. The reverse is true; for a complex shape has more character than a simple one – try drawing first an old face and then a young one and you will see what I mean. Mondrian knew this when he proceeded from his complex living tree to his simple abstracted one.

Secondly, there is the objection of discipline. Take a sheet of paper and cut out two abstract shapes – say a triangle and a circle. Now place them in a balanced relationship to one another. How do you instruct your student, how do you tell him whether he is working well or ill? In the last analysis you can only do so by a judgment of taste. But that surely was the major fault of academic teaching – the attempt to correct the vision of the student, to give him an aesthetic and, moreover, an aesthetic which by the time he is thirty will be out of date. (I should add that this difficulty is one that has been, at all events, perceived by some of those who have taught the basic course.)

Thirdly, let me put an objection of a much more general kind. Having considered the history of art teaching can we really correlate it with artistic achievement? David was taught in the school of Vien, Michelangelo in that of Ghirlandaio; Van Gogh learnt from bad drawing books and Cormon; Henri Rousseau from no one. Of what use, then, is a new method? I do not quite believe this argument. There have, I think, been good schools and bad schools, but I doubt whether it is the doctrines that have brought out talent. Sickert taught arrant nonsense, but he was a wonderful teacher. I suspect that Louis Lamothe did likewise, but he filled Degas with an enthusiasm for drawing which lasted all his life. I am pretty sure that some of the people who are now teaching the basic course are having an admirable effect upon their students, but I am equally sure that the same methods in other hands would be worthless. Finally, after sitting on the fence until the iron has entered my soul, let me come down as nearly as I can in what I think is my true position. I do think that art schools need a shaking up and a chance to revise their ideas and I hope that as many as possible of them will be given the chance to do so. I also believe that some of the methods introduced by abstract artists have their dangers, especially if they are not adopted in a spirit of high enthusiasm and particularly when they are applied to children in schools of general education. I am convinced that it is men not measures that count in art education, and some of the best men entertain ideas which would break in other hands. Above all, I hope that, whatever new forms of education may arise, there will still be room for the model's throne somewhere in the art school. Undoubtedly, the model is a survival from the Renaissance; being, in an amateurish sort of way, an art historian, I do not like her the less for that. But the fascinating thing about her is that, despite every expectation, she is always new. Every pose, every angle is, one would suppose, hackneyed beyond endurance, a ready-made cliché. And yet, when one sits down and begins to draw, one is astonished by the complete unexpectedness of that which one sees. In some mysterious way, the oldest property of the studio is eternally new: the harmony of contours and volumes, the unexpected proportions of limbs, the fantastic luminosity of living flesh delight even though they defeat us. The model is indeed 'out of this world': we see her with a shock – a salutory shock, I think – and, measuring ourselves against her fantastically intricate problems, walk perforce with humility in the steps of the masters.

Form and Content

It will hardly be denied that we live in an age of aesthetic liberty, of a liberty which borders upon licence. Both the writer and the musician feel able to do things which would have seemed impossible fifty years ago; the painter – and by the painter I mean also the sculptor – is even more unrestricted than they. His predecessors were bound, loosely but effectively, to the image of the natural world with permission only to make comparatively modest distortions and rearrangements. *He* may invent whatever he chooses, using whatever materials may take his fancy. He may cover his model with paint and roll her upon the canvas, he may discard the brush and employ the watering can, he is the lord of the bicycle tyre, the gum boots, the sand blaster and the spray gun; there is no experiment that he may not envisage and few, so it would appear, that he has not attempted.

And yet, there are restrictions. The painter does as he likes, but there are some things that he cannot like to do. The still life, the landscape, the portrait even, may be attempted, but poetical fancies such as those illustrated later in this essay are, for a modern painter, out of the question. There is, when one comes to think of it, a whole territory of art upon which the modern artist dare not – will not – set foot: the nymph by the fountain, the sentinel of Pompeii, the mild domestic anecdote, the splendours of war, the comedy and tragedy of courtship, the peccadilloes of mischievous children, the faithful dog, the tavern scene, the period piece – all these are forbidden territory, they are all, to use a familiar term of reproach, 'literary'.

In this sense we have no literary painting today, no literary painting in which the story is as clear, and as directly connected with narrative, as it would be in a Meissonier, a Hogarth, a Daumier or a Jan Steen.

In the same way, we do not have the kind of art criticism which accepts the story of the picture as its chief message and which, therefore, confidently applies the judgments of literature to the art of painting, or, going further, applies the judgments of morality to the literature in art.

Of the former method Diderot may stand as an example; listen to his comments on Greuze's *Le Fils Ingrat* (see illustration 8):

Everything is clearly thought out and well grouped . . . the grief of the mother and her tenderness for a spoiled child, the old man's indignation, the different actions of the sisters and of the little children, the insolence of the youth, and the old soldier's feeling of shame, as he shrugs his shoulders and goes off . . .

Ruskin carried the method a stage further in this criticism of *Many Happy Returns of the Day* by Frith (see illustration 9):

A taking picture, much, it seems to me, above Mr Frith's former standard. Note the advancing Pre-Raphaelism in the wreath of leaves round the child's head. One is only sorry to see any fair little child having too many and too kind friends, and in so great danger of being toasted, toyed and wreathed into selfishness and misery.

Such criticism is unimaginable today. A few years ago I had occasion to write about this work and, although I cannot now find, nor wholly recollect what I then said, I know that I paid particular attention to the asymmetric pattern of the gazoliers and their relationship to the pictures on the wall, the extension of this complex of forms through the heads of the men on the right and the women on the left to the group below, the projection of the line of the curtain through the skirts of the little girl standing by the old gentleman, his function as a *repoussoir* giving added emphasis to the central highlight, and so on. (I will discuss the dangers of such a mode of criticism later on.)

This limitation of the functions of the artist and of the critic may be traced back to the realist reaction against Neo-Classical and Romantic painting which began more than a hundred years ago and which seems, first, to have limited the subject matter of

165

Courbet and the Impressionists, turning them increasingly against the romantic scene, the anecdote and the classical 'history painting' of the salon artists; and then to have focused the attention of critics more and more upon the formal qualities of painting. The process finds its most uncompromising expression in an art which is completely abstract and in a form of criticism which rejects, first, morality, then the story, and, finally, the image.

'Let us remember,' wrote Maurice Denis, 'that, before we can consider it as a war horse, a nude woman, or any kind of anecdote, a picture is essentially a plane surface upon which colours have been arranged in a certain order.'

This was at the end of the nineteenth century.

In 1913 Clive Bell goes further: 'What we have to remember is that the problem – in a picture it is generally the subject – is of no consequence in itself.'

A generation ago these ideas, distorted and simplified by inaccurate repetition, could, not unfairly, be summarised in the following propositions:

The essence of art is design, the painting differs from the carpet or the crock only in that its patterning is subtler and richer. What matters in visual art is 'significant form' (Bell) and 'plastic harmonies' (Fry). There is, therefore, no essential difference between music, architecture and painting, and the fact that the latter has in the past been so much involved in the business of illustration is irrelevant and regrettable. The critical methods of Diderot are therefore absurd; those of Ruskin are grotesque. The proper study of the art critic is form, not subject matter.

Forty years ago these arguments directed the aesthetic thinking of a great many people; they are important, even today. I want to examine them and to consider to what extent they still command respect, but before doing so it will, I think, be useful to try to answer the question – What is form and what is content?

Is there such a thing as pure form?

If, by 'pure form' we mean to describe a work of art which cannot suggest any kind of content to anyone, then I don't think that there is. There have been and perhaps still are objects which can be sold as works of art – things such as a piece of wallpaper, or, better, a blank sheet untouched by any hand, or, again, a pedestal which supports nothing save air – and these do seem to arrive at a condition of complete purity. Nevertheless, those who exhibit, sell and buy such works seem able to see in them a wealth of meaning.

Our tendency as critics is to emphasise content partly perhaps because it is so much more describable than form, and a critic may do this even when, theoretically, he insists upon the primacy of form.

Herbert Read has pointed out, rightly, that Clive Bell's writings contain a very definite comment on life, an apology for *l'homme moyen sensuel*, a nostalgic regard for the eighteenth century and for the kind of world that the Impressionists painted and enjoyed.

Roger Fry's attitude was never as unreservedly formalist as that of Clive Bell and in fact Fry, at the end of his career, was looking for a synthesis between form and content. He was even more literary in his criticism. I would like to give one example; he is describing the *Bénédicité* of Chardin. This is what he writes:

The mother, as she helps the children, looks up to see whether the younger child is saying her grace in the proper spirit of reverence. The girl has just the puzzled, anxious deprecating gesture of a child who half-fears that she has got into trouble – the older girl looks down at her with the exact air of self-righteous superiority from which all younger children suffer. The very slightness of the theme makes the miracle of its exact notation all the greater and perhaps Rembrandt is the only artist who could have expressed it with greater intensity but even he, perhaps, would have overshot the mark of playful and tender malice which is so characteristic of French feeling.

Like the critics, the painters also seem ill-satisfied with an art so restricted as to exclude literary values. They avoid the overt and plainly comprehensible story but literary suggestions, the pathetic content in the work of Picasso, Matisse, Francis Bacon or Kitaj, are quite easily perceived, and even artists who seem engrossed by pure abstraction are likely to claim a literary and even a didactic purpose.

'The basic tenderness of the large and small form, or mother and child, proclaims a rhythm of composition which is in contrast to the slapping and pushing of tired mother and frustrated child through faults in our way of living and unresolved social conditions.'

Thus Barbara Hepworth with dubious grammar, but impeccable sentiment, explains the message of her art. Her intentions, at all events, are not unlike those of Greuze. The uninstructed spectator might be astonished to learn that she had any.

There has, in fact, been a reaction since the days when significant form was a novelty, but it has not been a complete reaction. It has been accompanied by a certain confusion of thought and inconsistency of action which stems partly, I think, from our situation in the history of art and partly from our terminological vagueness concerning the nature of content.

I hope that I may already have done a little to clarify our thinking by offering a, no doubt, very imprecise definition of content, but perhaps I can take the argument a stage further by stating the case for a revision of what used to be the attitude in the matter of 'pure form'.

Nearly all painting and sculpture is concerned with meanings which lie outside the work; that is to say, with the affairs of life rather than of art itself. It is only within very recent years that some artists have attempted to produce self-contained art: hitherto most works of art have been magical instruments didactic, designed for ostentation, or illustrative. Art is usually concerned with symbols and appearances, and one of the tendencies making for literary art in our time has been the increasing interest of art historians in the work of art as a rebus or enigma holding concealed messages for the initiate. Again, the history of art turns our attention to literary import because it presents us with an academic scale of values which, although ridiculous when considered in its pure form, does contain a measure of what we feel to be the truth. The gigantic figures of art history have not been content with minor themes; the artistic vehicles which have been made to carry the most profoundly moving designs are built also to carry profound literary meaning. Even Chardin or Cézanne, who seem able to contain the grandest emotional power within pots and pans, apples and napkins, seem to show by their excursions into other fields that in some way they have managed to crystallise their sentiments, the sentiments that is to say of heroic art, within these humble properties.

I think that we are also beginning to learn that the kind of geometric criticism which consists in imposing a diagram upon a picture and commenting upon the relationships of forms is at times unsatisfactory and misleading.

For example, consider illustration 10 in terms of pure form. Let us provide it with the kind of geometrical framework (illustration 11) with which some writers on art like to explain the constructions of Poussin or of Cézanne. Thus assisted, you may perceive that it is based upon a series of horizontals – the altar, the steps of the altar, the architecture in the background, the legs of the figure on the right, the alignment of the heads and hands on the left. These horizontals are connected by a series of ascending movements of which the most noticeable is that provided by the nude. This is projected on the right by the carved figure, and on the left by the drapery, and is again repeated by the hem of the monk's robes, the mouldings on the wall and the line of the roof above the window. Against this ascending movement is a regular series of nearly equal intervals which are connected with the verticles of the steps, the altar and the pilasters. The division of the light . . .

At this point I cannot but suppose that some readers will be saying, all this is very fine but what the hell's going on?

You may well ask. This is St Elizabeth of Hungary discarding all her worldly goods to the greater glory of God, and to the infinite satisfaction of Philip Hermogenes Calderon, R.A., and no doubt of the public which was able to witness this interesting transaction at the Academy Exhibition of 1898. It is the kind of picture which the twentieth century most dislikes, and we dislike it, not because we find fault with its geometry, but because we consider it prurient and hypocritical. This, surely, is what strikes the beholder at once – it is 'sexy', and its sex is disguised as piety; no consideration of its formal arrangement will persuade us to admire it.

It was the existence of pictures such as this, pictures which in one way or another pandered to trivial, false and disreputable emotions, that produced a reaction against the 'story' in art at the beginning of this century, although frequently that reaction was rather against bad literature than against literature itself. When we examine a work of art which presents us with vivid and unmistakably sincere emotions (say, Fra Angelico's *Annunciation* in the convent of S. Marco), we may, and in the 1920s would, have expressed our appreciation in terms of formal harmonies – the system of rhyming curves, the disposition of the figure lend themselves to formal analysis. But here again such an analysis would by itself leave far too much of the picture – the delicacy of its genuine and untroubled religious emotion – undiscussed.

And yet this picture may be cited in evidence on the other side of the case. How far is the literary element in Fra Angelico important? How much of it do we *not* perceive as we look at a reproduction?

Very little so it seems to me, and yet what we see in a photograph is but a pale shadow of the original. Indeed, if a Ruskin or a Pater had described this work, might we not have had all, or nearly all the literary message that it can give us, without seeing the picture itself.

I would now like to request your co-operation in an experiment. I want to describe a work of art which you will probably not have seen and from the slight indications that I shall give you, ask you to envisage the picture before seeing it.

It represents Paolo and Francesca. They are seated upon a parapet and behind them is a tremendously poetical landscape, desolate hills and a grey castle; these are seen imprecisely by the fading light that is dying in a broad, still, cloudless Italian sky illuminated by the pale radiance of a crescent moon. Paolo, who has something of the air of the young Raphael, has laid his mandoline aside and is about to embrace Francesca. She still marks the pages of her book with one unconscious hand while she surrenders herself, half reluctantly, to his melancholy ardour. Of all the romantic details of this intensely romantic scene, the most perfectly in period is Francesca herself; she belongs not to Dante but to the year 1830 and it is *her* ringlets, *her* shoulders, *her* pensive oval face which take us most decidedly away from any world of reality to that of poetic fiction. She is a victim, not of incestuous passion, but of Scott, Byron, Schnorr von Carolsfeld and Moore – her sweetness and sensuality could have been conceived only by the nineteenth century. One detail adds tension, terror even, to an otherwise idyllic scene, four fingers, emerging from the left-hand side of the picture, grasp the balustrade; Lanciotto Malatesta is there.

Now when we look at the picture itself (illustration 12), which is by William Dyce, you will, I hope, have had a fair idea of what sort of literary conception to expect. What you did not perhaps expect, and I could not precisely have described, is the roughly pyramidal shape of the central element in the composition. To give an exact description in words of the way in which this pyramid is broken by a re-entrant form would be tedious, nor is it altogether easy to make a verbal comparison of the structure of this version by Dyce and related works by Ingres and by Flaxman (although if you had known these works, and I had mentioned them, you would from the memory of their form have had a much more precise notion of the compositional structure of the picture). The fingers of

Malatesta, which loom so large in the literary programme, are barely noticeable in the picture itself.* We do not see them until we have studied the painting with a good deal of attention. What I am suggesting is that the content, in some cases at all events, is divisible from the form, which is, as it were, a residual element. We may see this again when we are confronted by a work of art the content of which is unknown to us; as, for instance, in the art of Pre-Columbian America, where the plastic harmonies are very apparent, but in which, lacking the archaeological knowledge necessary to a proper understanding of the content, only the residue remains.

Now this residual quality, this pure form, is something which is not confined to pictorial art. If we look at a picture and then at its frame, the emotions that lead us to say that this is a very bad picture but that is a very handsome frame are not dissimilar, and the same kind of value judgment will continue to operate when we pass from the frame to the wallpaper, from the wallpaper to the proportions of the room, and even when we look out of the window to the landscape. The excitement provided by harmonies of colour and form is, in fact, a very wide-spread emotion, and one which does not appear to be confined to our species. It can, by itself and without content, provide a sufficiently important element for the creation of works of art.

It is, I think, possible to find works of art which succeed as literature while remaining completely uninteresting as form. This is the case with much caricature: David Low frequently arrived at the most brilliant literary inventions, inventions which were fully expressed in graphic form and had in their pungent economy that artistic quality which one associates with brilliant oratory or epigrammatic verse; as plastic harmonies they hardly exist. Nevertheless, they have obviously to be connected with form of a kind.

Now, in considering such works one is forced to make the kind of distinction which arises in literature between apparent and associative meaning. In considering Goya's 'black' picture of *Saturn Eating his Children* (illustration 13) one needs no programme. One may be helped to a fuller understanding of his meaning by a knowledge of the legend of Saturn, but the picture is enough; no additional information is required. It is not often,

*Originally, Dyce included the entire person of Malatesta. The device, which appears so deliberate and so effective, was in fact an afterthought.

however, that a picture can speak with so little aid from without. Consider the painter Charles Le Brun's *Têtes d'expression* (illustrations 14 and 15) designed to serve as a vocabulary of the emotions for students. In the simpler examples we need no captions, but when the artist deals with more complex sentiments it is hard not to sympathise with that extremely impolite student who declared that he has confused fury with magnanimity, stupidity with heroism, imbecile vexation with serious modesty and injured innocence with constipation. Explicit content, in fact, soon comes to its limits; the painter needs to work within the frame of a known story or to supply an explanatory text.

Consider illustration 16, a caricature of the last century. To someone raised in another culture the political implications might be completely invisible. Imagine a Chinaman looking at it and being told that this was a picture of the Empress of the French. He might still completely misunderstand the artist's meaning: seeing her represented as a crane, the symbol of longevity, he might well suppose some flattering pun – the graphic translation of the phrase 'Long Live Her Majesty'. In fact, however, as we know, the pun is of another kind; La Grue here undoubtedly means The Prostitute. Explicit content, in fact, soon comes to its limits. The painter needs to work within the frame of a known story or to supply an explanatory text.

And yet painting seems to convey its most subtle and powerful literary emotions when it retreats from the explicit story, and even from the symbol: a description of rocks and trees, water and grass and shrubs, when it comes from the hand of Claude Lorraine may be as interesting, as superbly 'literary' as all the naughtiness of Boucher or the *Terribiltà* of Michelangelo. Painting, which is but a shallow vessel for narrative or comment, may be infinitely profound when it is used to contain a mood.

Literary painting, then, would seem to be of three kinds: the manifest or explicit kind that will immediately convey information – as in a picture of a man running or a tree falling; the referential or implicit kind, in which the picture may be a sort of enigma, the meaning of which may be apprehended by those who know its iconographic language, and, finally, the pathetic kind in which the subject may be so charged with emotion that a feeling different to but hardly separable from pure formal emotions is so conveyed that it has a distinctly literary flavour.

From this discursive meditation – I will not attempt to dignify it with the name of argument – it may perhaps be possible to disengage three propositions:

1. That the dislike that we most of us feel for literature in painting is connected primarily with what I have called explicit content – the manifest and unequivocal story; and, even here, the objection is strong only where the story is of an unpalatable kind, so that the argument against 'literature' in art tends to resolve itself into the tautological statement that bad literature is bad literature.
2. That the critical method based entirely upon a consideration of 'pure form' has this advantage: that it is of universal application in that all visual works of art must obviously have form; but, equally obviously, it disregards a great deal of the information that the artist supplies.
3. That the limitations and distortions that must arise when we adopt a purely formal method of criticism would be even more serious in a purely literary method.

If I now explain that everything that I have said is but a clearing of the ground to make way for my chief argument I fear that I may damp your spirits. Things, however, are better than they may seem: that which remains may be quite briefly expressed, for although I have felt it necessary to re-examine a territory that has already been explored by abler adventurers than I, I want to conclude by pointing out that the primacy and universality of form is not a matter that need bother the critic. His main job, as I see it, is to write about works of art in a way that will enable others to share his affections. To this end, he has three main duties: to be sincere, to be readable and to be intelligible. The fact that his criticism may be based upon a theory which can be demolished will not prevent him from being instructive and delightful.

Theories about form and content are therefore important only in so far as they assist or hamper the critic in the expression of genuine emotions. Considered in this light I think that the distrust of literature in art has not been happy in its effects. As we have already seen, the theorists themselves have not been able to resist the temptation of returning to purely literary methods of approach. In this inconsistency I think that they showed wisdom; formal relationships are the most intractable materials for critical discussion. We can all hope to be interesting when we discuss the relationships of human beings; with art we may extend that interest to a great part of the visible world, but the desire of the ellipse for the parallelogram, of the rhomboid for the cube, however passionately they may be apprehended, cannot easily be transmitted save by the painter himself.

But the nature of much recent painting obliges the critic to attempt this most difficult literary feat, and he is hardly to be blamed if his prose becomes a little dull; nor should we be too censorious if, faced by so unrewarding a situation, the critic takes refuge in pompous and obscure verbiage. Nevertheless, this is one of the characteristics of much modern art criticism.

On the other hand, some of the most readable criticism of our time is entirely concerned with values which can hardly be classed as aesthetic: questions of symbolism, of attribution, of the place of particular works of art in the history of ideas, in which the absolute value of the works as means to aesthetic enjoyment is not discussed. And, in the same way, some of the most valuable criticism that has been handed down to us makes aesthetic assumptions which we cannot entertain. Works of these kinds seem not only more readable and more comprehensible than are most appreciations of formal harmony but, for me, at all events, more useful in giving a notion of the intrinsic value of the work of art. I find it hard to explain why it is that a critic who turns his back upon questions of form should in the end enable me to look at form with greater intensity; I would only observe that we may here have something analogous to the creative process itself where the disregard of taste, or rules, of all that we usually think of as aesthetic values, seems at times to engender just those qualities that cannot often be attained by conscious pursuit.

Art and the Elite

I

The words elite and elitist have become so familiar and have been so ill-used during the past twenty years that, at times, I have been tempted to forbid their use in student essays. I desisted because I could not see how the essayists would manage without them. But it seems worth trying to see what, if anything, these words mean, particularly when they are used in connection with the visual arts.

It is, of course, true that my students and I use the word incorrectly. An elite must surely be a chosen body. Congress, the police, the final heat of the Miss World contest, and the Bolshevik Party are elites, whereas an aristocracy or a plutocracy – unless one believes the rich and the nobility to be chosen by God – are not. Nevertheless, when we use the word elite in connection with the visual arts it is certainly related to, though not synonymous with, class. An elite is usually a group within a relatively prosperous class. The patrons of the Renaissance were, presumably, at the apex of the social system; on the other hand, the patrons of the Impressionists belonged to a comparatively humble section of the middle classes. But it will be found that an aesthetic elite does always enjoy certain advantages of wealth and leisure and education.

What is elitist art? If we mean art produced by members of an elite, then we can only note that, in recent times, most of the painters and sculptors whose names we know came from some part of the middle classes, a very few from the working class, and hardly any from the aristocracy. Turning to more remote times and cultures, I must confess that I know too little to discuss the social history of primitive art. It seems that the artist lacked status in the Hellenic world and in Europe before the Renaissance. I believe that the *hetairae* of Athens painted vases; both in China and the West, ladies of good family were taught by drawing masters and so were some young gentlemen; landscape was a part of the training of the cavalry officer. None of which helps us very much. But often, in the great body of anonymous art, we do not know what the social position of the artist may have been. There is insufficient evidence to allow us to make generalisations. Art that is produced by members of an elite is not distinguishable from art that is made by the masses, so that the term can hardly be used to any purpose.

Take an obvious example: the jewellery of Fabergé. This was surely elitist art; it was made to please the Russian aristocracy, it was costly by its very nature, it was designed to please a fastidious taste; but beyond knowing that the men who made it were skilful we cannot (or at least I cannot) know to what class they belonged. All that they had to do was to satisfy the client. A whore with an elitist clientele is in much the same position, but this does not mean that she enjoys the privileges or shares the ideas of those whom she serves.

It is better to start with the work of art itself. Here in many cases we can be quite sure that a work of art has been made for a specifically elitist market. There is, for instance, a painting by Botticelli in the Uffizi the subject of which is, and always was, incomprehensible to the great majority of spectators. Botticelli has painted a group of people, some clothed, others naked, engaged in some violent and totally mysterious action. If, however, we 'know our Lucian' we shall at once realise that the painter is trying to reconstruct a lost masterpiece – *The Calumny* – by Apelles. No doubt the intellectual elite of Florence understood and enjoyed it, all the more so because it flattered their erudition. It is this which makes a work of art elitist, that it is destined for the elite and perhaps for no one else.

Note that Botticelli was not simply a painter of elitist pictures, he painted much that was readily comprehensible to the man in the street. Note also that, despite his learned subject matter, we cannot be certain that the painter himself perfectly understood his own programme. It would not have been difficult for a patron to have given him instructions. Thus we find that the elitist work of art is not necessarily the work of an elitist artist – and vice versa. Decidedly it is better to start with the art rather than the artist.

II

It was a very hot morning, hot even for Greece in August. I stood in one of the rare and precious shadows beneath the great Lion Gate of Mycenae, surely one of the most impressive as it is also one of the oldest of European monuments. Far below me, shadeless and shuddering in the heat, was the car park. Vast green buses in ever-increasing numbers discharged loads of tourists who painfully ascended the stony road towards the citadel. The crowd wilted, waited, and straggled; mentally I divided it into three groups. There were a few who seemed to be consumed by the sheer effort of walking; they glanced up at the gate without interest and glanced down again at their poor feet; some, much to my astonishment, did not even do that. Mycenae was for them part of the package: it had to be done and so they did it; but their minds, as I surmised, were set upon the possibility of ice creams and a dip into the sea at Nauplion.

These were a minority; the majority – to which I myself belonged – was at least able to stare, to admire, and, perhaps, to wonder. The French archaeologists of the last century who found these splendid beasts before the site was fully excavated concluded that these were the leopards rampant of some Frankish invader. We knew that they were wrong, we knew that the carvings were immensely old, immensely vigorous, immensely impressive; and that was about all that we did know.

But there was a third group, another minority. They had done their homework, read their guidebooks properly, and could talk with easy authority about Clytemnestra, Agamemnon, Schliemann, and other such heroes of antiquity. This was the elite. I admired and respected them, they were getting more out of Mycenae than I was. I wished that I too could parade a little learning. One of the emotions that the elite inspires is envy.

The Lion Gate is now elitist art; but was it elitist art when it was all brand new? It seems unlikely, for surely no one puts up a large piece of sculpture in a public place just for the private giggle of an in-group. But it is, all the same, possible. Let us turn to an example where we know rather more.

Consider, then, Gainsborough's portraits and Hogarth's *Mar-riage à la Mode*. Gainsborough, like Fabergé, was working for an upper-class elite and giving it, surely, exactly what it wanted. His pictures are intended for the drawing room and in that situation they are perfectly at home. No one, not even Vandyck, has made the British upper classes look so elegant. Contemplate his great ladies. How charming, how intelligent, and how distinguished they are. Sitters are notoriously tiresome, but could the most difficult of patrons ever have complained that Gainsborough failed to do them justice? Probably they did; but he remains the greatest of all great flatterers.

Hogarth, on the other hand, painting with Dutch coarseness and robust British honesty, seems to voice the indignant feelings of an honest bourgeois disgusted by the foppish and corrupt society of his social superiors. He worked not for an elite but for the multitude, his pictures were disseminated by engravers to every public house in the three kingdoms. He is the type of the demotic artist.

Now I think that these statements were historically true. Politically the two artists are opposed to each other. But in the course of time the producer/consumer relationship has changed: both Gainsborough's portraits and Hogarth's genre scenes can now be reproduced and widely disseminated, and I think that it will be found that both are acceptable to a fairly wide public. But if the public were to choose between the two it would choose Gainsborough, for Gainsborough has now become more demotic than Hogarth. After all, Gainsborough's fine ladies are thoroughly agreeable and accessible objects. Their class does not matter to us, and who could be moved to revolutionary indignation by the spectacle of a pretty girl in a becoming dress standing before a stormy sky and rendered with the most brilliant and engaging brushwork imaginable? Nor is there anything here to puzzle us, nothing that demands a high degree of education, nothing that will appeal only to the elite.

One cannot say the same of Hogarth, for here the social situation on which the painter's satire depends has changed. To appreciate it properly we need to sympathise with the artist's point of view, to climb back into the past, to realise, for instance, that the industrious apprentice, who seems to us a rather priggish character, represented, in his time, an inspiring social ideal. Nor is this all. Even when Hogarth painted his *Marriage à la Mode* series, there were details which some of his audience must have found a little difficult. No doubt in *The Countess' Levée* they would have been quicker than we are to notice the reference to the woman taken in adultery painted in the Dutch manner on a screen, but would they have appreciated the reference to Correggio's *Io* on the wall behind the countess? Or the double pleasantry in the foreground where a little black servant giggles as he unpacks a statuette of Actaeon antlered and thus symbolising cuckoldry. Nor is this all. Hogarth loves to guy the prevailing mode, to make fun of the *cognoscenti*, to ridicule the rococo; but to appreciate his ironies we require historical knowledge. In short, Hogarth is now, to some extent, the property of the elite.

It would seem then that there are two kinds of elitist art: that which, like Botticelli's *Calumny*, is deliberately obscured from vulgar minds and that which, like the gate at Mycenae, has, fortuitously, become incomprehensible to the majority. But in all the examples that I have cited there were images, images recognisable to a fairly wide social group; there was also a quality of design and of colour which, arguably, is understood by all.

It has to be admitted that, as tokens of social exclusiveness, the visual arts are at a grave disadvantage as compared with literature. It is very hard to make painting and sculpture utterly meaningless to the uneducated. The social devices of literature, the recondite allusions, the foreign phrases, and the artistic baby talk which give such a reputable cachet to the writers of our century are not easily reproduced by artists who speak the demotic language of form and colour.

These considerations present us with an interesting question. I have said that I envied the elite at Mycenae, that it had been granted a richer and more varied experience than the rest of us. But perhaps Demos has a simpler and a more purely aesthetic experience than the *cognoscenti*. For the elite the apprehension of a work of art is not a sensual but a cultural experience; it is confused with and perhaps distorted by all sorts of extrinsic emotions, historical speculations (which could after all be wrong), sentimental associations, and, of course, by the satisfaction of being able to identify and to talk knowledgeably about the work of art.

This, it seems, is the possibility that Roger Fry had in mind when, in discussing the hubbub caused by the First Post-Impressionist Exhibition, he refers to the 'vested emotional interests':

I tried in vain to explain what appeared to me so clear, that the modern movement was essentially a return to the ideas of formal design which had been almost lost sight of in the fervid pursuit of naturalistic representation. I found that the cultured public which had welcomed my expositions of the works of the Italian Renaissance now regarded me as either incredibly flippant or, for the more charitable explanation was usually adopted, slightly insane. In fact, I found among the cultured who had hitherto been my most eager listeners the most inveterate and exasperated enemies of the new movement. The accusation of anarchism was constantly made. From an aesthetic point of view this was of course, the exact opposite of the truth, and I was for long puzzled to find the explanation of so paradoxical an opinion and so violent an enmity. I now see that my crime had been to strike at the vested emotional interests. These people felt instinctively that their special culture was one of their social assets. That to be able to speak glibly of T'ang and Ming, of Amico di Sandro and Baldovinetti, gave them a social standing and a distinctive cachet. This showed me that we had all along been under a mutual misunderstanding, i.e. that we had admired the Italian Primitives for quite different reasons. It was felt that one could only appreciate Amico di Sandro when one had acquired a certain considerable mass of erudition and given a great deal of time and attention, but to admire Matisse required only a certain sensibility. One could feel fairly sure that one's maid could not rival one in the former case, but might by a mere haphazard gift of Providence surpass one in the second.

Roger Fry is surely right when he suggests that the elitist game is played rather with the cultural framework around the picture than with the picture itself. The initial response to Matisse – a response based upon certain cultural assumptions concerning art – does seem to be contradicted by the natural taste of Demos, that kind of natural taste which is made evident in the work of very simple people and of children. So that one might hope, as I think Roger Fry hoped, that Matisse would strike a responsive note in the hearts of people who had, somewhere within them, the kind of sensibility which is evident in his painting. Nevertheless, I find it difficult to believe in the enlightened housemaid. I have no doubt that both the duchess and the housemaid were shocked by

Matisse: what he produced was so very different from that which they expected to find in a picture. But as a matter of historical fact it was the duchess, not the housemaid, who was the first to recover from the shock, or perhaps to discover that she enjoyed being shocked. An innovation is usually more easily accepted by educated people, partly because, having a wider experience of art, they are not so surprised by innovations for which there will usually be some historical precedent, and partly because to appreciate that which it is difficult to like marks one as a member of the elite. It is not until the duchess has begun to express an admiration for Matisse that the housemaid will begin to find him socially acceptable and therefore admirable. When she does so, the work of art is vulgarised (I do not use this word in a pejorative sense) – it ceases to be elitist and becomes demotic. This, of course, is the reverse of that process which seems to have occurred in the case of the Mycenaean Gate; it resembles the kind of evolution which has made Gainsborough accessible to the masses, but it involves a more drastic change. Given the opportunity to see his work, no one was ever likely to find Gainsborough bewildering or objectionable; but this is not true of Matisse or of Renoir. For *them* to become demotic it is necessary that what I have too loosely described as the 'demotic language of form and colour' should become widely comprehensible.

A new form of art confronts us with a new pictorial language. It took time for the public at large to understand the Impressionists' use of colour. Roger Fry once pointed out that, in a Raphael drawing, areas that were in shadow would be indicated by the use of parallel lines which might be drawn straight across a face. These, of course, do not exist in nature, but we have no difficulty in reading them as shading. He prophesied, and rightly, that we should become equally familiar with the paint symbols of Cézanne and Van Gogh.

If we now pause and look back, what ground have we covered? We have found that if we are going to talk usefully about art and the elite it is the consumer and the goods rather than the producer who must provide our point of departure. Elitist art is simply that kind of art which is in some way suitable for use by an elite. Art can achieve this condition fortuitously as the result of an historical accident; but art can also be made incomprehensible to the masses by means of a more or less deliberate action either by patrons or by the artists themselves. In as much as people who are not members of an elite wish to share the socially reputable tastes of their 'betters', there is likely to be a continual tendency for art to become vulgarised and thus to lose its elitist character.

Incomprehensibility is therefore a prime social asset in a work of art; the social weakness of art has hitherto been either that it dealt in images or that it had formal qualities which could, immediately or eventually, be understood by everyone. A completely elitist art form would be one that contained neither imagery nor any kind of formal value; this, as I hope to show, seems now to have been achieved.

III

Demotic art is conservative. In the Western world, since the Renaissance, traditionalist sentiment has been modified by the social imitation to which we have already referred. Nevertheless, I believe that there has been a constant affection for the imitative techniques developed in Europe in the Renaissance and in the seventeenth century. The idea that painting and sculpture should provide a counterfeit of nature is still very strong and, if one may judge by the writings of Pliny, very ancient. Thus, if we look at the shops where they sell pious images, we shall find that imitations of Raphael or Carlo Dolci still command a market while, in the department store, Constable and the Dutch compete with pastiches or reproductions of the Impressionists. It is true that, during the past seventy years, we have witnessed an increasing demand for nonrepresentational art so that, in a sense, the abstract picture has become demotic. Big business, government, the Church, all the organisations that may, roughly speaking, be called the Establishment, commission large abstract paintings and sculptures; again, in the homes of the middle class, we are very likely to find an abstract over the mantelpiece. Nor, I think, does abstraction have any power to shock anyone of any class; as decoration it seems perfectly acceptable. What I rather doubt is whether it is received with positive enthusiasm by the masses.

In 1891 Mr Luke Fildes, as he then was, painted a picture called

The Doctor. It is a picture of a room in a poor home, an oil lamp reveals the doctor, an impressive figure, studying the countenance of a sick child. The child is sleeping, perhaps dying. It is clear from the physician's intensely thoughtful expression that we are at a crisis. All the details of the room (they are most carefully painted) lead us to suppose that he has been called in to deal with an unexpected emergency. In the background the anxious figures of the parents can just be perceived for they are faintly illuminated by the pale and uncertain light of dawn. The painter has appealed to our noblest emotions and relies upon a simple and uncomplicated response; there is nothing sinister, nothing disquieting about the picture. It is taken for granted that we shall feel rightly and simply. The picture was an enormous popular success.

It is recorded that when Sir Luke Fildes took a cab to his home in St Johns Wood, the cabby said to him:

'Isn't this where Sir Luke Fildes lives?'
'I happen to be Sir Luke Fildes,' replied the painter.
'It was you who painted *The Doctor*? Oh, Sir, I don't think I want to charge you for driving you.'

Mr Rothko and Mr Pasmore have achieved an international fame unknown to Sir Luke. In the eyes of the elite they are more valued than he ever was. But if they believe that they can get a free taxi ride as he did they will find that they are very much mistaken.

Abstract paintings lack by their very nature that quality of mimetic skill or common humanity which made Luke Fildes a favourite of Demos; but, for the same reason, abstract art is unlikely to be offensive or emotionally disturbing, while it may well have attractive qualities of colour and design. Thus, although it may hardly become entirely demotic, it need not remain entirely the property of the elite.

Socially speaking, no work of art can be entirely satisfactory which offers opportunities for vulgar admiration. If this danger is to be averted it is best that the public at large should be given nothing to admire. The art must lie not in the artefact but in the celebration of an artistic rite in which the artefact plays a completely subordinate role, it being taken from the rubbish bin or any other receptacle for the unconsidered trifles of our civilisation;

or, again, the object may be destroyed or simply left to the imagination. It really does not much matter. What does matter is that the entire operation should be incomprehensible and economically futile in order that it may remain socially inviolable. In fact, we have here something much more like an elitist religion than 'art' in the usual acceptance of the term.

Some years ago Piero Manzoni had the excellent idea of selling his own breath; the breath was sealed into balloons and sold for 60,000 lire per balloon. A public gallery purchased one of these balloons only to find, as the years went by, that there was a gradual wastage; the divine afflatus had escaped, and the museum was now left with a shrivelled bladder. The artist could not refill it for he, poor fellow, had ceased to breathe at all. But neither would the gallery supply the missing breath from the lungs of an attendant, nor even a director, for this would have been a kind of fraud. When one considers that the original distended balloon might easily have been inflated by one of Manzoni's friends (or enemies) and that no one could possibly know whose breath was inside the balloon, and that it would make no earthly difference to anyone whether there had or had not been a substitution, the essentially religious nature of the entire transaction becomes apparent.

Perhaps 'religious' is the wrong word – 'fiducial' might be more accurate, for it is the consumer's faith which determines the value of the art; very likely the artist will inspire more trust if he himself believes in what he is doing. But his sincerity or lack of sincerity need not affect a valuation which is determined simply by the condition of the market.

How such a state of confidence is obtained I do not know; clearly it is nothing to do with the artefact – or very little. For if I were to try to make a living by blowing up balloons it is clear that I should soon be out of business, even though my breath is every bit as pneumatic as that of the late Mr Manzoni. In many cases there is no artefact, only faith; but even where there is an exhibitable and tangible object the elitist character of the 'work' requires that it should, in itself, be of negligible interest; otherwise the product might be admired by the wrong people.

In a society which respects money above all things, the mere fact that an apparently absurd operation can be richly rewarded makes it less absurd, so that the artefact, if there is one, may gain the kind of respect that we feel for currency. It is therefore conceivable that even this form of art may ultimately become demotic. Meanwhile, I, personally, shall continue to prefer *The Doctor*.

Autolycus: A Demotic Art

Sculpture is, or at least was, the most conservative of the fine arts. It came to us from the Hellenic world and it was dominated by a few Italian giants. Unlike painting it could be reproduced, and reproductions of approved examples could be found in any art school in the western world. To a large extent, sculptors confined themselves to the study of the human figure. Those disruptive and stimulating intrusions which brought such variety and novelty to the tradition of Michelangelo were felt to a much lesser extent in three-dimensional art and although Giambologna, Bernini, Houdon, Canova and a few others did refresh the mainstream of the European tradition, they brought changes far less drastic than those which affected the art of painting when they came from Venice, Flanders, Holland, England, the Impressionists and the followers of Cézanne.

In the nineteenth century, Europeans began to import unconsidered trifles from the coasts of Africa, from Polynesia and from Latin America. Unconsidered trifles purchased or stolen from the natives by traders, missionaries, soldiers, sailors, ethnologists, etc., were at first considered mere curiosities: the ugly idols of the ignorant heathen. It was the painters and sculptors who perceived that they had qualities that might be admired and imitated. Then indeed the results were remarkable. It was the painters who first sat up and took notice; it was the Fauves who first began to study exotic sculpture. And it was not until the 1920s that Henry Moore, a student at South Kensington reared in the schools of Italy (for which he never lost his affection), looked at a book by Roger Fry, saw photographs of Mayan sculpture and changed his own art and that of the world.

When Commodore Perry steamed into the harbour of Yedo he was followed by European importers who no doubt anticipated that Japan, now that she had opened her doors, would sell us valuable porcelain and lacquered furniture much as China had done – and so she did. And most of it is, by present-day standards, pretty dull. Then someone noticed certain rude, popular prints, a very demotic form of art, which it is said were used as packing material for the more obviously costly wares of the Orient. These fell into the hands of Parisian artists and art lovers. They saw a form of art that they could understand and which was highly relevant to what the *avant garde* was doing. Within a quarter of a century the Japanese print had revolutionised the art of Europe.

At about the same time, another discovery was being made: it was a form of sculpture. Characteristically, as one may say, it was not a revolutionary discovery and one of the things which made it so immediately popular was that it was a new manifestation of the Hellenic tradition; aesthetically, then, it was not a novelty, or, at least, hardly a novelty. The objects which were now discovered were small, cheap statuettes made of clay; some had been put into graves, others broken and thrown upon rubbish heaps. Either way, they had been buried for about two thousand years. In the nineteenth century they were dug up by those snappers up of unconsidered trifles, the archaeologists; the archaeologists were followed by Autolycus, the tombarollo or grave snatcher.

In this process the archaeologist can be of enormous value. Unlike the grave snatcher he is not looking for a market, unlike the aesthete he is not looking for beauty; he is looking for truth, a neutral quality. He is interested in almost any relic of the past. He throws nothing away.

An example may be helpful. Visitors to the National Gallery will have noticed a painting by Margaritone, a predecessor of Giotto. It shows us the Virgin enthroned and, on either side of her, scenes from the lives of the saints. It is a bold, decorative schematic picture, not a masterpiece but sufficiently lively to catch one's attention and no one today would be likely to question its aesthetic value. In 1857 when this picture was bought for the National Gallery in London no one, so far as I know, doubted that it had no aesthetic value whatsoever. Lord Normanby, in his official report observed, 'The unsightly specimens of Margaritone and the earliest Tuscan painters were selected solely for their historical importance.'

Sir Charles Eastlake, director of the gallery and one who in such matters was particularly enlightened, agreed. 'Its chief use will be to show the barbarous state into which art had sunk even in Italy previously to its revival.'

In fact, the Margaritone was purchased simply for historical and educational reasons.

This process of discovery and evaluation can only occur when there are people who regard art as a subject for dispassionate enquiry and are not committed, as so many art historians are, to the investigation only of that which they believe to be good.

It is thanks to the archaeologist, the ethnographer, the anthropologist that during the past one hundred years the curious idols of the Negro, the Polynesian, the oddities of Pre-Columbian America and primitive man have become accessible, and thanks to the elitist character of our culture that we have learnt to admire them. An enormous number of things which, emphatically, were not art, have become art because society for one reason or another could accept them as art.

I want to look here at one example, a particular genre of sculpture which is interesting because it has been through the entire lifecycle of an artefact. It began as one of the lowest forms of art, it rose to great heights and then, for a variety of reasons – some of them very instructive – it dwindled again to a secondary position.

Its original condition could hardly have been more humble, for it began, virtually, as mud.

When men first began to make images, they perceived that one of the most expressive media lay beneath their feet. Presently they discovered that some mud was better than other mud, but that all alike suffered from the weather; the sun cracked the clay image, the rain completed its ruin – only the peculiar habit of working in caves preserved the first clay models of primitive man intact. Later on, after I don't know how many thousand years, men learned that a small object, if left in the fire, would harden sufficiently to become weatherproof. From the dawn of history we find models of men, gods and animals made of terracotta; and from about the sixth century B.C. we find the model makers using a mould, itself probably of clay. Thereafter, any number of copies could be printed off from one original. The sculptor working in other media – marble, bronze, stone or even wax – would probably make his first essay in clay. It is eminently the designing material of sculpture and for this purpose it is wonderfully suitable: it has the immediately responsive quality of pencil and paper, it takes the slightest movement of the hand, a correction is effected in an instant – no medium is more expressive, more intimate in its effects. Moreover, as the water in it evaporates, it passes from the condition of butter to that of cheese, from cheese to that of chalk and, passing through the furnace, to that of stone, so that it may be worked in its successive stages with the finger, the stylus, the knife and the file. It will take colours and all the varied textures of glaze.

Every now and then someone has had the wit to show us how superb a medium it is: the Chinese of the earlier dynasties, the temple sculptors of Bengal, the Etruscans, the della Robbia family, the portraitists of the seventeenth and eighteenth centuries (so much more expressive in clay than in marble), and that neglected master Dalou. But for all its beauties and possibilities, and despite the fact that it can be made to outlast the centuries, it has been very much neglected. Why? Because it is plebeian. How true this is we can see by mentioning its grand relation: porcelain. A porcelain figure is, almost by definition, a luxury article; an earthenware figure is not.

Sculpture is a public and an official art, sculpture celebrates the achievements of gods, heroes, generals and members of parliament, and when a committee meets to commission a monument, is there not always a member who says: 'Now gentlemen we are subscribing a large sum of money, I may say a very large sum of money, involving not less than a halfpenny on the rates, and we want the best that money can buy'? We know very well what the committee member means. He has his decent commercial pride, he wants no cheap or pitiful doings, and if you were to suggest that the job might be done in terracotta, he would explode. 'An earthenware statue, my dear sir. We should be a laughing stock, mark my words. Why, you might as well suggest that we buy a cart load of bricks.' And so the lively sensitive image of clay is expensively translated into cold comfortless Carrara.

The ancient Greeks are a case in point. Let us face it, they were snobs. They didn't think much of their sculptors, even when they worked in marble. But as for the makers of terracotta figurines – they were but dolly makers, contemptible creatures.

It must be admitted that this artisan was probably an unimpressive figure. He dealt in moulds and very likely they and the original patrix were made by someone else. A family might set up in the business with an oven and a dozen or so moulds. A child could learn to press the clay into the matrix and then gently release it when it had dried a little, and he could turn out six dozen gods or goddesses in a day. I dare say children did. Mama could lute the limbs together with liquid clay if the pieces were ambitiously complex, papa could tend the kiln and another child could paint the figures when complete. A little artistic initiative would be displayed in making each figure, while it was still moist, vary slightly in attitude from the others, and this was done. There were, it should be said, considerable variations in quality (and no doubt in price). The gilded figure of a hermaphrodite in the Ashmolean certainly looks as though it were intended for a wealthy and discerning purchaser, and some pieces were considered of sufficient importance to be signed. Still, the original model was probably made by one of the big-time operators, the men who worked in marble.

These little figures, seldom more than 9" high, were made for *ex votes*, or grave offerings, or as dolls, all round the eastern shores of the Mediterranean: east as far as the Crimea and westwards to Gaul. Then, about the beginning of the Christian era, the trade died out and the little gods were forgotten. In 1873 there was a big find at Tanagra which has given its name to the entire genre and almost at once they were acclaimed as being, if not the finest, at least the most elegant, the most charming works of Hellenic civilisation. Their success was immediate and enormous. Today, when their reputation has sunk, if not quite to the original level, still low, that great outburst of enthusiasm may call for an effort of historical sympathy.

So far as England was concerned, the finds at Tanagra could not have been better timed. In the middle of the century, our painters had turned to realism, as had the French; but it was a very earnest and moralising kind of realism involving, amongst other things, the rejection of the pagan world and of that Italian art which was thought to be a revival of paganism. When the Pre-Raphaelites escaped from the reality of their own age (which they did rather often), it was never to classical antiquity that they turned. For the ancients, it was held, celebrated not the soul but the body, a circumstance which worried Ruskin a good deal; and I am sure that it was with a full consciousness of the libidinous, the naughty side of antiquity, that Swinburne reproached his century in 'Dolores':

> We shift and bedeck and bedrape us,
> Thou art noble and nude and antique;
> Libitina, thy mother, Priapus,
> Thy father, a Tuscan and Greek.

Most happily, Libitina has been confused with Venus, the nude *par excellence*, and at the same time connected with grief (which kept Algernon happy); as for Priapus, or Icthyphallus, he was, as Lemprière remarks, the patron of licentiousness with special responsibility for the male genitals. Altogether Swinburne was, as they say, 'going it', for this was written in 1864 when our ancestors were, both literally and figuratively, very much bedraped and bedecked. The painters, in particular, were dreadfully shy. Even Swinburne's friend Dante Gabriel Rossetti, whom no one will accuse of insensibility to feminine charms, never, or very seldom, attempted to paint a naked figure of either sex. That multitude of stunners – Lizzies, Fannies, Janeys, etc. – are not merely clothed, they are muffled in their draperies. It has been said that Rossetti's paintings of the fifties show 'a sense of luxurious enjoyment in woman's beauty'. So they do; but enjoyment starts at the top knot and ends at the collar bone. It is the face, the eloquent messenger of the soul, which speaks to us or, as sometimes happens, gazes into space with an air of quite understandable tedium. That which is true of Rossetti is even more true of Holman Hunt and Ford Madox Brown. As for Millais, he did once embark upon what Du Maurier calls the 'altogether': in 1870 he painted a picture of a knight in armour liberating a young woman whom some inconsiderate person had tied naked to a tree. There was an awful fuss about it and he never tried anything of the kind again.

But Swinburne's poem is dedicated to a Pre-Raphaelite of the second generation, Edward Burne-Jones. And Jones, who was much more interested in Italian painting before Raphael than any of those who can properly speaking be described as Pre-Raphaelites, looked with interest at Botticelli and Mantegna and at that Mediterranean world which first flowered in Attica. Burne-Jones, perhaps because he had practically no academic training, considered the human body with enthusiasm. In the 1860s, we find him copying Michelangelo, Marc Antonio Raimondi and Roman relief studies – of which his master Rossetti would never have been guilty – and, thereafter, the human body – a rather mannered, elongated, epicene human body – becomes the centrepiece of his pictorial repertoire.

Burne-Jones's progression towards a more directly sensual and Italianate form of art was, no doubt, the result of his own personal development, but he moved in harmony and in company with a number of other British painters. In the 1860s, young Mr Poynter came to London enthusiastic for the classicism of Paris; Mr Leighton was turning from his austere German masters towards a more strictly academic form; Mr Alma-Tadema, having specialised in the rather cheerless home life of the Merovingians, was beginning a profitable commerce with Greece and Rome; Mr Joseph Albert Moore, having been a follower of the Pre-Raphaelites and a friend of Whistler, had begun his grand attempt to synthetise the glory that was Greece with the elegance that was Japan. The classicising movement of the seventies and eighties was under way.

This movement – or perhaps it would be more accurate to call it this tendency – cannot be regarded as a major event in art history, but it does mark an interesting change in national sentiment, and I believe that it owes a great deal to the artisans of Boetia. Every generation tries to reconstruct classical antiquity, in accordance partly with the known facts and partly with its own social ideals. During the first half of the nineteenth century the known facts were becoming increasingly numerous, but they were not altogether of a kind to encourage the British artists of that time. Lord Elgin had brought fifth-century sculpture to London – a rather shocking experience for those who had supposed that Graeco-Roman copies were the only true originals – and later discoveries made us acquainted with the severe school and the mysterious austerities of the sixth century. Such importations were highly interesting but, at the same time, slightly discouraging. The great masterpieces of Greek sculpture have a calm perfection, a sublimity, a gravity which inspires an awful respect; but they're not cosy. Now, in their painting as in their novels, the Victorians loved the sweet amenities and miniature dramas of social inter-course, the endearing misdemeanours of children and of animals, the lesser misadventures of true love and domesticity. In fact, at heart they were never academic as, say, Poussin is academic – their true passion was for genre, for the Dutch and the Flemings. What they needed was something that would cut antiquity down to life size. This was exactly what the Tanagra figures did.

Tanagra offered a quiet genre which was neither heroic nor improper; elegant young women, chastely but revealingly draped, play knuckle bones, converse and gossip, there are some fetching children, some grotesque actors, a few animals. They were coloured. We don't like the idea of colour on a marble statue, but on a terracotta figurine it may have charm, and, by a fortunate chemistry of time, all that might have been garish or startling was rendered sad, quiet, subfusc and refined. This was a version of classical antiquity that might have been expressly designed for the late-Victorian drawing room.

To what extent the Tanagra figures actually inspired the artists of the period I do not know. It is said that Whistler was influenced by the figures in the Ionides collection and it is hard not to believe that they provided source material for the later works of Alma-Tadema and of Albert Moore. Undoubtedly, they made a contribution, a very large contribution, to the aesthetic imagination of the age.

At no time, I suppose, have they been considered serious rivals to the great masterpieces of the Parthenon and of Olympia. Marcus Huish, writing about 1900, said that 'the reappearance (of these works) has been as startling an irruption as that of Japanese Art'. This surely is an exaggeration; and yet, by the turn of the century, it was pretty widely felt that there was no more refined, sympathetic and tenderly human monument of the ancient world.

'There, framed by the doorway, simply dressed in white, she resembled some old Tanagra figure . . .' How many heroines must have walked, brave yet blushing through the pages of third-rate novels with that archaeological tag tied round their pretty necks. Tanagra, which had once been trash, became art; that is to say, it acquired the status of High Art, partly because it was old, partly because it met the aesthetic needs of the age. And because it was high art, it became very expensive. In the end, its price was its undoing.

First comes Autolycus the archaeologist, and then comes Autolycus the tomb robber. Originally, perhaps, a simple peasant, he is not so simple when he finds out that his land will yield something much more precious than grapes or grain. Child of a quick-witted race, littered under Mercury, he looked for and speedily discovered a market. In 1877, four years after the first discoveries at Tanagra, the Greek government had to place guards on the site of the excavations, but already it was too late. Writers on Greek art complain that it is impossible to date these figurines because they have been taken without any regard for their environment. The tombs were broken open by night and in a hurry; the figurines were snatched; and other things – bones, shards, even pottery – were thrown aside or wantonly smashed.

A chain of communication was established all the way from the simple-minded tombarollo with a pickaxe, by way of middle men, officials, dealers, to the expert with his certificate of authenticity. It would seem that when an ancient Greek bought a statuette as an *ex voto* it would (after a decent interval, one supposes) be smashed, usually beheaded, by a priest so as to keep up demand. The modern collector also likes to have his wares intact – a headless Apollo or a Venus *sans* legs may be archaeologically interesting, but it looks inartistic; and so the ravages of age were repaired by modern ingenuity. 'It is now quite certain,' wrote C. T. Newton of the British Museum, 'that an immense amount of fraud has been perpetrated of late years. Terracottas are found to be made partly of plaster, to say nothing of false moulds and arms and heads borrowed from other figures.' This was in 1877.

Her Britannic Majesty's Consul at the Piraeus wrote, as it were, in reply:

The simple truth about the statuettes is that, as you say, a head may have been borrowed from one, and an arm from another, in those selected by me. But I don't think you will find any plaster of Paris in mine, or any fake ones, or any serious restorations. I have always set my face against it and warned Xacousti, Lambros and Rousopolis that retouching the colours was dangerous. A rage however for very highly coloured statuettes arose in Berlin and Paris. The lady with the retouched eyebrows and fresh lips met an admirer and modesty was at a discount. However the dealers have quarrelled with each other, Xacousti who was the most barefaced restorer, finding he was exposed abused the others. Envy hatred malice and all unrighteousness are the cause of more than 9/10 of what has been said about forgeries. Of course there were a lot of real forgeries. They took moulds of bronzes on clocks and made any amount of them. But these were easy to recognise when once you knew them. As to the wrong heads being on the wrong shoulders, why, tis the way of the world. How few men have the right head on their shoulders.

Between the tombarollo, the grave smasher, and the forger there is, so it seems to me, a world of difference. The former destroys, the latter creates; and although I suppose that it has to be admitted that forgery is, in a sense, immoral, it can hardly do anyone any harm. Either we know what is forged and what is real (in which case we shall not be defrauded), or we don't know (in which case we are as satisfied as though we possessed the genuine article). To my mind, the forger of antiques should not be prosecuted but rather furnished with a UNESCO grant so that he may do something to bring badly needed currency to the historically wealthy but economically poor countries. This is a hobby horse of mine and I must not ride away upon it, but in defence of Xacousti, Lambros and Rousopolis, it must be said that their activities were, when they became really skilful, hardly of a kind to be called forgery except by very pedantic people. The original image maker had a mould, he had some clay, and, without being an original artist, he made a model. When, in the early years of the century, Sir Martin Conway found a factory for the production of forgeries near Myrina, a noted source of the most elegant originals, he found the workers almost exactly repeating the actions of their remote ancestors: they had original moulds, they used clay taken from the same beds and, unless they painted their figurines, these were almost indistinguishable from those that had been made in the same fashion two thousand years earlier.

The trouble was that they ended by killing the market. Almost every great museum has a collection of admirable frauds and frequently it is only by the use of very modern techniques that these can be distinguished from the genuine articles – many thousands more must have passed into private collections. And then, of course, there were some pastiches that were not so admirable: enterprising artists produced wares which were rather too charming, too sweetly perfect to be true. On top of this, public taste began to change and the craze for Tanagra was replaced by a taste for the geometric austerities of the Cycladic period. Tanagra has been devalued, and today it is thoroughly out of fashion. It is too amiable, too humane, too comprehensible an art form to be popular today.

And so the cycle is complete, a demotic art has had its moment of glory and has been raised almost to the status of High Art, only once more to become, if not wholly demotic, at least a minor form.

Did something of this kind occur before? The decline of the clay image about the beginning of our era puzzles me and I don't know enough to argue against those who claim that it died because it was so essentially pagan, or that it was destroyed by the mass production of cheap bronzeware – although I must confess that neither reason seems to me quite conclusive.

But certainly in the Hellenic world it did die, possibly because it was too easy, too cheap to produce; in fact, too demotic. It lingered on in Gaul where there seem even to have been Christian adaptations of the form. Did it perhaps survive in remote districts? When I was very young I spent the autumn and winter in what was then considered a very remote French town. So desolate was it that on those distant beaches one needed no bathing dress. I gather that bathing dresses are still unnecessary, but for another reason. The town was called St Tropez. At Christmas, whole collections of crudely painted, crudely modelled figures appeared in the market place costing next to nothing – the ox, the ass, the Virgin, St Joseph, and so on. Could this conceivably have been the last tiny offering of an incredibly ancient industry? I suppose not, but it would have been nice if we had bought and kept a few of them, which, of course, we failed to do. What we needed was a snapper up of unconsidered trifles, an Autolycus.

Canons and Values in the Visual Arts: A Correspondence

Sir Ernst Gombrich has provided the following explanatory note:

In my Romanes Lecture on Art History and the Social Sciences *(Oxford, 1975) I defended the traditional notion of a canon of excellence in the arts. These lectures are given in the Sheldonian Theatre at Oxford, and I therefore used that building by Sir Christopher Wren with its ambitious ceiling painting by Streeter to remind my audience of the light which the social sciences can throw on the origins and the significance of such works. Yet, I argued, no 'value-free' scientific discipline can deal with the claim made at the time 'that future ages must confess they owe to Streeter more than Michael Angelo'. Not only does this boast make use of the canon of excellence, it cannot be refuted without reference to it. It would be insufficient to demonstrate by means of statistics that the prediction did not come true because Michelangelo remained more famous than Streeter. We cannot evade the problem of the reasons for Michelangelo's greater fame, in other words, his greatness. Thus while the history of building and of image making is properly the domain of the social sciences, the history of art as a history of mastery remains inextricably linked with the values acknowledged by civilisation. Any social scientist interested in exploring and explaining the history and sociology of art must sooner or later consult the existing canon, if only to select the data against which he wishes to test his theories.*

12 May 1975

DEAR ERNST,

I should have written before to thank you for the Romanes

Lecture, but I had to read it not once but twice and am indeed inclined to think that I ought to read it a third time before trying to measure the generosity of your gift. What did indeed strike me at first reading, and again at second, and is clear as daylight is the sheer triumphant elegance of your essay – the ingenuity, the clarity, the speed with which you so enviably do it; and this does indeed make it a delight. But with the pleasure of reading you and enjoying your ingenuity and your fun there goes a feeling of worry about your main argument, or what I take to be your main argument.

In this question of relativism I feel as Dr Johnson did about determinism, 'all human reason is in favour of it, all human experience against it' (probably I have misquoted). In other words I sit on the fence, and when I see anyone descending in too decided a fashion on either side, I utter shrill cries of alarm.

'The history of art, in this light, is rightly considered to be the history of masterpieces and of the old masters . . .' Yes, certainly, but of how much else. I wish I knew more about Egypt but little as I know I do get the impression that, from the Old Kingdom to the Ptolemies, with only one notable deviation, there is a steady and equal flow of talent and achievement – no mountains, no foothills, no genius, no epigones. Perhaps if I knew more the ground might look less equal, but was there in Egypt the kind of variation that distinguishes Streeter from Michelangelo? Surely not and, if not, are we to say that really there is no history of Egyptian art? I suppose we may, but after all this didn't prevent you from writing an excellent and illuminating chapter in *The Story of Art* devoted to Egypt. But supposing I am completely wrong about Egypt, suppose there are really vast differences of excellence, does this – the extent of our valuation – make history possible?

I am putting this badly. Let me try another tack. You have a good deal to say about Michelangelo and, if I understand you rightly, you say that we have to place him within a canon based not on reputation but on absolute unquestionable value. If we are to make sense of art history, it is not enough that we should say that Michelangelo is better than Streeter in the eyes of the world but that he is in some absolute sense better – and this I find hard to take. Supposing by some appalling catastrophe everything that Michelangelo ever made were destroyed, or worse still, supposing nothing remained but those horrible presentation drawings. Let us suppose that this catastrophe had occurred about a century ago so that one had to take Michelangelo as one takes Apelles, on trust. Could one in any real sense say that one felt his supreme merits? With only the *Fall of Phaëthon* to judge by, the words would stick in my throat, they would be insincere. But I could always sincerely say that Michelangelo had been one of the great art historical events – something which having happened, changed the world for ever – and I could do this without liking his work or being in a position to make any judgment about it.

About seventy years ago my father and my mother were dining in Kensington. The talk turned to Rubens and Van Dyck. Of the large and highly cultivated party at that table only my parents doubted the superiority of Van Dyck. To everyone else it seemed self-evident that Van Dyck was more refined, more sensitive, more civilised, more clearly 'of the company' than his master. There was something coarse, something brutal about Rubens. If these people could have known that by the third quarter of the twentieth century it would be generally accepted that Rubens was the greater man, I think they might have said: 'So much the worse for the twentieth century. Clearly if this happens it will mean that you have lost some of our culture, our refinement, our powers of discerning certain shades of feeling.' And can we say that they would have been altogether wrong? What they saw and admired in Van Dyck is to us much less important than what we can find in Rubens. In terms of objective truth we can say that both Van Dyck and Rubens exert a vast influence upon their contemporaries and their followers. Does it really help us to include or to exclude Van Dyck from the canon? And surely it is this consideration – I mean the magnitude of the artist as an art historical event – which saves us from the need for the random sample and the graph. If one compares Whistler with all his many British imitators of the last decade of the nineteenth century, it is quite clear who is imitating whom, even though it may not always be clear who is painting the best paintings.

I suppose this business of valuation, or at least the association of values with art historical judgments, is one of the bees in my bonnet. There is another which you also fluttered when you refer to the value that may be expressed in monetary terms. This you call cynicism, but I am not sure that this is quite fair. The Sheldonian is not yet for sale, neither is Chardin's *Retour du Marché*, unless the

Louvre has changed its policy very much. Nevertheless I don't think that I am guilty of a completely absurd statement when I say that I feel that, despite its 'bourgeois' subject and the fact that everything has no doubt been 'paid for', this picture is only remotely concerned with money, whereas Quentin de La Tour's portrait of Mme de Pompadour is – that is to say that it reflects a certain expensive life style, it is intended for an elite which is either rich or has to pretend to be rich, and in this it resembles a great deal of courtly painting, furniture, and architecture. To go back to the Egyptians, surely it is not pure cynicism to say that there is a vulgar, an ostentatious quality about their work, an apparent belief that one can buy one's way into a future life which is wholly civilised and which we recognise in ourselves, the ancients, and the Chinese.

Well I must not get started on another page having written far too much already. It is impossible though not to look at any argument presented by you with attention and admiration, even when one finds oneself in disagreement. My only real regret is that I have nothing positive to offer in return.

I do hope you are well, as I am almost, and as we are I believe the same age, looking forward as I do to a busy retirement with a minimum of committee meetings.

Yours ever
QUENTIN

Cobbe Place
Beddingham

13.V.1975

DEAR QUENTIN,
Thank you very much indeed for your kind and interesting response to my Romanes Lect. I don't know if you realise how rarely I get a real reaction to the stuff I send out. The majority of recipients don't acknowledge at all, and I don't blame them, for I frequently don't either. The rest mostly write a word of thanks, but give no evidence of having read the thing. You have read it twice, as you say, and that alone makes me proud. I did not write the thing for everybody to agree and to sign on the dotted line; on the contrary, I knew that it was controversial and rather explosive. Moreover, though the lecture is too long, it may not be long enough, and I may have failed in the end to put down what I

wanted to say with sufficient clarity because I tried to answer beforehand such objections as I could think of.

I wonder if I could persuade you to engage in a kind of public discussion with me about these important issues – though I realise that we both may not have enough time and leisure to follow up this wild idea. I have been much urged by the journal *Critical Inquiry* to write something for them, and this might be a suitable topic – though to retract right away, I *must* first get the *Ornament* book into shape. How would the idea strike you in principle?

I fear I won't be able now to answer in full detail; let me try to start at the end. There are people who don't believe art historians should be concerned with value at all. I think neither you nor I belong in that category. There are others (Michael Levey, I think, wanted to make that point at the Association of Art Historians) who think that the responsibility for our critical judgment rests entirely and solely with each one of us, and we have to make up our mind alone and unaided in our confrontation with every work of art of the past. I don't happen to believe that either; it sounds grand, but it is not only unrealistic, but also vainglorious. We never start from scratch, we have not invented our civilisation and our values in any case, and we should not pretend we have. If we tried we would find that we could not possibly justify our predilections because these likes and dislikes are indeed largely subjective. So I believe, first as a matter of sheer observation, that our civilisation transmits to us a canon of great poets, composers, artists and that we are in fact appointed to pass it on to future generations. Not, to be sure, uncritically, but with a certain humility.

The canon is not the same as a ranking order. I am sure the kind of discussion you tell about, whether Van Dyck or Rubens is greater, is also part of civilisation, and I don't think it speaks against my proposition. There are followers of various Gods and divinities in every religion; I am sure these were both great masters, and one can empathise with those who find Rubens too robust.

The main point I really wanted to make is that we cannot start from scratch and that anybody who wants to know about the history of art, whether social scientist or amateur, really uses these 'guidelines' (ominous words!). Freud wrote on Leonardo and on Michelangelo's *Moses* because he wanted (rather unhappily, as it turned out) to test his psychological theory. I have no doubt, by the way, that Apelles was a great master. I take this on trust, as I take so many things on trust, for instance that Miltiades was a good general. How do I know? I don't. We cannot examine everything all at once; as little (and this was part of my argument) as the scientist can or does. But though I know I cannot prove Michelangelo's greatness in the way de Piles tried, by the awarding of points, I can select him for my canon on the grounds (as I wrote) of faith and hope. I am sorry you find the presentation drawings so horrible. I find the portrait of Quaratesi ravishing. Of course there is something almost repulsive in Michelangelo's mastery, but my awe is not much connected with my 'likes'.

Now about those Egyptians – I would be prepared to bet that their craftsmen were not all equally good (or bad) and that there were renowned masters among them, much like the 'cunning' craftsmen Solomon engaged from Phoenicia for his temple. In the Middle Ages Nicholas of Verdun was such a one in the twelfth century. I am sure even we can tell differences in quality there: but I have to concede that it is unlikely that the Egyptians had an 'art' in the sense the Greeks had it. In *The Story of Art*, to which you so kindly refer, I start with my doubts about the universal validity of that term (to which I return in the Lecture), and I also say, somewhere near the fourth page of the twenty-fifth chapter, that 'it is obvious that an Egyptian artist had little opportunity of expressing his personality. The rules and conventions of his style were so strict that there was very little scope for choice. It really comes to this – where there is no choice, there is no expression' etc. etc.

On the other hand it is true that Egyptian art as such belongs to our mental universe, to the furniture of our mind, and long may that be the case. Whether we 'understand' it may be a different matter. Few people share my faith in the possibility of understanding a work of art or even think it makes sense to talk about it. This might also be a topic we might debate if it ever came to it.

You see, I realise that in calling in the canon I am advocating something like a retrograde step towards an 'Academic' interpretation of art, but I am less worried by this consequence than many people would be. Have you not also argued for something like a canon when you pleaded that the Pre-Raphaelites should not be ignored? I may 'like' them less than you do, but I don't find this all that important. I once shocked an American student of mine whom

I had sent to look at the Raphael cartoons and who came back explaining she did not like them at all. I told her coolly that I was not interested. It was perhaps cruel, but it did the trick.

I recently was invited to talk about 'Art' at the Institute for Education of our University. There was a well-intentioned teacher there who put forward the view that we had no right whatever to influence the likes and dislikes of our pupils because every generation had a different outlook and we could not possibly tell what theirs would be. It is the same extreme relativism which has invaded our art schools and resulted in the doctrine (which I have read in print) that art could not possibly be taught because only what has been done already can be taught, and since art is creativity (they used to call it originality) it is not possible to teach it. Q.E.D. – I recently asked my history finalists what 'Quod erat demonstrandum' means and they did not know . . .

Sorry, I am starting to ramble, and I must close.

Many many thanks, once more,

Yours ever
ERNST

19 Briardale Gardens
London, NW3

May 15 1975

DEAR ERNST,

Your letter arrived this morning and has had a most demoralising effect. For today is a free day, by which I mean that I have no teaching or committee work and am therefore 'free' to sit down and mark twenty-five scripts. I long for the A.U.T. to tell me I must not,* but so far they have not done so, and I was fully determined this morning to get the odious task done. I will not attempt to describe my own motives, but I'm afraid that they are purely self-indulgent and lead me to sit down instead and attempt not an answer but a what do they call it? – *accusation de reception*? – acknowledgment of yours.

I think it might be very interesting and a valuable mental exercise if we were in some way to publicise our differences, or at least in some kind of joint pamphlet to discover what those differences are,

---

*The Association of University Teachers threatened at this time to call its members out on strike.

for I must confess that I have not any settled convictions. The only drawback that I can see is that from an editor's point of view it might seem dull. What the public wants I imagine is a gladiatorial display, and we are both of us much too sensible to be gladiators. Still, shall we mention the possibility, making it clear that this is in fact no more than a possibility, to *Critical Inquiry* or some other journal and see how they react? Obviously you will want to deal with *Ornament*, obviously I can hardly think of such things until term is over.

But I think that there is a good deal more to discuss. Although I don't think that words like 'retrograde' or 'reactionary' have very much meaning within this kind of context, I must say that I am a little worried to find that you accept Apelles like that, as it were. I find a good deal of difficulty in accepting Miltiades, accepting him, that is, as I accept a general like Sherman or even like Caesar. One knows so little of what the general actually did, what actually happened, that to me it seems that what one really does take on trust is Marathon. This is the military masterpiece that makes the fate of the world. And in the same way (but I know far too little about Greek painting) I think there may have been a kind of Marathon of the arts to which names like Apelles, Zeuxis (can't spell) etc. have been attached, but perhaps wrongly attached. And just as it is to me pleasing and poetical and somehow tremendously appropriate that Rembrandt should have painted a chaotic military conversation piece in the depths of the night, it is after all quite wrong, and my fine feelings rest upon error. Nor need I be too much ashamed of such a blunder. Did not Mme de Staël say that the very essence of British literary art was to be found in Ossian, and were not all the painters and poets of Europe in love with that spurious genius for a generation? What I am getting at I think is that in the end surely your canon must be alterable by the historian. I had not really meant to involve us in further argument but only to say that there is more to be said (on both sides no doubt) and it might be a good plan if we could find a way to say it publicly.

I must however take up one point. Your teacher at the Institute, is he really a relativist? Isn't he a kind of religious zealot? I used to teach school children. With me there was a much better teacher (better in that she could interest and control a class and organise things and was in fact a very admirable and sensible person). One day she came into the room where I had been teaching and found a series of (to my mind) the most surprising and beautiful water colours. 'What are these?' said she. I explained that they were copies of Raphael made by eleven and twelve year old children. I would have gone on to explain how interested I was by their resemblance, not to Raphael but rather to Simone Martini, for they had all the shapes beautifully right but none of the internal drawing or the sentiment, but I was checked by her look of horror.

'You've made them copy from Raphael?' she said. Her expression was exactly that of someone who had been casually informed that I had committed a series of indecent assaults upon the brats. And in fact in subsequent conversation it appeared that this was very nearly what she did feel. For her, what she called 'self expression' was as precious as virginity.

The irony of the thing was that these creative virgins were coming to school with traced drawings of Mickey Mouse and pictures from the lids of cereal packets and had indeed been violated 1,000 times over before I ever introduced them to the forbidden delights of the Divine Urbinate, as Claude Phillips used to call him. I wander and I must stop. I simply must deal with those waiting scripts. 'Take but degree away, untune that string.' It may be naughty, but I wish I could. In another six weeks I shall, and then let us think of a joint effort. (I should be enormously proud.)

Yours ever
QUENTIN

Cobbe Place
Beddingham

19th May 1975

DEAR QUENTIN,

I am sorry about those scripts. I have wriggled out of mass marking. I, too, must not allow myself to be tempted away from the straight and narrow path, however. But I am 'seduced' by your story of copying Raphael: (a) to ask you whether you know the charming book on children in the Brera which reproduces a good many delightful copies of this kind; (b) your story has brought it home to me once more (I had made this 'discovery' once and forgotten it again) that autobiographically and so-to-say psychoanalytically *Art and Illusion* may partly have sprung from my reaction to this prejudice. In contrast to an elder sister who was and is very imaginative and produced very imaginative drawings much admired by my parents, I had taken to copying pictures of animals in a favourite animal book. I was quite proud of my efforts and somewhat mortified when I discovered from the tone of voice in which these drawings were duly 'praised' that my parents disapproved of copying. Those were the days of Cizek in Vienna . . . As you see, I never got over this grievance. To work!

Yours ever
ERNST

19 Briardale Gardens
London, NW3

Lucca*
July 30 1975

MY DEAR ERNST,

I think that I owe you a letter but, even if I do not, I now feel ready to try and get this correspondence restarted. It so happens that I have been seeing things which have a bearing on our previous letters. The 'things' were not in this delightful neighbourhood but in London. You will remember that I had said that: 'really there is no history of Egyptian art' and you, while conceding that it is unlikely that the Egyptians had an 'art' in the sense the Greeks had it, would 'be prepared to bet that their craftsmen were not all equally good (or bad)'.

It was not, let me assure you, in the hope of laying long odds on a 'cert' that I visited the Egyptian galleries of the B.M. In fact it would, as I now see, be rather hard to know who *had* 'won' the bet; it is possible, as one passes from one smart glossy mummy case to another, to fancy at all events that some of their skilful sign writers and decorators had a little more address than their neighbours, although I still think that, so far as finished works go – I mean the properly finished 'morticians'' goods – one is never startled, never shocked until one passes through all those thousands of years to the Ptolemies and the quite different, high spirited, downright 'amusing' vulgarities of Roman Egypt. Of the monumental work it is harder to speak fairly, so much of the British Museum Collection seems to be taken from the twenty-fifth Dynasty; but, recollecting the sculptures in Paris and elsewhere (I have never been to Egypt)

---

*This at least was where I began writing; I make the point because I had no works of reference with which to check my statements.

one does get an impression of overwhelming sameness, greater because more precisely skilful than, for instance, the vast collection of almost identical funerary urns at Volterra. The Egyptian sculptor does seem to have taken his completed images from an inflexible and eternal mould, the same original block of stone pointed out in exactly the same way to give exactly the same effect, the same inane stare, the same reticent smile. 'And all you hold,' I muttered to myself, as I stood for, heaven knows – perhaps the thirtieth time – staring at those frozen poker faces, 'all you hold is a pair of threes.'

And in this I was entirely wrong.

The staggering thing is that, if only the Egyptians could be persuaded to show their hands, they were, I am convinced, almost unbeatable.

Do you know – but I'm sure you do – those little drawings which they made when they were off duty? The museum has gathered a number of them together in one case, and the effect, on me at all events, was staggering. They are rapid, expressive, sensitive drawings, drawings by men who could disregard outline and convey all that was needful by the use of accent, scribbles that remind one of Rembrandt – perhaps that's going too far – but of Tiepolo, of the freest, most perfectly adroit of European hands. The effect, when one sees it surrounded by all that pompous, polished gravity, is not unlike that which one sometimes finds when one can compare a rapidly finished sinopia with a completed work; but, much much stronger, for here the contrast is between something that is intensely alive and something which is more than half dead.

Perhaps this individual and imaginative art was, as it were, an underground accompaniment to the official art of the Pharaohs, never finding its way into public monuments except during one brief revolutionary epoch during the eighteenth Dynasty. How profoundly shocking that revolutionary period must have seemed, how grossly the artists then violated the canons of their art.

Perhaps it is not quite fair, in this context, to speak of 'canons'. But there was surely a generally respected custom which tied all public and presentable art to a set of unbreakable rules, and this, I suppose, is almost bound to be the case where art is so much a part of religion. What is unusual, I fancy, is to find two such very different notions of art within one society. In most societies one is a traditionalist because it doesn't occur to one to be anything else; in Egypt the tradition must have been adhered to as the result of something like a conscious choice.

I don't know that this 'proves' anything; but it does help me to explain (to myself at all events) some of my misgivings about any form of 'academic' authority. At the risk of being tiresomely autobiographical, I should perhaps add to the list of circumstances which make it difficult for me to accept the idea of a canon as something desirable. As you know, I am not an art historian in the sense in which you are, and I suspect therefore that, for me, the painting of the High Renaissance has not the central importance that it surely has for you. I was born into an artistic milieu which was, or had been, very much concerned to challenge the existing cultural establishment; my own efforts as an artist have been largely concerned with the making of earthenware; my first attempt to write about an aesthetic subject took the form of a theoretical work on fashion.

These last two points need to be expanded a little.

Of all the 'useful' arts, ceramics stands nearest to the 'fine arts'. Indeed the work of the potter extends very naturally into that of the painter and the sculptor. It can carry almost as heavy an emotional charge. It was the chosen form and indeed a most capacious vehicle for the delicate and staggering aesthetic burdens of the celestial artist. In fine, the potter is or can be a creator of the highest genius. And yet, we have only to glance at the history of ceramic art in order to see how rare, how unusual a being he is *as an individual*. The individual studio potter is in fact a modern invention; in most epochs he is merged in the factory, the workshop, or indeed the entire culture in which he labours. Wedgwood, Spode, and Worcester are entities quite as distinct as Leach or Morgan or Palissy, and a word like T'ang is used to describe the very different artistic personality shared by heaven knows how many thousands of artists over a vast area for a matter of – what is it? – 250 years.*

With these facts in mind it is not easy to see art history as a history of 'masterpieces and of the old masters' without wishing to make certain additions and qualifications.

This does not mean that I reject the idea of a canon as applied to

*19 August. Only about 50 years out.

the history of ceramics. In fact I think that there are examples which come to mind when one is trying to throw or to decorate a pot and which are at once an inspiration and a threat – an inspiration because there are qualities like honesty, elegance, and so on which are all the better for being exemplified; a threat, and in the case of pottery a very real threat, because it is so very easy to end by making a pastiche. But the canon here is of course composed not of the work of great individuals but of great collective achievements. Moreover, even more remarkably than in painting, we have during the past century and a half set our canon topsy-turvy. In our grandfathers' time the triumphs of the potters' art began in antiquity with red figure ware; in China it was the modern work of the Ch'ing dynasty, famille rose, etc. which provided the canon which was imitated by the great European factories. The earlier dynasties were hardly known, and our modern admiration for peasant wares, the geometric style, Hispano Mauresque, and all the rude, crude, deeply expressive wares of the older cultures would have seemed very strange. Indeed I think that we have gone too far in this direction and undervalue the frivolous, delicate, and highly decorative pottery of the eighteenth century.

All is flux – this brings me to my other interest which I tried to discuss in my first book: *On Human Finery*. One must no doubt be careful in attempting to apply the generalisations which one can draw from the history of clothes (unlike ceramics, a shallow container of aesthetic feeling) to the history of art in general. I have recently been rewriting that book and, in an appendix, trying to see how far such a proceeding is justifiable, so I won't attempt to enter into any detail; but I would say that the phenomena of dress have obliged me to think in terms of classes and class relationships rather than of individuals and that I have learnt a good deal both from Plekhanov and from Veblen, despite the fact that they both talk a great deal of nonsense. Status, expense, and all the various sublimations of expense do seem to me to exert a profound influence on the aesthetics of dress in a relatively static society while, in a dynamic society, one in which there is competition between classes, the first principles of taste are governed by fashion. As fashions change, our conceptions of value change, that which was good becomes bad and vice versa; and these revolutions of feeling result, so it seems to me, from the evolution of conflicting classes. This, I have argued, does not force us to accept a complete relativism; but it does mean, I think, that we see the fashions of our own day and even, to some extent, those of the past, through a distorting glass, a distorting glass which is for ever moving in front of our eyes.

This letter threatens to become inexcusably long. What I have been trying to do is to formulate my difficulties in accepting a canon but, as you will have observed, I have already implicitly admitted that I can accept the idea. Thus I do accept the highly academic notion of a hierarchy of the arts; I believe that the art of the modiste will not carry as high an aesthetic voltage as the art of the potter. More importantly when you oblige me to ask myself the question: 'Could not Streeter, in certain historical circumstances, become a greater artist than Michelangelo?' I have to answer 'no', whereas it seems to me that a consistent relativist must answer 'yes'.

As I said in my first letter: I sit on the fence. If you will bear with me, I will try to say what kind of a fence it is and in so doing find out how far I can agree with you.

You are right in saying that we both disagree with those who say that 'art historians should not be concerned with value at all'. It is almost true to say that art history is concerned with nothing else for it is the devaluation of old values and the discovery of new forms of excellence which concerns us; this surely is the very stuff of art history. Nevertheless I think I understand the point of view of those who do say this; they have been afflicted, as I have been afflicted, by a kind of art history which might more properly be called 'art appreciation' and which consists in a kind of aesthetic exhortation: the student is to be told what is good and what is bad, and 'history' becomes a kind of apology for the good. I have taught students who have received this kind of instruction (it is common enough both in schools of general education and in schools of art) and who were genuinely puzzled when, for instance, I have insisted that no account of painting in England in the eighteenth century could be complete without a discussion of the portrait painters. The boys and girls had been taught that Reynolds and Gainsborough were 'academic', pretty, and elitist; they could therefore be neglected and forgotten. This in fact was the kind of pseudo-history that I had in mind when, in my Leslie Stephen Lecture, I blamed those historians who, on much the same principle, omitted the Pre-Raphaelites. Like them or not, the Pre-Raphaelites are a part of art history: they existed, they were influential, they cannot be dismissed. You suggest that, in urging this, I am in fact 'advocating something like a canon'. And it is here, and again when you say of Michelangelo: 'my awe is not much connected with my likes', or again, when you point to the irrelevance of a student who announced that she didn't like the Raphael cartoons, that we enter a territory where we can agree.

On these terms I can accept the canon. Take a concrete instance and, returning to Michelangelo, let me admit that, not only do I *not* like the presentation drawings, I suffer from still worse deficiencies. I am staggered by his power, but I never have and never will love any work by him as I love the School of Athens; worse still I find a comparatively minor figure such as Giovanni da Bologna much more sympathetic, much more congenial. But if I were trying to form a canon, obviously Michelangelo would have to be a centrepiece thereof; I might even be obliged to allow that Raphael was a shade less tremendous, and certainly I could not claim a place for Giovanni amongst the giants.

I think that it boils down to this: what does one mean by a canon, and what does one do with it when one has it?

To my mind the canon is a fact of intellectual life. As you say one cannot start from scratch. One is bound to inherit some kind of body of opinion, and this must provide one's starting point even when one is going to dispute its validity. The canon, you suggest, may be large enough to contain some internal contradictions. It allows the admirers of Rubens to coexist with the admirers of Van Dyck. We may treat it with scepticism and accept it only with strong reservations; but it remains a part of our cultural impedimenta – useful even to a person born blind, inevitable by anyone born in our kind of society – but by no means immutable in its character. Seventy years ago it would not have included Cézanne or even Piero della Francesca; today their position seems secure, more secure than say Carlo Maratti or Guido Reni.

If this be the nature of our canon, then indeed I can take Apelles on trust, for by this reckoning it is only his reputation that matters. It does not matter that, if we did find a picture by him, I might be disappointed. It doesn't really matter if he didn't really exist at all.

The trouble is that by making the canon acceptable to myself I may have made it unacceptable to you. To the true canonist the canon is the ark of the covenant; I have turned it into a public convenience, which is not quite the same thing.

In the 'ark of the covenant' values must, I suppose, be constant. The meaning of 'bonus' must be clear beyond all peradventure and that being clear one can, if one is a true academician, know the correct value of everything.

But I'm quite sure that you don't claim to know the correct value of everything, and I rather wonder whether anyone ever has made such large claims. Poor old De Piles always gets remembered for his unlucky 'Balance des Peintres', but De Piles was in fact anti-academic, a Rubenist of liberal views.* And although I suppose there have been hard and fast, cut and dry academic theorists, I believe that they have been few and that we imagine a dogmatism which had little existence in fact. Probably you can correct me on this. What I am really driving at is that a canon, taken in the sense of 'the ark of the covenant', is too rigid, too absolute a structure to be accommodated to the catholicity of human taste. We must have an entity which will serve as a guide, but we cannot altogether accept it. In short, we sit on the fence. I believe that it is the only possible position for me and I suspect that your own position is not so very different from mine.

Intellectually a fence does not make a very comfortable seat; but it affords a wonderful view of the scenery. I hope we may meet there.

Yours ever
QUENTIN

Castel Giuliano
11 August 1975

14th November 1975

DEAR QUENTIN,
Your letter raises so many questions that it would need several books to do justice to it, and it is you who would have to write these books. In any case it is a pleasure to welcome you sitting on the

---

*19 August. I cannot resist transcribing, now that I am home again, de Piles' actual remarks about his 'Balance des Peintres': 'J'ai fait cet essai plûtot pour me divertir que pour attirer les autres dans mon sentiment. Les jugements sont trop différents sur cette matière, pour croire qu'on ait tout seul raison.'

fence of my garden – and since you mention the 'ark of the covenant', let me assure you that I do not regard my garden as a sacred and closed precinct. I often like to stroll beyond its fence, though when I feel I am losing my way, I am glad to return to my familiar grounds. I would not even consider the fence immovable. We can all go and test a post here and there, and even move it a little, if we find that it 'gives'. My point remains simply that we must acknowledge that by ourselves we could never have staked out the area, planted the garden, and built the fence, nor could the greatest critic have done so on his own. We were born into our civilisation and we owe our orientation to that tradition which happens to be in bad odour just now. Of course we should be critical of what we are told, but informed criticism means focusing on one point, and you can't focus on every point at the same time either in science, or in the humanities or – for that matter – in criticism. The historian who investigates the reliability of a chronicle cannot doubt all accounts of the past without giving up his trade. One of the traditions not even the most radical revolutionary can dispense with is language. Up to a point what I have called the 'canon' is an element in our language.

An Italian barber in Cambridge (Mass.) once told me, while he cut my hair, that he had lost all pride in his craft. When he had arrived from Tuscany he did his work with care and deliberation only to be upbraided by his boss: 'Who do you think you are – Michelangelo?' I don't know whether either of them could have named many of Michelangelo's works, but they still knew what they were talking about. You and I have followed the rumour of that greatness to its origins and have tried to come to terms with it, but neither of us would have discovered Michelangelo in a civilisation without memory, without a tradition – without a canon.

Of course every generation tries to revise it. Berenson so disliked the meticulous style of the 'presentation drawings' (which make you uncomfortable) that he deleted them from the canon, and only Wilde re-instated them, without convincing everyone. Which brings me to your remarks about ancient Egyptian art and your preference for the spontaneous sketches over the official monuments. I need not tell you that this reaction has its own history which goes back at least to the cult of genius and of Platonic frenzy (Vasari's comparison between Luca della Robbia's highly finished

Cantoria reliefs and Donatello's inspired sketchiness is a *locus classicus*). The Romantics went to town over this, and Ruskin introduced a new element, his hatred of the dead precision of the machine killing the spontaneity of life. But I know that you have read through the whole of Ruskin's Collected Works which I have not, so I'd better steer clear of him. No doubt there is a real shift in our system of values here. There is a story in an ancient author (Diodorus Siculus I.98) of two Greek sculptors who had mastered the Egyptian system of proportions so perfectly that each of them could carve half of a colossal statue in his own town and make them fit without flaw. It is not a test of excellence we would find very convincing, although technicians might be impressed. But has not the shift away from rational perfection gone a little too far? Are the sinopia really better than the frescoes, are the sketches by Rubens and Constable always superior to their finished works? We need not come to an agreement here, for the very fact that we can pose the question in this way demonstrates at any rate the usefulness of the canon as part of our language.

I fully agree with you that this frame of reference, these landmarks in my ground also include anonymous achievements. The canon may have arisen from the notion of famous inventors, but there were not only the Seven Sages but also the Seven Wonders of the World. There have always been centers of renowned excellence in the crafts, honey from Hymettus, blades from Damascus, Cremona violins. These names stand for something, so does the canonic name of Stradivarius. We shall not want to quarrel over definitions here.

There is one word, though, which I should perhaps have used with more care. My revered friend George Boas has objected to my use of the term 'relativism' because I do not wish to deny the relatedness of things and values. Maybe I should have used the term 'radical subjectivism' for the attitude I find untenable in criticism. Imagine that an undeniably authentic painting by Apelles turned up tomorrow and would look strange to us at first sight. I think we would think twice before we proclaimed to the world that 'Apelles was much overrated'. The cheap joys of debunking are neither to your taste nor to mine. We would probably rather try by an act of historical empathy to find out what the Greeks saw in his work.

May I here trail my coat properly in conclusion of this letter which got longer than I intended it to be? Old Winckelmann in his *Geschichte*, (part I, ch. 4) denies that we should approach Greek art without prejudice. On the contrary, he says, 'Those who are confident that they will find much beauty will look for it, and some of it will reveal itself to them. Let them come back till they have found it, for it is there.' Brainwashing? Yes and no – but more no than yes. We are still free to tell him that it is his confidence which deceived him – as it certainly did in the notorious case when he fell for a cruel hoax and went into raptures over the fake antique paintings Mengs had concocted to show him up. But, as you know, I have taken the line in 'The Logic of Vanity Fair', which I wrote for the volume on K. R. Popper, that we must expect such mishaps since trust is a necessary ingredient in any experience of art. Those who cannot lower their guards can never surrender to any spell. Not that we must therefore fall victim to any impostor. What was said of astrology may also apply to the canon: 'The stars incline, but they do not compel.'

May I write: 'to be continued'?

Yours ever
ERNST

19 Briardale Gardens
London, NW3

Retrospect: An Autobiographical Essay

I was born in August 1910 and am therefore coeval with the First Post-Impressionist exhibition. In fact, I might almost claim that we were twins, conceived about the same time and in much the same part of Bloomsbury. While the British public was howling with rage at Van Gogh's sunflowers and Cézanne's bathers I too was howling, but in a much more rational way. I did not like the universe in which I found myself and showed a marked disposition to give the whole thing up as a bad job. We have both survived, grown old, and become respectable.

But when we were young – say, up to the year 1930 – neither the Bells, nor the Van Goghs, nor the Cézannes were wholly respectable; that, at least, was how it seemed to me, for I spent much of my time in an English public school. There the Impressionists were regarded as daring modern innovators. A connection with Post-Impressionism was but one item in a catalogue of crimes committed by my parents, crimes of which I, as a child, disapproved.

I loved my parents (and I had more than the usual number to love) but there were times when I could have wished that they were more like other people, respectable people who went to church, believed that all Germans were monsters, and had pictures that showed things as they usually looked.

The war ended, my parents began to seem a little less eccentric, and it appeared to me that in the matters of pictures we were right and the rest of the world was wrong. Why should a picture look like something else? Why should it not look like itself? From this it was but a step to deciding that pictures ought not to look like other things. I decided that I would be a painter: I would be a very modern painter, I would give up the task (which in truth I found difficult) of trying to make things 'look like'. My works should 'look like' nothing whatsoever and be, in consequence, master-pieces of modern painting.

Then one day when I was about thirteen, Roger Fry took me to the National Gallery and asked me which pictures I liked best. For a moment I thought of saying that I didn't like any of them, for clearly they were not a bit modern and all of them seemed to be imitations of nature. In the end I plumped for a Taddeo Gaddi (it looked pretty unlike life), and, later, for Uccello, partly because he seemed to have got his perspective all wrong, partly because I found the *Rout of San Romano* most enjoyable. But then, would you believe it, Roger went into ecstasies over *The Virgin of the Rocks* – he seemed to me to be batting for the wrong side.

I perceived that this business of art was more complicated than I had imagined. At school one day someone produced the cover of a magazine which had been decorated by Vanessa Bell. It was shown around, and everyone who saw it went into fits of laughter. It was the silliest, stupidest thing that ever was seen. Ought I to have stood up and said, 'My mother did that and it is first rate'? I was ashamed at the time that I did not protest or make my connection with the disgraced work public. But of course it would have done no one any good. Indeed, it would have con-firmed the philistines in their low opinion of me and of it. But I wonder if I were now to find the offending decoration and to seek out my aged alumni, would they smile, would they feel even the slightest interest in that which once startled them into contemp-tuous mirth? I doubt it.

But while in the company of right thinking philistines it was hard to see that Post-Impressionism had made any headway at all, there were indications in other places that Cézanne, at least, was no longer a subject for derision – so I should not have been surprised at what I found in Paris in 1928.

I came all eager to be trained as a soldier in the battle for modern art and had no doubt that it was here that the final engagement would be fought. It seemed easy and obvious; one would arrive at the Gare St Lazare and ask one's way to the battlefield.

'Yes,' they said, pointing in the direction of Montparnasse, 'this was the battlefield but the battle is over. We won the war about

1914; a pity that was the moment they chose to start another one – things might have been so pleasant.'

Things were in fact pleasant in Paris in the year 1928, but they were not very exciting for an artist. The great men – Picasso, Matisse, Braque, Léger, Rouault, etc. – were still there and at work. They had won their laurels; now they could rest on them. There were others: Derain, Vlaminck, Marie Laurencin, who had also gathered laurels in their time. But they seemed now to have lost something of their freshness. They had become fashionable painters and some now had nothing but fashion to recommend them.

Where, then, was the path to modernity and perhaps to salvation? The Surrealists seemed to provide an answer. It was slightly disconcerting to find that, unlike their parents' generation, they had arrived without having to struggle. Success seemed to be given to them free of charge; but, after all, this might simply mean that people had grown more enlightened. They were like the young Raphael: they found the age waiting for them. Yes, but in some other respects they seemed rather unlike the young Raphael. He thought it enough to delight his age, they had to shock theirs. They were the Salvator Rosas, the Fuselis of their time – the fat boys of painting. I did try to paint like a fat boy; indeed, I managed to be quite horrid, and it was fun. But after a time the fun palled and I began to reflect – it may sound priggish – that this was not quite the way in which to use the inheritance left to us by Cézanne.

But the interesting thing was that the Surrealists really could make one's flesh creep. I remember being deeply impressed by *Un Chien Andalou* which was made, I gather, by Buñuel with Dali's assistance, and feeling that this really was something new and important and that, had I been disposed that way and had wanted to make films, those were the kind of films that I should have tried to make. I have never felt that I wanted to paint like Dali; and, in a way, the Surrealist film makers put the painters out of countenance by doing much the same thing – but how much better.

From a theoretical point of view – and these are supposed to be the memoirs of a theorist – that rather sad vision of Paris in the post-war years was instructive.

'Never, since the eighteenth century has public taste been so happily informed,' thus Clive Bell. 'It will lead to no good, Clive lives too much in and hopes too much of the "Beau monde",' said

Roger Fry; to which Clive replied, 'Roger is at heart an old puritan, he does not think that we can be both good and happy.' I myself was inclined to side with my father. There were, after all, so many historical examples of a prosperous and pleasure loving society which, nevertheless, was ready to support the arts handsomely. I had not then learnt that history never repeats itself.

Some artists did, though, seem to have been corrupted. As Vanessa put it, 'When one has made a first effective looking sketch and knows that one has weeks of toil and misery ahead of one finishing the thing, how is one to resist a dealer who says, "Let me take it. I'll give you 100,000 francs for it."'

I knew Derain well enough to realise that he was an exceptionally intelligent man, a very good judge of painting with a fine sense of humour. He must have known that his later paintings were disgraceful, the product, not of failing powers or ineptitude, but of corruption, the lie in the soul. How could he do it? Was he desperately in need of money? I don't know. When one thinks of his early works, some of which really are tremendously exciting, the contrast is quite horrible. It was an object lesson.

But the real fault lay with us, the young: we were short of ideas. We lacked a leader so gifted that he could challenge the old gang, put MM. Picasso and Matisse in their places and start something new. So far as I could see then (or now for that matter) there was no one.

I found a letter some time ago in which I told my mother that I thought the proper task for a young artist was to return to abstraction, and I remember how in those days – the very late twenties and early thirties – Robert Medley and I studied the work of Gleizes and Metzinger and tried to learn from them how things should be done. I remember my pleasure at meeting a young, totally abstract painter, Hugh Slater, who had a positively religious belief in what he was doing. Why, I asked Vanessa, did you give it up? Roughly speaking her answer was because, having done it, there seemed nothing else to do, and then one discovered that one was, after all, in love with nature. In the same way, Hugh Slater gave up painting altogether.

His experience was perhaps repeated in that of the 'objective abstractionists' who also looked away from nature only to return and, as did the Euston Road School, to return to her with a fine enthusiasm. My own first experiments in abstraction convinced me that it was too difficult a form despite, or perhaps because of, the fact that it was too easy. It left me with a number of extremely dull paintings and a growing belief that there is no single right way of painting.

There was a roaring and a screaming in the streets. It emanated from an ugly crowd of frightened men on the steps of the Bourse. There had been bad news from America. Soon there was bad news from Europe and the Far East. There was unemployment as never before. There was war, fascism and a new curiosity as to what was happening in Russia. Was this a matter of interest to painters? To some of us it was.

Before the 1930s, although I should certainly have called myself a socialist and an artist, I made no serious attempt to examine the relationship, if there was a relationship, between socialism and the visual arts. Now I felt compelled to answer the questions, should I, as a socialist, paint in any particular way, and should I accept any particular theory of art? In the thirties there were at least two groups of artists proclaiming they were at the service of socialism. When I first knew anything about them, the Surrealists wanted to be affiliated to the Communist Party. The Party would have nothing to do with them. One could hardly blame it. I read their manifesto. I tried to read *Poisson Soluble*. I was aware of their demonstrations as, for instance, when they broke up the furniture at the Closerie des Lilas to cries of 'A Bas La France!' I was there when they yelled abuse at an actress until they were thrown out of the theatre (that was at the Répétition Générale of *La Voix Humaine* by Cocteau – no, that must have been later). I could see no political sense in what they did nor anything that was politic. Politics, said Talleyrand, is the art of the possible. They made a point of being impossible. In the late 1930s they arrived in London, where they had a great social success. They no longer wooed the Communists, but called themselves anarchists, which seemed more appropriate. (I do, however, still remember and admire their outrageous float in the May Day Procession of 1939.)

The Social Realists were in most ways the opposite of the Surrealists. They were committed to, and accepted by, the Communist Party, even though I think that they had reservations about official Soviet art. They believed that the history of painting was determined by economic forces (a proposition with which I personally could agree) and that all art was a form of propaganda (which I thought doubtful). Their own art tended to be frankly propagandist; in aesthetic terms it seemed to me of questionable value.

As a propagandist, any competent political cartoonist could be much more effective (even though the political cartoonist might, as an artist, be wholly uninteresting). It was, indeed, on the aesthetic rock that they foundered. They believed, or tried to believe, that by their propaganda they would not only help the cause of socialism but would create better works of art. I could see nothing that would lead one to suppose that this would be the case. Apart from some argumentative meetings, I had little contact with Social Realists and may have done them an injustice. But I did see something of their next of kin: the artists of the Euston Road.

These painters who, when their school had been closed in November 1938 were named by my father the Euston Road School were, in a true sense, reactionary. I suppose that they reacted against their own brief affair with abstraction, but, more important, they reacted against the Ecole de Paris which seemed incapable of generating anything new save fashionable triviality. I don't think that they ever denounced those leaders of the *avant garde* who had maintained their own integrity from the 'heroic age'. In fact, so far as I know, they issued no collective statements. One of them, Graham Bell, did produce a pamphlet, *The Artist and his Public* (1939). It is political in that clearly it is a socialist document, but it is not, nor, I think, was it in any way intended to be, a manifesto of the Euston Road School. It is in the main a very personal avowal of aesthetic faith, and, as such, moving, but it does not constitute an argument.

As one who was, for a time, a student in the Euston Road, I should say that, in so far as they had a doctrine, it was based upon beliefs in the importance of seriousness in painting and in the value of humility before nature. It had its affinities with the doctrines of Sickert. It distrusted all kinds of pretty or decorative painting, had an affection in its choice of subject matter for sobriety, insisted upon exact drawing and an exact statement of tonal values. The work of our teachers was never, to use a catch phrase of the 1920s, 'amusing'. It had at times an impressive authority which made some contemporary art look shallow. The School provided an admirable example of what could be achieved by a simple-minded devotion to the art of painting; perhaps, for that reason, it offered little to the theorist.

There was, however, another way in which the Euston Road might be useful to those artists who were not above accepting political guidance. I do not think that it was in the minds of those who established the School, and it was probably for reasons which have nothing to do with politics that these painters devoted themselves to a comprehensible form of art. Nevertheless, the mere fact that one is expressing oneself in a manner which can be understood by the public at large constitutes a political gesture.

To explain this fully I need to approach the matter obliquely. There was a time during World War II, about 1943, when people discussed the reasons for and against bombing Rome. It was an untidy argument because Rome means so many different things. It would have been simpler had the discussion centred upon Florence or Venice, but it was Rome that I discussed with the intelligent and amusing man who taught me the little I know about looking after pigs. His view was more or less this: 'It's all very fine for you to say don't bomb Rome because that city contains masterpieces which, if lost, can never be replaced. But why should I listen to such arguments? What matters to me is the probability that if we don't bomb Rome the war will last longer and we shall have greater casualties. Pictures don't matter. I was never given the education to understand them and, if I had been, I'd never be given the price of a ticket to Rome unless I went in khaki.'

Is there a reasonable answer? I don't think there is, unless one is in a position to make believable political undertakings; and even then one's answer must sound feeble enough.

One might say something of this kind: I can assure you that these things which matter so much to me can eventually be made to matter to everyone. This can only be done by socialising the treasure that is now in danger and that involves the creation and education of a society in which your children and grandchildren will discover that works of art are matters of the first importance. If we lose them now, our children will never forgive either you or me.

When the war was over the argument continued in other terms. If one serves, as I have done, upon committees which buy works of art for municipalities, one is likely to feel that one has fallen amongst the philistines; or, at least, that one is serving upon a body in which they are well represented. To do them justice, one must allow that, for the most part, they are fair-minded and reasonable people who will listen to an argument. Often they will accept that, having appointed experts to administer their galleries and museums, it is sensible to listen to the advice that those experts may offer them. But although they may be convinced by such arguments, they may not actually be persuaded to act upon them. Town councillors, after all, are not elected by aesthetes, and they must listen to the voice of their constituents. There are some things which a committee cannot accept or can accept only when those things have been revalued by the market. I know of one northern city which was offered and refused a Picasso. That was many years ago. Today, any council would accept a Picasso and none could afford it.

But if councillors are often guilty of rejecting works of art until they become impossibly expensive, the main fault lies with the artists, the dealers and the critics.

The dealer has to satisfy a clientele which, unlike that of eighty years ago, is not frightened by incomprehensible 'modernity' – indeed, this is what it wants. The dealer therefore may look for some young man or woman who may or may not have talent but certainly has a gimmick, some amusing novelty which will please the elite; and the fact that this is what town councillors will not like adds to its market value. In buying it, one shows the world that one has better taste than the common herd. One also nurses the hope that like those who purchased works by Matisse and Picasso when they were relatively unknown, one is 'on to a good thing'. But our young artist grows older; he or she may not be able to find a new gimmick; that which he has goes out of fashion and there are other young people to draw the crowds. This is hard on the artists, but this is what the market is like.

My advice (entirely unsolicited) to a young painter would be: look past the current fashion. If you look around you will find plenty of men and women who were thought to have genius before they were twenty and now, before they are thirty, are forgotten. If it is absolutely necessary to you as an artist to paint in an incomprehensible language, then of course you must do so, and perhaps one day you may be understood. But incomprehensibility is not in itself a virtue. If you can say what you need to say and are ready to tackle the difficult but rewarding task of making yourself understood, not by a coterie but by a mass, then good luck to you. It can be done; the Euston Road did it.

This digression, which has taken me away from the thirties and away from my search for an efficient theory, is, I believe, justifiable in as much as any theory should in some manner be related to practice. But now I must return to our perplexities in the years just before the war.

The young painter who was in, or travelled along with, the Communist Party was worried, but also intrigued, both by political and by theoretical problems. The political problems were concerned with the rise of fascism, and it was the vigour and enthusiasm of the Communist Party which, at grass roots, despite dreadful moments of wrong-headed folly, excited admiration. On the theoretical side, Marxist doctrines were, for artists, perplexing, discouraging, and enormously interesting.

We read Plekhanov but, speaking for myself, I should say that it was when he was not talking about painting that I liked him best.

Does anyone in this country read Plekhanov today and do most people know who he was? I doubt it. He was born in 1856, the son of a landowner in the province of Tambov and educated as a scientist. When he was twenty he joined a revolutionary group, was twice exiled and, while in exile, he became a pamphleteer, from 1895 preaching Marxism to the Russians. From 1899 he published a series of *Letters without Address* which dealt with historical materialism and art. These letters seem a convincing statement of the Marxist case, but are based upon his considerable knowledge of anthropology rather than upon a study of art history. *French Dramatic Literature and French Eighteenth Century Painting* (1905) seemed more accessible; it contains much that is true, but also some curious lacunae. But it was *Art and Society* (1912) which, for a painter of my generation, posed the greatest problems. Here he deals with French and sometimes with Russian literature and painting during the nineteenth century. For the most part, he deals with literature and is concerned to denounce Théophile Gautier and the doctrine of art for art's sake, together with the aestheticism and decadence of the late century.

Plekhanov does not turn to the art of painting until the very end of his study, and perhaps it is because he was concluding what was originally a lecture that he leaves so much unexamined. In describing the painting of the last century he looks only at what was uncharacteristic of that age. That which was normal – the 'bad art' of the time – he ignores. The nineteenth century is peculiar in the history of art. The art of the academies and the salons, the art that was commissioned by the leaders of society, by the Church, the State and the wealthy was the work of painters most of whom are today forgotten. Look at the evidence and you will find that the style and the content (a most important ingredient then) is to a large extent homogeneous. If one is looking for the art of the bourgeoisie that surely is where we shall find it. But Plekhanov looks only at the dissidents, the *avant garde*, which presents a more difficult problem for it is heterogeneous. Degas and Monet, Toulouse Lautrec and Cézanne, Rousseau and Odilon Redon, Seurat and Carrière: they were contemporaries, but how much in common did they have? Only this: that they were rejected by the Salon. In France, we have a vast majority of painters who were concerned to celebrate the fashionable life, erotic themes, anecdotes and orthodox piety; in England, it was much the same, with less pornography and military history and more landscape. How did it happen that this solid phalanx of socially conforming artists was challenged by a small group of dissidents? I would suggest that this odd division was caused by a large creation of new money which produced a large number of *rentiers* and the growth of new fortunes in new social areas. Thus it was that some artists could depend upon unearned incomes, incomes which made them independent, while there appeared a few capitalists who were so 'uneducated' that they would patronise the *avant garde*. Such were those Americans who bought Impressionists and those English industrialists who bought Pre-Raphaelites.

Here, at least, was a fertile field for speculation, but Plekhanov never considers it. He has other fish to fry. Having convicted the writers of what we should have called escapism – that is to say of shirking their proper duty, which is the propagation of revolutionary ideas – he turns upon the painters, or rather the *avant garde* and accuses it of the same faults. This kind of painting, he rightly observed, was becoming increasingly taciturn. There were some large exceptions which he does not notice, but it *was* one characteristic of the *avant garde*. Plekhanov is ready to allow that the Impressionists could paint good landscapes, 'But landscape does not comprise the whole art of painting.' Moreover, even if the Impressionists were realists, 'their realism was entirely superficial; it never went below the surface of things.'

'In brief, what we have already observed in literature is repeated in painting. Realism collapses as a result of its own lack of content. Idealist reaction triumphs.' And that triumph is horribly consummated in what was then the latest manifestation of modernism, abstract art.

Plekhanov, I feel, was deeply shocked by the Cubists and, like so many of his contemporaries, aesthetically shocked. He considered them not only ideologically wrong, but also downright ugly.

But matters were complicated by the intervention of another Marxist, Lunacharski. Lunacharski defended the Cubists and accused Plekhanov of using an absolute criterion of Beauty. He, in his turn, was accused of extreme subjectivism. We do not have, or at least I do not have, a clear record of the exchanges which took place after Plekhanov's lecture. Historically, the important thing was that they were in opposite political camps. After the abortive revolution of 1905, Plekhanov had joined that Menshevik group which opposed Lenin while Lunacharski stayed with the Bolsheviks.

After the revolution of October 1917 Lunacharski was in a position of power, he became commissar for education. Plekhanov, who returned to Russia to oppose Lenin and to persuade the Russians to continue the war against Germany, remained for a short time, fell ill and died in a Finnish sanatorium in 1918.

Lunacharski's position in the government cannot but have favoured the modernist painters who flourished in the years following the revolution. But, despite his commitment to the Mensheviks, Plekhanov was neither condemned nor forgotten. His earlier polemics were still remembered with enthusiasm and, when Stalin took power, Russian modernism fell out of favour and the official art of the regime became an art in which content was of the first importance; in fact, it became very similar to that nineteenth-century establishment art of which I have already spoken. I think that Plekhanov would have considered it greatly preferable to Cubism.

To us it must seem tragic that a promising modernist school was destroyed and replaced by a kind of art which was in the worst sense of the word academic. But if the revolution were to survive, its leaders had to make use of a form of art which would persuade the masses that the government was invariably benevolent and wise. Not an easy task, and one for which the modernists were useless – their paintings were either incomprehensible or terrifying. The regime did what a capitalist firm would do if it were trying to sell rubbish: it employed writers and artists who would, in the most convincing manner possible, tell lies. Also, it would seek an aesthetic lowest common denominator in which to express its falsehoods.

We, the artists in the West, cared even less for Soviet propaganda art than we did for the art of the advertiser.

Having said that, I must also add that when the Russians used the cinema for propagandist ends our reaction was very different. I can still remember the overpowering effect of Eisenstein's film *October* when I saw it almost by chance in a German cinema. It seemed so immensely superior to anything that Hollywood had ever done or dreamed of. It is no doubt a proof of my gullibility that I accepted – or nearly accepted – a kind of propaganda on film that I would at once have dismissed if it had been on canvas. A great artist can make one suspend disbelief.

But, as painters, we remained critical and sceptical. We felt, moreover, and this I think is a common emotion in people circumstanced as we were, the need for the moral support of artists who were to our way of thinking. We found in Courbet and a few others a source of strength. Amongst the moderns, we found encouragement in Picasso and also in Diego Rivera (although I personally had some misgivings here). But this attempt to enlist the great artists on our side was, as I think we most of us soon realised, a futile business. For one thing, the company whom we might reasonably hope to enlist was very small (even if it had been larger, it was not going to fight any real battles). For the most part, the old masters seemed to take no interest in politics or, if they did, they held their tongues.

The fact that so few painters had expressed political views and that, after all, it is not their business to express themselves in words, led me to discover what I believe to be the central fallacy of Marxist thinking in so far as it relates to visual art. Marxist theorists assume, because the painter is affected by the class struggle and practises an expressive art, that there is no substantial difference between the painter and the writer. This view was exactly expressed by my old friend, colleague and sparring partner the late Hans Hess: 'The visual arts are no different from other symbolisations such as language and writing.'

But they are made in a different way, valued in a different way and sold in a different way. We have only to think of those close relatives of the painter – the potter, the designer, the decorator – to perceive that, whereas a writer, when he expresses his views, uses the tools of his trade, the painter need be no more vocal and persuasive than the cobbler or the plumber.

To return to the 1930s. I remember a meeting in Duncan Grant's studio one evening when I read a paper in which I attacked the Surrealists and then, for good measure, the Marxists. I said the kind of things that I have been trying to say here, no doubt even more imperfectly and, when I had finished, a bright, intelligent young Communist got up and said that I was very old-fashioned; I had given them the old Bloomsbury story: content is nothing, it's form that matters. Form, he allowed, does matter, but it is inseparable from content. There is a dialectical unity between these two opposites but what we, as socialists, had to consider was content – the message to the world. If we looked after the content the form would look after itself. This was the gist of it.

I replied, and probably I am putting this in the light of later views and discoveries, that in fact he was wrong; form could be completely separated from content, so far as the beholder was concerned. Go into the house of Dives the collector and you may find that he owns an El Greco, a Benin head and a Sisley. The Spaniard and the Negro are no doubt expressing something which to them is of great importance (whether Sisley is expressing anything that might be put into words I doubt). But does Dives understand or even guess at the message which these highly expressive artists are trying to express? There is no reason to think so. Is it not much more likely that Dives hangs them on his wall and is proud of them because, like his motor car and his mistress, they are enormously expensive? And is it not true that a large majority of those of us who go to look at such things in museums are equally uninstructed?

It is a peculiarity of the visual arts that their content can be completely divorced from their form. For centuries, Europe and America have been importing Chinese porcelain. Is this because the decoration of such ware is likely to have a large symbolic meaning, which, in fact, is often expressed in decorative form? Of course not. Chinese pots were imported and sold for large sums because they were manifestly luxury goods. We buy the form, not the content.

So much for the unity of form and content. Needless to say my opponent remained unconvinced.

But that example of the Chinese pot deserves further examination. When we buy something, the content of which is unknown to us, we may, in fact, supply a content of our own which is completely unlike that which the artist himself intended to express. When Giovanni Bellini painted his *Feast of the Gods*, he represented Ganymede and Hebe bringing nectar, not in a Grecian urn, but in a Ming bowl. The Doge happened to have one and Bellini must have admired it; also, one presumes that his patrons saw no incongruity in using it. Why? It was in a formal sense beautiful, but there was more to it than that. It was, technically, finer than anything that Europe could then make, it was fragile, but had been carried across Asia with infinite care. It was immensely expensive. In fact, it had social qualities far removed from any literary qualities that it might contain.

Here, then, was a kind of value which is peculiar to the work of the visual artist, something conveyed by the form of the object and yet not in the ordinary sense 'aesthetic', but related to social value.

Can we go further and find a connection between those social valuations and the economic structure of society? I think we may. One of the remarkable mutations of taste which we have witnessed during the past two hundred years is a kind of devaluation of virtu, in the sense of high technical excellence. To return to our Chinese porcelain. Had you found some in a gentleman's house of two hundred years ago it would have been the luxury articles of the Manchu period: graceful, perfect, and, to our modern apprehensions, a little boring. In this century, the amateurs and dealers have imported wares of a very different character: bronzes and ceramics of the earlier dynasties, things which would not have found their way into a gentleman's house in previous centuries, things that would have lacked the polite qualities of Famille Verte and Famille Rose and which would have been considered crude and barbarous. How did they arrive in the market?

I would suggest that something of this kind happened. The perfect finish and elaborate workmanship that was so much admired in earlier days was increasingly rivalled by the products of the machine age. With modern methods, the most perfect finish and the most intricate patterning can be produced by methods which involve very little labour. Soon the time came when quite poor people could buy a plate which, formerly, would have been the result of long hours of skilful work. The value of skill was considerably shaken. The term 'hand made' received a new value and aesthetically minded people, feeling that technical virtuosity was no longer the asset it had been, began to look in new directions: to the primitives in painting, to peasant crafts (which now had the added value of rarity) to the hitherto unregarded productions of children and savages. In fact, we began moving towards that vast catholicity of taste which has had so profound an effect upon art and the aesthetic thought of our own century.

I think that it was in 1939 that a party of friends was staying with me in Sussex. We were all 'lefties'. One of us pulled a small red volume out of the shelf and read aloud.

Much of the charm that invests the patent leather shoe, the lustrous cylindrical hat and the walking stick, which so greatly enhances the natural dignity of a gentleman comes of their pointedly suggesting that the wearer when so attired cannot bear a hand in any employment that is directly and immediately of any human use.

Those who know him will at once recognise the hilarious irony of Thorstein Veblen. Rereading Veblen I am struck by the amount of sense and the amount of nonsense that he talked. He shows in the clearest way the manner in which our social ambitions deform and indeed determine our sense of beauty. He examines with devastating effect the forces which impel us towards the wildest forms of ostentation. He examines the mechanism of fashion very thoroughly but weakens his case, so it seems to me, by reference to an ideal beauty, a canon of aesthetic values which he never defines very clearly. Also I found it necessary to add to his categories Conspicuous Consumption, Conspicuous Leisure, Conspicuous Waste, another – Conspicuous Outrage. What I had in mind was the kind of behaviour which we associate with the Restoration (Plekhanov also notices this) when a section of the upper class deliberately sets out to outrage the puritan middle class by profligacy in manners, speech, dress and conduct. Perhaps the smart set of a later generation might provide an example of greater purity, for outrage need have had no overt political motive.

But, of course, the same motive, the desire to belong to a small, distinguished and fashionable group, an exclusive club or fraternity (in the American sense) or to join some body like a hunt, which has its own distinctive dress, customs and language, a fashionable religion, or again to be connected with some esoteric coterie which admires some fashionable kind of art, all provide examples where one can discern a social impulse, a desire to distance oneself from the crowd.

In the history of dress such motivation seemed to me important; it helped one to understand the macaronis of the eighteenth century, the aesthetic dress of the nineteenth and those attempts to carry the fashion to the borders of indecency which we find in our own century.

Dress has always seemed to me a rich field for social exploration. When I had leisure to think, as I had when the war took me into the fields to drive a tractor, I began to write. Leonard Woolf and I were at one point engaged in a rather sharp exchange concerning Marxism (for which he had very little use) and I attempted in a paper to explain my own views using the history of dress as an example. He suggested that I expand my views in a book. I did so.

This is where we came in.

Notes

BAD ART

This essay began as the Twelfth Annual Foundation Lecture given at Bretton Hall, Wakefield, in 1962. Four years later, I read 'Bad Art: A Revision', a paper correcting and modifying the views expressed in my first lecture, to the British Society of Aesthetics (published in the *British Journal of Aesthetics*, vol. 7, no. 1, 1967). The two have been adapted and amalgamated in the present text, although it should be said that some of my tastes have changed in the meantime (and on Albert Moore I now feel I was particularly harsh).

p. 17: 'in marine painting . . .': *Encyclopaedia Britannica* (London, 1911), p. 501.

THE ART CRITIC AND THE ART HISTORIAN

The Leslie Stephen Lecture, delivered at the University of Cambridge in 1973.

p. 27: 'People who . . .': Leslie Stephen, *Studies of a Biographer* (London, 1902), vol. III, p. 87.
p. 34: 'this obsession . . .': *Burlington Magazine* (February 1973), no. 839, vol. CXV.
p. 35: '. . . no hurry to do so': see Michael Levey, 'Botticelli and 19th Century England', in *Journal of the Warburg and Courtauld Institutes* (1960), vol. XXIII, p. 291.

CONFORMITY AND NONCONFORMITY IN THE FINE ARTS

This was a contribution to *Culture and Social Character*, ed. Professors Lipsett and Lowenthal (New York, 1961), compiled to criticise or to complement David Riesmann's *The Lonely Crowd* (Y.U.P., New Haven, 1950).

ROGER FRY

An inaugural lecture resulting from the creation of a Chair of Fine Art and of a course which combined art history and studio work at the University of Leeds, 1963.

p. 66: 'In this essay . . .': Roger Fry, *Cézanne* (London, 1927), p. 88.
p. 68: 'I don't like . . .': Virginia Woolf, *Roger Fry* (London, 1940), p. 79.
p. 69: 'immensely grave . . .': Roger Fry, *The Artist and Psychoanalysis*, (London, 1924), p. 16.
p. 69: 'We confess . . .': Virginia Woolf, *op. cit.*, p. 112.
p. 70: 'the reckless prophet . . .': *Morning Post* (16 November 1910) letter from W. B. Richmond describing the Post-Impressionist exhibition at the Grafton Gallery.
p. 71: 'The accusation . . .': Roger Fry, *Vision and Design* (London, 1920), p. 192.
p. 72: 'The space . . .': *ibid.*, p. 44.
p. 74: '. . . to paraphrase': see Virginia Woolf, *op. cit.*, p. 263.

SICKERT

Parts of this essay have appeared in *The Times Literary Supplement* (14 May 1976) and in the *Burlington Magazine* (April 1987); and much was written as a preface to a book about Sickert's writings which has not been published.

p. 76: 'The opinions . . .' and three quotations ff.: Clive Bell, *Old Friends* (London, 1956), p. 12 *et seq.*
p. 78: 'I remember . . .': Walter Sickert, *A Free House* (London, 1947), pp. 23–4.
p. 78: 'Monsieur Blanche . . .' *ibid.*, p. 97.
p. 95: 'the august site' and 'smartened up young person': *ibid.*, p. 59.
p. 99: 'The pretension . . .': *ibid.*, p. 4.

DEGAS: *Le Viol*

The annual Charlton Lecture, given at the University of Newcastle-upon-Tyne, 1965. A tradition had been established that the Lecture be devoted to the examination of one work of art and it had attracted some terrifyingly distinguished visitors to the University.

p. 103: '1867 or 1868': see *Exposition Emile Zola* (Paris, 1952), p. 114.

p. 103: '. . . *circa* 1871': see Jean Sutherland Boggs, *Portraits by Degas* (Berkeley, 1962), p. 91.

p. 104: 'Was Degas . . .': Camille Mauclair, *Degas* (London, n.d.), p. 14.

p. 105: 'M. Wilenski . . .' Tabary, *Duranty* (Paris, 1954), p. 149.

p. 105: 'mon tableau de genre': Henri Rouart as reported by Henry P. McIlhenny. A study for *Le Viol*, now the property of John S. Thatcher, is inscribed by Marcel Guérin., 'Très precieux car c'est tout ce qui reste en France de cet admirable tableau que Degas appelait "mon tableau de genre".'

p. 106: For Herriot on the resemblance to Manet, see *Discours Ministeriel à la Sorbonne*, 6 October, 1927.

p. 107: 'You paint . . .': Jeanne Févre, *Mon Oncle Degas*, (Geneva, 1949), p. 73.

p. 108: 'a variation . . .':. J. Meier Graefe, *Degas*, trans. Holroyd Reece, (London, 1923), p. 28.

p. 108: 'No modern artist . . .' 'Degas' in Bruno Cassirer, *Kunst und Kunstler*, (Berlin, 1902), p. 28.

p. 108: 'I do not find it necessary . . .': Walter Sickert, *A Free House*, *op.cit.*, p. 150.

p. 109: 'Below the stark ruff . . .': '*Carlotta Grisi*', in *Yet Again* (London, 1909), p. 308.

p. 109: 'I wish above all . . .': *Archives de l'Impressionisme*, ed. Venturi (Paris, 1939), p. 129.

p. 109: 'It has the expressive face . . .': Boggs, *op. cit.*, p. 51.

p. 110: Degas' poem: Lafond, *Degas* (Paris, 1918), vol. I, p. 132.

p. 111: The Ducros portrait was compared with *Le Viol* by Paul Jamot, *Degas* (Paris, 1918), p. 70.

p. 111: 'The girls . . .': *Anacharsis* (ed. 1838), T III. p. 40.

p. 112: For Cabane's views, see *Gazette des Beaux Arts*, 6e periode, 1962, pp. 363–6; for Mlle Fevre, *op. cit.*, p. 29; and for the evidence of Degas' 'sight' see Arsène Alexandre, 'Degas, Nouveaux Aperçus' in *L'Art et les Artistes*, N.S. xxix, no. 154, Février 1955.

THE LIFE ROOM AS A BATTLEFIELD

This essay was originally four lectures given to the National Society for Art Education at its annual conference in 1962.

p. 118: 'Seeing that the antique . . .': De Piles, *Cours de Peinture par Principes* (Paris, 1707), pp. 404–5.

p. 118: 'wrinkles, pouches . . .': *The Nude* (London, 1956), p. 4.

p. 120: 'there is no excellent beauty . . .': *ibid.*, p. 16.

p. 122: 'the short-lived academy . . .': Whitley, *Artists and Their Friends in England, 1700–1799* (London, 1928), vol. 1, p. 17.

p. 122: 'Portrait painting . . .': Sandys, *History of the Royal Academy of Arts* (London, 1862), vol. I, p. 27.

p. 124: 'Raffaele, it is true . . .' and quote ff.: *Discourses*, Sir Joshua Reynolds, ed. Fry, (London, 1905), p. 7.

p. 124: 'it may be laid down . . .': *ibid.*, p. 9.

p. 125: 'it will not . . .': *ibid.*, 15th *Discourse*, p. 428.,

p. 127: 'As I have . . . to mock': *The Works of Sir Joshua Reynolds, Knight* (London, 1798), copious MS Notes by William Blake, vol. I, 3rd *Discourse*, p. 55.

p. 127: 'Why should . . . whore': *ibid.*, 4th *Discourse*, p. 146.

p. 127: 'It is not easy . . . the sublime': *ibid.*, pp. 56–8.

p. 128: 'It is from . . . from the imagination': *ibid.*, p. 60.

p. 128: 'In the midst . . . an Artist': *ibid.*, 7th *Discourse*, pp. 241–2.

p. 132: 'paint a figure . . .': Haydon, *Lectures on Painting and Design* (London, 1844), lecture 4, p. 177.

p. 137: 'Only think . . .': Haydon, *Correspondence and Table Talk* (London, 1876), vol. I, p. 449.

p. 138: 'an unseemly altercation': Sir George Clark, President of the Board of Trade, in reply to William Ewart, see *Hansard*, 25 July, 1845.

p. 138: 'The Figure Master . . .': *The Times*, 14 May, 1845.

p. 141: 'I apprehend . . .': evidence before Select Committee, 1849, q. 3.

p. 143: 'The main thing . . .': I. A. Sparkes, International Health Exhibition, vol. xiv, Conference on Education (London, 1884), Section B, p. 272.

p. 143: 'The tap root . .': Ruskin, *Laws of Fesole*, Library Edition, vol. XV, p. 344.

p. 144: 'And the purpose . . .': *ibid*, pp. 435–6.

p. 144: 'I flatter myself . . .': Reynolds, *op. cit.*, 2nd *Discourse*, p. 19.

p. 146: 'Of all English ports . . .' and 'It is certainly . . .': *Turner: The Harbours of England* (London, 1876), vol. xiii, pp. 60 and 62 respectively.

p. 148: 'So then . . .': *Modern Painters* (Orpington, 1888), Vol. 2, p. 103.

p. 148: 'He has involved himself . . .': *ibid.*, Vol. 3, p. 22.

p. 149: 'It should be allowed . . .': *Elements of Drawing*, Library Edition, vol. XV, Preface, p. 9.

p. 150: 'That dark carnality . . .': Ruskin, *The Relationship between Michelangelo and Tintoretto*, Library Edition, vol. XXII, p. 104.

p. 152: 'I was sitting one night . . .': Sickert, *A Free House* (London, 1947), p. 325.

p. 153: 'What he wanted . . .': *Grave Imprudence* see *Archives de l'Impressionisme*, ed. Venturi, *op cit.*, p. 296.

p. 155: 'The artist is he . . .': Sickert, *op. cit.*, p. 277.

p. 158: 'For two hours . . .': Virginia Woolf, *Roger Fry, op. cit.*, p. 263.

p. 158: 'I very early . . .': *ibid.*, p. 228.

FORM AND CONTENT

A lecture delivered at the University of Hull, 3 November 1965.

p. 165: 'Everything is clearly . . .': *Diderot*, ed. Adhémar and Seznec, (Oxford, 1957–67), vol. II, p. 157.

p. 165: 'A taking picture . . .': Ruskin, *Academy Notes*, (London, 1856), vol. xiv, p. 53.

p. 166: 'Let us remember . . .': *Théories*, 1870–1910 (Paris, 1920), p. 1.

p. 166: 'What we have to remember . . .': *Art* (London, 1920), I, iii, p. 68.

p. 167: For Herbert Read's views on Clive Bell, see *British Journal of Aesthetics*, vol. 5, no. 2, April 1956.

p. 167: 'The mother . . .': *Characteristics of French Art* (London, 1932), p. 67.

p. 167: 'The basic tenderness . . .': Barbara Hepworth, 'Carvings and Drawings' (London, 1952), n. 5.

ART AND THE ELITE

Published in *Critical Inquiry*, vol. I, no. 1, September 1974.

p. 180: 'I tried in vain . . .': Roger Fry, *Vision and Design* (London, 1920), pp. 192–3.

p. 183: 'Isn't this where . . .': L. V. Fildes, *Luke Fildes, R.A.: A Victorian Painter* (London, 1968), p. 123.

AUTOLYCUS: A DEMOTIC ART

This paper is the result of an enquiry which can hardly be dignified by the name of research into a form of art which, because it has some affinities with my own work as a sculptor, interests me profoundly. My enquiry led me to the British Museum and to the Ashmolean, where, despite my manifest ignorance, I was received with patient kindness. Those who look for scholarship will not find it here, although they may discover in my notes a starting point for serious study. The paper was received with excellent good humour by a very intelligent audience in the University of Southampton on the evening of 4 May 1976.

p. 188: 'The unsightly specimens . . .' and 'Its chief use . . .': David Robertson, *Sir Charles Eastlake and the Victorian Art World* (New Haven, 1978), p. 178.
p. 193: 'the reappearance . . .': *Greek Terra-Cotta Statuettes* (London, 1900), p. 4.
p. 194: 'It is now quite certain . . .' and 'The simple truth . . .': Higgins in *Apollo* (1962), vol. 76, p. 57.

CANONS AND VALUES IN THE VISUAL ARTS: A CORRESPONDENCE

This exchange of letters between Professor Sir Ernst Gombrich and myself discusses, but can hardly be said to deal with, the question of value judgments. The editors of *Critical Inquiry* thought that it would be interesting to publish our letters as they stand (vol. 2, no. 3, spring 1976, University of Chicago Press). To begin the piece, Sir Ernst provides a summary of the Romanes Lecture which provoked the exchange.

p. 212: Fn.: *Cours de Peinture* (Paris, 1707), pp. 489–90.
p. 215: 'The Logic of Vanity Fair', in *The Philosophy of Karl Popper*, ed. Schlipp (Illinois, 1974), pp. 925–57.

RETROSPECT

p. 225: 'But landscape . . .', 'their realism . . .' and 'In brief . . .': G. V. Plekhanov, p. 24, *Art and Social Life* (London, 1953), p. 214.
p. 227: 'The visual arts . . .': in *Marxism Today*, October 1973.
p. 230: 'Much of the charm . . .': Thorstein Veblen, *Theory of the Leisure Class* (London, 1949), p. 171.

Index

239